# LAWLESS
### and the
# FLOWERS
## of
# SIN

ALSO AVAILABLE FROM WILLIAM SUTTON
AND TITAN BOOKS

*Lawless and the Devil of Euston Square*
*Lawless and the House of Electricity* (July 2017)

# LAWLESS
## and the
# FLOWERS
of
# SIN

WILLIAM SUTTON

**TITAN** BOOKS

Lawless and the Flowers of Sin
Print edition ISBN: 9781785650116
E-book ISBN: 9781785650123

Published by Titan Books
A division of Titan Publishing Group Ltd
144 Southwark Street, London SE1 0UP

First Titan edition: July 2016
10 9 8 7 6 5 4 3 2 1

William Sutton asserts the moral right to be
identified as the author of this work.

Map illustrations by William Sutton.
Map design by Rebecca Lea Williams.
Map typography by Titan Books.

A CIP catalogue record for this title is available from the British Library.

Printed and bound in the United States.

# LAWLESS
### and the
# FLOWERS
#### of
# SIN

# LONDON
### 1863-64

PADDINGTON

Baker Street

Oxford Street

MAYFAIR

Hyde
Park

Shepherd
Market

Rotten Row

Kat
Hamil

KENSINGTON

*ubi mel*
*ibi fel*

Westmins

Portsmouth
& Petersfiel

Our sins are stubborn, our repentance vain;
We make ourselves pay liberally our oaths,
And blithely head back on the filthy path,
Believing worthless tears may cleanse our stains.

Charles Baudelaire, *Les Fleurs du Mal*

# PART I
## PRISM OF DELIGHT

### NOVEMBER 1863

A very little key will open a very heavy door.

Charles Dickens, *Hunted Down*

# SENSATION

If you're after one of those sensation novels, you had better look elsewhere. A prettified heroine flutters her lashes to bewitch the eligible bachelor; he never guesses at her guilty past until, strolling gas-lit alleys, she makes confession of her sins, turning doe eyes upon him, as the organ-grinder's ballad reaches a lonely climax.

Trumped-up potboilers purporting to cut to the heart of our diseased society, throwing us through precipitous chicanery with never a moment to examine the characters' inward lives, they titillate our fancy, turn our stomach, leave us empty. Too trite, too comforting, these maids falling from grace, men besotted with aunts, purloined identities, revelatory memoirs; they give the glow of gratification, but their revelations are gossamer-thin. If that is the kind of tosh you like, look elsewhere. Pontificate, as you sup from your dainty cup on the plush divan, on the scurrilous morals of today's authors, so bent on scandalising us that we will not be able to wait for next week's instalment. Oh, let us have it sooner: let us have it today!

Bah.

But turn down the blind, follow the street seller home to his bloodied spouse—follow your own husband, or your wife, equivocating on their destination of an evening—and you shall find scandal closer to home. How near disaster lies. Ruin shadows us all, however grand, however insignificant. The streets are paved with the bodies of the trampled, and you and I, if we pay no heed to such warnings, are as like to fall underfoot as anyone.

My story is not one of these sensation tales.

My story has eyes blackened by blows, crinolines ripped to reveal voluptuous flesh bruised by careless knuckles. Gas lamps smashed to give cover of darkness, deluding the common man that nobody sees his weakness, and if nobody sees, no one will know how low he sinks in the mouldy bedroom of a Pimlico penny brothel, with filthy pictures peeling off damp walls, as the rickety bed creaks and jilters, while wealthy gents watch through peepholes for three and six an hour.

Do you think me jaundiced by my profession? Are my protests gauche? There are those in the police who blacken their hands in the filth that once appalled them. Now that penny dreadfuls are *de rigueur* in the drawing room, no depravity is too shocking for entertainment. And what is wrong with that? These gratifications distract us. The fleeting glow of shock lulls us from the greater crimes around us every day, crimes so familiar we no longer notice them.

This is not one of those sensation novels.

Nor is it one of those so-called detective stories that fill our newspapers and railway stations. There was nothing to detect. The facts were plain before my eyes. I had only to dig into the teeming fecundity of colours laid before me—and I failed.

There is no right place to begin such a story; and yet I must begin.

This is the story of a man. And of a girl. A host of girls. The Flowers of Sin. Flowers of evil, grown in the London filth. Entrancing flowers that bloom in the spring and are withered by autumn, devoured in the compost by this voracious species of worm to which we all belong.

It is, most of all, the story of Felix.

## WELCOME ARRIVALS

The girl whooped. Bubbles bobbed and weaved beyond her outstretched arms. She skipped after them across the blanket of virgin snow, the Quarterhouse quadrangle unused to such frivolity. She clasped her dainty hands upon one, and it vanished. She darted into my path, as I headed for the porter's lodge. I moved her aside, my curt smile ill masking my vexation.

Where the hell were Molly and her troupe of entertainers?

I strode through the great stone archway and glared out into the square. Along the ancient walls, fine carriages crowded to drop off the gentry for our charitable do. Before they could be ushered safely into the Master's Lodgings, shoeblacks and nostrum vendors clamoured for their attention, chastised continually by my colleagues. A fruitless harassment: these lurkers' services were as useful as ours. But such skirmishes abounded wherever the "two nations" met, the thresholds we police continually patrol between have and have-not, ease and malaise. Whom we are protecting from whom is seldom explicit.

Where were Molly's bloody tumblers and strollers? If she let me down, the commissioner would be sorely embarrassed; and if I embarrassed Sir Richard, there would be hell to pay. I stared out across the cobbled square glowing in its fresh sheet of snow. Infuriating that I, a detective of Scotland Yard, should be at the mercy of this ragamuffin and her ragtag rabble.

As I was cursing Molly's damnable timekeeping, two worn-out nags entered Quarterhouse Square dragging tumbrel carts, and trudged towards the gates.

Observing this, as he leaned against the gateway, a curious

old fellow stood puffing at his pipe. He nodded to me genteelly. For a moment, I thought he might be the porter; I had better reassure him that I, as sergeant in charge, could vouch for this unholy congregation. Noting the contrast between his noble face and threadbare suit, I realised he was more likely one of the Quarterhouse Brothers. The Quarterhouse, once a monastery, was long since become a home for elderly men fallen on hard times. Selected on rigorous (though secret) criteria, these impoverished gents enjoyed a comfortable life in this, the most refined almshouse in London—more charitable club than almshouse—endowed by some old financier grown rich on ordnance and usury.

As the East End bells chimed the hour, I waved Molly's carts into the archway. There they disgorged the strangest human cargo I had ever seen. The old gent and I watched the dwarf acrobats, crippled jesters, half-dressed dancing girls tumble out; lean sinews, strong brows, trumpets, timpani and flashes of flesh. As I sought Molly's ginger mop amid the cavalcade, the old fellow addressed me.

"There's something refreshing about their flaunting of physical defects, wouldn't you say?" His accent was clipped, so precise and English that he must be a foreigner. He nodded to a pair of peepshow grotesques. "They are as God made them. Criticise and be damned."

His companionable tone cut through my mood, and I couldn't help but smile. The grey old fellow set about stoking his pipe—not without difficulty, for his right hand was disfigured—clenching the tobacco against his overcoat. I was about to offer assistance, when he flipped the pouch into his waistcoat pocket with the ease of long practice. The pipe whirled into place between his lips. I looked him up and down. An engaging old fellow. Besides this dexterity and his old world overcoat, there was a music to his movements—

"Lucifer, old man?" Molly clapped me on the back. She

loved to creep up on me unawares; it was her way of proving an urchin knew the streets better than any Scotland Yard sleuthhound. She patted my stomach familiarly. "You're in rude 'ealth, by the looks of it."

"My health isn't the rudest thing in the vicinity, you wee street Arab."

She ignored my insult and struck a match for the old fellow.

I ruffled her mop of ginger hair, which annoyed her. "I can offer you lessons in reading a clock."

"Have I ever let you down?"

I simply looked at her.

She rolled her eyes, then fanned out a deck of cards with a friendly wink. "Choose a card, sir, any card."

The grey old gent smiled, chose a card, showed it to me for confirmation, and slipped it back into the pack.

Molly put her fingers to her temples, her mind-reading pose, and declared portentously, "King of hearts."

"I'm afraid not, young lady."

"Queen, I meant." She frowned, her face falling. "Jack?"

He shook his head kindly.

She sighed, putting away the cards with a tragic air.

"Consummate showman." I aimed a kick at her backside. "Get on with it."

"I promised you a show, Watchman." She puffed herself up to her full height, five foot nothing, and marched off into the party. "By Beelzebub, you shall have one."

"Speechifying at eight, Moll," I called after her, "if you can learn the time by then."

The old gent laughed, at her bravado or our complicity. "Pipe, young man?"

"That's kind of you, sir." I anxiously surveyed the quadrangle. After the hectic preparations, I would have liked nothing better than to dally. Oh, for a moment's peace. How a little snow throws Londoners into consternation: the butchers of Smithfield refuse to deliver a pig all of two hundred yards; champagne doubles in price; reputable thespians cancel all theatricals. Hence Molly and her troupe: these misshapen performers hastily sweeping the snow aside, unrolling their rustic dance floor, erecting stalls for mulled cider, peepshows, and the World's Smallest Theatre. No, I could not shrug off my responsibilities yet, not until Molly's scoundrels and ne'er-do-wells won over our glittering guests. "Perhaps later," I sighed.

"Of course, Sergeant."

I had not introduced myself, but the gent, perceiving my haste, withdrew to finish his pipe in the square, leaving me to commence battle.

## THE WORLD'S SMALLEST THEATRE

The girl was still chasing bubbles. She gasped as a vast, roiling bubble rolled toward her, produced by a louche gent to amuse his talkative clique, in high spirits as they raided the punchbowl early. The rest of the revellers emerged from the Master's Lodgings, where, rather than doff their coats they acquired extra scarves and gloves. All around, a squadron of tumblers and stiltsmen began cartwheeling through these statesmen, tradesmen, jostlers and journalists. While Molly fussed over the World's Smallest Theatre prior to the curtain-raiser, I exchanged an inspiriting word with caterers and serving staff.

The lass gazed through the bubble's rainbow whorls, veiling the scene in sapphire and emerald, gold and vermillion. She reached out, laughing. People in their finery turned toward that youthful laughter, as flowers toward the sun. She reached out her fingertip, resisting temptation, resisting, oh—

The bubble burst. The most delicate of touches. The girl clutched at her taffeta dress and burst into tears. She turned her eyes upon me in mute appeal. All around, fops and functionaries, ladies and waiters looked toward me, as if the girl was any concern of mine.

I snorted. She might be with the caterers, a sister hauled along to sell biscuits and cider. She might have been one of Molly's lot, but for being here before their arrival. With fashions today, she might even be some royal cousin or niece attending Prince Bertie and Princess Alix; I never could keep up with the Saxe-Coburgs' efforts to dominate the globe (if I interpret Mr Darwin correctly).

The girl wailed.

The onlookers held their breath in distaste. I laid a hand on the girl's shoulder and crouched beside her.

"Don't fuss," I said. I was tempted to remind her that she was the agent of her own downfall, but she gave me such a look that I held off moralising. Was she servant or guest? No parent was evident, and the caterers paid her no mind. "Who are you with?"

She stared in disdain, then recommenced her wilful wailing. I had misjudged, if not her age, her sham innocence. In my haste to quiet her, I pulled from my pocket the first thing I could find. A penny. I exhibited it between my fingers, then, as Molly had taught me, snapped my thumb—and it vanished.

The girl broke off her wailing.

The crowd about us relaxed. We were part of the show, rather than a disruption.

The girl stared. She prised off my hat and peered beneath. She turned her attention to my whiskers. Before she could tug them off, I snapped my fingers again, peered at her—and drew the coin out of her ear.

She began to giggle, like sunshine burning through fog.

"Bravo, Sergeant," called the smarmy gents who caused the bother with their childish bubble-blowing.

Snatching the coin, with a penurious look, she wriggled

away and vanished among the revellers. The chief bubble-blower made a ribald comment, then turned back to his punch. I gazed after her, blinking. Such an odd blend of childishness and self-possession. Her lucrative exit suggested she had known poverty; no, this was no princess. "Shift your dish, Watchman." Molly elbowed me aside, taking up position as Master of Ceremonies. "Sir Richard hisself is after you, in them cloisters there."

"What does he want?"

Molly rolled her eyes. She had tolerated my complaints for months, long before this charity ball was dreamt up. I was *persona non grata* at Scotland Yard ever since resolving a case underground, a case which caused disruption and death, which saw my inspector retire under a cloud—and of which I am not permitted to speak. Voices high up cast me as the troublemaker. I spent a year pursuing dead-end causes, while the knotty puzzles were handed to Darlington and the juiciest adventures to Jeffcoat, my competent, uninspired peers. Not that I'm the jealous type.

Sir Richard finally took pity. Seeing my glum face pass his door each morning, he made me organiser of this charitable shindig as a tonic, to get me out of the Yard's drear backrooms. It would be simple; it should be diverting. To launch a new charitable fund, the Phoenix Foundation for Fallen Women, some kind-hearted old musician fellow—one of the Quarterhouse Brotherhood—had persuaded the capital's wealthy to help the capital's vulnerable. The Brothers might be poor, but they were well-connected.

With the snow, however, and still November, the city had ground to a halt. My party suppliers came a cropper one by one. If it hadn't been for Molly's links with the theatrical underworld (and other underworlds I needn't list here), my efforts for this worthy cause would have fallen flat. Sir Richard owed me. But what recompense would he offer?

"My lords, ladies and gentlemen." Molly blasted me aside with her ceremonial tones, as two strongmen deposited a Punch and Judy stand so tiny you could barely believe anyone would fit inside. "The World's Smallest Theatre presents a tragical comedy: *Natural Selection*." The curtains fell away; the puppets were revealed. A farmer was cuddling up with his plump prize pig on a frosty winter's eve. We all laughed. "Later on," she continued, "after speeches for the Phoenix Foundation, will follow a most pitiable rendering of *Orpheus and Eurydice*, a fallen woman indeed. Thereupon the ladies withdraw, and Miss H's dancing academy conclude the entertainments."

The audience, though accustomed to sophisticated dramatics, warmed to Molly's nonsensical patter. As I weaved through the crowd, the pig won us over, snorting through the agricultural year: spring turned to summer, the pig loved, was wooed, married, and was grown fat with child. By the time I crossed the quadrangle, the pig bore sextuplet piggy finger puppets, to hoots of laughter from the suits and gowns.

Hors d'oeuvres were served. The scene changed. The audience chomped into the saucisson and bacon vol-au-vents. Some had the grace to look sheepish, as the fiddle struck up a ghoulish lament, and six tombstones, emblazoned with piggy faces, arose on the tiny stage to dance a dance of death.

## COMMISSIONER PAYNE

I scanned the rear cloister, peering in at the rough-hewn windows in search of Sir Richard Payne, commissioner of Scotland Yard. The quadrangle, with revels now in full swing, was surrounded by sandstone cloisters, as antique as any Oxford college. These were surmounted on three sides by the monastic cells that housed the Brotherhood. At the corners overlooking Quarterhouse Square stood the Porter's Lodge, for servants, and

Master's Lodgings, where gentry came in. At the far corners, the chapel, kitchens and refectory. Beyond this rear cloister, enclosing a walled garden, rose a dilapidated glasshouse. Despite the snow, I had resisted extending the party thither: exuberant behaviour can ruin glasswork and rare plants, and drunken toffs are more heedless than drunken tramps.

I spotted him lurking by the kitchens, warming his hands at the brazier where the tidbits and dainties had been kept hot. Yes, I knew why Sir Richard wanted me, more or less, but not what he had to offer. It had better be good. A month it had taken to organise the party, then this early snow, and I had to organise it over again. Now, as the snow sparkled around socialites, servants, and ramshackle players, a terrible pride welled within me. I would present to my commissioner a face sour as an old goat. Fists tight, breath clenched, my determination to get into Sir Richard's good books was eroded to a grim belligerence. He would not dare to summon me now, unless he had a worthy commission.

"Good God, need we encourage such things?" Sir Richard appeared to be talking to himself. He smoothed his mutton chops by the glow of the brazier. "*O tempora, o mores.*"

"The times and the morals were just as bad in Cicero's day." The grey old gent was there, and a policeman beside him. "In pursuit of lofty, elevated things, who are we to deny anything to any man? You love literature, and I music. If some enjoy more wayward muses, shall I criticise them?"

"Such sums, for such filth?"

"The Library keeps our books, Sir Richard, not our morals." His smile was barely discernible in the shadows of the ancient cloister. "These scholars seek nothing less than rapture."

Payne snorted. "Voyeurism and debauchery—" I coughed, lightly, and Sir Richard started, turning upon me with a scowl. "Bloody hell, Watchman. Must you creep around so stealthily?"

"It's what you pay me to do, sir." I did my best to disregard the policeman who stepped from the shadows: my usurper in the echelons of the Yard, Sergeant Solomon Jeffcoat.

Payne gestured. "Solly, would you mind?"

Jeffcoat touched the grey old fellow's arm to escort him out. The gent bowed discreetly, gave me a warm smile, and limped off.

I stared after him, puzzled. Not any old gent fallen on tricky times, he knew Payne; he was privy to intimate debates. "Sir, that fellow—"

"I was just speaking about you, Watchman." Sir Richard cut me off. He examined his watch, with a sidelong glance at me, and shook it in irritation. "And your manifold talents."

I was known as Watchman around Scotland Yard, as I'd spent my youth apprenticed to my watchmaker father; they were glad to abuse me for free repairs. I took his watch with a sigh. "Why does that fill me with foreboding, sir?"

"Nonsense." Payne laughed. I was waiting for him to condemn Molly's troupe: the disquieting humour, costumes, and handicaps. "Your soirée has raised a thousand pounds and a deal of publicity for Felix's charitable endeavour. Well done, young man... The Phoenix Foundation, indeed." He tugged at his moustaches. "The thing is, Watchman, we all need good news."

"We, sir?"

"The police force. The government. Damn it, the whole country needs a boost. And you're the man to give it to us."

I gazed at him impassively.

"Don't be like that, you impenetrable Scot." He waved me toward the sandstone shelf that ran along the cloister's inner wall. "Sit down, for God's sake."

I perched on the cold stone. Determined to hide my anticipation, I picked open the casing of his watch with my old pocket-knife. I examined it in the dim light. Cogs and springs I could handle; the reverie soothed my craftsman's soul. Sir

Richard's hyperbole gave me the shivers. It was the way I'd been treated, perhaps. You give your all and are punished for it. Unjust? Certainly. Typical? Perhaps: we're all cogs in a machine that none of us understand. Yet Sir Richard knew the dangers I had undergone, the indignities I'd suffered. I was relying on him. I needed to be reinstated at the heart of the mechanism.

"Look, Watchman, you're a good sort. The charity's bigwigs are grateful as all hell to you. You mustn't get in a tizzy when they lap up the plaudits: Mauve, and Brodie, and Felix himself, though he's a genial soul." Gabriel Mauve was our political contact, a cabinet minister, J.W. Brodie a newspaper tycoon, and Felix the Quarterhouse Brother who'd dreamt up the whole shebang. I'd met none of them during my efforts; I knew my place. Sir Richard began pacing up and down. He was ill at ease. "Our battlegrounds are no longer in China or Russia, nor the mills of Lanark and Preston. The war this great nation is fighting today is in our souls, indeed our bodies—well, you know what I mean, Watchman. Everybody knows. You've only to stroll the Haymarket of an evening, or any train terminus. Charitable efforts, like this, are all very well. But I've called for a Commons Enquiry. And you, Lawless, are our man."

I stared at him.

"To persuade a Commons Select Committee to act, I'll need a brand-new survey." Sir Richard was inspired. A rousing speech, almost as if he intended to stand for parliament. "We'll count every house of ill repute. Itemise every last working woman. On the streets. In bordellos. Everywhere. A census of sin."

Was this the commission I had dreamed of? I shivered involuntarily.

"None of your cynicism, Watchman."

He gave me a smile that made my heart sink, for I saw a trace of pity behind it. "Much has been done since '57 and the last appraisal. You may take great satisfaction in quantifying exactly how immorality has declined."

"Declined? Sir, are you joking?"

"So many good works. Cholera. Poverty. Pleasure gardens closed, slum alleys patrolled. Law and order bolstered and extended into the darkest corners."

Yet he always complained how government constrained his police finances.

"All improving the poor's plight, you see. Removing temptations from women's paths. Warning gentlemen of the ills caused by lapses moral and sexual."

Pah.

"This commission is crucial to the government's plans. I wouldn't trust it to anybody else."

A backhanded sort of a compliment. Perhaps he really was going into politics. "Jimmy Darlington's our man for vice and immorality, sir. I wouldn't dare tread on his capable toes."

"Darlington's been transferred. He's to shut down the filthy bookshops, but he'll show you around the night houses."

"Shut the bookshops?" I had sent a couple of these publishers down the previous year—pornographers, they were calling them now—but they popped up in new premises the moment they were released. I looked at Sir Richard more closely. There was something he was not telling me. "Some job Darlington will have. Is this shake-up coming from on high, sir?"

"I'll tell you, Lawless, but you mustn't let on to anyone." He lowered his tone. "A certain politician has a particular friend. They had a tiff. She's vanished. He's asked me to find her."

"You want me to find some politician's missing friend?"

"Lawless, Lawless, I say," he beseeched me. It was not like Sir Richard to beseech anyone. "Don't get on your bloody high horse." Payne put his hand to his brow. "Not any old politician. The Prime Minister."

Mistress, more like; after all, Palmerston was known in the press as Lord Cupid. "I see, sir."

"An impossible task, I fear. I told Darlington to seek her out. He laughed. Laughed. It's not how we do things, says he. We police, we make our presence known. But no details, thank you very much. Better that way, he says." Payne snorted: so Darlington was out, and I was in. "The PM must accept his loss. But things must change. We know bugger all. Without a detailed picture, what are we? A benign overseer, toothless, checking the worst excesses, with no chance of saving a single sausage. I've promised him we'll get a grip on what drives this netherworld: types of house, where the women come from, what age, what trades—"

"Hold the bus, sir. What are you asking me to do? Count the brothels? Or close them?"

"That's what I like about you, Lawless. Never afraid to speak your mind." He pointed through the frosty glass at the dancing couples. "Look. Things are changing. Here's London society, clamouring to contribute, to save those wretches from their baser instincts."

Outside, the Prince of Wales was gallantly turning Princess Alix, his Danish bride. (It was her fault that we'd persisted in holding this blasted party outside despite the snow, for in Denmark, they think nothing of such wintry sport.) I knew Prince Bertie well enough, and his baser instincts, and I couldn't help smirking at Sir Richard's utopian homily. "Let's start with counting them. How long will you give me, sir?"

"Six months."

I laughed despite myself. "Six? And how many men?"

"Watchman, the last reckoning of London's loose women numbered eight or nine thousand. It won't take—"

"Reckoned by whom?"

"The City Police."

"Whom you wouldn't trust with your laundry money. What does Darlington reckon?"

Sir Richard muttered under his breath.

"I'm sorry? Was that eighty thousand?"

"Darlington's a gambler. He includes every parlour maid and ballet dancer. Boosts his opinion of himself."

"Let's talk about closures." I sighed. "If I am to close one single brothel, I shall need henchmen. Heavyweights. A cohort of them. I'll need a ban on newspapers: one sniff of this, and the blasted *Bugle* will make a scandal of every gent turfed out *sans culottes* by my efforts. I'll need lawyers to avert the owners' wrath over diminished profits. Always remembering, sir, that those owners may be here tonight. Not to mention on your Commons Select Committee—"

"Don't be an ass, Watchman." Sir Richard glared at me, his frustration palpable; but he was the model of restraint, and guile crept into his eyes. "You'll be an inspector one of these days, Sergeant Campbell Lawless."

"If I toe the line, you mean?" I turned my attention back to his watch's workings. "I'd rather pack it in."

"Nonsense."

I screwed up my eyes; there was grit in the mechanism, jamming the hands. This was just a new way of consigning me to oblivion: totting up numbers to be ignored and consigned to filing cabinets.

"Believe me, Watchman, your report will be taken seriously. The Select Committee will rely on it to demand an enquiry, I'm telling you."

A year in the shadows, and this was what he offered me in recompense. Late nights in dens of iniquity. Angry exchanges, with fallen women and their customers. One hell of a challenge. But I didn't mind hard work, or reluctant collaborators. I relished all that. Getting at the obscure truth, when people wanted to keep it obscure, that's what I loved in the job. Persuading. Observing. Devising solutions. "Why ask me to tell lies, then?"

"That's not what I want."

I kept working at the watch. He was sending me into a world where the strong were entitled to behave as they pleased, while the weak were powerless and dispensable. I might give my all and make not a scrap of difference. I would need to rely on him. "Fudge the figures, then."

He tore himself away from the warmth of the brazier and loomed over me. "I never said that."

I slid the knife blade into position. I nearly had it. I would not let him intimidate me.

He subsided on the stone ledge beside me, his tone all at once unguarded. "Do the job your way, you recalcitrant beggar. It's worth doing. And it's important to me."

"I won't do it at half-cock."

"If I wanted a duff job," he snapped, "I've plenty of others I could ask. But I'm asking you. Turn over some stones. See what scuttles out."

I liked the old bugger, despite it all, all my disappointments and let-downs; I liked the fact he knew he could count on me. I clicked the watch casing smoothly back into place. "Give me a year."

He clapped me on the back, surprised and relieved. "Let's try for nine months or so." He seemed genuinely delighted. "Impress me. As for the newspapers, we've J.W. Brodie on our side, don't you know?" He gestured to the quadrangle, where the newspaper impresario was deep in conversation with our grey old pipe-smoker. If Brodie decreed it, the press would keep silent, all right. I was almost persuaded. Payne exhaled, tired of my grouching. "Now, a word about that urchin friend of yours."

"Molly?"

"You're fond of her, I know you are. She and her associates have done well enough out of this knees-up, eh? The statute book could be thrown at her for misdemeanours, current and prior." He leaned toward me, his mutton chops glowing dimly.

"I'd hate to see such pettiness. Wouldn't you?"

A low blow. Molly had come a long way since I first encountered her, a snub-nosed tyke entangled in an illicit gang. That gang was disbanded now, thanks to my previous investigations. An underground misadventure wrenched her from her friends, and I'd vowed to keep an eye out for her. This charitable party was the first work I'd found her in months. She jumped at the chance, mustering every lowlife and cripple she knew to help me out. Whatever Sir Richard might suggest, there was nothing untoward about my relations with Molly; she was only thirteen or so, for God's sake, though she behaved more like thirty. I had a duty to keep her from the sway of the criminal element.

"Sir Richard." Molly materialised before us. Typical timing. Her face gave no hint that she had been earwigging. "The speechifying is upon us."

"Be a sport, Lawless. I'm relying on you." Sir Richard stood up and laid a hand on my shoulder. I would recall that moment in the months ahead: a friendly sort of a warning, or a veiled threat. He shushed Molly away. "Besides, it's Brodie who's paying for this grog fight. Have a drink, man. You're off duty."

"Don't forget your timepiece, sir." I lifted the watch into the light, but kept hold of it a moment. "You don't honestly think our morals are better?"

"Watchman, I'm no fool. Politicians have a duty to convince us that we are improving." Outside, applause. He brushed down his lapels. "There'll be pose and pretension tonight, I grant you, but that doesn't mean it's all idle posturing. You and I know we're all flea-bitten apes, and more liable to brain our neighbour's wife than to write her sonnets; but we share a duty to tell people that they are better."

"In the vain hope we may become so?"

"In the hope we may curb their wickedness."

As he stood to go, the light from without cast a soft radiance over his features. I blew the dust from the watch casing and handed it over, ticking anew.

Payne looked suitably grateful. "I'm not asking miracles, Watchman. It's a dirty business. I need something that plays well to stalls, dress circle and the gods. A message to well-heeled parents that their sons won't be tempted; and to the lower element, that the ruination of their daughters is not inevitable. Do what you can."

## POLITIC CHATTER

Of the frenzy of self-congratulation that ensued I will say little, except to thank God I am no politician.

Gabriel Mauve, MP, with precise enunciation and a deal of self-satisfaction, launched into an encomium on modern society. He followed the very script Payne had touted to me: Progress Technological corrupts, unless intersown with Progress Moral; how much we hear of Social Evil, the base element to blame, our moral guardians at fault; look instead to this wonderful alliance organised by Scotland Yard's Commissioner Payne (viz. me), publicised by society darling Mrs Mauve, financed by magnate J.W. Brodie, no less.

And there he was: Brodie himself, rarely seen at public events. The reclusive financier said nothing, leaving Mauve to make a damned fool of himself. Oh, Mauve and his ravishing wife were untouchable then. The most lionised couple in the land, their parties were the parties to be seen at; their pronouncements echoed across the town. Her hairstyle was aped, his opinions parroted. Times change and change by turns; that is how London works. There was no point in resenting them. Their day in the limelight wouldn't last. My poor impression of Mauve stemmed from his earlier activity:

blowing bubbles ill befitted a cabinet minister.

Brodie, though, I found myself admiring. He had the decency to stay quiet: no swagger, no boasts, though it was he financing the stramash. He stood simply to the side, content to hold the puppet strings, as they summoned the final founder to the platform: Felix Sonnabend.

I looked on astonished as this old fellow limped on. This Quarterhouse Brother, a former musician, modestly declared his thanks. He mentioned me by name, demanded an encore of Molly's theatricals, and wished us all to enjoy these wintry revels. The mysterious Felix Sonnabend, founding father of the Phoenix Foundation for Fallen Women, was none other than the grey old gentleman pipe-smoker.

## SYMBOLS AND SIGNS

As the curtain fell, women dabbed at their eyes. Men strained to speak in level voices, lighting cigars to mask their emotion. I must admit, my heart had sunk when Molly announced the main drama. Drama? A mere puppet show.

Quite how their marionette Orpheus won our sympathies I cannot explain. The mystical musician pursued his dead wife to the underworld. With a toe-tapping gypsy serenade, he bewitched the boatman, guard dog and queen. But he turned back, forgetting the warning, as she vanished back amid the shades, crying, "Orpheus!" The audience stood aghast, many among them openly weeping. I pulled myself together and went to see the players.

Molly elbowed me aside, brushing off my congratulations. "Allow me to present Bede and the Pixie, together trading as the Oddbody Theatricals."

Two figures tumbled out from the World's Smallest Theatre. The Pixie cradled her elfin violin to her side. Bede, a cripple, rested where he fell, volubly analysing their performance. I reached out to help him stand up, only to realise his hands were withered. On his knees were boots, inverted, since his feet were stunted.

As the Pixie set him upright, I complimented her artistry.

She looked at me, gesturing with her violin, but made no reply. The little waif was mute.

"Wait till later." Bede gave an obscene wink. "You'll be able to view a lot more of our artistry in the after-hours show."

The Pixie made signs to Bede, some query about me. Together, I supposed, these two mites could function, almost as one able-bodied soul.

"No, Pixie." Bede observed me uncertainly. "I doubt it very much."

Molly had an uncanny knack for knowing when she was being discussed. "What's this unspeakable allegator alleging, Bede, old fellow?"

The boy blushed. "Nothing, Prof. She just wondered if you and, er, your sergeant here—"

The Pixie nudged Moll, running her finger down the curve of her violin with silent laughter.

"Certifiably not." Molly glanced at me, wavering between disgust and scorn.

I wondered how much of Payne's task for me she had gathered—and his vague threat. Her knowledge of the underside of London could be invaluable to me, but I had better watch my step.

I looked askance across the crowd. When Prince Bertie writes the guest list, what can you expect but Masons and magdalens, Delilahs and dandies? Rich men, poor men, philistines, pressmen. Fijian footballers, Red Indian raindancers. Aborigines in cricket whites, Patagonians in tail coats. Scientific atheists and soporific aerialists. Yankee abolitionists. Groggins, the elocutionist. A Baltic Sea heiress, a Battersea cellist. Garibaldi's Colonel Peard, in bright blue cape and ginger beard. George Eliot with a puss so sour, it turned the cream in the Eton mess. Wilkie Collins and unwed spouse, on opium tincture for his gout.

Everybody was scandalising each other. They flaunted fascinators and florid waistcoats in violation of the Queen's mourning. Ladies gossiped of the latest sensation novels, gents of dirty chapbooks.

"Still reading *Lady Audley's Secret*?"

"*The Female Spy*'s better, but *Aurora Floyd*'s a hoot—"

"Isn't that a dirty book?"

"No, that's *Maria Monk*. Tosh!"

"With the invigorating engravings?"

"If you like that, try *Indiscreet Jewels*. The ring describing where it's been…"

I exchanged glances with Molly over this endless giffle-gaffle: chatter of conquests and concubines, bawdhouses and laudanum. I'd even heard rumours of some salacious index of prohibited books doing the rounds of the flash gents.

A gentle laugh acknowledged my discomfort, while making light of it. The grey old pipe-smoker stood at my side. None other than Felix Sonnabend.

"Mr Sonnabend. I had no idea—"

"Oh, please call me Felix. That's how we do it among the Quarterhouse Brotherhood."

"Felix, then. When we met earlier, I didn't—"

He wafted my excuses affably away. "They do go on rather, don't they?" He gestured to the society chatter around us. "It's today's social milieu, I suppose. In my day, we discussed opera and poetry, not scandal and share prices."

I nodded. "Fashion, eh?"

"You're right." Felix gave me a disarming smile. "We must forgive them. After all, what are their lives worth? They fight their way to the City every day to trade slips of paper. Return to sterile homes, where perfectly dull wives organise perfectly drear dinners. Let nanny raise the perfectly dreadful children, destined for Eton, Oxbridge and the cabinet. Or anything equally turgid, as long as Papa approves."

Molly's Oddbody friends, normally a tough audience, tittered at this diatribe.

"I'm not scandalising you, am I? The Brothers tell me I must watch my continental candour." He brushed back his silvery hair. "They moan about slavery in Manchester manufactories and Shadwell workrooms; but is the moral degradation of the rich any lesser?"

"How so?" I asked. His forthrightness was refreshing amid the chatterers and chunterers.

"Well, they've written themselves a cheque they never can cash. Driven always to outdo, they must be distrustful at work, envious always of their neighbours. Expectations of abundance, but lives barren. The manufactories may be a form of slavery, but at least they foster camaraderie."

"Fine words, sir," said Molly, "and there may be something in 'em."

Bede piped up. "What is it you do, may I enquire, makes you so different?"

He smiled in self-reproach. "Guilty as charged."

It tickled me that he devoted the utmost attention to these street children, quite ignoring the aristocrats clamouring for his attentions. Journalists were waiting to talk to him about his Foundation, fine ladies admiring his profile.

Felix didn't notice any of them. "I'm a grumpy old Austro-Hungarian refugee, never content, always criticising these Englanders who welcomed me so kindly. I am an artist, like your friends. Retired now. But I'm—I was once a violinist, like your little friend."

Miss H's Dancing Academy appeared. As the hoofers took

to the stage, Molly gave her friends the nod. "Back in your schwassle-box and disport yourselves shamelessly."

The Pixie swept up Bede in her arms and carried him to the peepshow, where they would give their after-hours display: rather lewder, I imagined.

"I almost forgot, my felicitous friend." Molly reached quizzically for Felix's jacket and pulled a card from the top pocket. "Jack of diamonds?"

Felix was suitably impressed. "The very fellow."

Moll marched off with a triumphant gait.

"Quite a performance," Felix smiled, drawing me confidentially aside. The socialites waiting to congratulate him turned back to the entertainments. "I do apologise, Sergeant. I shouldn't dismiss a life I never led. I just feel a dreadful lack—don't you?—at the heart of London society. The dearth of—how can I say it?—of rapture." His eyes sparkled. "I see I am frightening you with my wild talk."

"Not frightening." I glanced at his crippled hand. "Only puzzling."

The shadow of sorrow passed across his face. "I have been blessed in my work. In my life."

"And this?" I looked across the quadrangle of revellers. "The Phoenix Foundation for Fallen Women?"

"My way of expressing gratitude. I benefit from charity: the Quarterhouse Brotherhood house me and thirty fellows like me, fallen on straitened times. Why not help poor women still less fortunate?"

"Forgive me, but how can an impoverished artist start a charitable foundation?"

"My artistic contacts I still have, though my performing days are done." He spread his hands in apology. "Money men—like Mr Brodie—like to share their good fortune, and what's more, to be seen doing it. I suppose he is speculating on Quarterhouse's charitable capital, gaining readers, and influential friends. It costs him little. I see no harm in it, indeed considerable advantage on all sides."

I found myself mesmerised. It was as much the honesty of what he said as the magical timbre of his voice. But it was time for me to shoo away the ladies tarrying roundabout, near enough to absorb his musicality, or smell his cologne. The puppet show had been decent enough, but this dancing was not for them.

"Go, of course," Felix bade me. "Lawless, I do hope you'll join us later. At Brodie's, you know. I could do with an ally."

As I ushered dawdling ladies back to the Master's Lodgings, I glanced back at him. Why should I be so taken with Felix? I had the foolish conviction that he was sharing intimate notions, never to be repeated, never expressed, were it not for the esteem in which he held me and my efforts on his behalf. Such contentment he exuded. No, not contentment; that is too level a word. Vitality that needs no stoking. These chattering people might be too conceited to see it, vying for witticisms to outdo each other. Felix cared nothing.

"What a life he has led." A lady addressed me calmly. While the other women hurried past us, she asked me what I knew of Felix, for she had observed us chatting.

"Nothing," I admitted. Much as I wished to hear more about him, I could not take my eyes from the lady. I am not blind to feminine charms: the shapely waist, the delicate neck. As I stood, pointing her peers to safety inside, she spoke unhurriedly, her low thrilling voice setting me aglow. She told me of Felix's life: music, Italy, love and loss, war and exile.

Our first encounter. I won't describe her. Only that the gaslight betrayed strands of grey amid her dark hair. Her tear-shaped eyes hinted at sorrows, but laughter welled quickly within her. But I promised myself I wouldn't describe her.

The trumpets sounded a salacious change in the tempo. With mock alarm, she excused herself, grasping my hand.

Rather forward, but there was no longer anyone to witness, the women within, the men absorbed in the shows. "I'm afraid I've bored you."

"Not at all. What a lot you know about our patron, Felix."

She tilted her head in modesty. "I am fanatical for music."

"I should like to know more." Suggestions and implications danced in the air between us. At last, I relinquished her gloved hand. "Shall I see you again?"

"You shall, Sergeant—"

"Lawless. Campbell Lawless."

"—if you'll permit me to write to you, care of Scotland Yard." She indulged me with a smile: I too had made an impression on her. And she was gone, muttering only her name. "Alexandra."

## SURVIVORS

Bawdy laughter behind me. Across the quadrangle, Gabriel Mauve was tossing a silver coin up and down, pouting. His cronies lolled by the back cloister, as the servants carried out the brazier and brought benches around it. The girl, with no more bubbles to chase in the dark, was turning cartwheels. Mauve winked again to his clique of sycophants. He flipped the coin high into the air, to land on the sullied snow. Sure enough, he hooked his prize. The girl pirouetted over. She snatched it up—whether a florin, or half-a-crown, it was a sight more than she'd filched from me—and turned a celebratory cartwheel.

The gents applauded. The remnant of the merrymakers huddled around, and I joined them, as the servants stirred up the brazier to roast sausages and mallow sap on the glowing embers. A party in the snow, confound the folly of it.

The girl lowered her head, bashful, and threw herself into

a double spin. As she wheeled, her dress fell up and over her knees and thighs, and she had not adopted the modern style of drawers and petticoats; that is to say, she showed more than she ought.

The younger men gave a roar. I averted my gaze, though I could not help but see that she was still more grown-up than I had thought. Gabriel Mauve, cabinet member and our voice in the political world, gazed at her unabashed. "Like a breeze," he said to me. "She's like a breeze."

It was true. The girl didn't even know she was beautiful; and yet a suspicion of the spell she cast was dawning on her, which heightened the titillation. She lowered her shoulders and stared at us, for an instant mature and womanly; then the shoulders hunched once more and made her girlish again.

Mauve smirked. "You're Lawless, aren't you? Not a bad effort, this bash. I'm grateful, too, for the efforts you're about to embark on." He bit his protuberant lip. "Sir Richard has spoken to you, hasn't he—?"

"Gabe! There you are." A full-bodied gown twirled from the cloisters, as colourful as a peacock. Only now did I recognise his tutting wife. These were the days before every scandal was luridly engraved in the illustrated press, and every headline adorned with portraits of the latest politician, the latest singer, the latest dustman, styled as Greek heroes. "Gabriel Mauve, are you drinking? You know what happens when you lush." Without a glance at me, she shook back her luxuriant locks, reached down and rubbed his groin, unabashed. "Remember Brodie and his blasted news hounds. Well, well. A woman will be satisfied." The celebrated wife strutted off, shaking her finger.

It was Mauve and his wife who made this the hot ticket in town. That he struck me as an odious crawler and she a vainglorious ostrich scarcely mattered. The Prince of Wales and his Danish poodle were too *dernière saison*: when Queen Victoria's son and heir offered to throw the party himself, it was deemed unroyal for Bertie (now married and respectable) to launch a fund for harlots and hussies, though harlots and hussies were dear to his heart.

There indeed sat the prince, dancing girl on his knee, his young wife gone to bed. The faithless cad owed me a favour from his bachelor days, when he was prone to errant impulses. When Inspector Wardle retired, Bertie had asked for me as his personal aide; his mother preferred a toad-eating flunky to report his indiscretions directly to her. Pimping for a prince was delicate work, and I was better off out of it. Yet, since that crisis underground, on the new Metropolitan Line, I'd been consigned to the worst jobs in the Yard. Policing was not always thrilling. It could be menial work, with poor reward. I'd done my share of filing, night shifts, court time, parliamentary duty, and informing the bereaved, while Darlington monopolised vice and Jeffcoat earned glory untangling enigmas. Of my new commission from Payne I was unsure, but it would at least see me back in the wicked world.

"A breeze across a wheat field," Mauve muttered again.

I frowned. "But who is she?"

"There's always hangers-on at these things." He smiled. "To cater to all our needs."

The girl stood mesmerised by the falling flakes; they fell on her dark hair and stayed intact for a moment before melting from the heat of her body. She scooped up a handful of snow and ran forward, but stopped short of us, wary of Mauve's ribald gaze. She seemed a delicate creature. She sized me up, judging me a kindly old sot. Just as she threw her snowball playfully up to me, Mauve pinched her cheek.

She flinched away.

I caught her snowball and held it out to her.

She hesitated, just out of reach.

"You have an admirer, officer." Mauve snorted. "Some have a way with children. I have five—or is it seven?—and

I never have got the hang of them."

"And yet," I said, "you reform our education laws year after year."

Mauve walked off in search of his wife.

The girl stood dumbly before me, hair tied in bunches and eyes shining.

"Dear lady," I said, "your snowball."

She reached out, but it fell at our feet, turning to slush. She squealed, wheeling away in delight, only to slip and fall in the snow.

Mauve's toadies made ripe comments.

"Gentlemen." Feeling like an aged schoolmaster, I helped her to her feet. I wrapped a scarf around her neck, and away she waltzed.

Rosy hints of dawn to the east. In the half dark, muttered conversations, glimpses of bare thigh. Molly's players mingled with the surviving gents. They had saved the day, gyrating tassels and suggestive refrains. If the dancing academy had given offence, nobody was complaining. At this time of the night, there was no problem in the social orders mingling. The dancers were scandalising the gents with picture books.

"Ah, a contortionist."

"That's a python, I presume?"

How many of these women would I end up counting for Sir Richard Payne? The pleasures they offered were far from the rapture that Felix spoke of. But my new duties need not begin tonight, nor my euphoria be tainted by my ludicrous task: to improve the irredeemable. Tired of enchantments, I slumped on a bench near the brazier and leant toward the warmth. The Pixie took up her fiddle, and Bede, grinding an organ, reprised Orpheus's doleful serenade. We all leaned toward that plangent rhythm, huddling together, with the music and the sausages. Felix watched them from the shadows, wiping away a tear.

I breathed in the cold night air. It was marvellous. As I

began to forget my woes, I felt the gentlest of nudges on my elbow. The cartwheel girl shrugged off my scarf and pressed a cup of cider into my hands; she must have seen me shiver. The music stilled my mind. Before I knew it, the girl had insinuated herself onto my lap. I laughed. What harm in it? She peeked inside my jacket, where she found my policeman's badge.

"Yes." I rolled my eyes. "I'm a policeman."

Pointing her fingers, she made the noise of a gun, her voice a surprising rasp.

"No pistol. Only a cosh." Laughing, I showed her the truncheon hid in my inside coat pocket. "Is there someone you need to fight off?"

Wide-eyed, she drew her finger across her throat.

I glanced around theatrically. The head caterer was still at the brazier, toasting the last of the food. "Is it him? Kill him, shall I?"

She opened her mouth but thought better of telling. The caterers were done and Molly's troupe packing up, but the girl kept perfectly still, as if praying nobody would notice her bedtime was long past. I cast my eyes into the embers. The organ music swelled; my gaze darkened. The girl pinched a fold of my trousers at the knee; back and forth she rolled it, in rhythm with the music, stroking the nap against the seam. It was the habit of a child playing with her blanket, an intimacy so heedless that I was thrown into a reverie. Yet she was heavy on my lap, and whatever Mauve said, she must be with someone.

The mesmeric music filled me with peace. I could recall words softly spoken, utterly familiar, at another fireside long ago, as if I could hear again my mother's voice. As a child, sat on her knee, by the fire in Morningside, I would lean into her shawl, as she pinched a fold of my nightshirt, rolling it back and forth between her fingers; such solace it brought me that even here, years later, everything was right with the world.

Flash! Pendants of ice sparkling on the old stone walls.

Bede's music faltered. Flash!

I started to my senses—and the girl was gone. It was the confounded photographer, her apparatus set by stealth to capture these last loafers. Flash! Must everything these days be preserved for posterity?

"Taken unawares, Sergeant Lawless?"

With a familiar mix of pleasure and discomfort, I looked up to see Miss Ruth Villiers, my librarian friend. More than friend, I might nearly say.

I blinked at her. I had written her an invitation, knowing this kind of charitable nonsense appealed to her, not to mention her aunt; but I was not sure I had sent it. "I feared you had not received my invitation."

"I didn't." She eyed me frostily, as if it were I who had been avoiding her. "I came with the photographer and Aunt Lexie."

"Oh."

Our spat of last year she had not forgiven: that ordeal underground, Molly's gang embroiled. I could see in her face that Ruth still blamed me for letting the truth be hushed up.

I sat up, blinking. "Glad to see you, is what I mean."

She offered me a skewer, white syrup toasted on its end. "Marshmallow?"

I accepted this olive branch. The sugary confection invaded my rotten Scots gums, and I suffered immediate toothache.

"My aunt is lolling somewhere abouts." She glanced around, toying with the ringlets of her dark hair. "You haven't seen her?"

She had grown it longer; how fine it looked against her pale neck. "I—ah—I don't think so."

She caught me admiring her hair. Her smile was unexpected beside her brusque words. "Admirable to see you too, hard at work, as always."

A typical jibe. I knew better than to protest. Trying to establish my decorum, I reached out my hand. "May I at least escort you home?"

"No, no. We must dash for the first down train."

"The train?"

"I'm living out of town now, you may recall."

"Of course, with the dreaded aunt—"

"Besides, you have more important people to spend your time with." And, with that final barb, she was gone. Did she mean Mauve and his cronies? Perhaps she was alluding to the silly girl on my lap.

Confound her. If only I'd known she was there, we could have had a quiet talk, set aside our disagreements. Now she was vanished away, back to Sussex, and her infernal aunt's, rendering futile my hopes of rekindling our friendship; for the year before she had been very dear to me, and I to her, I think. Could I pursue her? Too late. Apologise? Too late. As usual, I was always too late.

# THE CARCASS

On to J.W. Brodie's bash. I would not have dared to go, except that Felix sought me out to chum him along. When would I ever chat to him again, if I passed up this chance? It was not his celebrity that drew me; I'd known nothing of that before Alexandra spoke of it. It was an inner light. I liked his blindness to social class, his excitable talk.

As we rolled out of Quarterhouse, the merrymakers pelted each other with snowballs. Down Quartern Lane they tottered, singing a raucous ditty, and up St John's Street. Felix touched my arm, guiding me up the back lane, a shortcut to Brodie's place on Corporation Road.

The snow was dirtier on these alleys known only to locals: a darker world than the Quarterhouse quadrangle. Felix talked of the evening, but with none of Payne's unrealistic hopes or Mauve's hyperbole. Promises, collaborations, compromises,

even, were worth it, if they aided the needy. His desire to
share his good luck was strong enough, but behind it I sensed
a sadness. I thought to ask about his injured right hand; but I
found myself fretting aloud about the do chez Brodie.

"I hate these things too." He laughed. "Brodie will show
off his latest contraption, no doubt. Everyone will kowtow,
so his newspapers speak well of them. How vexing to know
everyone is polite only to get something out of you. All
desperate to impress, none daring to speak his mind."

A thrush was singing on a pollarded tree as we passed
Jerusalem Court. The last autumn leaves rustled in
Clerkenwell Green, metallic and dry. On past the house of
detention, dark and looming, we reached Corporation Lane.
The noisome revellers appeared at the corner. Between us, the
Finsbury Bank, and opposite it, a policeman guarding Brodie's
ceremonial portico. But fifty yards from those marble steps,
the stinking alley we had negotiated seemed the gateway to
an entirely different city.

But Felix had not made it through beside me. I found him
gazing down at a bundle of blankets in the shadow of the
prison wall. He was holding his hand to his face, staring at the
heap of clothes. He gave an unearthly groan, as if looking into
his own grave. I went back, stooped and peered under the
blanket: a pitiful excuse for a human being. After the cider
and sausages, the stench made my stomach lurch. It was a
sight common enough of a winter's evening, but I reproached
myself for not having seen it, investigated before he saw it.

Did Felix know her? Foolish thought: the face was obscured,
wrapped in rags.

The fallen woman—fallen, indeed—was collapsed in an
inhuman posture. Her head was twisted against the doorway
of Jenner & Cox, the tobacconists, her arms bent at the elbow,
like a conductor poised for a symphony. She was frozen, as
if the winds had changed, in this reverent pose. Her clothes

thin as paper. Snow on her petticoats. The flimsiest of dresses barely covered her chest, but it was her legs that made one recoil. Nobody could sleep in such an attitude. This was the body of love, tossed on the dust heap.

I laid my hand on Felix's shoulder to draw him away. "Felix, sir, I will—"

"No." He looked up in a kind of panic, stumbling forward.

I grasped his arm. "Won't you come along to Brodie's? Warm yourself."

"You go ahead, Sergeant."

I looked at him in dismay. There was nothing to be done for her.

"Please, see that this unfortunate... I can't bear—" He reached in his pockets for coins.

"Not necessary, Felix. I'll enlist that policeman at Brodie's and remove the body."

"I must... I cannot..." He turned away, overcome, and stumbled down the alley, back towards the haven of Quarterhouse.

## THE SECRET CHAMBER

I did not mean to stay at Brodie's bash, only seek help with the corpse; besides, arriving without Felix felt fraudulent. But blasted Jeffcoat was at the door, welcoming me with gruff bonhomie, though Payne's favoured sergeant knew how I felt about him. He thrust out his knife-blade nose and told me Brodie wanted a word.

"Brodie can wait," I said. "There's a corpse down the road."

Jeffcoat insisted he and Darlington would deal with it; I'd done my duties for the night, and Brodie didn't like to wait. I yielded, unwillingly. Felix had been so distressed, I would have rather kept my promise; but I made sure Jeffcoat had money enough for a cab to the mortuary.

In the basement, the carousing centred on the billiards table. No sign of the master of the house. I took a whisky, to relieve my mood and the toothache. Such a grand salon, like a gents' club, where one normally housed the servants: politicos and parasites betting wildly on every frame, duelling over swerve shots and droll ripostes.

I found myself perusing Brodie's cabinet of curiosities: arachnids; fossils; a murderer's skull phrenologically annotated; embryos in aspic. Not a collection for polite company, but acceptable in a gentleman's rooms. In between the baize-lined cabinets, I spotted hinges. A nice mystery.

Gabriel Mauve teetered over. The last person I wished to speak to. He launched into an anecdote about a dress house. This particular brothel was popular with men and women, upper-class, married and unmarried. One lady, lacking marital spice, came seeking tastier morsels. She eyed the well-made bed in alarm. Could she truly forsake her vows? With a gentleman unknown? The latch clicked. A glance. A gasp. Mauve nudged my elbow. "The man who had come in—it was her own husband. Can you credit it?"

I admitted, it was hard to believe.

"It's the truth," he protested. "Every word."

"Can you be sure, sir?" A useful preface to the world I was about to enter. "Gents' clubs are full of apocryphal anecdotes."

"I'm sure. Because I was there." He blinked away a tear. "And it has proven the salvation of my marriage." He fell, insensible, into an armchair; his wife had told him not to drink, and I could see why. But how could he be sure it was his wife's first visit to that well-made bed?

The billiards players grew scarcer, conquered by drink and bankruptcy. A stout-chested man stood by, admiring me as if I were one of his specimens.

"You like my collections, huh, boy?" J.W. Brodie's inscrutable expression I recognised, his ash grey hair and neat moustaches, but his accent took me aback, American twang laced with Old World ice.

"The casings are superb—"

"The casings?"

Not the praise a collector would appreciate. I bit my lip. Before I could revise my sentiment, he burst out laughing.

"Forgive me," I said, "if I admire hinges and casements. I'm a watchmaker by trade."

"A watch man? Right. I got nothing against tradesmen. My father worked down them Scottish mines. Say, ain't you Payne's Scotch boy at Scotland Yard?"

"You have me." I was surprised that he should know of me, flattered even. "Watchmaker by apprenticeship, policeman through habit and circumstance."

He grinned. "And in this sleuthing capacity, you made a discovery, right?" Our eyes flickered to the hinges. Brodie glanced about. The few gents still on their feet were tight with gin. They were more interested in cannoning balls and spider rests. "Would you care to see my real collection, Mr Scotland?"

Why was I accorded this tour of the inner sanctum? I suppose a man like J.W. Brodie can simply own pieces of the Colosseum, and sometimes wants to show them off. His secret chamber was adorned with photographs: Brodie with Garibaldi, Brodie with the Czar, Brodie with Abraham Lincoln. These were impossible to doubt. Less easy to accept was the scrap of the Turin Shroud, recently returned from analysis at the University of Oxford.

I resisted touching it. "A forgery, of course?"

"That's what they're telling us." He winked. "That's what they want you to believe." The consummate newsman: no need to lie, just let us believe.

Brodie showed me a panoply of wonders so strange, I would have doubted them in any other house: Genghis

Khan's scimitar, a first edition of *Don Quixote*, carnal writings of mediaeval popes. Brodie winked. Now I saw: this wall of his secret chamber was an erotic library. The bookshelves stretched from floor to ceiling. If Darlington was hunting dirty books, these were titles I should alert him to: *Sodom*, *The Cockchafer*, *Le Courrier des Fouteurs Ecclésiastiques*, *Fanny Hill*; and a luxurious black volume titled in a strange language I struggled to decipher: *Efliter… Efterces… Eflrcesym*, or something like it. The significance of this tome was lost to me, surrounded by so many diversions.

A novella in a yellow jacket sat wantonly open:

> …*au naturel*, as the French say. Her waist was little,
> enhancing the delicious bulge of the minx's hips and
> posteriors. Miss Lucy soon gave way to her delight.
> "How nice! It's better than the other way, go on." The
> duke, exhausted with delight, cried, "*Quel plaisir*. This
> must be what the serpent teach Adam and Eve! The
> forbidden fruit, *ma belle* Lucy!"

It was as if Brodie had set up his display to taunt me, to bewitch me. For only then, shaking myself free from the dirty books, did I notice the chess automaton.

Brodie sat before the cabinet and casually shifted the white pawn to king four.

The carved wooden face of his opponent inclined slightly, the eyes shifted left, then right, and its wooden arm swung mechanically across the board. It hovered over the pieces. It shifted a pawn.

I couldn't help but gape. I was a keen competitor in the Yard's after-hours league. All chess fanatics had heard tales of this device, though I thought it was long gone.

Brodie lit a cigar, lapping up my consternation. The New Turk was a miraculous mechanism, by any standards. A machine, idly playing its master at chess. Over the next half hour's moves—a King's Gambit, if you are interested—Brodie related how he acquired this machine. In the Turk's heyday at the Schoenbrunn Palace defeating Beethoven, Goethe and Napoleon, how the press speculated, how the priests damned. The demon had toured Europe, defeated countless English masters, and astonished the States, before falling from public favour. Brodie had purchased it cheap. He showed me a newspaper cutting that declared: TURK DESTROYED BY FIRE IN CHINESE MUSEUM.

"Nice story." He grinned. "All the more miraculous for it."

Not destroyed, merely damaged. A few repairs and Brodie had resuscitated the marvel. Now the American prodigy Paul Morphy was coming out of retirement to challenge the European masters, Brodie's newspapers planned to whip up a carnival in which his New Turk machine would challenge the winner.

"Darn it." Brodie winced, as the Turk's mechanised hand planted its rook to the eighth rank. Checkmate on move thirty. "Care to play?"

I walked all round the machine. Brodie wheeled the cabinet around, opening each panel one by one to display the workings. I am an aficionado of cogs and clockwork. No trickery was apparent: the cabinet was too small for a man; were there a sentient opponent hidden in elsewhere, working it by remote means, I should hear the pulleys and see the strings working the mannequin. No hoax. No tricks. An automaton chess fiend.

I chose the Evans Gambit, a modern variation. The Turk's face, rudely carved, suggested archaic wisdom. Ten moves in, I was mesmerised by the movement of the mechanical arm. By the twentieth, my kingside was stymied and my queen disarmed. I gambled on a knight sacrifice, but the fatal blow descended, delivered by his bishop, while castles pinned my king.

I blinked in wonder. "Let me examine this prodigy."

"You got to be kidding, boy. I'm going to lend it around the aristocracy. Our friend Gabriel Mauve, cabinet minister, has asked for it."

I made a face.

"He won't blab, believe me. He'll never know how it works." J.W. Brodie drew on his cigar, eyes twinkling. "If my papers have any influence, it's a sensation. I won't have some nickel-and-dime flatfoot explaining how it's all just levers and pulleys."

"Is it all just levers and pulleys?"

Silence.

I stared at the Turk's impassive eyes.

"Ain't we all just mechanisms," said Brodie, "propelled by forces we cannot fathom or control?"

I shook my head. "It plays so like a man. As if there were a homunculus inside."

"A minuscule chess master?" He laughed. "Remind me of that, Mr Scotland, next time it needs repairing. Come on. My New Turk has defeated us both. We may stand to be winners in another respect. Old Payne has dealt you a problematical hand, ain't he? Count up the capital's cathouses. Whoa, now. I'd say you could use some help. Junior reporters, maybe, to run a little legwork. Touch of discretion here, blast of indignation there." He stroked his moustache, looking sideways at me. "We all need help sometimes."

"Sometimes we do. If we can afford it."

"A murder a day is all I ask."

To sell his salacious rags? "I can't imagine a businessman like you would ask me to break police rules."

"I'm not asking you to commit the murders."

I looked around his chamber of secrets, gave the New Turk a final glance, and stood up.

"Come on. You've something I want; I've something you need. Sure we can come to an agreement, Mr Scotland. Take another shot of whisky, why don't you?"

"I'll be on my way, Mr Brodie." I looked him in the eye. "I rarely drink much."

# PART II
## KEEPER OF VICES

### DECEMBER 1863–JANUARY 1864

Folly, lewdness, sin and minginess
Bewitch our spirits, and exhaust our sides.
We cultivate our genial regrets,
Like beggars nourishing their parasites.

Charles Baudelaire, *Les Fleurs du Mal*

A modest woman seldom desires any sexual gratification
for herself. She submits to her husband, but only to please
him; and, but for the desire of maternity, would far rather
be relieved from his attentions.

William Acton, *The Functions and Disorders
of the Reproductive Organs*

Boldness is one of the most essential qualities in getting
women. Not much harm can result from it, if not good. A
man can but be refused, and women don't tell of sexual
requests to them. Not one virtuous woman in a hundred
would tell anyone but a confidential female friend if a
man said to her, "Oh! I'm dying to fuck you," and she'd
feel in her heart complimented by his desires—though she
wouldn't tell that.

"Walter", *My Secret Life*

# A COMPLAINT, FROM GABRIEL MAUVE, MP

Your blasted Lawless was so fascinated with the chess automaton. It has nothing to do with it, damn it to hell and back. That's not been thieved. I can't understand why he kept poking about at it. Leave off, I told him, and sharpish. Idiot.

That's right. It's not mine. Borrowed from Brodie. Yes, Brodie, the newspaper chappy told me about it at the party last month. He cadged it off some Yankee sideshow halfwit. Oh, he'll make a killing with exhibition matches next year; chess fever, all right, with Morphy versus the world, Staunton lured out of retirement, don't you know. But this is all beside the point. My point is that I have been robbed, and your deuced officer wasted precious time on half-cocked queries and pointless cross-examinations of household members, when he could have been hotfooting it after the thieves.

I am calm, damn you. I'll tell you when I'm not calm.

No sign of breakage. Yes, no obvious sign. My Secret Cabinet—I must make a clean breast of it, I suppose—my *Camera Secreta* is a repository of papers and private artefacts, priceless not only to me but to the nation. I found it open while fetching some literature, after a late night with the Flash Songsters down the Cyder Cellars. No, I don't know exactly what's been took. Stop bloody well preaching about your difficulty in catching the blighters.

The Cabinet. Allow me to explain. It's a closet, accessed from my office, an old Catholic chapel where papists hid from their just deserts. Large enough to stable a donkey. Thick walls, no window. Dank. Ancient flagstones. Ideal for manuscripts, so Panizzi of the British Museum tells me, of which these bastards have taken several: de Tissot's *L'Onanisme*, and Wilmot's *Nymphomania*. The door, quite invisible from the house. No, no servants know of the room's existence; I alone have a key; I never, ever leave it open. My wife? Oh, my wife on occasion I've allowed in. For the room's upkeep, you understand, filing and cleaning. No secrets between spouses. There's nothing untoward in that, despite your impudent look; our marriage is a modern one, and I will stand no aspersions upon it. Your Lawless fellow spotted the door, I admit, only because I had left it ajar in my distress, which I never, ever do.

Confidential papers I do keep there at times; recently the Education and Workhouse reforms. Untouched, yes. The point is that this is a matter of state security. And your blasted Sergeant Lawless kept badgering me about the automaton. The details of what has been taken I will confirm anon: private papers, certainly, and rare books. Is that not detail enough?

No, the money has not been took, nor the jewels. Nor has the rare engraving of Venus and Mars *après l'amour*—which shows the thieves are fools. Except that the papers... Their value is not financial, exactly, not intrinsically financial. Only that they could prove an embarrassment to me. And to my wife, yes. She knows of their contents. Some of their contents, rather. The rest, if you must insist, yes, there may be potential for blackmail. I'm sure I speak in confidence, as man to man? I have, as many gentlemen do, recorded amatory highlights of my life. A life such as mine is lived with passion. Besides the pleasure in recording such passions, there is instruction for posterity. I am proof men of our generation, whom some think bloodless and dispassionate, are the equal of the great lovers of the past: Byron, Casanova, Catullus. Good God, no! I would not want the papers made public. Not in my lifetime. Do you want to ruin me?

No, I see that it's difficult for you, of course, without details. One feels so angry. Violated.

To prove these memoirs were mine? It would be a stretch, I suppose. They will seem the wildest fiction. Only I would know, and my wife, if they were published, and I feel shamed. If anything should come before the courts, with my being a minister, such is public prurience these days...

No, as I told you, no sign of a break-in. Which made your idiot Lawless claim that the thieves must have been already inside, dash my wig. He examined the little pull-down bed— for when I fall weary over cabinet papers, you understand.

Not the bloody automaton again? Yes, I borrowed it. Brodie lent it me temporarily. It only runs for a couple of days, then must needs retune or rewind; recharging, that's what he calls it. Bloody Yank plays his cards close to his chest. It's a marvel, all right. Beat me in nineteen moves. Tired of it then. I should have returned it to Brodie, but the Justice Bill has occupied me totally. I'll call Brodie's cronies to fetch it. No, no, a few urchins delivered the thing. Yes, they helped me bring it inside the Secret Cabinet, but they were there only moments. What do they matter? Catch the blasted thieves, won't you? Of course you have something to look for: my blasted amatory memoir. Is my signature on this report not example enough?

I see. I see the obstacle. True, I shouldn't want it divulged among the republic of thieves and dirty booksellers that such a document is afoot. We'd be doing their blackmail work for them. I see. No rewards, then, for God's sake.

This Lawless fellow, though: unacceptable impudence. I would wish him dismissed. See to it.

# THE PATH OF FILTH

"Get 'em off," cried a man nearby. We were in the Argyll
Assembly Rooms, entrance fee waived.

Darlington grinned. "Watch this, Watchman."

It never ceases to amaze how much fiercer is the hold of
the partly clad body than its naked counterpart. Mask a face,
veil an upper arm, and the suspense begins. Cover a thigh in
satin, adumbrate a bosom with tassels, and any man who is a
man falls prostrate, and many women besides.

I have friends, educated friends, who assert that any woman
earning her living through parading her form is a prostitute.
She is a corrupt tool of the system, corrupt economically and
morally, whether actress, dancer or courtesan. Using her God-
given form to expedite lusts, she is culpable for furthering the
spiral of sin and decay.

The actresses, dancers and courtesans I know tend to
disagree. Many speak of the thrill of performance, when they
hold so many souls in their hand, delighting and frustrating
with the hem of a skirt or the fringe of a corset.

"Get 'em off." Another catcall.

I kept my head low.

"You'll get the feel for it." Darlington's dirty fingernails
described curvaceous shapes. "Allow me to show you the lay
of the land, and I shall open your eyes—and a few doors."

Darlington had grandiose notions that he could lift the
lid on the hotpot of vice broiling beneath the West End. I,
and innocents like me, might pass evenings ignorant of the
temptations on offer; but the flash gent saw opportunities on
every corner, and he could show me how. I might as well
humour him.

Darlington was a buffoon. True, he and Jeffcoat had dealt
with the corpse that night at Brodie's. The corpse turned out to
be the very woman Payne had been asked to find by the Prime

Minister. But this grim news somehow seeped out beyond the walls of Scotland Yard.

"A conspectus." He sketched it out in the air. "Your typical swell's passage round the nether nightspots."

Conspectus, indeed. The 1857 conspectus of prostitution counted eight thousand, six hundred prostitutes. If I was to follow Payne's demand that I annotate each unfortunate woman's age and trade, where to start? This was our sixth stop, and we'd annotated bugger all. At the Royal Opera House, Darlington had pointed out boxes empty but for a bottle on ice; the ladies were not the prettiest, he said, but the retiring rooms were famed for excellent locks. At the Alhambra, I had never noticed all the women in the circle. Wives wouldn't be seen in such places; these could only be mistresses. On to Barnes's, where oysters were served before we sat, with rump steak to follow; I would have been more grateful, if not for the toothache.

Nowhere did we wait for admission; nowhere did we pay. Though not in uniform, we were known as policemen. Darlington revelled in the respect shown him, and the perquisites. At the Cyder Cellars, the chorus warmed up with profane chants:

> *Mother H, she lodges*
> *The best fillies of the nation:*
> *A tidy passage down below*
> *A hairy situation.*

Beneath the Alhambra, gents crowded to express admiration to the dancers. The waiter whispered. Darlington grinned but sent him away. Tonight, at least, he was resisting the darker treats on the menu.

Now we had removed to the gilded upper chamber of the Argyll. Artistically clad women held *poses plastiques* in velvet alcoves, temples of voluptuousness based on classical art, though stirring the psyche rather more directly.

The lights dimmed. The ensemble struck up an exotic rhythm. Onstage chugged a miniature train, driven by the famous Chouchoute. She sweated as she stoked the furnace, the orange glow glistening on her brow. She bent over, flesh gleaming through choice gaps in her attire, as the train-rhythm grew hotter.

What was he hoping to show me? Did he think my Edinburgh upbringing so provincial I should never have seen the like? True, Edinburgh is small: that makes the louche night spots closer and affordable to frugal apprentices such as I; my schoolfriends were well acquainted with the Cowgate, beneath the castle, notorious for explosive displays.

My irritation with Darlington was hard to disguise. They'd done competent work that night, he and Jeffcoat: identified the dead woman; traced her to a Kensington side street well known to flash gents; found the boarding house she'd most recently worked in (an address familiar to Lord Palmerston, amongst others). Jeffcoat's report was painstaking; he even credited me for finding her. Yet the *Bugle* picked up the story, giving it disproportionate coverage, given that fallen women met unfortunate ends all the time. It wasn't long before all the papers were nosing around. Nobody said she was the PM's mistress, but the scurrilous slurs were obvious. These articles infuriated Payne, marring his political ambitions when he had promised the PM discretion. I wished I had dealt with it myself. Brodie had asked me to find a murder a day for his scandal rags, but after my lukewarm reaction, I never heard from him: maybe I wasn't the only one to whom he made overtures that night. Darlington was an incompetent; Jeffcoat was the one I suspected of selling stories to the *Bugle*.

Chouchoute threw off another garment. Hat, jacket, shawl, chemise. She stood before us, gleaming golden in her bodice, gloves and new-fangled bloomers. She looked up at us and wiped her brow.

"Get 'em off."

She squared up to us, much as a navvy might look at a pile of dirt. A flutter flew through the audience; the separation between viewer and viewed seemed flimsy. Chouchoute threw down an immaculate white gauntlet. The music faltered, the house lights rose; she peered out from the stage, offended, and raised a finger.

"Who?" she said abruptly, gazing down lasciviously. "Who has spoke?"

"Him there!" Jocular voices called, and the guilty gent was shoved toward her outstretched finger.

Chouchoute drew a cane from her high boot. She leant down, catching the hapless fellow's chin with the tip of the cane. His gaze was directed onto the twin orbs above him, brightly lit, swelling beneath the bodice. There was no escape. The music resumed. She kneeled on the edge of the stage, drawing him forward in rhythm, until his face was against her muscular thighs. The fellow's eyes were bulging.

"Such close inspection." She spoke in a faux French accent. "One really should have shaved." Her eyes flashed. She whirled around and knelt, the stays of her corset within his reach. The fellow gaped upward, practically panting. Chouchoute gave a quizzical frown. "Is he trying to see what I ate last night?"

This show, I admit, was more shameless than Edinburgh's equivalents.

"Get 'em off," cried Darlington.

Chouchoute glanced over her shoulder, right at us.

I froze. My worst fear was to be dragged onstage. Of this danger Darlington seemed heedless. He was heedless of so many dangers, I would realise soon enough.

Holding our gaze, she untied the bow on her corset lace with a flourish. The fellow's hands were trembling as he reached for the lace. She grabbed his hands and had him pull the stays asunder. Inch by inch, the ivory skin of her back was revealed, arching up from her waist. The crowd bayed for satisfaction. The corset loosened; her milk-white breast was sure to be revealed; she winked at me.

The lights went out.

A flash of light. We caught our breath. The show unfolded in a series of photographic flashes. Flash: she turned. Flash: his face against her bosom. Flash: her legs wrapped round him. We gasped.

Flash: the bloomers—gone.

Pandemonium.

## KATE HAMILTON'S

At midnight, as the music halls emptied and the dancing salons cleared, we passed through the throng. Where next? Night house or accommodation house? *Maison de convenance, maison de tolérance*? Or straight to the finishes, like so many before us, hoping to clinch the deal.

Blazing lamps illuminated the Haymarket, its Turkish divans peopled by troops of elegant courtesans: the girl fresh in from the north, the bloom of her cheek not yet dimmed; the pale milliner in her lace; the prima donna's rustling silks; the haggard old fury in a doorway.

A woman slumped into the dirty slush, dizzy, and bloated with disease.

Felix sprang into my mind. I recalled his distress, seeing the dead woman that night, and my heart juddered. Londoners pass by horrors every day, and remain unmoved. His distress cut me deep. Had I ever seen someone so unhinged by grief? So changed in a moment? And for someone he didn't know?

In front of us, a girl lifted her skirts from her ankles as

she stepped from the pavement. It was an innocent-enough gesture, to keep the hems out of the dirt. Darlington quickened his pace. What was he trying to do? Impress me with his worldliness? And his ridiculous long coat, as if playing the part of a stage detective.

I was tired of his posturing. "Jimmy, what does this sauntering around the West End achieve?"

"Achieve, Watchman? What did you think to achieve?"

"I asked you to show me the ropes, before handing over. Payne demands that I reckon up every last prostitute and every blasted brothel. All you've shown me is that there are more at the trade than I ever imagined."

"That's lesson enough, ain't it?" Barely heeding me, he feigned a furtive look, as if stopping for a stolen moment when he ought to be somewhere else. "Others have made this reckoning before you."

"They certainly have." I pulled out my pocket book. "Fifty thousand in 1791; eighty thousand in 1839; Dr Acton reckoned two hundred and ten thousand in '51."

"Acton did well," Darlington said, grinning, "to interview so many."

"But Payne's last return, in '57, counts just eight thousand six hundred."

"An oddly precise figure. I've been at this game a year, Watchman. Thankless. You ask yourself, in the end, what is a prostitute? Observe." He whistled at the girl ahead of us, to my embarrassment, for she looked quite respectable.

Sure enough, the girl looked back over her shoulder. She turned a sultry gaze on each of us in turn, weighing up which had whistled. Darlington smirked. He pulled open his coat, just enough to show his police truncheon protruding, and winked.

The sultry pose gave way to a scowl, and she vanished into the night.

Darlington put an unwelcome arm around my shoulder.

"Here on the streets, Watchman, you'd be surprised how many women will answer a whistle. Would you have counted that girl? In the Burlington Arcade on long winter afternoons, where all the men in London walk before dinner, must you count every shop girl? What of courtesans, from Kensington to Ship Alley? Are they prostitutes, or employees? Or simply unwed mistresses? The sailors' wives, with five husbands each. The milliner augmenting her stitching with irregular antics. The upright lady whose licentious urges may bring profit, my friend, or simply pleasure."

I pulled my coat tighter, eyeing the streams of night people around us. This city of strangers, unknowable, innumerable. "So what am I to do?"

"Do the rounds. Give the impression that we police keep count of this flesh heap, and it will regulate itself, mostly. Then go home, stop thinking and try to stay in your right mind."

Two steps from the dens of Soho, a dark entranceway was fringed by two ill-trimmed laburnums. You do not feel the eyes watching you as you approach. You imagine slipping from view into the passageway that leads to the silken palace. A moment of uncertainty, then you push your way in. The passage envelops you with a steamy warmth: the welcoming embrace of Kate Hamilton's.

Darlington went to push aside the heavy plush curtains, his truncheon tucked beneath his winter coat. A voice accosted us. "Not on duty," he replied, "but rather attending personal business. By appointment with Kitty H. herself."

The bell was rung, velveteen drapes pulled aside, champagne thrust into his hand. It dawned on me, Darlington wasn't trying to shock. He wanted me to know that he knew everyone. That champagne, before we were seated, meant he had done his job.

At the heart of this pageant of bodies, nestled in the

palace of ottomans and pale rouge divans, beneath a soft dome illustrated with lurid Olympian daubings, sat a vast ungovernable whale of a woman, a queen of the Orient, enthroned above her minions. Kate Hamilton herself.

Darlington winked.

"Long tempo, nanty vader, Jimmy Darlington," she crooned. "Roll up, roll up, my lover boy. Choose between Lila, layer of lords, Cora, comfort of commodores, and Sabine, saviour of seamen."

"Nah, Kitty," a pale woman with ample bosoms piped up, lolling on a gent's knee. "I never saves none of it."

Kate Hamilton erupted, a blancmange Vesuvius. "Cora, kindly entertain the gentlemen. Jimmy does respond to your particular endowments."

In a recess off the main chamber, illustrated with the judgement of Paris and more pretexts for nudity, Darlington drew out a set of chessmen, but disdained the board laid into the table. Instead Cora shed her gown and lay back on the ottoman. The Oriental lamplight threw enticing shadows on her. Scarves wrapped around chest and hips, her stomach lay bare. Neatly inscribed, from hipbones to ribcage: a chessboard tattoo.

Darlington swiftly laid the pieces on her tum, flat as an ironing board and walnut brown. As he advanced his pawn, Cora lay quite still, draped in diaphanous silks. I would normally look away from such an exhibition of flesh—but one must stare intently at the chessboard.

"Excuse Watchman, Cora. He's admiring your artwork."

"This in't nothing," said Cora, her pronunciation a mélange of East End and the Orient. "Lila's got a map of the world on her back."

"You always know where you are," Darlington nodded, "with Lila."

We played out a King's Gambit (accepted, Berlin Defence). Cora had to hold in her laughter, for she spotted illegal moves before we did, and anticipated my checkmate, pinning Darlington's bishop against his king. As his fingernails lingered vainly over the puzzle, I asked him what we could glean from these girls.

"Hard to get a straight answer." He gestured towards Cora and her remarkable form. "Observe. Cora, how did you come to be whatever you are?"

"*Moi*?" She stretched carefully. "Oh, I'm a ruinated daughter of a priest." This tale seemed as likely as any, but she would elaborate no further.

Darlington shrugged. "See?"

Hearing my Scottish accent, Kate Hamilton sent over a whisky.

A sterner bell rang: an alarum. Glasses were swept into crates, bottles hid under carpets and false walls. The lights rose. Whatever had been going on moments before was reimagined, with an earnest air. Cora sat up, disrupting my victorious position, to make her attire respectable. Before I could protest, she proceeded to set up the position again on the table, the pieces exactly as they had been on her stomach.

I goggled at this feat of memory. She shrugged it off languorously. Cora did everything languorously.

Tea was served just as the uniformed police waltzed in.

"F Division." Darlington pulled his hat low. "Amateurs."

Cora spotted my whisky. I'd had enough to numb my toothache; more and I might yield to temptation. Without a thought, Cora upended the dram into the pot plant. (I took note of this trick of Cora's, which would save me from many ills.) As the police made a show of looking around, like villains in a thrupenny drama, she was genteelly filling my glass with peppermint tea.

"Care for a cuppa, officer?" Kate Hamilton boomed, holding out a box of cigars.

The leading copper took one. He was leaning forward to

kiss her when he noticed us. Darlington shaded his eyes as the copper's mocking glance took in me, Cora and the board. "Wasting your time teaching that simpleton to play chess."

"Chess masters may teach anyone," said Cora levelly. "And don't call my uncle a simpleton."

The wag ventured no further into the interior. They promptly withdrew, a bag handed to them at the door; coins jingled in my imagination.

"Shambolic operation." Darlington stared after them. Within two minutes, normal stations were resumed: carpets, drinks, girls, et cetera, and Cora's déshabillé.

"Cora." I gave a low whistle. "You're a quick-witted little liar."

"Not at all, you silly uncle." She arched her eyebrows, placing a hand on her chest as she set the pieces for the next game. "I was youth champion of Lower Armenia, 1861."

Demoralised by another swift defeat, Darlington introduced me to the madam.

Kate lit a cigar and handed it to him. "Chivalrous gent, is he? Just 'ere for the chess?"

"More interested," I said, "in delights other than those of the flesh."

"Ennui, is it? Plenty here to stave off the ennui." She pronounced the word as if it were a venereal disease. "If you dispense champers to Cora, Maura and Mehetabel, no one will begrudge your *delectatio morosa*, that is, a certain lustful brooding."

Darlington laughed. "Watchman is my successor, Kitty. On our salary, champagne's at your discretion." He winked and strolled back to Cora.

Kate Hamilton stretched. Her bosom strained beneath mountainous folds of material. "Will you be a more demanding overseer than our Jimmy here?"

"On the contrary. Lend me a modicum of help, and we might dispense with the farce of these inspections."

A hush fell around us. "And of what might that modicum consist?"

I considered. "Let the girls speak to me. Tell me their true histories."

"Ain't that our business and none of yours?"

I wanted neither to convict, nor convert, I assured her. Such a well-run establishment I saw no need to police. After all, boys will be boys. I simply had to deliver a census. Let parliamentarians witter on about reform. "Tell me how many girls work for you. Let them tell me how old they are, where from, how come to the profession, and I'll leave you be."

"We might manage that."

"I'd be grateful."

"Grateful enough to free us from F Division's nosy parkers? Customers don't like it, I'm sure you understand."

"I can be persuasive."

She inspected me intently, her face as weather-beaten as a naval pilot's. "Is that an equitable exchange?"

"Well. Since you're asking." I clapped my hands together. "I shall be taking a reckoning of the houses neighbouring. Could you help persuade them to talk to me?"

"We can do better than that, my lover, if you're serious." Kate sat back, like the *Great Eastern* returning to dock, though more amply bosomed. "Why not regard us as your West End office? A glass of Scotch for the Scotchman here. You and I shall come to an arrangement, as sure as Almighty God is sitting on his throne." She clinked her glass against mine, her pig-like eyes twinkling. "A most favourable arrangement, my lover."

## THE 9.23 CLUB

My face burned with shame; my blood was boiling—how on earth could I tackle this mission?

I was at the Yard, as it emptied out, on a brittle afternoon, long before my nightshift, struggling to tot it up. I must soon set out upon my labours. I set myself nightly goals. Studied maps. Walked miles. Lurked. Stalked. Felt a fraud, a busybody, a peeping Tom. Wandered Waterloo tenements, doors always on the latch. Counted the footfall in Islington alleys. Took tea in Kensington, only to be thrown out for having more questions than cash. We won't tell you nothing. Why would we tell you? What are you anyhow, gospel-grinder, sawbones or copper?

"Going well, Watchman, by the looks of things." Sir Richard Payne popped his head around the door. I had a Stanford map spread out, spilling over the corners of my desk. Jeffcoat and Darlington hovered behind him, full of clubby bonhomie, doubtless heading out for a drink to celebrate solving Palmerston's little problem, a drink to which I was not invited, because my duties, of course, were about to begin for the night.

"It's quite an undertaking, sir." I kept my eyes on the map: at the moment of Payne's interruption, I was finishing up Pimlico's measurements. I'd divided the whole of London into sections, to estimate the magnitude of the task. I looked up to see them already marching down the corridor. I brandished the ruler, as if to spear the commissioner between the shoulder blades. I bit my lip and calculated again.

I cried out in exasperation. I calculated anew. I checked the figures. Again. And again. I had begun so well. I scoured the boroughs, spoke to local divisions, made first reckonings. All this energy, all this optimism, and it was futile: by my calculations, at this rate I would finish my enquiries in seventeen years.

I put my head in my hands, exhausted. I snatched up my pen, to hurl it against the wall. I wanted to smash my reckoning into a thousand pieces and see the ink trail down the wall, a chart of my fruitless endeavours. Suppressing my tantrum, I crushed the pen against the paper until the nib snapped. Black ink splattered the map. I leapt up so violently that my chair crashed to the ground. The registrar looked at me oddly, as I charged out of the building onto Whitehall.

"Ahoy, Watchman." A deep familiar voice. "Coming to the 9.23, you miserable beggar?"

"Oh, God." I turned to scowl at a considerable beard. "Not tonight, is it, Collins?"

"As you well know. Too long since you've graced us with your presence."

"I'm on night duty. Thanks all the same."

Wilkie Collins placed his bulk in my way. "Pull yourself together, man."

"I can't afford the time."

He grabbed my shoulders and looked gravely into my eyes, as if he were deciding whether a beloved but ragged old overcoat was worth keeping or not. "On the contrary, you old sleuthhound. I'd say you can't afford not to."

It's thanks to Miss Villiers that I was inveigled into the 9.23 Club, fearful shower that they are.

Miss Ruth Villiers, with hair so dark yet face so pale. Ruth, librarian at the British Museum Library, who gave me such assistance last year. She ransacked archives, unpicked puzzles and deciphered coded threats. Without her insight, I should never have solved it in time. I was in awe of her, and most fond. Brilliant as I thought her, and beautiful, I had failed to pursue her as she perhaps wished to be pursued. To be frank, we had fallen out. Molly and Co. had been exposed to horrors, and Ruth felt they deserved recompense. She was right, of course, that they deserved a better chance in life; but what could I do about it? One lowly sergeant's protests brought nothing to them—and only trouble to me.

Ruth withdrew, in a state of dudgeon, to live with her dreaded Aunt Lexie in some country backwater. We saw little of each other now, but I heard her words in my mind in times of need, in particular, her stern injunction that I must find some friends to talk to.

"But I talk to you," I had said.

Ruth rolled her eyes. "A chap needs to share his woes with other chaps. There are things you shouldn't trouble a lady with."

"Are you saying I abuse your capabilities?"

"I'm saying you irritate me."

She wasn't joking. She still commuted to the Library, irregularly, but no longer sought me out. I missed our tête-à-têtes in the tea rooms of Great Russell Street. I missed more than the tea and scones.

Through her introduction, however, I was thrown on the mercy of this impromptu salon. Wilkie Collins was a novelist, a merry devil of a soul, outcast from polite society for his untoward marital arrangements. Collins liked nothing better than to drink all evening, and explore the city's darker quarters all night, as if voyaging to the equinoctial regions.

Henry Mayhew had struck up his acquaintance while investigating the same night spots. A journalist, long penniless, of lugubrious disposition, Mayhew had lately captured the public imagination with *London Labour and the London Poor*. These exotic tales fascinated everyone, as if myths of Hindustan, yet these real-life characters lived on our very streets.

Collins and Mayhew played rackets at their club. Despising the crush of after-work nabobs, they booked a court for eight every Tuesday, aiming to reach the pub by nine.

I turned up at nine every week.

Our occasionals drifted in soon after: Lemon, the *Punch* editor; Lear, the filthy landscape painter; and his heretical pre-Raphaelite friends. Dickens often said he'd come, though rarely did; he gave as excuse charitable duties at

Urania Cottage, which doubtless meant he was visiting his mistress. What made us laugh was the way Mayhew and Collins strolled in, rosy-cheeked with exertion, at twenty-three minutes past nine on the dot, without fail and without a word of apology. It was of course I, the Watchman, who noted this aberration.

I often thought, I haven't the will to chat tonight, I'm in a mood, I won't go, or I'll go but sit sullen and silent, or I'll just drink myself into comfort. Half an hour of their effervescent foolery, and I was restored to humanity. What nonsense we cajoled out of each other. Mayhew would fulminate over the latest injustice. Collins would goad him about it, only to prove historiographically that the past was worse still and we really ought to be celebrating progress. Whereupon I would pat Mayhew on the back, and he would weep, admitting he was melancholy, not from the grimness of interviewing street folk, but because he had argued with his wife.

"Six pints of your finest ale, sharpish. I'm off to the worst job in the world."

Collins laughed. "What's got into you, Watchman? You need a dose of laudanum. You're normally as expressive as a bagpipe."

Normally, I sat quiet as the literary men debated issues of the today. Today, I told them my woes: how I had been landed with the Yard's most intractable task; I must be as clinical as a chemist, saintly as a priest, and reductive as a tinpot major; and all to be reported in nine months. "Payne knows it's impossible, yet he lets me flounder. It's ridiculous. It's indefensible." I expected them to agree.

"It sounds bloody marvellous." Collins downed his first pint and rubbed his hands. "By God, I can think of a few places I could help you count."

Mayhew was suitably repulsed. "Show us the figures you have." He frowned at the tables in my pocket book. "How on earth did they make these old reckonings?"

"That's just it. I can't see how, with fewer police, and worse managed."

"Bet you five guineas," said Collins, "they made half the numbers up. One, two, miss a few, ninety-nine, a hundred."

I shook my head, showing Dr Acton's figures from the last decade.

"William Acton?" Mayhew knew him. "He'd better vouch for this evidence."

"Why, damn it, Lawless?" Collins studied me closely. "Why are you at it?"

"My blasted commissioner's orders."

"Nonsense. You're too bloody-minded. Orders be damned. There's something else."

I drank deep of my ale. I had stayed on in London after the underground disaster, against my better judgement. I was hoping to see my efforts rewarded; I was crying out for something new. Now Payne sent me to oversee the oldest vice in the world. It queers your appetites when you spend your nights in brothels, but it hadn't dented my determination.

I talked of Felix. Of Felix's gentleness toward Bede and the Pixie. His indulgence for Molly. His preference of the Oddbody Theatricals over chattering society. About our walk to Brodie's house, when Felix could go on no further, because... well, because of griefs he could not express.

Poor wretches. Not just that woman. How many like her across the city? Tossed aside, and never a thought spared for them. When I came to London, I was shocked by the poverty, the naked indifference of rich and poor rubbing shoulders so close. Edinburgh wore its inequalities with Presbyterian shame. London was so shameless, it made us Londoners callous. Felix made me see them again: the disregarded, the exploited.

"You hope to change something." Mayhew patted my shoulder. "But what?"

I gave an impression of Payne, bellowing, "Close all the brothels down!"

"Unnatural hope." Collins exhaled. "Shut one, another opens."

I laughed hollowly. Payne's more realistic demand was that, besides venues, I tot up the women, noting age, origin, and whence come to the trade. "Even if I make rough valuations, that will shock Sir Richard's Commons Select Committee. The lawmakers and reformers don't know the half of it."

"Save one woman," said Mayhew, "and you have done something."

"Something?" Collins guffawed. "You have salved the conscience of the rich. What have these girls left except the workhouse? Stop them selling themselves, and they are without a trade. More ale!"

I stared into my glass. Molly always complained that governments legislate and reform, careless that each reform impoverishes more of the destitute.

"Buck up, Watchman." Mayhew thumped the table. "I interview street folk, beggars and criminals in order to goad the rich out of inaction. Despite his posturing, Collins writes to shame us out of hypocrisy." He turned his maudlin features upon me, lyrical in his cups. "Your calibration of carnality can change hearts. Assess the figures, as they are, and you compel us to tackle causes. You beg the country to stop punishing and start helping."

Collins grinned, proud of our friend's outburst. "We each of us fight the system, and are one by one defeated. You shall experience sinful things, my friend. To tackle those sinful things, you shall need my help."

Another hour, a pitcher of the house ale, and my plans were made, the map repartitioned, my helpers settled.

I told them of Kate Hamilton's offer; they agreed it could do no harm.

I told them of Brodie's hinted offer, and my evading it.

"His newsmen to gather information for you, in return for dibs on the latest murders?" Collins snorted. "I trust J.W. Brodie about as far as I can spit him."

"We have more reliable helpmates." Mayhew's work on prostitution, alongside the assiduous Etonian, Bracebridge Hemyng, meant he knew all the societies: societies for suppressing vice, for protecting young females, bringing peace to the penitent and refuge to the degraded.

"I'm sure they are well-meaning and charitable," I sniffed, "but they will hardly hand over all their researches to the police, whom they hold culpable."

Collins butted in, promising to inveigle Dickens and his painter friends to tour the boroughs in their sybaritic jaunts. "This very night, I shall take you to St John's Wood. No! No shirking now. Your commission is quite thrilling, taken in this light. The things we'll get up to. I shall ask questions, while you take shorthand. Even the closest madam will divulge her character when you hint you may include her in a novel." With Collins soaking me in ale, the siren call was more alluring than at Kate's or the Argyll Rooms, where I could resist the demon of temptation easily enough: find a girl, hear her tale, the job is done. "But the best notions of all, Lawless, are staring you right in the face, and you're missing them entirely."

I stared at him.

"Molly," said Collins simply. "Engage the help of your Molly and her theatrical urchins. They have underworld connections, haven't they? Inestimably more approachable than the likes of us. And how have you forgot your most instructive ally?" He nudged me suggestively with his elbow. "Your friend, Skittles."

I had once mentioned, in my cups, that I knew the courtesan, long before she was famous and her handkerchiefs fetched hefty sums among society gents. Collins's ribald allusions made me regret this indiscretion. I cast my eyes down. Go hang; if they want to believe I was Skittles's darling, let them.

"Is this true?" Charles Dickens appeared behind us. "My goodness." He clapped a hand on my shoulder and studied me penetratingly, smoothing his beard. "My dear Lawless, are you really acquainted with the illustrious Skittles? Let us pay her a visit. What stories she'll tell us. More ale? Or is it time for a dram?"

# DAINTY MISS SKITTLES

The remarkable thing about Skittles—Catherine Walters, the horsebreaker Anonyma—was that she was not the greatest natural beauty. Nor was she dainty, however the song puts it. She was a solid, buxom girl, with upper arms made to steer horses or carry trays of beer, her thick hair without refinement, worn *au naturel* aside from that singular damask rose. But what did that matter? She was enchanting. I defy any man to talk with Skittles for four minutes without declaring he is a little bit in love.

How did she do it?

That is just the thing: I'm not sure she was doing anything. She was behaving as God had made her: attentive, effusive, amused; oh, always amused by what you said. Musical laughter burst from her lips, as if she appreciated not just your wit but the fascinating intimations you left unexpressed. Her head tilted; her brown eyes fixed you with that wry smile of hers. She did enjoy men's company; she was unashamed to show it. She was so quick-witted that, when the company was dull, she could enliven it, without ostentation, so she made you feel you were the entertaining one, when in fact she was conducting the tempo with effortless flair. If her intimate relations were as warm (and I am told that they were, indeed, more so), then every man who came close to her must have felt he was a master of sensuality, an emperor of love. And who does not desire that?

Back in my early days at the Yard, I often accompanied my old inspector to his train at Paddington Station. One day, I saw a young lady, as I supposed her, weeping at the pie counter. I engaged her in conversation, telling her I was a policeman, with no intent to harass.

"A mutton shunter is still a man," she replied with a twist of the lip. "In't he? Therefore I would request that you sodding leave me be."

She made me laugh. I assured her I had no designs upon her—though, truly, she was striking, hypnotic, lovely. Her dress had a provincial elegance, as unlike a Haymarket doxy as a dairymaid to a duchess. She turned those full, frank eyes upon me and at length, restored by tea, teacake and bar billiards, told me her tale.

Skittles was from Liverpool, not the most poetical spot. Tiring of her parents' tawdry little lives, she took a job serving at the station refreshment bar, where she hoped she might see life. A gentleman who frequented the station wooed her and, soon enough, frequented her. She told this tale of wilful ruination with disarming candour, not so different from a sensation novel or erotic fantasy. I warmed to her at once: I had never known a woman to speak openly about such things.

The gent, having conquered, deserted. She was here at Paddington on a promise to meet his friend, who had offered her lodgings, promising to make the cad do his duty. She suspected this offer for what it was, a heartless seduction, and mocked her own folly. What the friend did not know was that her monthly courses had stopped; without a swift solution, she would be soon be undone.

I told her to return to her parents.

She laughed. "Even if they were not so dull, God bless them, I could not return now, with my ruination evident." Besides, she was tired of selling tarts—and desired to know more men. She would take a new name and seek a wealthy gentleman sponsor. I thought only low women talked of such things; but in Skittles's mouth, there was nothing coarse about it, only an earthy honesty.

She delivered her story readily as she trounced me at bar billiards, taking singular delight in my accruing penalties for knocking over the skittle pins guarding the pockets. I christened her Skittles, and gave her a little prize money, to protect her from maltreatment; for I too had been an incomer, overwhelmed by the big city's bustle and noise. The dangers were graver for a woman, especially a large, handsome woman like her, with leather boots and silk stockings beneath that quaint taffeta skirt.

There was the end of the story.

Except that, through her undeniable talents, Skittles had risen to become a watchword about town, still delighting in the nickname I had conferred on her. I heard rumours that she had bedded a duke and might even wed him. The pretty 'horsebreakers' were at the height of their notoriety; this euphemism allowed ladies who, on foot, would be thought objectionable, to ride through Hyde Park on horseback, scandalising society ladies and delighting society men. I was passing through the park, when a warm voice called out to me from Rotten Row.

"Sergeant? I believe I owe you a sovereign."

I squinted up at this vision in green. Down she leapt from her mighty steed, without waiting for help from her well-heeled companion. She wore a rich velvet suit lined with crimson, gold lace and embroidered buttons. To complete this ensemble, her breeches fitted her shapely limbs tightly, pearl-white stockings showing over the diamond buckles of her red-heeled boots.

She clasped my hand, a picture of jaunty elegance. Hand on hip, she recounted her adventures since that day in Paddington. Finding favour at Kate Hamilton's, she was fast established as a courtesan in the grand French style. What a life she was leading making the most of her talents, she said. All thanks to my kindness that day.

I was delighted for her. But what would become of her? Need she stay in the gay life? She seemed so persuasively a lady now; she could surely find employment, or love, and leave the life behind.

"I'm happy with my calling." Her cheeks were flushed with vigour; there was no doubting her sincerity. "I have all I want. I have learned the piano; I meet ministers, dukes and financiers, maybe a prince, if I'm lucky; I sing; I ride—accomplishments of great use to a girl. I tell you, all those years ago in Liverpool, I was as much to blame as my seducer, I so wished to escape the drudgery of my life. I thought I was better than selling tarts in the provinces. Now I am three and twenty. I am fond of dress. I take an interest in science and telegraphy and even politics, for I have studied the globes, you know. And the old fool loves me to excess."

Her old fool sat aloof on his horse, peeved at my intrusion; no doubt he wished to study the globes before the afternoon was out.

She told me she had had four men since the first she yielded to. "I tire of them after six months, so we mutually accommodate. My father and mother don't exactly know where I am, though I send money each quarter. What will become of me? You awkward old bird, what a question. I could marry this one tomorrow, if I pleased." She said I might always enquire after her at Kate Hamilton's, for Kate's functioned as an agency of sorts for circles loftier than the common night houses. "But I'm no longer known as Skittles. Every flash gent claims to have brushed with Skittles; few have. Ask for me by my new sobriquet: Anonyma."

Damn it all: so the famous Anonyma, mysterious equestrian of the bridleways, was good old Skittles. The *Bugle*'s society pages were full of Anonyma's antics. She presented me with a handkerchief, embroidered with her insignia, and repeated her hint about meeting a prince, for she knew I had worked for the Prince of Wales. I still saw Bertie once in a while, and he jumped at the invitation to one of Anonyma's afternoons. Ever an admirer of alluring women, he brought her ten cases of tea, which was a sure way to her heart, if not further.

Skittles didn't remember to pay back that sovereign: it was too much when I gave it; now she was celebrated, too little.

# ENQUIRIES

The next time I saw Felix was at the theatre, early-December. I greeted him jovially, hoping I might offer him a drink after the show.

He looked done in, white-faced and wild-eyed. "The Quarterhouse curfew, you know," he muttered, by way of excuse. "Do come and call on me, would you, if you'd be so kind?"

I promised I should visit soon, before Christmas.

Felix's agitation preyed on my mind. Nor could I shake off the memory of the night we'd met, and his distress in the shadow of the prison walls. Not that I thought him involved, and I had combed through Jeffcoat's report (praised most sincerely by Payne; our commissioner never thought to blame one of his own for the *Bugle*'s meddling). Felix's mercurial behaviour was a mystery. Who could enlighten me? I would ask the 9.23 Club.

# THE WOMAN

All I know of her, still, is her name, Alexandra, and no further
will I pry. And yet I know every inch of her, more intimately
than I know myself.

I found her in the Casino de Venise, commonly known as
the Holborn, as promised in her playful note, at five o'clock
on Friday the fifth:

> *VIENS, VOLONTAIRE, VOLONTIER.*
> *VENISE, V VENDREDI V. A*

Willingly, wilfully, I came. She was absently stroking the
mahogany rail that encircled her booth, her thoughts elsewhere.
It is not ideal for a lady to await a man unaccompanied, but
there are corners of the West End where it is unnoticed or
overlooked. Only her natural bearing gave her away; in that
dark shawl, one might otherwise have taken her for a loose
woman. That was perhaps her intention, and the best way to
remain anonymous in a place where one might encounter
gentlemen one knew from polite society.

She lost no time in making her intentions plain. Surely I
knew a place?

I knew and was known in too many. I chose a neighbourhood
house I had inspected on my rounds. We passed by a row
of coffee houses, their windows advertising rooms. Turning
down Titchfield Street, I tapped at the innocuous door. The
pasty-faced owner admitted us without a word, preserving
the gentrified air. Where was the harm? I had visited her
establishment, but could not see how to include it in my
reckonings. Neighbourhood houses are merely unregistered
hotels, rooms by the hour; whether assignations are
commercial or merely clandestine is impossible to judge.

She was tense as we mounted the stair. We met nobody,

but heard voices behind doors we passed, and creakings. She hesitated on a landing, as if to turn back; I did not urge her on. A moment, a doubt, and she took my arm again.

We found the room at the top of the building, with a view out over the rooftops. A cheval glass, a washstand, a chamber pot; not overlooked, no need to draw the curtains. Nothing distracted from the bed. The sheets were fresh, the pillows plumped; one almost felt ashamed in sullying them. I was about to say as much, when the urgency of desire overtook us. Words were beyond the point.

"I hope you don't think badly of me."

This was later, an hour after our meeting. I laughed. "Do you care?"

She considered this. Her bare shoulders rose in a shrug. "Not really."

We both laughed. I reached out to stroke her face but held back, fearful that this was too great an intimacy. She responded fervently to my touch. We were lost again.

The room was furnished with an elegant simplicity. I almost commented on it, but I did not wish to advertise my familiarity with the décor of brothels. No boxes of laundry, no tired wardrobe. None of the fussy décor of a middling house of accommodation with suggestive prints from Holywell Street mouldering on the walls, lurid wallpaper, too many mirrors with rococo gilt edges. No, this room was a boudoir fit for a lady.

After another hour, she arose languidly. The ballet of her body was entrancing; I watched her dress with barely a word. I couldn't help asking if this was a common sport to her.

She smiled in reproach: no, I was the first whom she had chosen like this. "But, please, we don't need to discuss my life, do we? You are a detective, I know. I pray you, don't investigate me."

"Why not? Would I find dark secrets?"

"Not dark. Not at all, I promise. When a woman is older…"

She laughed. "Allow me my air of mystery. Do me that kindness, will you?"

I would, I promised her. I was curious by nature, and by profession; but if it pleased her that I restrain my inquisitiveness, I could.

Her farewell kiss promised more. The grace of her movements enchanted me, languishing still on that bed, as she glanced back from the doorway. When I in turn arose and tried to pay, I found she had settled the bill and reserved the room for the same time next week.

# MELANCHOLY

Wet snow, everywhere. I was sick of it. London was sick of it. December's sleet dissolved to slush the pristine white coverlet formed by November flakes. Each night it froze over. Choosing your footwear became a matter of life and death, when walking the pavements or hurrying for the omnibus. I am no expert on women's clothing, but I wager it was that winter of '63 which ended once and for all women's free access down below and instigated the new fashion of bloomers, or drawers with a split. I knew one woman who— But I shall speak of that later.

A month into my task, my hopes of accomplishing it were shrinking.

A policeman's lot is solitary. Even constables with a companion on the beat remain distanced allies. With my nocturnal agenda, I was endlessly tired, peevish, and afflicted with one influenza after another. I liked nothing better than walking alone on these untethered days between my nightly researches.

Mauve's complaint of stolen papers was no isolated incident. Over the holiday, peculiar thefts occurred at more illustrious addresses. Darlington puzzled over one, Jeffcoat another. But the world was conspiring against us. Jeffcoat was engaged on his own secret commission for Payne that took him to the furthest reaches of the city, and beyond; something to do with missing persons, though nobody would talk about it freely. We worked opposite hours, and Payne had taken our reports on the thefts, so we could never compare notes.

The river is a melancholy companion. The greatest of London's parks, and the filthiest, along its mudflats the hurly-burly of London life is evident as nowhere else. As the markets ran short of potatoes and London ran short of patience, children and indolent parents filled the malodorous spaces, such as survive Bazalgette's improving works. I strolled on the half-finished Embankment, sifting my salty researches for pearls.

I was one of many forgetting their troubles by the Thames. A mother kicked a dirty football eagerly past her little ragamuffin, only to stop, embarrassed to be seen too sporting, and let him take it. "Ma," the boy called. "I show you how the real football men, they kick it." Aiming a great thwack at the sodden leather, he upended himself on to his backside, leaving the football behind him, quite unmoved, in the mud.

I knew how he felt. My mission was distending, my confidence diminishing. I walked the streets, annotated maps, observed, enquired, peeped and pried. The more I learnt, the more I understood my ignorance.

In the sanctuary of Kate Hamilton's, she would send another girl my way. Just like the last, I prised her out of my lap, took drab notes of her drab story, and ended by losing to Cora at chess. I penetrated no further into Kate's premises. Yet every night, the girls rolled in, each with a fresh story: my notebook accumulated numbers in columns. The West End was in my grasp. Kate herself winked, clapped and sent over another tumbler of whisky. I accepted it; but wary of drunkenness, after witnessing Darlington's habits, I crumpled a sheet of blotting paper in my pocket, to soak it up and set a roaring fire when I got home; or else, well, Cora's pot plant was steadily wilting.

This expedient had two effects. First, it made me smell of whisky, bestowing an air of dishevelled Scots bonhomie that loosened folks' tongues; second, it convinced Kate that I was under her sway as firmly as Jimmy Darlington had been.

To tackle the wider boroughs, I relied on my researches alongside the 9.23 Club. I asked them about Felix too. Collins knew him slightly and thought him a queer old fish. He remembered reading a book about him, or even by him, and promised to look it out for me. He wouldn't remember, of course, after our night of "tailing" as he termed it.

Any regrets about these outings I put aside; for whatever the others' sins, I never neglected my duties. After several rounds of ale, Collins would unleash the whisky monster. Our sybaritic jaunts took us to bawdy houses from St John's Wood to Waterloo. The Pre-Raphaelites chummed us along whenever they could, and Dickens joined in on occasion.

I soon learnt that the girls told fibs until they were paid, being reluctant to make clients glum.

Watching Collins exert his charms was a lesson in beguilement. Not that he treated everyone as equals, nothing so false; rather, he attended high and low equally, especially those with a furtive aspect. Consequently, everyone loved to reveal their secrets to him. He gave his word he would pass them on to nobody—except in his novels that the nation would devour.

## THE GLASSHOUSE

I could see Felix as I emerged from the rear cloister of Quarterhouse, seated in a wheeled wicker throne amongst the tropical frondage. How different was from the crisp wintry evening when we first met. Quarterhouse was an oasis in

London's densest square mile, a pool of generosity hemmed in by the rapacious East End.

Felix spotted me, gesturing enthusiastically. A glazier was measuring up the glasshouse doors. The whole edifice was undergoing and overhaul: iron stanchions repainted, glass panels replaced. The Brothers might be impoverished but Quarterhouse was flush.

The taciturn glazier stood aside and beckoned me in. A wave of hot air hit me. I tried to keep in the heat, closing the door so firmly I nearly shattered it.

"My dear fellow." Felix rose and shook my hand warmly. "Thank you for coming." There was something odd about him, an elation of sorts. He lost no time in heaping me with thanks. What a party I had got up; how much we had raised to save poor unfortunates; a flying start for the Phoenix Foundation.

As I took off my coat, dripping with sleet, I listened in fascination. At the Foundation party he had seemed a man at peace, gently ironising the follies about him, after a life embattled. Now his eyes were bright, though distracted; his handshake firmer; his declarations more vigorous and sincere. He had been reborn.

Outside, the Yuletide snows heaped up against the glasshouse were turning to slush from the warmth. I stared at the flowers blooming beneath the spreading plane trees. If Quarterhouse was a charitable establishment, the endowment must be spent as much on nurturing flora as humanity.

"I know, I know, it's a wild luxury. Sometimes nature needs a helping hand. Keeps the old buildings habitable." He tapped his nose, gesturing toward the glazier. "I believe our friend Brodie's contributed to this renovation. None of the Brothers complain, I can tell you."

By the stove at the centre stood two leather armchairs, like outposts of civilisation forgotten in a jungle. I moved gratefully toward the warmth.

Felix barely seemed to limp as he bustled me through the teeming leaves. He took out his tobacco pouch, flexing his damaged hand; it was not healed but he was using the fingers, which I would have sworn was not the case when first we met. "You are well, Sergeant?"

"Passably well, thank you, Felix." I had a cough, a canker sore and a headache, but moaning didn't help. "You seem to be flourishing in midwinter."

He beamed at me. He took a breath and clenched his fists amiably as if preparing to make a declaration of some kind; then he bit his lip and began again, more moderately. "I am, it's true. I'll admit, I have had some good news. Potentially good. I mustn't say more. Not superstitious or any of that bosh. Just I wouldn't want to jeopardise my sources."

By God, he was changed. Barely a fortnight since I had seen him at the theatre, wild-eyed and pale. Now he was bursting with life. The city outside was frozen; Felix was spirited and virile. Of these changes, he made no mention. Was it my place to question him? I frowned as my trousers began to emanate steam. "I'm glad to see you so cheered. The night we first met, you were sad. A little mysterious, too. I wished I could be of more help."

He puzzled for a moment, then remembered. "The poor wretch in the street."

"All dealt with, sir. You may have seen it in the papers."

"I believe I did." The shadow of a frown crossed his brow. "Do you know, I'd forgotten all about it? Isn't that terrible?"

"I don't know, sir. We're inured to horrors in this city."

"You poor chaps must be, out on the front lines of poverty and squalor. We are terribly protected. Not just we Brothers, in the haven of Quarterhouse here, but all of my class, swanning back and forth from dinner to dinner, from opera to club; and everywhere we pass hundreds of poor wretches, like that woman, ready to drop with exhaustion and starvation, tossed aside by some careless husband or bawd house bully. It's a disgrace that two such different worlds can exist side by side. An outrage. Not even side by side. Intermingled. Except the only time one side acknowledges the other is the fast gent abasing himself in the world of gaming and loose morals."

"Or the loose woman displaying an ankle to attract such gents."

"For which they can hardly be blamed."

"Oh, I have gone beyond blame and appraisal. I enter numbers on charts."

He smiled. "And your numbers, are they eloquent?"

"They declare that the oldest trade is in no danger from governmental austerities. Whatever opinions we espouse when we are on top of the world, we never know how we will bend those morals when life trips us up."

My unaccustomed pronouncements stoked Felix's fervour. He grasped my shoulder, told me I was the very man and demanded to know more of my census.

"It is a strange world to visit, and stranger still to annotate dispassionately." I hesitated. "Distressing, at times."

"I'm sure the women say the same." He leaned forward, his eyes bright, and asked that I relate tales heard in the netherworld.

These were the tales that haunted my sleep. Sweating in the unaccustomed heat, I told him of the woman with the delirium tremens who wanted to do herself in, but hadn't the wherewithal. I told of a seduced factory girl whose child starved in her arms. To counterbalance the misery of my theme, I even told of Skittles, her fall and rise.

He gripped the side of his chair, following my tales with a vivid intensity.

"Felix, are you all right?"

As if to emphasise how distant were our lives from those I had been telling, a servant chose that moment to deliver him a letter upon a tray, along with coffee and warmed brandy. A luxurious almshouse, indeed.

Felix downed the snifter, staring into the middle distance. He poured the coffee, inspected it and asked the servant to try again, with an effort at joviality. "Would you mind terribly? I'm the European chappy and I like it to taste of coffee."

I sipped at my coffee, nonetheless, and found it strong enough. "Felix, sir, I'm sorry. These tales I hear every day. I forget how disturbing they can be."

"What now? Yes, of course. Forgive me. It's only that such things have been weighing on my mind recently."

"In establishing your foundation for fallen women, no doubt? I should like to pay a visit, see how it works."

"The Phoenix Foundation? Well, how it's run, the details, I haven't a clue. Beyond my diminishing energies, I'm afraid. I'm just a name, you see. A moth-eaten old figurehead." He blinked, but it struck me that his energies had never been more fulsome. Behind this retreat from responsibility lay something deeper. "We have employed the best people. They assure me we are finding those on the brink... those vulnerable to..." He blinked again and spluttered for breath.

"For goodness' sake, Felix, have another tot of brandy." I offered my glass, which he gratefully took. "You are too tender a soul to administer the Foundation yourself. You established it, that's the important thing. The good it does may never be apparent to anyone."

He smiled palely. "You're a good sort, Lawless, old man. A good sort." He tore open the letter. He took out a cheque book, signing a couple of pages distinctively, with a flourish like a violin. He wafted them in the air, then tucked it back in the envelope. He saw my eyes upon him. "Payments, to be countersigned. For the Foundation. Looks fraudulent, I don't doubt. I rely upon the charity of Quarterhouse; then I sign off charitable monies to fund my Foundation."

"Not at all. These are donations, from your musical admirers and illustrious colleagues, I'm sure."

"The last I can eke from my artistic standing. It is all I can do." He sighed. "I only wish we could raise enough to help every last one of the poor lost women you encounter. One's funds only go so far."

"And the problem is so widespread. No need to explain to me. You find the funds; women shall seek out the Foundation."

He nodded, placated. A trail of organ music announced a service in the chapel. "I am expected at evensong. Quarterhouse is an Anglican establishment, nominally, with few rules, but it was once a monastery, and we are expected to be monkish in a few ways. They tolerate this old papist humming along in dissonant tenor. You've cheered me up immensely. Thanks for your visit."

This was palpably untrue. I found him in a mood of elation and was leaving him downcast. "But hadn't you something to discuss?"

"There was something." He grimaced, as if he had a dreadful confession to make, but again he thought better of it. "It can wait. I'll make a clean breast of it one of these days. Yes, I'll tell you next time I see you. We'll have a glass of brandy and I'll tell you all about it. I may need your help, your insight into the illicit world." The organ swelled. He took an apothecary's dispenser from his pocket, tipped out a pale blue pill and made a face as he took it. "From the diabolical to the heavenly. I must attend chapel or I shall be fined a shilling, you know. Won't help the finances."

He stood, filled with strange energy. The fellow brought over my coat, now quite dry, and I offered to drop off Felix's cheques, for I would pass Coutts & Co. on my way back to the Yard.

Felix gazed out at the wintry garden. "Looks wintry, eh, and dead? But the roots nurture their secret life." He squeezed my shoulder. "I do value your labours. Growing up in Europe, those wars we endured... We have all seen terrible things, things we would rather forget. If your census can make these poor wretches more than numbers on some chart, they are no longer worthless. They are not disposable. They have a voice. It's a terrific thing you're doing, whatever Payne and the others think, just by giving it your all."

# PROGRESS TO REPORT

"Watchman?" Sir Richard Payne grabbed me as I was trying to sneak in early of a morning. "Deuced hard to smoke you out, you wily Scot. What a state you look."

"Long night of it, sir." I had spent the entire night, for the first time, with Alexandra. My heart was singing though tinged with melancholy, after seeing her to a cab to take her to Waterloo and home.

"Investigations proceedings apace, I've no doubt?"

"Yes, sir. I'm dropping off my notes before knocking off."

"Right-o. Well, pop in before you leave. I want a word."

If he heard my groan, he gave no sign of it.

I was shattered. I had kept my promise to investigate nothing of her life; but I could not help imagining her returning to a putative husband, and thinking not of me until the next time, although she would think of me, I knew. It was the first night I had neglected my researches, and the taste of shame was in my mouth as I hovered in Sir Richard's doorway.

"I've had complaints, Watchman. It's not like you to ruffle feathers." He held up a sheaf of papers. "Rather a lot of feathers."

I waited for him to go on.

"Don't be like that, you daft Celt. Sit down." He was about to offer me a drink. He kept a bottle of gin in his desk. A second glance at my worn features and he thought better of it. "I'm not telling you off. I want to get to the bottom of it. Mauve, for instance." He perused the first sheet with distaste.

I did not sit down. I knew he had read the report; I had read it too. "Mauve, sir, was less than candid with me. Which, in investigating a theft, is irritating, sir. An evidently impossible theft at that, and a theft where one may not seek the stolen goods because one is told nothing about the goods, except that they are not in themselves valuable, unless as a weapon of blackmail. Not just irritating, sir, preventing a full examination of the scene, but obstructive. In my opinion, sir."

"True enough, Watchman, true enough. But I rely on you to be—"

"Subservient, sir?"

"Diplomatic, dash it. You've observed the peccadillos of the great and good. I don't ask you to indulge them, just to show a modicum of tact."

"Tact, sir?" I gasped. "If Mauve told me what was in the papers I'm meant to be seeking, I would show tact. But he didn't tell. I haven't the time to waste in guessing. As it is, your census of sin is sinfully behind schedule. You have other sergeants. Why was I even called to a theft, I'd like to know?"

"Because, you great oaf, you are trusted. It is known that you worked for the Royals; it is not known what you did for them. Thus, evidently, you show discretion beyond your fellow officers' capabilities."

The echo of his voice hung in the air. As he read over Mauve's complaint, Sir Richard could not help the corners of his mouth turning upwards. He set down the paper and gestured at it.

"All right. This fool of an MP has done something he oughtn't. What matter? Saint Paul had his sins. What's worse, though, Mauve has set it down on paper, thinking to relieve or absolve his soul through confession. I don't wish to know. Instead, said confession is whisked away. Someone somewhere is rubbing their hands, waiting for the moment that the threat of revelation will hurt most—and pay the best dividend. Is it any wonder if Mauve behaves like a pompous ass? Sometimes, Watchman, you must indulge your—"

"Elders and betters, sir? Yes, sir." A damn sight easier when they behave as betters.

He leafed through the other sheets, his face darkening. "But you can't be interviewing gentlemen when they are, shall we say, at their leisure."

"In disreputable places, you mean?" Now I drew back the chair and sat down. "Oh, I must, sir. Not to shame them. To find out where else they go."

Sir Richard's expression pulled me up short. A moment's silence. "You are making progress, Watchman. Let us set a date for this Commons Select Committee." He opened up his book. "I have the spring in mind."

"Not so soon, sir. We said a year."

"I said maybe nine months, but things have changed."

"I'm only fathoming the depth of the problems—"

"You have accounted for several hundred brothels already. The '57 census counted four hundred and ten in total. Ergo you must be nearly concluded."

"That was only resident brothels, sir. We have to include the night houses, and accommodation houses, and board houses." I was ranting. "Introduction houses, lodging houses—"

"You will be done by April. Ample time not only to write your report but also to reduce these figures in advance of the Committee. Which would delight the ministers. And reflect well on all of us." He made a note and shut his book with a triumphant clump.

I got up to go, but stood there a moment. I was so tired, I couldn't help heaving the truth into his view. "There are more brothels, sir, ten times more, you know as well as I do. And it's lodge houses that are the most numerous, if we open our eyes. To count up the courtesans in Kensington Gore, housed in splendour at their lovers' expense, this is a task I haven't cracked. Nor how to count the Thameside wretch and the Haymarket hag, too lowly for the lowliest house. Would you want me to view the topmost rungs as beyond the law and the lowest as beneath it? These too must be numbered. You asked me to do the job, sir, and you want me to do an equitable job. Else why appoint me?"

"Oh, Watchman." Payne sat back, rubbing his whiskers. "I knew you might upset people. Close down a popular spot, or denounce the antics in the boxes at the Opera House. Instead, this irksome diligence." He poured himself a gin, tight-lipped, and leaned forward. "Get your numbers, Watchman, by all means. But complete the census, and soon. I don't care how you do it, with clairvoyants or circus monkeys. Enough questions. No more complaints from gentlemen."

He fell silent. I was evidently dismissed. I preferred Payne blunt like this. When he smiled and wheedled, he seemed a lesser man, under the influence of politicians or bankers, seeking advancement or even a peerage, after all he had done to transform the police. I had a sudden intuition: he was headed for retirement. This Commons Select Committee was to be his crowning glory, demonstrating statistically that Payne's police not only had the measure of the Great Social Evil but had it tamed, and would one day vanquish it. If he could leave the Committee with that fervent fiction, that would be enough; as to the truth of it, he gave not a fig.

I swore then and there that I would do it; the 9.23 Club and Kate Hamilton's girls were just scratching the surface. I would follow Collins's bidding, and call up the troops. Engage Mayhew's societies. Engage Molly and Bede and their Oddbody Theatricals: the misshapen miscreants knew every draggletail doxy and Haymarket harlot, and they were smart. Them I would visit on the morrow.

I would seek out Skittles—though of late, I'd heard nothing of her. I was afraid she might have met a bad end.

There was one more person whose help I could use: Jeffcoat. I could go next door and ask him. What murky corners of the city might his backstairs researches illuminate? But I couldn't bring myself to cease my quarrel with him.

All this I thought. I went to leave, but found myself standing in the doorway. "Whether there be one board house by Waterloo or fifty makes no difference, I suppose, sir, nor whether ten girls lodge there or a thousand. But I know that a thousand girls work here, there or under the very bridge; and I shall count them and talk to them and include them in the records for the committee, God damn it. Then you and your politician friends can decide what to do about it."

## ODDBODY CONFAB

After Sir Richard's complaints, I longed to see a friendly face. I used to head for the British Museum, and the solace of Miss Villiers' bright conversation. Being no longer in her good books, I turned instead toward the Adelphi Arches, beneath which Molly held her impromptu court.

"Watchman, old cove, that's a melancholy face." She broke off pinning and repinning bits of paper across a corkboard. "Hast thou hexertions with which we might hassist thee?"

"Oh, Molly, I fancy I am beyond hassistance."

To distract me from my woes, she showed me her ingenious Oddbody system of messages, professional, personal and cryptic. Each member of their loose collective had a patch of wall, adjacent to their friends' patches. Here they scratched messages social and occupational in charcoal or chalks. Thus anecdotes, scandals and job news circulated with rapidity among the city's theatricals, showmen, cripples and beggars.

---

# WATSON'S MUSEUM OF
# LIVING CURIOSITIES REQUIRES:

## FAT BOY, WORLD'S TALLEST WOMAN, AND AUSTRALIANS

**ART PHILLIPS** seeks a Living Mermaid

**MUTE GIRL** requires dwarf, able-bodied, for private shows; flexibility essential

**HARVEY'S MIDGETS**: need accommodation; current too small

---

To express interest or appreciation, members initialled messages, inscribed their personal symbol or sketched a self-portrait.

Cheered by their invention, I told her my troubles. Overwhelmed by the census of sin, I could not think straight. I was exhausted, and found myself complaining about the theft at Mauve's house, and his pig-headedness.

"What else was found in your man's room?" Molly loved a good mystery. A locked chamber, mysteriously thieved—this puzzle was right up her street, and she delved for details. I divulged a few tidbits, though I hedged over mentioning Mauve and the sensitive nature of the stolen papers; I was sworn not to mention the chess automaton, but mentioned that a borrowed contraption was in residence. Molly smiled at these evasions. "Anything similar at these other thefts of yours?"

I hadn't mentioned the other thefts.

"Saw 'em in the papers, didn't I?" Thinking that covered

her gaffe, she began rolling out a poster for Ang and Ana, the Siamese Siamese Twins. "Clear as day. Someone's hidden in the room."

None of the thefts had been mentioned in the papers: not the theft I was called to, nor Darlington's, nor even Jeffcoat's, though he might yet sell his tale. I blinked. "Nobody was in the room."

"Misdirection. That's what you're meant to think." She bit her tongue between her teeth. She knew something. "But I wouldn't want to spoil your detectional fun." She returned to her work on the wall, connecting seekers and sought, offers and pleas.

Such were the differences between Molly's help and Miss Villiers'. Ruth was an indefatigable ally, deploying her remarkable intellect and insights on my behalf. She could not resist tireless researches. Molly, on the other hand, liked me well enough, but she knew where her loyalties lay: I could not expect her to welch on colleagues. Besides, I had omitted telling details. If there were a connection, Payne must have spotted it. The automaton? Even if it had been in each room, it was too small for a person to hide in. "Heard tell of a chess automaton, Moll?"

She sniffed, as if surprised by my changing the subject. "Couldn't say I have."

"Bluff and flam, Molly. There's this automaton doing the rounds. A contraption so miraculous that those who borrow it must swear to keep it secret."

"Don't this oath apply to you?"

"I'm asking your advice."

"You'll never make a card player." She tilted her cap back. "Sounds like the typical newsman's trick, don't it? 'You mustn't tell; you must never tell.' Bloody advertising done for them." She spoke in her best posh voice. "'Have you challenged the automaton? Oh, you simply must.' Worst kept secret in London."

It was true. As the American chess master Paul Morphy's European tour loomed closer, the fervour over Brodie's contraption grew ever greater.

Molly kept her eyes on her work. "As for your calculus of courtesans, we'll be unable to help. You're hampering their trades."

"I'm not—"

"I shouldn't like to be complicit."

"I got your lot into that Phoenix Foundation party."

"I like that. Our piggy puppets saved your bacon."

"Darlington's found you a job on Holywell Street."

"Oh, yes? Filthy books, is it?"

"Lexicographical position, I believe. Slang dictionary. The only filth required will be your irrepressible Londoner's tongue."

"Hark at you, with your tongues and positions." She drew a caricatured smile below the Siamese Siamese Twins, and an arrow to suggest they contact an Indian boy(s) with two bodies and one head. "Look, give us your lexical contact. Come back for the get-together in the New Year. That's our omnium-gatherum." She scribbled the date, signing it with a caricature of her own fizzog: mop of unruly hair, snub nose, cheeky grin. "They're well connected, my cripple convention. They're all scroungers, in need of sponsors, and it only takes pennies to make 'em voluble. What do you say?"

# THE CASK OF HATE

A boy was found dead in a queer house on New Year's Eve, just a stone's throw from Kate Hamilton's. A punter found him, and I was summoned. The case was handed over to Jeffcoat, for his expertise in missing persons.

Nobody had paid any mind when the boy vanished over Christmas. He might have been visiting relatives. He might have been, but he wasn't. He was crumpled in the bottom of a closet beneath a heap of clothes, until his body's decomposition defeated the winter's cold and they smelt him out. It looked accidental, except the closet was locked. He was barely clothed. No bruises. Something blocking his windpipe. Misadventure, indeed.

How could such indignities come to pass in this day and age? Because most night houses, unlike Kate's, were itinerant brothels. Nobody to count in or out, no thought to stave off disease, no one to save you from harm, nobody to care or call the doctor at the last. It was shameful.

What difference could I make to a boy like this? My census was a politic tactic, Sir Richard placating elements of society who cared nothing for such people: "Scandalous that such places should be allowed, and such people exist," they would say, "and better for all if they die." This netherworld little affected families like that, oh so fine and lovely; except that contagion spreads. A disease inadvertently caught, a pox visited upon a wife by a gentleman caller. How little it takes to persuade a good girl to step out: the hour is late; she accepts hospitality, a beverage, drugged. Shamed and ruined, she can never return to her respectable home; she is trapped in the penumbrous half-world of bordellos and workhouses. Boys too, shamed by wayward urges, lured into lives that would shock their families. Still, when did the state become responsible for nannying aristocratic boys and girls out of their naughty habits?

## HOW STUBBORN OUR SINS

I followed the route, so familiar already, through the back alleys, skirting Leicester Square, until I spotted the entranceway. Kate Hamilton's curtains hung crimson and lush, located between Appenbrodt's Sausage Shop and Bennett's Pies, where meat is dressed to your liking, lamb or mutton to taste, and nothing ever stales, with old beasts turned out to die of rots, bots and glanders.

"Watchman, my lover, business or pleasure?" Kate boomed.

"Commingle the two, may we, Kate?"

"Commingling's what we does best." Laughter rippled through her; her formidable bodice put me in mind of the buffalo in the Zoological Gardens. "Scotch for the Scotland Yard Scotchman. Cora, you minx, this official needs relieving, can't you see? Working after midnight, I ask you, and holidays too. His commissioner ought to be ashamed, as Almighty God is sitting on his throne—though he don't shame easily, that one."

Kate was a wonderful monster. I intended to make desultory enquiries about the dead boy, but I held little hope of illumination. A game of chess was welcome solace from the frustration of these duties. Now that Darlington was reassigned, censoring the erotic book trade, and Jeffcoat occupied with his investigations, I was on my own.

Cora and I recommenced our companionable matchplay with few words. Girls never talked freely. Draped in diaphanous silks, Cora lay quite still, pieces laid out on her remarkable stomach, indifferent to her languid desirability, ever awaiting the summons to private rooms. The same antics occurred across the city, across the world, no doubt; but here there was a decorum, a sense of humour, that made it more tolerable. I had time for Kate Hamilton. They said she was once an art student, not so many years ago, with a talent for *tableaux vivants*: the winsomest girl in Mayfair. Now, mistress of madams, she dominated this most orderly of houses, sipping bubbly from midnight to daylight, alive to each tug at the far corners of her web. It was her pride that all felt safe here: gents never recognised, girls fearing no misuse.

"Hands off that bishop," said Cora. "You're in check."

"Cora, Cora, no news for me, Cora?"

"Nobody knows nothing." This was her reply whenever I

asked for rumours. The boy being found so nearby had made them all unsettled, though; it showed in her muddled strategy tonight, and I hoped she might divulge the local whispers. As my gambit led to domination of her kingside, she resorted to more imaginative distractions. When her hands began to rove, I queried her move.

"Another Scotch, and quick." Cora knew that I would accept no immoral favours. Many officers might have, not mentioning Darlington; it rarely led to the sack, but it was a quick route to the clap. Kate and I had an understanding. She thought I didn't like girls, but never ceased offering, with new variations to tempt me. That made no difference to me. I did like women; I'm just an arrogant bugger who doesn't like to be beholden to anyone. If she'd seen how I ogled Cora's midriff, she would have seen through me.

A commotion up above: a man stormed onto the landing in a silk robe and white crown. His words were inaudible amid the drapes, but there was something familiar in his theatrical posture and hectoring tone.

"If you'll calm down," a girl cried, "I'll fetch her for you, sir." Appeased, he was drawn back into the shadows. This was a drama frequently re-enacted: all part of the service, if you find bedroom disputes arousing. The girl leaned over the balcony. She was a Negress, wearing a mitre of red chiffon. "Cora, come sharpish, won't you?"

"Little chance of that, with him," Cora said and rolled her eyes. With Kate's eyes upon us, she swept the pieces from her stomach. It was the closest I would ever come to checkmating her, and she knew it. "You'll have to excuse me, uncle."

I sighed as she departed, watching her cinnamon curves, full posterior accentuated by shapely waist.

"Never fear, Watchman," Kate tutted. "I'll find you another. Never a shortage at Kate Hamilton's."

Oh, yes, Kate impressed me. Most houses were shambolic:

a girl might never come home, and no one would notice; I heard tell that a ruffian might kill a girl, if he was prepared to pay. Bullies ought to protect their fillies, but they cared more for their wallets. The exceptional thing with the dead boy was that he was reported, investigated, and not just slung in the Thames to be hooked out by the boatmen.

Kate's was different. A republic of the independent-minded. The women looking out for each other, making the most of their youth and beauty, under the protection of this vast benefactress, who scared off undesirables and punished malfeasants. Kate herself was wild and irascible and kind in her madness—as sure as Almighty God is sitting on his throne—and I felt no unease over our agreement.

When I paid the promised visit to F Division, the superintendent railed indignant against my complaint of corruption: his officers were not at fault if the bullies' code of signals meant that spirits and other illegalities were concealed the moment they inspected. I countered that two officers of Scotland Yard were ready to testify that said officers readily accepted bribes for such blindness. He compromised: if I would drop the charge, he would keep his "inspectors" away from Kate Hamilton's.

For every once I visited Kate's, I visited fifty other night spots. For every time I played with Cora—played chess, I mean—I interviewed a hundred girls. For each interview with Kate's girls, I confronted the superintendent of H or Q or S Division regarding their own inspections of brothels, a police duty variously interpreted.

Commissioner John Crow of Southwark took this task as seriously as I. He had accounts filed and ready to hand over. His method of annotating maps with numbers, addresses and summaries I adopted: henceforth I was never without a Stanford map folded in my pocket to tot up doxies of the 'Dilly and courtesans of Kensington.

By contrast, Commissioner J.P. Blackward of Hampstead was so obstructive, he must either have been a dimwit or (more likely) personally profiting from each brothel on his patch. Such are the ways of outlying villages.

Some had excuses; some made no apology. The clerks of Clerkenwell smothered me with details:

—Comical Lil, Jewess doxy-thief: entices to bed, bully rifles pockets;
—Ada Diamond, alias Costello, widely known to officers: bug-hunter (i.e. robs drunks in street);
—Cranky Pol, aka Henrietta Hall: fraudulent tea pedlar.

Across the city, prostitutes stood in the dock, in rags or in finery, charged with stealing chisels, shovels, a pair of trousers, five pounds of bacon, a feather bed, towels, candlesticks, plaid dress, cauliflowers, oats, a cow, a parliamentary edict, and beans to the value of twopenny-halfpenny. Where was the sense in jailing these unfortunates? There was no consistency; there could be no improvement, much less a metropolitan solution. Whenever I was abused, or threatened, or worn down by evasions, I had to remind myself: whatever Payne's motives, Felix asked me to do this. He asked me to do it for the good of the city, and for women, so that no more need end up dead in the gutter like that poor lost soul on the corner of Brodie's street.

In exchange for my warding off pestilential inspections, Kate sent girls to tell me their tales. This was the favour I asked of her. In other houses, I received short shrift. Pose a question and they turn silent and suspicious. Girls assumed I was clergy or temperance; bullies divined I was police. Madams fobbed me off with understated numbers, girls gave imaginary ages and fanciful origins. Every night, I had to cajole the truth from them, cut through their bush-beating and persuade them: the census was for their own sakes; truth-telling would lead not to punishment but protection.

When Cora was summoned aloft, I found myself unsupervised. I rose, hoping to slip unnoticed after her up the dimly lit stairwell.

"Oi, oi, saveloy!" Kate spotted my empty seat. "Where's our Scotchman?"

"Kate, Kate." I feigned innocence. "Just a cursory inspection, for my records."

"Inspect me any day, my lover," she roared. "Tickle his innards, Sabine. He stands in need of something damp."

An amply bosomed woman brought the next whisky. "This way."

I took the dram, as always. It was one thing to refuse girls week in, week out; to be impervious to women *and* drink was hard to believe. Sabine led me up the stairs, parted the decorative curtains and pushed through into the interior, an expedition into uncharted lands. The premises were more extensive than I'd realised: manifold stairs and balconies gave off a hallway of faded grandeur. Once an ordinary house, or several knocked together, this had become a labyrinth of a thousand rooms, a fecund body laid out beneath the respectable surface of Leicester Square.

"Changed your mind about girls?" Sabine joshed, as she led me past the inner chambers. "Or are you a devil dodger?"

"A priest?" I laughed. "No fear."

"You're the sleuthhound, are you?" Her eyes flashed wide in the semi-dark and she squeezed my arm. Perhaps the boy found in the closet had scared them. But everyone was a fanatic of detection these days; the shilling shockers of my youth had become serials for adults. Detective novels were everywhere—Wilkie Collins was planning one, and Dickens too. She leaned close, her cologne mingled with sweat and odours of the night. "Glad to make your acquaintance, proper like. You're called Watchman, ain't you?"

I looked at her, face powder ill concealing her mockled cheeks. "No rumours for me? About the dead boy?"

"You're the lilly law; ain't you solved it yet?" Winding corridors. Stout doors. Glimpses of untenanted rooms: dishevelled sheets, redolent of perfume, as maids hurried to clear the latest sullyings. "Can't Jimmy get to the bottom of it?"

"Darlington?" I followed, smiling. "Some chance."

"Where's Jimmy got to these days?" She gave me a sly look; unattractive, with her face, but she doubtless relied on her broader assets. "Likes to get to the bottom of things, he does."

What would she make of Darlington's job inspecting dirty bookshops? Jeffcoat's glamorous secrets would impress her more. Was I jealous, as I traipsed through cold nights from bawd house to finish and back again? Not at all. "Busy."

"Too busy to pay me a visit?" Sabine led me into a dim-lit chamber, stiflingly warm, and stood stroking her collarbone idly. She beckoned me over to the velvet curtains, putting her finger to her lips. She peered through where a glow of light showed through the curtains. She put her hand to her mouth, stifling a giggle, then bade me look. A peephole.

In the next room, pale white youths in scant costumes were arrayed across white-and-ebony tiles; facing them, dark-skinned girls in translucent red stood around the Negress, the mitre completing her meagre bishop's outfit. Cora was arched back on dark pillows, her tiara squashed against the floor. A familiar-looking man knelt at her splayed thighs, clasping her buttocks; the chess board tattoo quivered as this baby-faced king bumped against her derriere. His lips were pouting, his white crown nodding along to his rhythmical pants. Behind them knelt the red queen, in her crimson corset, smacking his backside with her sceptre; her dark luxuriant locks swayed as she moved back and forth astride a pale young knight, his face a picture of concentration beneath his horsehair plume.

I watched for a minute, drawn in, as if by a theatrical show. Could I imagine myself involved in such a scene? What made people indulge such fantasies? I barely noticed when Sabine fished my handkerchief out of my pocket. As she began groping at the buttons of my breeks I came to my senses, as if waking from a dream. I extracted her hand and retrieved the hanky.

"But you wanted to." She pursed her lips. "How d'you expect a girl to earn an honest shilling?"

I hastened from the room and leaned against the corridor wall, discreetly adjusting myself. "Tell me your story. Then you'll earn shillings, and my gratitude."

She fluttered her lashes, which drew attention to her powdered cheeks. "Seduced milliner, ain't I?"

"Oh, Sabine. Are you really?" Decided themes were emerging in these confessions. Mayhew's researches made a grim catalogue. By contrast, Kate Hamilton's girls rarely sparked my indignation: their origins were too uniform, too reasonable. I knew Kate was on my side, and I was grateful for her help, but I was beginning to suspect the line her girls fed me. "Is Sabine even your real name?"

She shrugged. "It's Stephanie. But Sabine sounds more licentious."

"What do you want from this life?"

She leaned close to me. "What do you want, Watchman?"

I held up a hand to stay her advances. "Forever fumbling at loose ends. Peeping at cabinet ministers abasing themselves."

She scowled. "You don't know nothing about me."

"Because you won't tell. I ask and ask, and none of you tell."

"Men don't give a fig. They only ask to salve their conscience before sating their appetite."

"I'm asking."

"I'll leave this life soon enough. I'm saving up to start a coffee shop." Sabine's look dared me to contradict her. The disquieting sounds from next door increased in pitch. She squeezed my arm. "Be a good boy and wait here, Watchman. I'll fetch you another whisky."

She bustled away down the corridor, tapping at one particular door. I followed, at a distance, espying more passageways winding off in every direction. Behind each door, muscles straining, fluids pouring. Flesh pulsating. Groans and gurgles. Cries. Sighs. Each room more fecund than the last. An argument sprang up behind one door. A shout, a slap, a yelp, a slap; the door thrown open, and I hid in the shadows. A silhouette, a hand clutched to her face.

"God help us!" She slammed the door behind her.

I recognised that warm northern voice. I stepped into the half-light. "Skittles, is that you?"

"Bleeding heck." She started. "Watchman?"

"Are you all right?"

She arranged her gown into a semblance of decorum, recovering her famed poise. "But can it be you, Sergeant, here?"

"Out of my natural element, of course. Merely working."

"Cora told me about the queer lilly law who spends the odd evening at Kitty's." She pushed at my shoulder. "Chessifying mostly, I heard."

I blushed in the darkness. "And you? What are you doing here?"

"Merely working, of course." She rubbed at her posterior.

"But your apartments? I thought you had long since graduated from Kate's."

"Sometimes you go up, sometimes—" There was a noise from the room; she gave a dark glance at the door. "Out of my natural element, and all."

"But your famous afternoons? Your handkerchiefs—"

"No time for idling. This isn't the place for talk." Skittles glanced down the passage. She pulled me into the shadows as we heard footfalls approaching. I confess, the blood danced in my veins as she grabbed me, though goodness knows I had no designs upon her. "Will you meet me? Dress more foppish, and less the Newgate mizzler, will you? Cora and Steph'll tell you where. Come with an open mind. I could do with your help."

The footsteps were upon us, but it was only Sabine with the whisky. She and Skittles exchanged a complicitous look. Then the famous courtesan kissed my cheek and marched brazenly back into the room.

# PART III
## CONFOUNDED CONFEDERACIES
### JANUARY–FEBRUARY 1864

The ruin of many girls is commenced by reading the
low trashy wishy-washy cheap publications that the
news-shops are now gorged with, and by devouring the
hastily-written, immoral, stereotyped tales about the
sensualities of the upper classes, the lust of the aristocracy,
and the affection that men about town—noble lords,
illustrious dukes, and even princes of the blood—are in
the habit of imbibing for maidens of low degree "whose
face is their fortune", shop girls—dressmakers—very often
dressmakers and the rest of the tribe who may perhaps feel
flattered by reading about absurd possibilities that their
untutored and romantic imaginations suggest may, during
the course of a life of adventure, happen to themselves.

Henry Mayhew, *London Labour and the London Poor*


There are but two families in the world,
as my grandmother used to say, which are the
haves and the have-nots.

Miguel de Cervantes, *Don Quixote*


We are keepers of books, not guardians of morals.

Keeper of the British Museum Library

# COMPLAINT OF WILLIAM DUGDALE & JOHN HOTTEN, EROTIC BOOKSELLERS

When your man Sergeant Lawless strolled in, I thought I was headed back to the Penitentiary. The things we do for books, eh?

It's just after *Lucretia, or The Delights of Cunnyland*, new edition, comes in the post: a notable addition to our Flower Garden. Eager to show off the delightful engravings, I run into the back room to tell Hotten and the girl.

"Dugdale," Hotten interrupts me, his eyes bright, "you must hear Molly's latest."

The urchin continues mid-anecdote. "This flash yob coshes the jailbird right in the inexpressibles. He kicks the bucket, only no one twigs he's croaked…"

How can one resist such argot? How full of slang Molly is, and told with relish. Hotten is transcribing these lexical gems, when—ting-a-ling—the fierce wind lashes in through the bookshop door. I peek out to see a bright-eyed sap come in, collar pulled up against the prying eyes of Holywell Street. (It's your man Darlington, but I don't know that yet.) He has the look of a Pantagruelian fantasist. He thumbs through the tamer prints, and asks offhand if we have *Fanny Hill*. Do we have *Fanny Hill*! This may have been the open sesame for erotic booksellers of old, but I need better proof of erotophilia before opening our secret Flower Garden, since my troubles with the judicial system.

Sensing my disdain, the sap takes a deep breath, and asks for *The Cockchafer*, *The Politick Whore,* and *Sodom*, by the divine Rochester. I look at him in a new light: this is sufficient abracadabra to unlock the special door. Locking it behind us, I show him our new blooms, the latest "republications from Amsterdam". *The Natural History of the Frutex Vulvaria* catches his eye; *The Sixteen Pleasures* piques his interest; but he's soon engrossed in *Venus School Mistress*. His eyes grow round. Sweating slightly, he peruses the tale of the Fukkumite Islanders and their underwear.

Ting-a-ling at the shop door.

I slyly open up *Cunnyland* at the engravings of the priest and the callipygian orgy. I suggest he latch himself in while I'm with the new customer. I pray he isn't a soiler: we need sales, not smirches.

Another blast of wind. In the doorway, an unwelcome face. Lawless of Scotland Yard. My heart sinks. "Sergeant, what a pleasure."

"Back in business so soon, Mr Hotten?"

"I'm Dugdale, as you well know, having sent me to prison for two years." I clench my teeth: I'm rather homely, Hotten's got less fat on him than a butcher's pencil. "Is it so cumbersome to distinguish between us?"

Lawless smirks—he's doing it to unsettle me, hoping I'll give the game away. "Trade going well?"

"No complaints from our customers."

"Reference books, is it now?" He eyes our respectable shelves. "I should hope so, after the time you spent in the Penitentiary. Millbank, wasn't it?"

Mere mention of the Tench makes me wince. "Blast it all, Lawless, we've just opened. Can't you let us alone?" I wonder if he knows that our ever-expanding list of customers includes

MPs, the PM and his commissioner. "Hotten has friends in high places, you know."

"I'm afraid The Obscene Publications Act deems the filthy books in your back room—"

"Back room? What back room?" I laugh; he points; I tut. "That's private premises."

"You have a customer in there."

"Not a customer. A friend."

Lawless laughs. He pushes me aside and rattles the handle of the Flower Garden. Thank goodness I told the sap to lock the door. "Darlington?" he calls. "Found anything?"

After a long moment, the door opens. "Sorry, I've been seizing certain items." The sap is rather red-faced. Clutching several precious volumes, he can't look me in the eye. "I shall have to confiscate these."

"You lying so-and-so."

Lawless takes advantage of my shock to nip around the counter and bother Hotten and the girl.

"Blasted police," Hotten protests. "We've a tradesman's entrance, you know."

Lawless begins his accusation. "Mr Hotten—"

"I'm Dugdale," says Hotten, just to confuse him. "That's Hotten behind you. If you'll excuse us, we're working. Your Commissioner Payne won't be pleased—"

"Oi oi, lilly law." The girl sidles out. Entertaining a pubescent youth in our accounting room suddenly looks a bit rum.

Lawless stares between the three of us. "What's going on here?"

"Writing a dictionary," says she, "ain't we?"

"And I'm the Poet Laureate."

Hotten's bravado is shaken. "This is not what it looks like."

Molly squares up to the policeman. "Are you imputing low morals to me? That's slander, that is. I'll have you in front of the magistrate, don't you doubt." Plucky little thing, she brandishes the manuscript at him. "*Dictionary of Modern Slang*, expanded edition. To which I am prime contributor. Incarcerate these gents, would you?"

"It wouldn't be Dugdale's first time."

The girl glances at me with increased respect. "You try to earn an honest wage, and the charpering coppers can't wait to spoil it."

"We've been harassed by authority, it's true," says Hotten, "but we are not ashamed. We are working in the interests of posterity."

Lawless smirks. "Is that what you call it?"

Darlington is still perusing *Cunnyland*, further confiscated volumes clutched under his arm.

Hotten takes the slang manuscript from Molly with a reverent air. "This evanescent vulgar language, rich and poor, honest and dishonest, this is the language of the streets, of the fast life, high and low, as old as speech and city congregations, full of pungent satire and always to the point."

"Nicely put, old cove." Molly applauds. "That'll make a tidy introduction."

Lawless gestures at Darlington. "And these other publications, Hotten?"

"We also promote literature which soothes woes and heightens pleasures. I stand by the right to read and our right to print."

"Literature?" Lawless scoffs.

Molly rises on her tiptoes. "Who gives you the right to judge what men may and may not read? And women for that matter."

I gather my courage, inspired by her defiance. "Why should the literature of love be banned, Lawless? You leave the pimps' trade unimpeded, while harassing our mere descriptions of pleasure. We men of letters are free to think, and write; and our words might even alleviate vice. Ban the lascivious acts, if you must. To prevent us describing the truth of the matter is to put the cart before the horse. The prudish may think it better that such thoughts should not be thought. But many, including prominent citizens of the world, enjoy such writing. And what harm does that do?"

Darlington nods, to Lawless's annoyance.

"How," Hotten chimes in, "is literature arousing sexual appetites worse than murder stories? Newspapers, full of knifings, and poisonings, and death, are purchasable by you, me and this child for pennies; but one mention of minette and gamahuche, and we are branded pornographers."

I stand by him. "Murders are mere sport for these detective novelists. The knife slices the belly, the blood spurts, the victim writhes in agony—unnatural violence. I describe a hairy mount, the most natural thing in the world, and I am jailed."

"True enough." Darlington grins. "We don't complain about books that make the blood run cold. Why must we confiscate books that make the blood hot?"

Lawless shakes his head, defeated. "Maybe you're right." To my amazement, he holds out his hand for us to shake. "We will grant a period of grace to finish your labours."

Hotten shakes on it without discussion.

"Not because I agree with your deviations," Lawless continues, "but there are worse crimes; and you are gainfully employing this indolent street child."

"Oi!" Molly demurs.

I blink back my astonishment. "You're letting us off?"

"On one condition." He takes a deep breath. "That you should inform me, if ever certain manuscripts should be offered to you, private papers in an erotic vein, papers you may suspect stolen from men about town…"

Hotten and I exchange a glance. Lawless has described, more or less exactly, the extraordinary collection of manuscripts we've just been offered by an Irish littérateur of our acquaintance. We say nothing; we accept his amnesty. I promise to let him know if we are offered anything suspicious. Lawless marches off; if he lets us trade long enough, we'll finish the slang dictionary.

His crony Darlington says he'll be returning for frequent inspections. I keep him happy by offering to send our next publication for his inspection when it comes out.

This is publisher-police collaboration, as I prefer it. Hotten was ready to scare them by brandishing our subscription list. Better keep that up our sleeve. If they get heavy-handed, we can call on heavyweight friends to fight our corner. The new manuscript—well, better it remain unmentioned, and we'll see if the subscribers complain when we serialise it.

The girl stays behind to finish her dictations. We crack open a bottle to celebrate our defiance. How can I resist? I can't. I simply can't resist telling her about our latest—and surely greatest—publishing venture.

## FLOWER GARDEN CATALOGUE, ANCIENT & MODERN, HOLYWELL STREET 1864

(appended to Dugdale-Hotten's complaint, for the perusal of Commissioner Payne)

*The Lifted Curtain*
*The Ins and Outs of London*
*Sodom, or The Quintessence of Debauchery*
*The London Jilt: or, the Politick Whore*
*Lucretia, or the Delights of Cunnyland*

*The Ladies' Telltale & The Lustful Turk*
*The Romance of the Rod*
*The Whore's Rhetoric*

*The Sixteen Pleasures, or About All the Schemes of Venus*
*The Natural History of the Frutex Vulvaria*
*Harris's List of Covent-Garden Ladies, or Man of Pleasure's*
     *Kalendar*
*The Crafty Whore*
*The Cockchafer: Flash, Frisky and Funny Songs, Never*
     *before Printed and Adapted for Gentlemen Only*
*The Cabinet of Venus Unlocked*
*Mutton Walk Cyprians*

# RENDEZVOUS WITH THE URCHIN LEXICOGRAPHER

By the time Molly joined us, Darlington was ordering his second celebratory pint. She appeared at our table as if by magic. "Top of reeb, thanks, Watchman."

I ordered her one happily enough. Top of reeb, indeed; it was Molly who taught me whatever backslang I know. Top of reeb, pot of beer—even a dullard detective could untangle this. Maybe a policeman shouldn't be buying a girl beer, but I too was pleased with our charade and hoped she'd share more of what she'd gleaned during her employment.

"Excuse my tardiness, Watchman. Couldn't leave the old churls till we'd chalked up the letter C. They're in clover with my canting cock and bull."

I smiled. "Cheese your claptrap, chatterbox."

"You ain't going to crunch 'em, you old crusher?" She fixed her eyes on me. "It's cushy coppers for me."

"I'd have thought your Oddbody Theatricals more profitable, no?" All the trades Molly had ever learned had been systematically banned: chimneys, night soil, toshering, mudlarking, even Bazalgette's sewer work. Dictionary-writing was a legitimate alternative, if only the publishers weren't offenders of the Obscene Publications Act. But maybe they were right: what harm did words do, when every day I must ignore criminality in night houses?

"Bede and the Pixie are otherwise engaged, the blinding cog-diddlers." She grimaced. "Dugdale and Hotten pay prompt and pay by the word. Don't put the old anti-queer-uns away, I beg you."

Darlington delivered the drinks, flushed with our success. He removed a volume he had secreted in his coat pocket, pleased with himself for discovering such filth in the booksellers' secret room. "We put the fear of God up 'em, all right."

"I get the impression," I nodded, "that Dugdale found the Tench uncomfortable. But it's information I want, about these stolen manuscripts."

"Oh, they'll give us it, if they want to continue trading," he grinned. "They'll do whatever we want, in return for my discretion."

Molly raised her brow. "You might want to watch your step. Hotten has friends in high places."

I looked at her. "How would you know?"

"Oh, you don't know the half of it, Watchman. But seeing as you've considerately allowed me to continue in their employ, I'll share what I've learned." She took two pamphlets from her pocket. "Exhibit the first: Dugdale-Hotten's catalogue for 1864, for the discerning erotobibliophile."

Darlington sniggered at the list of authors: Terence O'Tooleywag, Paddy Strongcock, and Timothy Touchit. "Where do they find this filth?"

"Erotic memoir, ain't it?" Molly sniffed. "Everyone's writing 'em, pseudonymously mind. Ain't you? Can't say I see the harm in it. Still, if I were you, I wouldn't reel him in just yet. Viz, exhibit the second."

This is when I first heard rumour of the vast erotic manuscript later known as *My Secret Life* by "Walter". Molly's exhibit was minimal: a few scribbled notes and chapter titles. But she explained that these represented snippets of memoir delivered to Dugdale-Hotten over recent weeks. The details they carefully hid from her, but they couldn't conceal their excitement. It seemed a memoir of extraordinary extent, describing every sort of salacious situation from the sensuous to the obscene, from youth to old age, the profound to the perverse. They were receiving the manuscript piecemeal from a secret source—which made Molly think it might be stolen, or some of it, at least. Dugdale had never read such a catalogue of sexual escapades. He was dying to serialise, for it would be a smash; but he had been warned to hold off for the moment. She promised to bring proofs as soon as they were typeset; I would leave Darlington to bring it to Sir Payne's attention.

I was already pleased with our ruse, but there was one more document Molly had shrewdly copied for me.

"Exhibit the third: the subscription list." With a glance about her, Molly pushed it along the bar. "The erotobibliophiles."

On the list, names I knew. Names everyone knew.

"It's a new publishing model," Molly said. "Gents sign up, and pay monthly, thus receiving each new Dugdale-Hotten edition."

I screwed up my eyes. Far too many names: bankers, businessmen, journalists, politicians, peers and policemen.

"Blimey." Darlington snatched up the list. "The head of the British Museum."

"Not to mention a prominent newspaper editor, and your very own Scotland Yard commissioner." Molly examined her beer in the murky light; it was cloudier than the January skies outside. God damn it: Dugdale-Hotten worked out how to keep us off their backs. "I imagine, Watchman old cove, it may aid your investigations, this list, eh? I ain't saying that reading is the same as doing. Nor imputing low morals to nobody.

Only that your literary aficionados take a profound interest in a subject, and if this lot are interested in your investigations, you'd do well to watch out."

# FOLLY

I remember every detail. Her skin and her hair. Every detail of her clothes and her underclothes, for she allowed me to help her remove every last layer. And the way she spoke. She had this way of going so far, then leaving the rest to the imagination. But her kisses said to me what words never could.

Titchfield Street was ever quiet. I pushed away the thought that Gabriel Mauve MP had encountered his wife in just such a place. It could be so sordid. But with her, it became always divine.

I cannot describe her here. I will not write of our intimacies. Oh, I could detail every movement, every reaction, but I lift the quill and torpor overtakes me. Yet I see now the pleasure of recalling to mind these golden moments, when we had the body of love, the hands of love, the touch of pleasure, skin so soft, her mellifluous voice, limbs entwined, our hearts afire.

The fourth time I met her, I found her sitting at the cheval glass in her night shift. I entered without knocking; she started a little. Seeing it was me, she kept on brushing her hair. She allowed me to study her, her back elegant as a violoncello, the swell of her breasts, and her spine inviting the touch of my fingers.

"You shouldn't have come."

I laid my hands on her shoulders. "You shouldn't have asked me."

She shivered at my touch, my hands chilled by the icy wind. "It was foolhardy."

"And last week?"

"I have been foolish all month."

# UNHOLY ROT

Gales, squalls, always the wind, and a murder a day in the *Ha'penny Gazette*. Brodie's papers went from strength to strength, in the wake of their insinuations about Palmerston and the dead woman. I scrabbled at this same coalface of depravity, for which his readers had voracious appetites. His rags overflowed with scandal, strangling and suicide: FRIGHTFUL WIFE MURDER IN BRISTOL, BURGLAR BITTEN BY A SKELETON. With butchery in the news daily, every halfwit in the country solved each mystery, sending their deranged cogitations to Sir Richard Payne by the penny post.

Brodie's papers were proud of their infamy. The *Ha'penny Gazette* sold best, with sketches of violence, alarmist propaganda and interviews with actual murderers. But now his empire suffered a setback.

It was another of his publications, the *Bugle*, that upset the apple cart. Jeffcoat had solved the case of the boy found in the queer house closet at New Year. Months before, he had investigated the son of a good family in Fulham gone missing. He spotted the connection between the two sorry tales and concluded the matter quietly, with consideration for the grieving family. (More plaudits for Jeffcoat; bully for him.)

Or so it should have been. Except that, just before Jeffcoat tied up the case, the *Bugle* cottoned on. They reported details of the son's flight—household arguments, monetary woes— in such minuscule detail that the family complained. Now the boy was dead, the journalists' meddling looked rum. The public lost patience: hadn't the family misery enough? I would have blamed Jeffcoat for the leak, but the family lawyer proved that the revelations were gleaned by improper means: butlers bribed, wastepaper turfed from bins, blotters stolen for experts to study the handwriting. Such methods were beyond investigative licence and illegal. The journalist was sacked, the editor castigated; and that was just the beginning. Scandal, testimony, and counter-testimony. In the preamble to the trial, an affair between the lady of the house and the journalist was hinted at. The hounds kept a-baying. The editor was indicted and imprisoned (briefly; he was after all a school friend of Gabriel Mauve MP).

Brodie settled the compensation claim out of court. But the public decreed that things had gone too far. Out of the woodwork sprang a thousand more grievances against journalistic impropriety. Families whose bereavement was trampled on. The scurrilous accusations ruining a prominent cricketer's equanimity, and his batting. An actress, followed to the house of a suspected amour. So many injustices committed in the name of scandal-mongering. The paper ought to be closed.

There was nothing for it, declared Brodie, ever the populist. He would close the *Bugle* forever.

A victory for fairness, crowed his competitors, admiring his methods—and envying his sales.

Brodie happened just then to have bought the moribund *Police News*. Rather than sack his poor journalists for misguided zeal, he magnanimously re-employed them, just in time to relaunch that august organ as the *Illustrated Police News*.

Garish engravings adorned each case, supposedly inspired by coroner's inquests. But the details were so accurate, the portrayals so realistic, we police began to recognise details never mentioned in the inquests. Brodie paid the victims to tell tales. Brodie even paid criminals. The writers cooked up quotations to fit their racy versions of events; the editor paid witnesses to put their names to them. Brodie's lawyers checked each story. Some painted us police as heroes; more made us idiots. Nothing to be done about it. Brodie's various papers made the most of each scandal, corroborating each other's facts like Mrs Gamp and Mrs Harris—"As discovered by the *Illustrated Police News*"—

while each produced by the very same editorial staff.

As always, Brodie triumphed. I made enquiries about him. His mother was American, his father a Scottish miner from the Fife coal pits. He was not the obvious business mogul so often encountered in these times, full of inflated ideas and swollen vanity. He had no need of personal glamour. He was a manipulator of crowds, suffering the population to call unto him for scandal, sensation, gaming and liquor.

He had told me to call on him. He had hinted that his reporters would help my census-taking, if I had something to offer him. He meant me to pass on information on violent crimes, to enliven his rags. I never did call on him—but someone did. Someone was dishing the dirt, and I was superfluous, because he was never short of his murder a day.

## THE DINNING ROOM

"Miss Sabine's table," I said, above the noise, "if you please."

The legend "Dinning Room" was inscribed on the wooden gateposts of this fashionable Leicester Square coffee house, adjacent to Burford's Panorama; the continental owner had insisted on it, overconfident of his spelling. The maître d' winked. The staff pretended to be French, to maintain their dignity. The clientele was genteel, yet the bully by the kitchen door kept his eye on us. I discerned consorts and courtesans, not from their dress (more demure than the wives, who tried too hard to be risqué), but rather their arched eyebrows and self-possession.

"Moisten your chaffer, may I?" It was Sabine, or rather Stephanie, the doxy from Kate Hamilton's with the pocked face and the ample bosoms. "You like to hear girls' stories, I'm told."

I looked past her. This was not our agreement. "You told me Sk—"

"Shush." She glanced about, then went on. "You wasn't

expecting nobody else, were you? Well, I'm a seduced milliner."

"And we must all go bald-headed, if so many milliners are ruined. Would a sovereign entice you to drop the usual flam?"

"Carry me out and bury me properly!" she cackled. "Money? What do I want with money? Stand me a white satin, though, and I'll make a clean fist of it."

I called for the gin happily enough.

While the waiter fetched it, she whispered that I must play along. "We've to talk a while before you give the bully a sovereign and we takes a room. Standard practice, you greenhorn." She drank the gin, straight off, and plucked at her taffeta pleats. "S'pose you might as well hear my real story. I don't care to tell you where I'm from, sir. Touches me on the raw, that does. I was so young when enticed." She was the daughter of a countryside vicar. Visited an aunt in the big city; met a gent at Hackney market; evening walks; a stop by his cousin's. "No wonder I acquiesced, charmed at such refinements, never suspecting a fault." She refused brandy, begged for a cab, took coffee. And when she awoke, she found herself ruined. "I wept. I ranted. Wanted to kill myself." Thence to Kate Hamilton's, where new opportunity knocked, several gents liked her, and she truly was saving up for that café, to leave this life and become a lady.

After a second glass, her voice grew lower and her tale bleaker. She wasn't brought directly to Kate's. She described sotto voce a house where girls were broken in: spirit tamed, body disciplined; trained up for the flash life, how to win gents, the ways of the flesh; how to please 'em, seduce 'em, marry 'em.

Finally, a tale I could believe. "I can't imagine how they tamed you."

"Lack of imagination on your part." She laughed.

"Where is this house? This branch establishment?"

"Such talk needs privacy." Her eyes darted rapidly about, and she squeezed my hand. "They make us sign a contract.

Drink up, and we'll go. We are closely watched, and Skittles closest of all." Sabine extracted my pocket watch, nodded, and shoved my hand under her skirts. "Oh, oh! My sweet," she gasped with mock outrage. "Follow me down."

I palmed a sovereign to the bully, who opened up the door by the kitchens. A stairwell took us beneath ground level. Haphazard doorways off the lower vestibule. Sabine pushed me against the wall, as one of Kate Hamilton's bullies strolled our way, pressing my hand to her backside. "In case they know you," she whispered. "As long as you're paying for my attentions, you'll escape theirs."

We circumnavigated an ill-lit bar, where dancing girls toyed with serious gents. From the snugs surrounding us, muffled gruntings and squeals. In a dark corner, a fracas arose. A figure was catapulted out.

"That, sir, is too far." It was Mauve, his eyes moony, his demeanour self-satisfied. If he saw me, he gave no sign of it. He pursed his lips. "Too far by half."

Sabine tugged me onward through the circles of the underworld, giggling to see me disconcerted. I thought I knew all the brothels of Leicester Square. "Where the hell are we?"

"The Alhambra, ain't it? Members' club, where enthusiasts may express their admiration for the dancers. At close quarters."

"Don't tell me this joins up with Kate's emporium."

"Maybe it does. Maybe it don't." She took my arm, led me chummily down another corridor, and bundled me into the first cubicle. "I've chose us a fair to middling room."

"No peepholes?" I smiled. "Costs extra, I imagine."

"You can always donate on the sly to my coffee shop fund, if you're pleased with my work." She dimmed the lamp and regarded me across the threadbare mattress. "I'm bursting to piddle. Stay here."

She grabbed a pot and disappeared through the adjoining screen doors. I sat on the rickety bed, glanced at the sheets, then stood again, brushing at my trousers. If this warren of corridors stretched all the way beneath Leicester Square, underlying the Alhambra, Dinning Room, Burton's Panorama and Kate Hamilton's, then for every miscreant we had seen dallying over their pleasure, a hundred more were pursuing personal depravities behind closed doors: a vast subterranean counterpart of the grand square above, like a harlot pinned beneath her gentleman caller.

A faded print on the wall portrayed a lady striving to rise from her whiskered fellow's arms: he lounged at the piano, playing some childish ditty; in her face torment and exaltation competed. I must get to Skittles. Sabine was testing my patience. This contract of hers intrigued me. Ignoring the sounds through the partition, more like hinges creaking than piddle in a pot, I called out. "Will you really leave this life if you can, Sabine?"

"Inquisitive party, aren't you?" Her voice, above the ruffling of skirts, sounded strange through the doorway.

"I don't mean to preachify. All my questions and queries—I hope they may make life better for you and your friends."

"I'll stick to the life till I'm a stiff 'un, I suppose. Where's the fun in suffering? That's my philosophy." Her voice was quite changed. In she came, her face shadowed, placed her rear gingerly on the bed, and turned to look at me. "But Steph'll escape yet."

I stared at the damask rose in her hair. "Sk—!"

Skittles put her hand over my mouth. "Hush, you old fool."

## A ROSE ENSLAVED

Skittles silenced me with a smacker of a kiss on my cheek.

"Your perfume," I hazarded, "is very nice."

"I'm not wearing any. Here, where's the gin?"

She had sent Stephanie-Sabine to divert the bullies' attention. A laudable scheme. With a new customer like me, they would earwig, like as not; Sabine's verbosity had blunted their vigilance.

"You may think her a moaning minnie. But I'll see Steph a-right, set up with her respectable café at Waterloo, if you can help me now."

What ups and down Skittles had undergone since that day at Paddington Station. Rising to elevated circles, with her own apartments. (I was charmed that she made time for me that day on Rotten Row.) Now she was reduced to this raggle-taggle cubicle. I studied her pale make-up. "But you had risen so far. I thought you beyond the clutches of these bullies."

"I carry myself gaily, but have never broke free of my doubtful origins."

"Skittles, are you all right?" I wondered what her powder was hiding. Sabine's bottle of gin quieted her sobs.

I will not record here everything she told me. My cosy view of Kate's was blinkered; but my wider researches should have prepared me for her revelations. Much came out before the Commons Select Committee's Enquiry; some still too shocking to believe. Some girls might be willing debauchees, but most were not. Skittles held back her tears. "You should see the little tykes they drag in, some of them tiny as sparrows."

There were dark forces at work. She herself had been tamed again. Her pet duke dropped her; the bullies picked her up straightaway, and had bent her again to their will. Their sins she hid with the powdery cosmetics, scars deeper than I could see.

"Walk away," I said.

"I signed papers on my first day at Kitty H's, giving them powers over me; I don't know what." She spluttered on the gin. "I'm grateful to them. The things they taught me. Riding. Piano and cribbage. Groggins dispensing fine talk, highfalutin manners. I've been content these last years. My fellows provided apartments and opera boxes. But my poor duke has been scared off marrying me."

He wouldn't be the first aristocrat to pull back from such a marriage.

"Oh, he loves me more than ever." She sighed. "Blackmailed. I know who scuppered our plans and why. They want more out of me; and I tell you, I am frightened, Watchman. I'm mightily come down in the world, without patron, or solace."

She would think of escape, but she had not a penny to her name; she had set aside earnings aplenty, but from their false accountants, she could not retrieve a sou. Her fellow had made arrangements, heartbroken, to pension her off, but what did she see of the money? Nothing. His family heard he had settled upon her three hundred pounds per annum; they questioned his sanity, and the money was withheld pending a writ of *de lunatico inquirendo* at Gray's Inn Coffee House.

"And here?" I asked. "What about your earnings now?"

"The meagrest portion is set aside as our share; the rest is counted against our clothes, victuals and lodgings. The moment we are ill or damaged, they drop us. If we escape, they track us down."

Did Kate's bullies, godlike, see everything? "They?"

"The organisation that—" Her courage failed her. She looked wildly about and needed calming; I had never seen her like this. She continued in a fraught whisper. "They track us down, make no mistake. They drag us back like dogs, with you police behind them. We have signed our lives away."

"Kate protects her women."

"You would say that," she said. "Men love the old battleship. You think her a champion of women; she cares only for profit. The monies paid for us Kitty takes. She pays off our protectors, and their protectors' unseen protector. So on, ad infinitum." Her bosom rose and fell. "Help me escape, Watchman."

"Do you mean it?" I half rose.

"Not now." She tugged me back. "They'd kill us both."

"I promised Kate—"

"Oh, she has you wrapped up too now, has she?"

"I owe favours to no one." It was not true. My census had me mired in collaborations. Was I compromised? I need not regret enlisting the 9.23 Club, nor asking Mayhew to enlist the charitable societies. True, I had benefited from Kate's help, even if her girls' tales were repetitious. I did repent of my chat with Brodie, but I had made no deal with him. I cast my eyes down. "It's not my business to meddle in things I don't understand."

"Oh, Watchman. It is your business." She gave a hollow laugh. "This is it, love. Do you want to save my life, or not?"

Whatever my debt to Kate, it could not prescribe my loyalties as a policeman, nor as a man. "Of course."

The lines around her pretty eyes softened. "Make plans for me. Most secret plans." She rose and adjusted her damask rose in the glass. "What it costs you, in time and money, I shall pay you back some day. I do not wish to presume."

"Perhaps you can." I explained how hard it was to gather women's stories.

"No wonder, if you keep harassing women with questions." She told me of girls she knew, and how they came to live the life: stories less sensational than the novels and less erotic. Girls preyed upon, lied to, promised the earth; enticed from slums, countryside, and abroad. Working girls, young girls, naive girls; girls such as Cora and Sabine, lured to the Great Wen to make their fortune. Girls drugged, kidnapped, coerced, tricked by loose gents, swayed against their will, forced through misfortune and cruelty; snatched, drugged, violated.

I sat on that meagre bed, mired in the smell of exploitation, as debaucheries reverberated through the thin walls. Skittles's shining eyes betrayed no exaggeration; if anything, she was understating the matter. I laid my hand upon hers, my great brutish paw on her slender fingers, but drew it back out of a sort of shame.

"And you?" I swallowed. "Were you too unwillingly ruined?"

"Not I. I'd had a fucking; I wanted more." She observed my shock. "Have I misjudged my lexicon, Watchman? Groggins told me off for my unscriptural tongue."

I grabbed her hand. Twice she had mentioned him. "The Irish elocutionist? How is Groggins mixed up in this?"

"That old rascal. Ah, he schools us entirely. No electrocution needed. Insists upon every detail from our vowels and consonants to our bowels and—"

"Skittles!"

"Too much detail?" She burst out laughing. Skittles changed my view of the whole census that night. If even Kate's girls were enslaved, or believed themselves enslaved, this story was likely repeated in every borough, with all colluding to whitewash it in the eyes of the authorities.

"Why not leave? You're not locked up."

"They don't need locks, Watchman. I told you: the contract. I should have asked my duke when I could—he works in the Law—but I was cocksure, and ashamed, all at once—"

"Give me it. I shall see if it has any force."

"You mustn't show it to any lawyer who might know—" She thought better of naming names. "If anyone learns of this—" She drew her hand across her throat.

"I'm the soul of discretion." I would tell Cora or Sabine when and where Skittles should meet me. She veiled her face. She would show me to the backstairs, which led into Burford's Panorama, a back route to avoid the bullies' gaze. "And the contract?"

She glanced about and drew out an envelope from under her bodice.

I smiled. "So closely watched." I drew out my handkerchief to wrap it in.

"My handkerchief of old?" It was her turn to smile. "You carry it still?"

"Everyone longs for a hanky imbued with Anonyma's perfume. Flash gents pay fifty guineas in the clubs."

"Spoony chumps. That perfume was just apothecary's tincture. Yours, on the other hand, shall have the genuine article." She grabbed it, fiddle-faddled at her skirts and handed the handkerchief back with a wink. "Genuine *cassolette du jour.*"

## AUTOMATON QUERIES

It was most inconvenient that my librarian friend, Miss Villiers, had moved to the countryside. She was never at the British Museum when I called, and I am not an assiduous correspondent. Her frosty postcard wishing me a happy Hogmanay inspired me to reply by letter. I made casual mention of the chess automaton. Might she rustle up something on the subject next time I popped into the library? Incidentally, my reader's card had expired and I needed a referee to commend me; could she think of anyone?

I awaited her reply eagerly. She could never resist a mystery.

My enquiries about J.W. Brodie turned up no more, until my toothache turned into an abscess. The dentist Sir Richard sent me to was a cheerful colonial, a devotee of the new ether treatment, and rather indiscreet. His tattle took my mind off the pain: Gabriel Mauve was one of his patients, and J.W. Brodie was his tennis partner. These two he held up as the poles of discretion: Mauve continually vaunted and flaunted his hobby horses; with his vast success Brodie was reserved. When the dentist had ribbed Brodie, however, about the debacle with the *Bugle*, Brodie couldn't resist an indiscreet boast. He didn't give a damn about it being shut down. Illustrated newspapers were here to stay. With engravings ever cheaper to reproduce, he had at a stroke persuaded thousands of penny readers into paying half a sixpence for his *Illustrated Police News*. No, no, Brodie didn't give a hoot about the scandal. In fact, he had encouraged the outcry, whereby his competitors advertised his papers for weeks on end. If heads had to roll, so be it. After all, for a newsman, *succès de scandale* was simply success.

# THE VENAL MUSE

Felix had implored me not to give up; Skittles inspired my next steps.

I lost no time in seeking out Groggins. An elocution teacher by trade, Sheridan Groggins was a chancer, a Dubliner riding his wits through London society, with qualms about meddling neither in the lowest echelons nor the highest if there was a penny in it for him. To find Groggins mixed up in this business was no surprise.

I knew better than to warn him of my arrival. I watched his doorway in Mayfair a while, noting the regular comings and goings. A finely clad lady slipped out; though of course ladies and courtesans can be hard to distinguish, and both may be anxious about their vowels. Pleased with her progress, she didn't notice me hovering near enough to catch the door before it closed.

Groggins' study door being ajar, I peeked in. He was scribbling so furiously, writing up florid annotations, that he did not notice me wander in. I had time to cast an eye over his bookshelves, where I was not surprised to see titles from Dugdale-Hotten's catalogue. On his desk stood a large black file, inscribed *M—S—L—*.

"Be-jaysus. Are you after giving me a heart attack,

Sergeant?" He scrabbled the sheets away into the file and locked it with a padlock. My amused look he could not ignore. "Not that I've anything to hide from the likes of you."

I sat, uninvited, in his armchair. I allowed the silence to hang between us. Groggins was a voluble soul. If I remained taciturn, he would not resist telling me what was on his mind. On the coffee table lay a cheap bound copy of *Lady Audley's Secret*, part two.

"Dreadful story," he blustered. "Only one gets so hooked. Could you believe the end of that second instalment?"

"I imagined your tastes above such sensational claptrap, Groggins."

"I have a theory, you know. Those bemoaning sensation fiction's baneful influence upon society, and on literature, are the very same voraciously buying the books." He glanced at his file. "And when the government passes acts against obscene books—well, doesn't it make you wonder about governmental reading habits? That old devil Palmerston, eh?" He wagged his finger. Seeing his own hand unsteady, he reached for the inevitable bottle of cognac. He poured me one too. "Funny thing, Sergeant. I was minded to call on yourself."

"Problems with the parade of flowerlike womanhood through your door?"

The blood drained from his face, as if I had just signed a warrant for his death. He drank down his brandy, coughed, and poured a second. "That's a peculiar expression, now, Sergeant, wouldn't you say?"

"I'm sure I don't mean anything by it."

"Ha."

I followed his gaze back to his file. "Business weighing on your mind?"

He drummed his fingers on the desk, straining to regain his equable humour. "The government bans lewd books. There's a positive explosion of the stuff. Why?" He blew out through pinched cheeks, and decided to confide in me. "Sensational literature is as popular in the drawing room as below the stairs, so your discerning gent feels the urge to dig deeper for titillation. Lo and behold, he hears tell of the French filth of the last century. But editions of the Marquis de Sade dent the bank balance. Hence the new publishing craze." He looked at me penetratingly. "You're aware of the self-published *mémoire érotique*, no doubt? The critics rubbish them; the public decry them; they sell by the cartload. Twitchy publishers leap on the donkey cart, sniffing for success. Invent us fresh misadventures, they tell impoverished scribblers. Seek out forgotten tomes, retitle and republish, they declaim. Or pretend you're republishing. Lo, a new profession is born: the libertine's scribe."

"A post you willingly apply for."

He sighed. "Here's a funny thing, Sergeant. The lovely courtesans, whose vowels I have coached for so long, abruptly find themselves in possession of a second commodity, equally sellable—and less frangible than corporeal beauty. Besides their curves and unmentionables, they have a wealth of stories."

I thought of Cora in her languorous chiffon. "An unquenchable supply."

"Jesus, they've only to recount their everyday habits." Leaping up, he paced back and forth by the French windows, regaining his swagger. "And such good recall they have, I tell you. A poetically minded whore can generate remarkable sales."

"No doubt rephrased with your inimitable wit?"

"You'd think so. You'd imagine the public want their tales tarted up. A little prettification, remove the dismal interludes, the emotional stultification, the violence. Not a bit of it. Turns out that readers love the tawdry minutiae of amorous dalliance: the roadside piss; the dirty underwear; the washing of the quim, or not washing; the food ordered so as to stay longer abed; the chance fuck by the Pleasure Gardens."

"No need to be coy, Groggins." I sipped my brandy, thinking of Skittles and her unscriptural language.

He barely heard me, gazing out through the frosty panes. "The disease inadvertently passed on to a wife; the chubby thigh, the ill-matched bosoms; the lumpy nymphomaniac preferred to the heavenly prude; an uncle fond of the birch; a Latin master whose handshake lingered; bath time with Aunt's straying hands. These ingredients, excised from erotic literature as cheap and vulgar, are the stuff of these new erotic memoirs."

"You revel in inventing this stuff."

"Inventing? No need. I simply set it down." He tapped at the file. "Country girls promised marriage by raffish rakes. Parlour girls enslaved. Wife meets husband in classy bordello. The inevitable vicar's daughter." He put his hand to his brow. "It sells. It certainly sells. Isn't that justification enough, that this is what people want to read? Should men seek more exalted dreams? We used to demand erudition. Enlightenment. Today's narratives titillate and disgust. Not just erotica. Sensation novels and detective bilge, spicing commonplace truths with sexuality. Priapic clowns bestride our fiction, evicting tragic heroes: Romeo with doublet unclasped and breeches round ankles, pleasured by sirens, nymphs and muses, orchestrated by cloven-hoofed satyrs. I considered myself unshockable. By these girls, I tell you, I have been shocked."

He pushed open the doors to the balcony, as if afflicted by these sordid tales. An easterly wind cut through the cosy room; Groggins didn't seem to notice. He leaned against the frame of the French window, toying with the hanging basket, where the lobelia was absurdly in bloom, despite the winter gales.

"Pleasure," he said, "is all. Pleasure justifies itself. If these tales of abasement and abomination disturb? Away with you. They're just stories."

I drank down the brandy. "Just stories."

"I do love my flowers," he murmured, clutching the edge of

the hanging basket. "I'm a fool for them, so I am. It's sinful."
He swallowed tightly, as if he had said too much. He glanced
at me, feigning carelessness, and set about watering with a
scarlet jug. "Who's sent you this time, Lawless?"

I mustn't land Skittles in deeper trouble. "Unless there is
more you wish to tell me, you've answered my questions."

"Have I, now? Then, if you'll excuse my language, get the
hell out of my apartments." He glanced out the window, and
gave a laugh. "I wouldn't wish my premises to get a reputation
for beastly respectability."

# AND LEWDNESS

The fifth time, she arrived late and avid for me, tearing off my
clothes within minutes. Not uniform; I never went in uniform.
She took her pleasure with delicious serendipity, covering me
with delicate, deliberate kisses.

The next time, we were both early.

The next, earlier still. After the first sating of our hunger,
we would dwell on each other's body, exploring and searching
and seeking each other's pleasure with a dreamy indolence,
until I felt I knew every inch of her skin, every imperfection
on her arm, every mole on her back. I would stroke her skin,
massage it, scratch it—how she loved to be scratched.

But I promised myself I would write nothing of these
intimacies. Only that to recall them is to relive them; now
that they can never be any more, such riotous recollection is
an indulgence. Her neck, her soft thighs, the delicate perfume
of her hair where I so loved to bury my face.

But this has nothing to do with the case. No indiscretion,
nor blackmail, as you might fear; as, perhaps, I should have
feared. Simply that I am not immune to the lure of the female
form. And the unease that grew to haunt me: that I am part of

the problem, not the solution. That perhaps we all are.

I knew nothing of her beyond her name. It seems wildly improbable, or foolish, but she had asked me, and I had kept my word. She was a lady—nothing could be gained by knowing more. If she were widowed, she might be too high to consider me a suitor. If she were married, that was only to be expected. If she were unmarried, then... we must answer further questions when they arose.

She entwined her finger into my lapel. "We should end it."

"You've tired of me." I smiled as she pulled me toward her.

## A SIGHTING

I saw Felix briefly on my rounds, as I ducked out of the gales into the Opera House.

He had popped out to call for drinks. The waiter was following him patiently, with champagne and two glasses.

"Lawless." He glanced about in nervous excitement. He was not discomfited by seeing me, but rather distracted; so different from our last meeting, it seemed strange not to comment on it. There were no anecdotes, no quips, though his warmth was unreserved. "Can't stop. Second act. Thrilling stuff."

I asked if he had news of his foundation.

All well, as far as he knew, but he had handed over the reins entirely. "My own energies are failing, you see. But, thanks to your party, I have able helpers. Such capable people. They have it working like a charm, I'm told."

"You haven't inspected?"

"No. Ought I?"

I offered to visit in his stead.

"Capital, young man. Yes, you do that, when you have a moment." He beamed, his silver hair gleaming with oils. His evening dress was ornate, far from the unadorned tweed he had worn when first we met. His eyes flickered past me. "Would you mind terribly, young man, if I excused myself?"

## AUTOMATON ANSWERS

Miss Villiers looked dramatic in her red winter coat. I was glad to see her, though she had her brisk air on, as if she would stand for none of my usual joshing. The angora scarf wrapped around her lustrous hair, to stave off the winds, increased her theatrical aspect. I found it easy to compliment her, for once.

"The dowdy clothes I wear for library duties are not of my choosing." Seeing me silenced by this bristly response, she softened her expression. "I must make haste. I am due down the line for dinner with the aunt. The original Turk automaton was never reliably exposed. In 1827, two boys claimed they watched for hours after the game, and saw a man climb out. The *Federal Gazette* identified him as Schlumberger, a German chess master. But would Schlumberger have endured such constraints? The *National Intelligencer* called it another promotional stunt. Historians have puzzled ever since. I've read the explications by Dr Silas Mitchell, Robert-Houdin, Fiske and Kummer. Not to mention our friend, Mr Edgar Allan Poe."

"Edgar Allan Poe?" I smiled. She had once lent me Poe's tales. His involvement not only gave the thing an air of enormity in Ruth's eyes, but it reignited our old detective connection. She knew me for a slow reader, and I was always grateful for her researches. "And have you a solution?"

"I have thought of little else all week. I have read and reread all the commentators. The mechanics are advanced. Of that there's no doubt. After all, the Turk inspired the Spinning Jenny, the analytical and difference engines. But to play chess? Could a machine beat a human? Mr Poe tested each theorem, through his powers of imagination. I'm convinced: he surmised the only way the automaton can be worked."

And she told me.

It was too audacious. It was so audacious that it was inescapably the truth.

I cast my mind around the criminal fraternity. Who had such a conjunction of attributes physical and mental? "It's so hard to credit any individual with the wherewithal to pull it off."

"Ah, but you make an assumption. Why an individual?" Her eyes sparkled. Ruth liked nothing better than a puzzle. "Might not two people work together? Imagine a diminutive couple, for example, with differing expertise. One agile, the other a chess fiend. Plenty of needy folk would endure discomfort and privations for the right fee. Do we know of a paymaster?"

The pleasure of discovery animated her pretty face. I looked at her. I could not tell her the full story, but I hinted at the dark waters of blackmail, without mentioning Mauve and the others and their foolish memoirs. "Whoever is the architect of the scheme has much to gain: power and influence."

"Keeping his hands clean of the entire business. I knew it."

"You have it. A mechanism controlled by forces we cannot fathom. Your perspicuity, as always, has set me right."

She narrowed her eyes, looking for the irony behind my compliment, but there was none. "How will you seek the perpetrators?"

"I shall begin by asking Molly."

Ruth could not restrain a smile. "Do."

I knew it. She must have already consulted the smudge-nosed little tyrant.

"But I must run for my train." She squeezed my hand with the old fervour of our previous investigations. In my excitement, I had forgotten to ask about my reader's pass. As I watched her elegant figure run up the Waterloo steps, a pensive mood overtook me. Oh, yes. She had intimations

of who was involved in the automaton racket, for Molly and
Ruth were pretty tight.

# A POOR LIFE

The winds brought an Arctic cold straight off the North Sea.
My police greatcoat seemed a thin cardigan. The shoots of new
endeavours were frosted on the branch, flowers nipped in the
bud. On and on it went. A winter too hard. Tempers frayed,
and people died in their beds. The river froze again, but those
who moaned were reminded they didn't know much: this
wasn't nothing like the old freezes London used to suffer year
in, year out.

It was weather to make the curmudgeon congregate.
Protests everywhere. One influenza followed another: cow
flu, sheep flu, Brazilian parakeet flu. Protectionists said we'd
all die from the next: too much commerce with the filthy East
and their bubonic plague; or was it the Indies? Wherever the
natives no longer wanted to buy our opium, which was a
terrific liberty.

I turned up early at the Adelphi Arches on the day appointed
for the Oddbody get-together. I was idling through a game at
their chess board. No sign yet of the promised congregation,
but Molly's timings were beyond science.

Bede shuffled in, disconsolate and alone. From every part
of his coat hung cheese slicers and nutmeg graters. This was
his trade when the theatricals dried up. Round his neck was a
sign: BORN CRIPPLE. Without the Pixie to dress him and shift
him, he cut a pitiable figure.

I could not help but marvel at his fortitude. Bede was
scarcely more than head and trunk. His arms and legs were
withered. His hands bent inwards, sinews contracted, fingers
curled like bird's claws. He shuffled on his knees, clogs on

leather caps strapped around thighs thin as wrists. He cast an eye over Molly's message board: auditioning for Blind Gospel Reader at Richmond would not make the most of his disabilities; Human Cannon Ball was a short-term contract; but Midget King Lear at Savile House might be more his line.

"Lost your partner in crime?" I said. "I was hoping for another performance."

He considered me with no alarm. "The Pixie enjoys employments denied to cripples such as I. She only needs me on occasion, to voice her desires." He frowned, evidently thinking better of this line of discussion. One glance at the chess board and he was absorbed. "Your Kingside's a disgrace, old man. Play me for a shilling. I'll straighten out that gambit."

His face was handsome, the ample forehead testament to his intelligence. Direct questions might send him scarpering. Instead, I asked Bede about his life. As we played, his cripple confederates began gathering around us. They showed little concern for my presence, which reassured me. As I have said, a policeman must be wary of learning too much about his friends: even gents have pastimes frowned on by the Law, and Molly's chums certainly dabbled in illicit trades.

Bede played a tidy game, countering my Evans Gambit with the Kieseritzky variation. Though Miss Villiers' solution gnawed at the back of my mind, I was swept up in his story for the moment.

What a life he had led. His mother was a nobleman's cook, her intellect weak: Bede was a lovechild. He never knew his father, who had soon sailed for Buenos Ayres. His mother fretted so, when she married a farmer of middling circumstances, that another servant took him on.

"No mother could have loved a child more." He advanced his knight's pawn. "Only her feelings were that strong, she could never bear to see me."

The servant looked after him well. His mother visited

once a year—or less—but sent £30 per annum towards his upkeep. She died four years back. Then the servant was seized by the cholera, leaving him all alone, cripple as he was, without a friend.

He tried running a tinware shop, with candlesticks and fire irons, but he couldn't get the money in; there was a deal still owing. He tried hawking brushes in the country, and kept a boy with a barrow for a shilling a week. His limbs ached so badly from walking that he got no sleep. His knees in heat, he could barely crawl upstairs. He could neither wash nor undress; his boy had to hold drink to his lips. The thought of his helplessness threw him into a fit.

"But it's the Almighty's will," he said, to my surprise, "and we must abide by it. Last winter, I was took bad with a fever. The boy was gone; I lay in my things all night. I was took to the workhouse, where they used me ill. They gave me gruel in place of tea, because I couldn't work. Better die in the streets than be a pauper. A year ago, I begged five shillings off them and sought lodgings. Some Blackfriars girls bought my things and never paid. I crawled the streets, four days and nights, fit to die with pain. If I got a penny, I stopped for a half pint of coffee till they drove me out. Dreadful it was, out on my knees day and night. I was walking on my bare bones. I would fall asleep, sitting with my things, until you police drove me on."

Bede stopped a moment in his story, his friends crowded round us. He never noticed the tears his tale had elicited. I studied the board intently. Something about this Evans Gambit piqued my memory; yet of all the tales I had heard on the London streets, this was the saddest. "And Molly?"

"I met her at Union Hall. She recommended me as an honest fellow for this confederation. I soon began communicating with the Pixie. She wheeled me to my aunt's in Ham to ask assistance. They're well-to-do but wouldn't look at me for my affliction. I told them I had no food. Her husband shut the door in my face and sent for the police."

He shoved a bishop crabwise across the board; he was thrashing me soundly. I had played an endgame like this before. Identical to this.

"Ashamed of scrounging, I learned to sell these nutmeg graters. But Molly urged us to use our talents—my memory and voice, Pixie's dexterity—to set up in show business." He brightened at this recollection. "The Pixie indicated I, being articulate, had as much to offer her as she me, with wheeling, dressing and feeding. I learnt her signage: no jargon but a full grammaturgical language, independent of English, shared by deaf and mutes across the capital. It shares words with Gypsy and the Argot. She can spell in Roman alphabet. I did as Molly asked: I wrote a scenario, Pix managed the puppets, I did the voices. We scored a hit. The Smallest Theatre in the World had quite the summer of it. We have struggled in these winter months, aside from your gig. The Pixie has returned to less savoury pursuits. I'd chum her along, but parties untroubled by muteness are often appalled by deformity, and vice versy." He scratched his nose. "Checkmate, by the way, old man."

He advanced the inevitable pawn. I glared at the board, thunderstruck. My king, already pinned by his castles, was pincered. An uncommon demise, just like my defeat by the Turk.

Bede saw my stare. The colour drained from his face, for a chess player as good as he remembers such an elegant victory. He realised too late: the checkmate he had just repeated was the same as the game I played and lost in Brodie's cabinet—against the Turk.

As Miss Villiers' researches had suggested, men come in all shapes and sizes. The original Turk may have housed a man. The New Turk, I could swear, would not, unless he could fit in a shoebox. But if you need a man to fit in a shoebox, somewhere in this great wide world you shall find him.

Too small to house a man—a full-grown man—but a boy

with only head and torso would fit neatly at one end, with the other roomy enough for his miniature accomplice, moving silently from chamber to chamber as Brodie displayed the mechanism. Edgar Allan Poe had declared that the Turk must be worked by a misshapen midget; the second obstacle is that the midget in that fearful box must be a chess master.

I had not expected my suspicions to be confirmed so indisputably. It was later I learnt how Bede watched his opponent's moves in a cunningly placed mirror; how he signalled his moves silently to the Pixie. She effected them via a system of pulleys. A deception to make you gasp in wonder, the demands on the perpetrators so great they could not be believed. Whenever the coast was clear, the Pixie could let them out to deal with their necessaries. They could endure a couple of days; the machine was then recalled to Brodie's.

"Bede," I began. "There's a case I am struggling with."

The atmosphere turned tense, as if the Oddbody confederates feared I would arrest their friend for trouncing me at chess. Bede shrank back. The Pixie leapt up and shooed away our audience in concern.

"Don't worry, my pet," he said kindly. "If we've done wrong, the fault is mine. Any judge would clear you of misdeeds."

I pitied him. "This has just confirmed my suspicions, Bede."

He shook his head. "What will my old mother say?"

"You said she was dead."

"Right enough. Still, the shame of it."

"Two things, and I shall let you be." I patted his shoulder. "The deception itself is no crime. But you two have been stealing. For whom?"

"Stealing?"

"Papers." I rolled my eyes. "Who told you to steal the papers?"

The Pixie made rapid gestures at him.

Bede sighed. "We couldn't say. We're just intermediaries."

"Who pays you?" I needed this trail to lead somewhere. To the top, I hoped. Someone was paying for these papers, someone moving in society circles, knowing that these men, who should have more sense, were writing down amorous ventures that they ought to blush at. I tightened my grip on his shoulder. "Who?"

Bede toyed with the chess pieces.

"For God's sake, Bede, the scandal could be vast. If certain blackmail cases result, you will be culpable."

Pixie made a conciliatory sign.

Bede coughed. "We don't know. We take the papers. We secrete them inside the Turk. We vacate. We don't know what's done with them. We don't care to ask."

"For the risks you take?"

"Better than sleeping on the streets."

"Come on. Who's pulling the strings?"

"I couldn't say, old man."

"You know who pays you."

The Pixie gestured urgently. Bede shook his head. She grabbed a chalk from Molly's board and began scribbling the name before he could interfere.

G—R—O—

I whistled gently. That name again, so soon. I must pay him another visit. "Before I arrest you both, tell me, would the Pixie do anything for a shilling?"

Bede controlled his alarm. "Oh, she earns a lot of honest shillings."

There was sniggering under the arches. I thought as much. "And can she report fully and faithfully what she has seen?"

"The Pixie's the full shilling up top. It's only her tongue as was cut out, back when mutes were in fashion."

I looked at the impish little girl: the things she must endure. I would not shop them in; I need not arrest them. Why should I? Yet I might use the threat to my profit. "Bede, listen carefully. You must tell me the full story. You were foolish to get involved in such turbid waters, but consider: to your paymaster, you are dispensable. You're in grave danger, and the Pixie even more so, whether you collaborate with me or not." I let this sink in. "Fortunately for you, I need you almost as much as you need me. And I'll tell you why."

## HYPOCRITE READER

I found it hard to sleep. After a long shift, I would fall asleep sitting up, only to wake thinking about Felix. There was something rum about the whole business. I couldn't put my finger on it; I just had some instinct. Molly was always telling me to trust my instincts, while Ruth begged me to doubt them; between us, though, we had solved the thefts—though what was to be done about it, I had yet to decide.

Darlington, though, wasn't sleeping a wink, his look furtive, black rings round his eyes. He said he was top hole. "Having a time of it, I am, Watchman." Which made me wonder. I recalled his louche attitude to policing the night houses; what benefits was he exploiting now?

As we walked from the Yard to Charing Cross, he made his confession. I was on my way to the 9.23 Club, he back to Dugdale-Hotten's.

"Attendance on the erotic muse is driving me dotty, Watchman."

I glanced at him. "Your new lending library?"

"The temptations are too much. I confiscate these damned erotic volumes, I read them, they stick in my head. I can't sleep. I read them again and again. I lay my head on the pillow and I'm still inside them with all their—pardon my French— minetting and gamahuching and hikerypikery."

He sketched out tales gleaned from loose chapters at

Dugdale-Hotten's: of three couples who played a game to see how well the wives recognised their husbands in the dark, by several means; and another from a French book he'd confiscated about an Irish priest, an altar boy and a boiled egg.

"Do people invent these scenes?" He was quite entranced. "Have they the gall to make them up?"

"Depraved minds, I suppose."

"Yet more depraved if they're true." He was truly disturbed. "Whatever you and I can dream up, I reckon somebody is already doing here in London right now."

I shrugged. "And worse."

He bit at his fingernails. "Oh, I can dream up pretty dark scenes, I tell you."

Silence. We were both wondering, who writes these memoirs? My first thought, of the low and uneducated, I dispelled, for who has the leisure and the money to pursue peccadillos? I recalled Dugdale's subscription list and I couldn't help picturing all those MPs and luminaries in Darlington's stories, in the darkened room, or at the altar. I ought to be ashamed, or envious.

"Do you ever think," he said, looking absently across Trafalgar Square, "that the whole city is alive, old man? I look around and see bodies. Entangled bodies."

"These lovers you're always reading about."

"I see 'em emerging from the pavements. An unholy parade, bodies in delight. Trains pounding through tunnels, panting engines beneath the skin, filth drizzling from water pipes, sewage, hydraulics, like animal spirits pumping around the body's cavities." As he was staring up at Nelson's statue, a woman with her head buried in a book trod on his shiny leather boot. He glared after her, aggrieved. "And they think it's acceptable to go round openly reading such claptrap."

"Teach the great unwashed to read, and they taint their minds with cheap filth." I glanced at his satchel. "Never mind what they get up to behind closed doors."

"But that's different. The tastes of gents, that's something loftier."

"*Maria Monk*," I said, "and her *Awful Disclosures*?"

"Not that modern tripe. No more scandalous than Lady Audley and her blasted secrets. But the pope's manual on the positions! I'll lend it you—"

"No. Thanks."

"The female body described like a landscape: skin fresh as snow, sullied by trampling boots." He gestured expansively at the spire of St Martin-in-the-Fields. He was all pent up, like a balloon about to burst. "Damned architects are obsessed. Columns everywhere. Domes and columns."

"I believe you are raving, Darlington." I led him across the junction as I would lead a child. "With such overactive imaginings, you'd best move to Devon with a bag of dispiriting pastoral novels to read."

"Better than these newfangled detective yarns."

"Why would people want to read about our irksome investigations?" I laughed. "Please God, there's a genre that won't catch on."

"Done to death already: *The Notting Hill Mystery*, *The Ticket-of-Leave Man*, *The Female Spy*. Tiresome, believe me. All copies, copies from life. It won't last. What next? Polar explorers, God damn you? Ships to the stars?"

"Vampyres?" I offered.

We burst out laughing.

This was where our ways parted. I was concerned about Darlington's ravings; I would ask the advice of the 9.23 Club.

"Here." He brought out a sheaf of his confiscated papers. "Like some?"

My face was stony.

"Not intending offence, Watchman, old man."

I hesitated. I might spot connections between Dugdale-Hotten's publications and Groggins' tales. It also flashed through my mind that Alexandra was not averse to such tales, for she spoke of paper-covered volumes from the Burlington Arcade. I nodded. "I shall seek clues about our thefts."

"Don't spoil 'em, now." He passed them over with a sly look. "Payne wants the volumes returned."

"To Dugdale? For heaven's sake."

"Word from on high. Something to do with the British Museum." Avoiding my protests, he slunk away down Holywell Street like an eel down a sewer. If he, a trained detective, could be so turned by his readings, what of the common man? I had better bring Darlington to the 9.23. They'd give him a talking-to.

I would rather have brought along Felix, of course. With his modulated tones and wit, his was the kind of gentle chivalry that would fit with these renegades and misfits. I would rather that than spend my time with Darlington talking of dirty books and prostitutes, but it seemed unlikely now.

## OFFENSIVE FRIENDS

"He's simply not sleeping." I told the 9.23 Club about Darlington. I alluded to his reading obsession, without mentioning Groggins' erotic *magnum opus*. "What is the remedy?"

Collins patted his pocket. "For your friend, I've something that'll put him out for the night. For society, as long as there are sexual relations, there will be pornographers. Wouldn't you agree, Acton?"

Mayhew had come up trumps. He had written letters to charitable societies across the capital, commending my work and asking them to share their own researches. He also brought Dr William Acton, author of *Prostitution, Considered in its Moral, Social and Sanitary Aspects*. Acton looked the born aristocrat, neatly combed hair matching his bow-tie, yet he had researched these murky subjects for years.

"I interviewed many young males," he declared, "for my treatise on masturbation and you'd be astonished—" People along the bar moved away, and he thought better of his topic. "Yes, Collins. Quite right."

I filled them in on my labours in the calibration of carnality. My figures so far already outstripped previous returns. The 1857 census had divided its 2,825 brothels into categories:

WHERE PROSTITUTES ARE KEPT: 410
WHERE PROSTITUTES LODGE: 1,766
WHERE PROSTITUTES RESORT: 64

Likewise 8,600 prostitutes comprised:

WELL-DRESSED, LIVING IN BROTHELS: 921
WELL-DRESSED, WALKING THE STREETS: 2,616
LOW, INFESTING LOW NEIGHBOURHOODS: 5,063

Collins guffawed and began scribbling wicked additions to the schemata:

COFFEE HOUSES/OTHER PASSING ACCOMMODATION: 10,000
WELL-DRESSED, IN PRIVATE LODGINGS:
½ OF KENSINGTON

What I wanted to know from Acton was how he had arrived at his higher estimate, in 1851, of 210,000 prostitutes.

"Simple, Sergeant." That year, forty-two thousand live births were recorded to unwed mothers. Taking this as the first step into prostitution, Acton estimated that each of these mothers worked as a prostitute, on average, for five years. "Thus my total."

My jaw dropped. "Does their misfortune make them prostitutes?"

"It's the first step, I'm afraid," he replied. "Some escape; others fall for longer. Your police figures are a mere palliative."

Mayhew sniffed. "Any woman who sleeps with a man outside marriage is technically a prostitute."

"Oh, Mayhew," Collins groaned. "A woman mayn't but a man may? You're an old Presbyterian."

"People may one day laugh at such attitudes," said Acton. "In my *Functions and Disorders of the Reproductive Organs*—"

"Acton," cried Mayhew.

We laughed. I called for a pitcher of stout. "Acton, I had imagined you to be a puritanical prude."

He smiled. "And so I am."

"Is there no way back for fallen women?" If not, my task was surely pointless: I thought of Sabine and her dream of a genteel Waterloo café.

Acton objected. "Many women only pass through prostitution, as if a station on the underground, emerging back to the daylight of respectable life. If they are detained in that subterranean twilight, it is because we guardians of respectability do not allow them to aspire."

Mayhew shook his head. "To me, William, any woman ruined, of whatever class, remains a prostitute."

"Nonsense," Collins bellowed. "A woman who sells her favours is using God's gifts to survive. What difference in my writing books, or in Watchman here unhinging mysteries? Damn it all, aren't we all prostitutes?" He thumped the table. The next table looked over. "I don't care if you style my writing thus. Make 'em laugh, make 'em cry, make 'em wait. That's my literary motto. Know where I got it? From a little minx in St John's Wood. She made me laugh, all right, and cry, for she could work a man's mechanisms; and, by God, she made me wait—"

"Collins," we protested. You could rely on Collins to overstep the mark—not by inches, but a javelin throw.

"Society ladies," said Acton, "weigh up their looks, breeding and dowry to find a husband. Not so different from prostitutes."

"Except," said I, "that they look for love."

The others looked at me strangely.

Mayhew turned his lugubrious eyes on me. "Acton is right that people enter upon a life of sin through poverty or desperation. If the Poor Laws would only feed and house people in need, it would halve the population of prostitutes."

Acton agreed. "We fret about charitable acts. Make donations. Your friend Felix sets up a foundation. But any of us may fall. We totter two steps from disaster."

We fell silent, thinking of others' misfortune, imagining our own. I thought of Skittles. I thought of the woman in the gutter. I thought of Felix's distress.

"There are pensions." Collins smirked. "If you are a gambling man."

Acton ignored his cynicism. "I take out insurance against fortune's blows."

Mayhew was gloomy. "You can afford it."

"Those who have the means ought to pay the premiums for the less fortunate." Acton became inspired. "A sort of insurance scheme for the whole nation. It need not cost the earth. Without it, we remain two nations living side by side, communing only during commercial transactions; hence the lower element's slang, so they may hide their paltry deceptions from us, because we have cheated them in spades, grasping all the capital and leaving them to flounder in the Great Struggle for Life."

Collins guffawed. "You old communist."

Our candour, political and sexual, had cleared the tables around us and we left. It did me good to make light of it all.

But I feared in my heart the story was worse than I'd accepted. I thought of Cora, of Sabine, of Skittles's tales of abductions and coercion. The prostitution trade depended not on a supply of debased women but the demands of debased men.

Collins chummed me down towards Seven Dials. "Let's research the topic in Southwark this very eve," he said, as if suggesting a Thomas Cook outing. "Come along, you mizzling old tuft-hunter?"

"Not tonight." I scuffed my heel against the pavement. "I'll just take a stroll."

"Want company?"

"Only my own."

Collins looked at me knowingly and hailed a cab. He leaned out the window. "That book about your man, Felix. It was something to do with *Secret Prisons*—"

And he was gone. I crossed to the opposite corner, where another cab awaited me. The door opened and I saw her. That impish face framed by lush ringlets with their hint of grey.

"Good evening, Sergeant. Would you care to accompany me?"

I got in and, lightly, took her hand. We headed for Titchfield Street in silence, bewitched by the touch of each other's fingers.

## OUR STUBBORN SINS

I was fascinated by her underwear. The chemise, the corset, the crinoline petticoats on a whalebone cage; bloomers in midwinter, then in the old fashion, once spring came, nothing.

That day, we did not make it to the bed. Afterward, I traced my finger down the nape of her neck, where her hair was soft as silk, tresses strewn carelessly across the pillow. Down, down over the bumps of her neck, the indentations between her shoulder blades, down to the hollow of the small of her back. The thrill went right through me.

I was thunderstruck by the thought: this will not last. One day, when we come to our senses, she will end this reprehensible indulgence. She shifted ever so slightly, half asleep, responding to the touch of my fingertips. Such is the compelling touch of flesh. Yes, this soaring joy will be taken from us. I wrapped my arms around her, skin against skin, reminding myself I hadn't lost her yet.

She told me I seemed preoccupied. I mentioned my work, a subject I usually avoided, and brought out the manuscript pages Darlington had lent me. I held my breath, lest she might be angry. Her cheeks flushed as she flicked through the pages.

I sat by, admiring her glowing skin. "Dr Acton states that most women have no interest in sexual gratification and only submit to embraces to satisfy their husbands."

"Dr Acton needs his head examined," she murmured absently.

"We have to confiscate such writings. You don't think them demoralising?"

She sighed. "When Dickens publishes his latest gory tale, do you accuse him of inspiring murders? These books give pleasure. They may educate the ignorant. Think of Ruskin and his poor wife, not least. What's so wrong with describing desire?" She pulled me to her. "It's not just men that shop on Holywell Street."

This indiscretion made me bold to ask of Felix. From our first meeting I knew that she admired him. I didn't express my concern; rather that I would like to know more of his past, and Collins had mentioned a book.

"His autobiography. *The Secret Prisons of Italy*. A bracing read."

"You've read it."

"Oh, that's how I know of his illustrious past, and the hardships he suffered."

"I should like to read it."

"Ah. It may be hard to find. It was fifteen years ago."

"But you have a copy?"

"Yes. No. Had." She bit her lip, tilting her head, a most becoming habit. "I gave my copy away. To a young friend."

"An admirer, you mean?"

"No, no. To my niece." This was the most she had ever volunteered about her family, and I smiled. She was angry. "Don't be jealous. It doesn't suit you."

# PREPARATIONS & DEDUCTIONS

The weather was exhausting. The winds would not give way, and spring's warmth was still unimaginable.

The Phoenix Foundation for Fallen Women was established in a disused tannery in Whitechapel. I can't say why, but I feared I might uncover something unsavoury.

I was mistaken. Everything was tiptop. The warden was an old fellow full of good sense, and his matron suave and competent. She showed me their ledgers, and gladly allowed me to take notes: a roll call of arrivals, possessions, previous addresses, concomitant donations and ultimate departures (with or without child).

I admired the system, which pleased her. She had been taught the technique of keeping such ledgers when she worked on a newspaper.

The whole place maintained an air of competence and efficacy. If anything it was too perfect.

I enlisted the help of the charitable societies Mayhew had commended me to: the Society for the Suppression of Vice, the Society for the Protection of Young Females, the Society for the Prevention of Juvenile Prostitution, the Society for the Rescue of Young Women and Children, London Female Preventive and Reformatory Institution, the Refuge for Deserted Mothers and Children, Urania Cottage, the Home for Gentlewomen in Reduced Circumstances, the Baptist Noel, the Home of Hope for the Restoration of Fallen and the Protection of Friendless Young Women, and the Friendly Female Society.

As predicted, these organisations collected information with all the detail I could wish. What I had not foreseen was how readily they would share it: that I wished to present it to the Commons Committee elicited alleluias all round.

The stories I gleaned from the societies were less rosy than the tales woven for me chez Kate Hamilton, sorry tales of coercion and violation, just as Skittles had claimed. Perhaps natural talents saw the cream rise to the top of the bottle, and Kate's girls endured lesser sufferings. Yet it tasted sour. On my visits to Kate's, I found Cora much changed, and unwilling to display her tattoo, for she said she was grown round through overindulgence.

At the 9.23 Club, a competition sprung up between Collins's team (writers and painters) and Mayhew's (journalists and doctors). They totted up numbers postal code by postal code, N, NW, EC and E (leaving WC to me).

Acton's calculations troubled me. So many unwed mothers: what became of their offspring? I must bury the hatchet and speak to Jeffcoat, for he was doing the rounds of the asylums and foundling hospitals.

The thefts by the chess automaton had stopped, to Payne's relief. I garnered no credit: I could not expose Bede and the Pixie, and I owed Molly a debt.

It troubled me. Brodie owned the automaton. Was it he who ordered the thefts? Did Brodie not know of my closeness with Molly? Would he have hired the Oddbody duo to conduct illicit acts under our noses? He was not so reckless.

Unless he wanted the ruse discovered; unless he wanted me

to know about the power he held over the rich and famous. And Groggins' tales from courtesans—were these fuel for more blackmail? I found myself waking in the night, mulling over foolish things I'd done in my life, cowering in my bed at the thought of exposure; and I had lived a careful enough life. Which of us is spotless?

Meanwhile, I was preparing to spring Skittles. First, I had that contract of hers checked by trusty friends. Then I begged a favour from Bertie—that is, the Prince of Wales. He was busy with his anxious wife and newborn heir, but he owed me that much.

# A YOUNG WOMAN

The next time, as I was dressing, she had news. "I saw Felix. At the theatre. *The Lady of the Camellias*. You're right. Something's odd..."

I waited for her to go on. "Odd?"

"He looked twenty years younger." She began pinning her hair back up, immersed in thought. "And dapper, as if he had been born again."

"Alone?"

She looked at me, her eyes bright. "He was with a girl. A young woman. Perhaps a relative. I couldn't say. He has such old-world manners."

"Did you speak?"

"Briefly. He was not his usual effusive self. Happy, though— and rather secretive. In his memoir, his family were dispersed. Lost, in all those European revolutions." She shook off her puzzlement, and gave up pinning her hair. "Don't let's talk now. I must soon be off. Come back to bed, Campbell."

\* \* \*

If only I could go to him and beg him: Felix, what is transforming you? I requested *The Secret Prisons of Italy* from Mudie's Lending Library; I read the description in their catalogue, but the sole copy was out on loan. I sent to Miss Villiers to ask her if she might look it out in the British Museum Library, and renew my pass while she was at it.

I often thought of him at the party. Society tittering indignantly over greed, power, lust and a dozen other disreputable themes: one quotes J.S. Mill, another counters with St Paul, the third umpires through Darwin. Felix laughs away their pretensions, like droplets off a swan's back. He was magnetic. These are the ones for me: people who sparkle.

Yes, Felix was some man. He had led an exalted life, consorted with kings, dazzled from Salzburg to Sebastopol. But it was not his celebrity that drew me. It was an inner light.

In the police force, one is subject to untold criticism. One expects curses from high and low, with London as it is these days, a hothouse of petty investors arguing over interest rates, tinpot speculators banging on endlessly of mortgages and margins and properties and bubbles, news hacks pandering to chauvinist readerships, street women impossible to distinguish from debutantes, and scandals hounding government, opposition, the church, the law and everyone's uncle to boot.

Adrift in this sea of bellyache, Felix seemed a beacon in the torrid waters of disgrace.

I contrived to see him again. Arriving at the Opera House at the second interval, I kept watch for Felix but could not espy him anywhere. I purchased a half-price ticket for the final act. The lights dimmed. I would see little of the audience. Yet, as the hero appealed to his lost love, a wild violin struck up: who should I see leaning over the upper box but Felix? And beside him, just visible, another, smaller figure.

I withdrew from the auditorium (with regret: the singing

was exemplary, the costumes bold). The waiters were lolling about. I tipped one to fetch an urchin who loitered in Covent Garden, one of Molly's associates.

Sure enough, before the audience emerged, Felix departed, shepherding beside him a poised young lady. I kept back, not wishing to embarrass anyone. At the entrance, they mounted a cab. I manhandled the urchin into a cab with me, and we set off in pursuit. They headed for Quarterhouse; but the rules of the order were strict, and I thought it unlikely that Felix would drive straight in for all the Brothers to see.

At the end of Quartern Lane, they descended. Of course, there might be nothing to it: she might be the daughter of a friend, or a goddaughter or something, but it seemed odd. I longed to see her. I was ready to risk any awkwardness.

I gave the urchin a box of matches and bade him accost them. "Lucifers, sir. Lucifers."

I could not hear what they replied. There was something in her movements that I recognised: a cultured laugh, half-covering her mouth, so as to suggest your joke has been, ooh, too much, but she appreciates your daring. As for Felix's manner to her, it was neither untoward, nor uncomfortable. On the contrary, he was attentive, and so delighted by her company that it was touching; his old face was lit up with her every comment, and the wee thing seemed to revel in her ability to bring him such joy.

They turned the corner into a sleepy little side street: Quartern Mews, the urchin reported. I gave him a ha'penny, promising another if he reported faithfully where they went, with further observations potentially profitable.

Half an hour later he rejoined me, where I waited in The Sutton Arms.

Felix had escorted the girl genteelly to the door of 17 Quartern Mews, EC. There the landlady admitted them without comment. She served tea, standing by in the front room.

As a chaperone?

Not at all, the boy reckoned. More in the way of a servant.

Indeed, it was Felix himself who saw the girl upstairs, after she had played him an air on the fiddle. He descended soon after, more like a doting father seeing his child to bed than one of the seducing fiends in Darlington's erotica. During his watch, the keen-eyed boy noted two other shapely young tenants of Quartern Mews arriving home, escorted by gentlemen older than themselves.

As Felix walked away back towards Quarterhouse, the boy reported, he breathed in the night air with the deepest satisfaction. He glanced back toward the house, where the girl stood, silhouetted in the window, waving goodnight. He waved back, then stumbled quickly away, seemingly overcome, gazing up at the stars in wonderment.

I promised the boy I'd report his good offices to Molly. His descriptions set me wondering, and I paid him half a sixpence.

## INCIDENT AT THE WINDOW

Irregular winds blew in the last week of February. On the last extra day of the month, I happened to be strolling past Quarterhouse with Molly. I was bending her ear on the urgency of my census.

"Your Oddbodies might want to help out."

"Might they, old cove?" She wrinkled her nose at me. "In return for?"

"In return for my discretion on other matters."

She pursed her lips, feigning unconcern; but I knew Bede had confessed his sins to her, and she knew I knew.

At that moment, we chanced to spy Felix up ahead, on Quartern Lane, ducking into the Mews. We followed him into the courtyard. I attempted a hulloah, but he did not hear me through the weather's blasts. He dived straight into the elegant little house, with no ceremony, as if he owned the place. Within a few moments, the middle of three doors on the balcony opened. He emerged with infinite sadness on his features.

"Ho there, Felix," I called up. "We saw you in passing. Ho there."

He stared about, in distress, like a bird discovering the nest has been robbed. On seeing us, his face turned white. "Who told you I was here?"

"Nobody, sir." I was taken aback by this unaccustomed tone. "As I said, we were just passing."

He shook his head and gave such a look to Molly that I thought he had gone out of his wits. He breathed an almighty sigh and blinked rapidly, as if a cloud of damnation had passed over him. "You must forgive me. This is very good of you. I should like to ask you both up, but the place is really not fit. I have been so... Well, I only ask that you ignore my ill conduct."

The pallor of his face was rapidly overtaken by a livid flush, spreading visibly up through his features; and as if fearing that a fit was taking him, he withdrew in terror. The fear on his face was so palpable, so graphic, I would have thought I had imagined it, had Molly not witnessed the same.

I had promised her a quiet supper of pie and mash at a Spitalfields hostelry, but we turned on our heel, and neither of us said a word all the way back to town.

## SIR RICHARD'S COMPLAINT

Of course, Payne had to call me in. Skittles would be at the Panorama at nine; I was in no mood for complaints. All was arranged. I was only stopping at the Yard for fear of a message from Bertie.

Jeffcoat was sitting in his office as I passed. Bloody Jeffcoat, cosy and intimate, chatting to the commissioner about their latest bridge game, no doubt, like the fearful Masons that they were. "Marvellous, Solly. Anything you need—Ho there. Watchman!" Payne spotted me slinking past. He barked his summons as if I were a yeoman on parade. "Lawless, get your backside in here. You're in trouble."

I paused at his door. Jeffcoat arose, eyeing the papers on the commissioner's desk with a pained look. He dallied as he passed me and spoke quietly. "Watchman, come and see me, will you?" My disdain must have been obvious, for he shoved his nose in my face and reiterated with sincerity, "I could do with your help."

I looked after him in consternation. To my mind, we were at odds, he in favour and I out of it.

"Get in here," Sir Richard barked, tugging at his whiskers.

I glanced at my watch, anxious about the timing for Skittles's rescue. On the corner of Payne's desk lay Buckle's instructive *History of Civilisation*, the bookmark far advanced; I picked it up to find the dust jacket was in fact covering *Lady Audley's Secret*. "You're getting to the good bit," I said.

He winced. "Don't tell me."

"Gets ludicrous after that. As if she hadn't planned the ending."

"I asked you for good news."

He laid the *Illustrated Police News* over the book and huffed. SCANDALOUS DISCOVERY, the page was titled; in the engraving, police held their noses, prising open a trunk to reveal a dismembered woman squeezed in like a children's puzzle set. Down the page, a SANCTIMONIOUS SCOUNDREL murders his own child, followed by CRUEL FATALITY OF THE IDIOT BOY: KILLED BY A CRICKET BALL—or perhaps these were two separate outrages.

"I'll tell you what the bloody scandal is," he muttered. "Painting us as twits."

"How effectively Mr Brodie's papers have been trammelled by the closure of the *Bugle*."

Payne looked at me sharply. "Enough of your smart talk, Watchman. Unless you have something to contribute. It's no wonder they make such headlines."

"A murder a day." My eyes flickered round after Jeffcoat. "Where does Brodie find them?"

My imputation—that these rags had peculiar access to police activity—Sir Richard did not heed. "Give Brodie good news and he'll splash that across the news stands."

"If you ask me, sir, J.W. Brodie—"

"I asked you for figures showing that prostitution and bawdy houses are on the decrease. Get me those; I'll ensure Brodie publishes."

"I'll bring you the figures, sir, in time for the Commons Committee —"

"Ah, yes. The Committee is to be convened ahead of schedule." He pushed the papers aside. I spotted a report written in Jeffcoat's hand—so the layabout did some paperwork, after all, besides tipping the wink to Brodie's newshounds. "As soon as possible."

"When?" I blinked. "Next month?"

"Sooner, I'm afraid. We have to take the opportunity, of course." Payne stood and began to pace. He looked harassed: pressure from above, no doubt. But someone was trying to sideline whatever I might discover. "Parliamentary situation's uncertain. Delay on our part won't do."

My mind was running in circles. I wanted time to tell of the outrages Skittles had outlined. I would struggle to sum up my first reckoning of the figures, even with the 9.23 Club's questings and the societies' figures. My report must leave no stone unturned. It had to be compelling. To force the Committee to act—

"What have you to say for yourself?"

I shook my head in dismay. "You promised, sir, to let me do this thoroughly. A balanced report. I've had no help—"

"Darlington's helped."

"You call that help?"

"You can't go round upsetting people, Watchman. Waltzing into a private room on business premises."

Now I saw it: the bloody publishers, Dugdale-Hotten, had complained. "Not a private room, sir. Business contravening the Obscene Publications Act."

"You need proof of that."

"I have proof."

"Why have I not seen it?"

"Because, sir, it is only the tip of a stinking dunghill."

The silence hung between us. I found myself squinting at Jeffcoat's report on the desk, where I read the words "infants", "unmarried", "forming".

Sir Richard sucked in his breath. He gave an airy gesture. "Drop it."

"It's a dunghill I am excavating to build our case for the Committee."

"We've had complaints."

"From Dugdale and Hotten?"

"From their clientele. They are rather well supported."

There was a time that a complaint made against me sent me into paroxysms of angst. These days I was disappointed when nobody complained. "Well supported?"

"Dugdale and Hotten remain at liberty to trade. For now."

"You're not going to favour them over me? Ha. I must remember to be well supported next time I break the law."

"Lawless, don't be an ass. Forget the dirty books. Back to your task."

"I am at that task, sir. I lent Darlington a hand with these obscene books to investigate those awkward thefts that you'll remember."

The wind rattled against the window. Sir Richard gazed out. "Let's say no more about it."

"They're connected to the wider crimes I'm taking census of."

He rubbed his chops, looking pained. "Dirty books, Watchman, they're just dirty books. For God's sake, setting a few words to paper, it's not really a crime."

"I agree, mostly." Of this, I was persuaded. As Collins and Alexandra put it, erotic writings were an outlet, not a provocation. But there was something shifty about Payne's defence; I recalled his name on Dugdale-Hotten's subscription list.

"There's worse on the shelves of any gentlemen's club. Volumes that have to be chained up so as not to be filched. And re-covered yearly." He laughed weakly. "Don't be such a starchy-arsed Scot. It may not appeal to you, but many right-thinking folk happily peruse these volumes."

I looked him in the eye. "Dugdale's struck a deal with you."

"Confound you, Watchman." He went to the door, to be sure it was closed. "It's the bloody British Museum, promised some almighty bequest. An antiquarian book collector offers a *Don Quixote* first edition. The fellow also collects erotica. He rests his offer on us letting Dugdale trade freely." He put his hand to his head. "The Obscene Publications Act was a rush job. People today, you and me, we can judge what is obscene and what is not. Never any need for bloody legislation."

Word from on high: Dugdale gets immunity to secure an old book for the library. I laughed hollowly. The old Whig. Why trust Payne, if his arm could be twisted so? Damn politics and his ambitions. What other enquiries might he forestall? Dugdale's complaint didn't bother me; this protection did. I decided in that moment: I would confide in Sir Richard no longer, not about these investigations, nor my fears of what I might uncover. "April, did you say? I shall be as ready as I can."

"Friday, I'm afraid."

"This Friday coming?"

"You're a sound fellow, Watchman." He opened the door for me. "Sometimes, you can be too fastidious. Leave Dugdale be, whatever filth he's peddling. We all need our friends in high places."

"I need to talk to you." Jeffcoat was waiting in the corridor. "About flowers."

Skittles would be waiting. I gave him five minutes.

What he showed me in those minutes shook me. He started with Acton's figures. Take the number of unmarried females giving birth. Compare the number of patrimony cases instigated, the smaller numbers brought to trial and the minuscule number won. Add in the number of infant deaths reported, plus suspicious deaths, dubious burials and so forth. The statistics failed to add up.

"Dark waters, Watchman. I would value your help in navigating them."

Jeffcoat hoped I'd share my researches to help solve these discrepancies. Not a smart move, if he was planning to sell the story to Brodie's rags. I kept my thoughts to myself. Jeffcoat was direct, amusing, unassuming. I repented of my long jealousy.

As I hurried out into the misty evening, the clerk called out that he had a note for me from a Mr Groggins. I thrust it in my pocket, but it would have to wait, if Skittles were to be saved.

## SKITTLES'S ESCAPEMENT

Cora's appearances at Kate's had grown irregular. First she hid her belly, then was sporadically absent; now she was vanished, and spoken of by nobody. The courtesans' code forbade speaking of the departed, for good or ill.

So it was with Sabine that I arranged my meeting with

Skittles. Her heart was set on that respectable café of hers, and took my message warmly; but Kate Hamilton's was no place to speak of retiring, even surreptitiously.

As the clock struck nine that evening, I drew up the carriage by Burford's Panorama, as arranged. Wisps of wintry mist gathered around the Dinning Room sign, as a demure lady emerged from the Panorama. She stepped up beside me, her face veiled. Amazing how she made herself respectable with a simple shawl drawn around her bosom. Still the damask rose in her hair, even tonight. I admired her for that.

"Skittles, thank God. That contract of yours: it's worthless." I had had it checked by her duke and Bertie's own lawyer. "Doubly so, as you did not know what you were signing."

"I may walk away?"

"They have no hold over you."

Her grip on my arm relaxed, and her dark eyes looked up at me. In this light, the make-up hid the bruises. "Still, better run for safety, eh?"

"Yes. We have all heard of girls thrown off Waterloo Bridge, as if a suicide. But you've nothing to fear tonight."

"Oh, I have everything to fear. They protect their investments."

She was right. Anyone might sell her out, even an honest cabby. But this was no ordinary cab, and I had her retreat meticulously planned.

The Prince of Wales had not let me down, despite his Danish in-laws' crisis. This was the royal carriage; to interfere with it would be treason. Bertie's own driver was to drive Skittles to Paris. There, Bertie himself would introduce her to people who would protect her and her reputation. If they encountered trouble, well, I had cooked up a plan with the driver, which he would explain en route.

Why go so far on Skittles's behalf? I might need an ally one of these days. Instinct told me I couldn't do better than

Skittles. Besides, she was worth it.

She kept talking about paying me back.

"It doesn't matter."

"I don't like to be indebted. I've arranged some interviews for you." She had put word around about my quest to hear girls' stories—their real stories. "I shan't forget your help, Watchman. Once I get a few bob together, I'll buy Sabine her café by Waterloo. Once she's established, she'll ask the girls there for you."

I gave her some banknotes, a spare shawl and a big straw hat. We were sat very close. I was about to comment on her perfume, but thought better of it. She touched my cheek, just for a moment, then I descended.

The doorman of the Dinning Room, a familiar bully, was watching the carriage as it pulled away; I made sure to stroll past him with a friendly nod and was tolerably sure I had been recognised.

# PART IV
## CIRCLES CLOSE

### FEBRUARY–MARCH 1864

The depravity of manners amongst boys and girls begins so very early... The precocity of the youth of both sexes in London is perfectly astounding. The drinking, the smoking, the blasphemy, indecency and immorality that does not even call up a blush is incredible, and charity schools and the spread of education do not seem to have done much to abate this scourge.

Henry Mayhew, *London Labour and the London Poor*

The children of the poor, almost as soon as they can walk or talk, are sent to the workhouse. For girls, these are the primary schools for prostitution... On the countenance of these girls, nothing but joy and animation can be seen, while the very vulture of misery is gnawing—hour after hour—day after day—at their hearts. Originally seduced from a state of innocence, and then abandoned by everyone who held them in any degree of estimation, they are left upon the world, and have no alternative but to go on in the way they have commenced.

W. O'Daniel, *Ins and Outs of London*

# COMPLAINT OF AN INTEMPERATE YOUNG MAN

"Officer, officer!" I call, as I catch sight of your joker, Lawless. My heart is pounding as I burst out of the doorway, pretty much *déshabillé*, onto Gerrard Street. A couple of girls are passing, French, or Belgian, I'd say, with their crinolines, satin mantles and pork-pie hats. They catch my eye and titter, for I'm *sans* breeches, I must tell you, clad only in my striped waistcoat. Thank God for the fog, eh?

Your half-witted slogger Sergeant Lawless is passing right by, his bullseye lantern useless in the fog. I grab at his shoulder. "There's been a theft," I say.

"Really, sir?" And damn it, if the blighter doesn't look over my shoulder, as though he'd rather be in the pub. He's on his way to some assignation, no doubt about it. "Do tell," he says, loath as you like, and looks at me as if I'm some kind of gigolo.

I'm furious by now, and the sorry tale pours out, as I steer him to the door. "The blighters are doubtless on the point of escaping."

"We'll do our best if you just slow down."

"Arrest 'em. God damn it, shift, man."

He drags his heels. "You say, sir, you went willingly to this woman's room?"

And the canting blockhead begins to tilt the whole blame

on my head. I tell him how she eyeballed me. The free drinks. Virtually ravishment, don't you know. I'm choosy about my fillies.

"You're sure you have been robbed, sir?"

I gesture at my bare knees, apoplectic.

"And this is the house, is it, sir?"

"Do you take me for an idiot?"

He doesn't answer, checks his watch and bangs intemperately at the door. "What are we saying has been stolen exactly, sir?"

"My money. My trousers."

"And your watch, sir." He nods at my chain dangling free.

"Oh, blast."

The door opens. A demure old she-goat peeks out. "What is it, officer?"

Is this the harridan I paid for the room? I try to push past her, but the policeman only goes and restrains me. "Is this the woman who robbed you, sir?"

"What do you take me for? Let us in, you old hag. Your floozy's stitched me up proper."

"My!" The harridan bats her eyelashes at the policeman. Shameless. "This is a genteel house. Tell this filthy yob to try his improper talk at a more suitable address."

She gave the plate by the door an ostentatious wipe— *Ladies' Finishing School*, my arse.

The police fellow sighed. "Madam, it will make less of a scene if we unravel it in your drawing room rather than on your doorstep."

The whole house was quite changed. I jest not. Within five minutes. And would you believe that the layout of a night house so usefully corresponded with a private ladies' academy? The parlour, whose sofas were filled with girls lolling perpendicularly, boasts two bespectacled frumps reading philosophical volumes. A wholesome lass arranges flowers. Upstairs, the erotic woodcuts have gone in favour of worthy engravings of the Seven Wonders.

The room itself, well, it's the same, but not the same. With the lamp low, the bedspread looked louche and continental. Under a less forgiving light, I must admit, it looks quite the boarding house standard. I stare about in confusion. Fresh linen, fresh pillows and a modest screen around the chamber pot.

He asks the harridan to give us a moment. She and I lock eyes: I know my story is true and she knows it; I know she knows. But out she strolls, brazen as you like.

To my amazement, the policeman hazards a guess at what has happened and hits the nail on the head.

The girl espied me at the Holborn, a little tipsy. She set her cap at me, outdrank me, put something in my gin, I'd wager. She brought me back to have her way with me. I have a well-heeled look, I suppose. Her frontage looked seventeen, but her rump and calves proved more mature. She stripped and I plugged her. Though young, she was well trained, and her free manner pleased me, even the way she washed, pissed and dressed afterward. "What's this?" she said, when I gave her a half crown. "More than you were promised," said I, for the room was dear enough.

All of a sudden, she demanded a sovereign; I'd not promised two farthings. She was incensed: look at her shape, she said, and her face; gents gave five pounds to see this beauty. What sort of a gent was I?

"A gent with no more than ten shillings," was the reply.

She stood against the door, limbs handsome in their bright silks, plump breasts squeezed into her stays. She fumbled in my pockets and roused my blood. I got my hand up her petticoats, until she gave her full attentions. Had she pleased me, I would have given her a half sovereign, but as the crisis neared, she called, "Mrs Smith, here's a bilk."

In came the bilious harridan, as I was buttoning up. She wouldn't have her girl insulted. If I'd no argent, they could pawn my watch. I raised hell till she called out, "Bill!"

Her bully, Bill, appeared and I lost my rag. He came on all menace and knavery, and I was sore afraid.

I tore aside the curtains and bellowed, "Police! Murder!" I smashed him about with the poker, but I was finally overcome and battered out of doors. Defrauded, detumescent, debagged.

As I go over the tale with Lawless, I find myself red-faced with fury.

The sergeant is sanguine. "Your possessions are miles hence with the perpetrators. Nothing to be done, sir. Some girls lift more than their skirts. If you'll excuse me, I advise you to throw yourself on this lady's mercy. Borrow a garment. Call a cab." He looks at his watch. "I'd speak no further on it, unless you wish to waste your time and money—and be known to your friends as the halfwit who hocked his hose to the Holborn hoofer."

# A PLEA

Skittles should be safe in Paris soon. After I'd seen her off, I breathed in the cold night air. Satisfied, I recalled the note in my pocket. Typically sensational, Groggins beseeched me to meet him at the Holborn at midnight. He would bring certain papers to make it worth my while, for he declared himself "in horrible danger".

I saw no harm in stopping by Groggins' place on my way. Nobody home. I thought of forcing my way in, but I had no reason to enter a property uninvited; and I had the sensation of being watched.

I cursed him. A long day I had had of it. With the Commons Select Committee looming, I longed for my bed. I went all the same.

A deep fog was descending, and the cold was fierce. I should have been at the Holborn for midnight, if it hadn't been for the intemperate young fool who stopped me in Soho: a ruddy goat, debagged and penniless, who I recognised vaguely from Kate Hamilton's. Typical scam. Girls never like it when a fellow bargains them down. A bilk, they call it. A fellow's slow to realise he's being duped at the crisis, trousers round ankles. It still impresses me how they transform the whole bawdy house just to make a fool of him.

Groggins never showed up. I waited an hour. Exhausted, I drank a glass of hot brandy. I sat, thinking of her, precious weeks before, awaiting me there at five o'clock on a Friday afternoon, before it all began.

## A TELEGRAM

I slept late the next day, and reached the Yard after midday. Payne called me in. He handed over a telegram.

"Dead floozy at the channel. Something to do with you?"

"Doubt it, sir." I blinked. Death at Dover. Woman drowned. Sent by Bertie's coachman. I put my hand to my mouth. "Though I knew her. Skittles, we called her."

"Distraught over a common whore, Watchman?" Sir Richard gave me a look. "Have you been up to no good?"

"She was to testify, sir. I persuaded her to head for Calais to keep her safe. They got to her first." I shook my head. "She wasn't a common whore, sir."

A full account of the disaster arrived in the second post, courtesy of Bertie's cab driver. This gave me a chance to conduct an experiment. Darlington was chatting in Jeffcoat's room. I told them all about the death, feigning I was in a state, for I feared it was my illustrious friend, Skittles. Sure enough, to my great satisfaction, that week's *Illustrated Police News* carried a full spread on it. The lurid engravings even referred to her friends in the police force being unable to save her.

As the paper told it—details uncannily like the letter—the driver stationed the carriage by the water to await the ferry. At the sight of some sinister men approaching through the mist, the lady took fright, crying, "I won't stand no more."

She descended in haste. Perhaps she slipped. The driver swore she threw herself from the parapet. The sinister men proved they had no ill intention by helping the Port Authority fish her out, but too late; only her shawl was recovered from the brine, while a big straw hat was spotted floating away. The driver, exonerated, went on to Paris. Of the sinister men there was no further notice.

Point proven: Jeffcoat was our bloody mole.

At the Yard that afternoon, I drew up lists for the Commons Select Committee: I would need facts, persuasive witnesses, and evidence. If Sir Richard thought to truncate my investigation by pruning back the date, I must force it to blossom sooner.

I studied Dugdale-Hotten's subscription roll and made a shortlist. I added Molly (for a netherview of the criminal method); Felix (for his Phoenix Foundation); myself, Darlington and even Jeffcoat; the 9.23 Club; and finally, Payne himself, Gabriel Mauve and Mr J.W. Brodie, who might have awkward questions to answer. Conjecture was insufficient, even perilous. Proof positive I must secure: the thefts, the memoirs, and the whole sordid world Skittles had described, I must tie together.

I sent word to friends in the House with an interest in the Great Social Evil. I shall be eternally grateful that Gladstone stood up to be counted. He may have been Chancellor of the Exchequer, but he had been a friend to Skittles, and he did not shrink from chairing this controversial Commons Select Committee.

* * *

Mudie's Library sent word the first volume of Felix's memoir was available. Despite my pressing duties, I picked it up on my way home and spent a fruitful hour or two perusing it in a tavern.

It covered his musical training, time with the Austrian military orchestra and establishment in Italy. My affection for him grew, as I sensed the sadness behind the text; for all his talents and achievements, his childhood had not been happy. The volume ended with his marriage, gleefully described, a hint that she was with child, and some presages of disaster.

This only whetted my appetite for the second volume, as there was no mention yet of his injury nor the secret prisons of the title. Where was his wife and family now? I sought in vain some clue to his recent behaviour. Sadness perhaps goes hand in hand with talent.

# THE FILE

It was my interest in Brodie's murder columns that brought news of Groggins the next morning. I paid Molly's lot to scan the *Ha'penny Gazette* the moment it came out. One boy, an early riser, caught me as I stopped in at the Yard after a tour of night houses.

Jeffcoat too was arriving early. He ushered the boy in, amused by my methods. "This boy wants to inform you of the unfortunate death of an Irishman."

Unfortunate death indeed, on the very night I was detained from meeting him. It was only the passing mention of his origin that gave it away. The paper called it suicide. He had hanged himself in a privy, at the club next door to the Holborn, exclusively for gentlemen. The *Gazette* delved no further, but the place was known for unnatural passions, and its privies for forbidden encounters.

The body was gone before I reached the morgue, but Dr Simpson told me it smacked of *suicidium manu aliena*. Involuntary suicide. Blackmailers often exploited illicit love; men who refused to pay met unkind ends. That Groggins was prey to such blackmail I doubted, for he loved women; Simpson retorted that one never knows a man's true passions.

Groggins knew he was in danger. He was Brodie's scribe. With my report to the Select Committee looming, and secrets to keep, this was no suicide.

I cursed my stupidity, and stomped straight in to see Payne, for I must comb Groggins' apartments before anyone else got to them.

The commissioner had loafed out to a cosy political lunch. I would have to drag someone down to Mayfair with me, both to give my search authority, and in case of danger.

Darlington was at his desk, but he was asleep. He was always asleep these days. He looked done in. I wouldn't trust him to tie his own shoelaces.

Jeffcoat saw me standing indecisive in the doorway. He sized up my anxiety with a glance that seemed to say, "Whatever it is, Watchman, I'll come. Whatever our differences, you can rely on me."

The furniture, furnishings, pictures, all were in place. But for such a man of letters, there was one thing missing. Books.

The place had been cleared of every form of literary endeavour. The shelves were bare, the files had gone, the desk lay empty, right down to the blotting paper. A local constable was nodding on duty on the landing. Nobody had took nothing, he told us, not since he'd been there. A theft and a suicide? Unhappy coincidence. I could not see such an egotist, however frightened, destroying his own oeuvre. That egotism had done for him: his life's work cleaned out on the very day he croaked it.

I thumped the desk in frustration. I was thinking of Groggins' large black file, the one inscribed *M—S—L—*. I must find it. It would thread everything together: the thefts and their ringmaster, the erotic memoirs and their perpetrators, and the women. Too busy with Skittles, and thinking of the Committee, I had let it slip from my grasp.

Jeffcoat stood by, so patiently and uncomplainingly that I felt the overwhelming urge to confide in him. "Will you sell this story to the *Illustrated Police* and all?"

He laughed off my accusation. "That'd be Jimmy Darlington you'd want to talk to. Have you noticed his new rig? Not to mention being tight half the time, and worse."

I rubbed at my eyes, recognising the truth now it was presented so starkly. I don't know if I was more ashamed of trusting Darlington or suspecting Jeffcoat. "Shall we say that I have not?"

The spring sun shone hazy through the mists over Green Park. We stood at Groggins' French windows and talked. First, the thefts. Mauve's memoirs, I knew, had been filched via the automaton (by Bede and the Pixie, though I didn't mention that). Jeffcoat confirmed: he'd visited an admiral and a lawyer who had been robbed while in possession of the borrowed chess machine.

The rest we guessed at. Groggins, scribe of filth, transcribed the stolen memoirs: so many confessions set down by men who should know better. Along with these, he took down a hundred reports of courtesans and ladies of pleasure. The encyclopaedia of love Groggins was assembling would be sold through Dugdale-Hotten to clandestine collectors—though darker chapters might be held back for purposes of blackmail.

"Now that manuscript is gone." I sighed. "And the one man who might have exposed the plan. Let's not tell Sir Richard. Not yet."

"Why?" said Jeffcoat. "Are you after his job?"

I hedged my bets. That Sir Richard could be pressured to protect Dugdale-Hotten was enough to justify caution; no need to tar him with graver doubts. "It will all come out, if this Commons Select Committee summons a judicial enquiry."

He nodded. "Loose threads. I'd like to pull at a few." He threw open the French windows, standing right where Groggins had stood, making his bibulous Irish confessions to me. Why confess? What had he feared? "Horrible danger," he wrote. He was no fool. Might he have hidden a copy somewhere?

Jeffcoat inspected the lobelia. "How on earth are these flowers still in bloom?"

"Green fingers." I clutched his shoulder. Those flowers, garish and proud, that Groggins loved so sinfully. I unhooked the basket, dug my fingers beneath the blooms and found— nothing. I cursed, putting my soiled hands to my head.

Jeffcoat lifted the soil from the basket. There, tucked between the tarpaulin inner and the hessian lining, quite dry in spite of watering, safe from winds and fogs and sinister men: a thin manila envelope.

We ran in to the desk, dizzy with hope. Jeffcoat pulled out handwritten paper, and a black gentleman's card, which appeared blank. The foolscap sheets bore tabular lists in Groggins' florid hand. The first sheet was titled *M—S—L—* Vol 1.

Chapter 1. *CW…VIM…GBM…WD…AESCG*
Chapter 2. *JCH…WA…AGMP…RM…GBM*
Chapter 3. *CJHD…WWC…P'zzi…ML…HM*

And so forth. Assigned to each chapter were several sets of initials, with the odd abbreviated name, as if to remind Groggins of the full details. Some initials appeared many times. One set of initials bracketed a whole chapter. The abbreviated names could not have been more provocative: Panizzi, keeper of books at the British Museum; the editor of the *Bugle*, now disgraced; and other figures of public controversy.

As for the initials, there were scores of them. The chapter list was endless. The work must rival *The Thousand and One Nights*. This was the kind of game Miss Villiers enjoyed—if only I could risk involving her in such murky waters; if only I still saw her. And I had Dugdale's subscription list, to match this against.

Why keep only this? The big black file was gone. What use the contents without the manuscript?

No doubt these chapter titles matched that black file marked *M—S—L—* where Groggins stored these erotic memoirs, some stolen, some dictated by girls.

Groggins was paid well for his work. He could not risk selling the material elsewhere. However, keeping a record of who had written what would offer him some clout. A dangerous sideline. Had he made injudicious comments or threats? Was he visited by the same men who chased Skittles into the Channel?

Most important was that title. I recalled the black volume I'd glimpsed on Brodie's bookshelves with its own coded title—what was it now?—*Eflesym* or similar. Had Groggins thought to assemble these memoirs off his own bat, or was he commissioned to do it? The thefts, the publishers, and Groggins: mechanisms propelled by forces we cannot fathom.

Jeffcoat brushed off the black card. He tilted it to the pale sunlight. It was not blank. The florid lettering, like a creeping lily, showed faint in the light, debossed in black ink upon black paper.

"What does it say?" I asked. "Flowers?"

# The Flowers of Sin

# TRUCE

"Jeffcoat, it's me, Watchman." I knocked tentatively. "Thanks for your help."

He observed me patiently. "Over your mood, are you?"

I bit back a sharp riposte. "If I have been a little—"

"Cheese your barrikin, you daft bat. Sit down." He opened up a Stanford map, annotated, like mine, with red and black marks across the metropolis. He looked at me. "We are two sleuthhounds, you and I, barking at separate holes of the same warren."

My quarrel with Jeffcoat was forgotten. If I had thought him taunting me, he had thought me aloof; if I had called him big for his boots, he had puzzled at my ill humour. I had thought Jeffcoat chummy with Sir Richard Payne; he had been digging out figures that would make uncomfortable reading for the commissioner.

I had more in common with Solomon Jeffcoat than I had imagined. The same age as me, he came to detection through his policeman father, while my experience came through watchmaking. He liked books; I liked the theatre. He spoke French; I barely spoke English (as those who disliked Scots told me often enough). He trained a tomcat named Thom to savage all other beasts in the environs of Scotland Yard; he was surprised when his colleagues complained of the carcasses it left by their beds.

We worked for three days straight. Over those long hours, we divulged everything we knew and everything we suspected. After that, I would have trusted him with my life.

Whatever Groggins' list meant, whomsoever it implicated, I was not safe in divulging it. Not until the opportune moment. By then I must assemble trustworthy allies. What I had not expected was that Jeffcoat's investigations might be grimmer than mine.

It was the first time I had really trusted another officer since my first days in the Yard, when I idolised Inspector Wardle. Jeffcoat had learnt his trade from Wardle too, and was just as upset when he left the Yard under a cloud. We both stood in need of an ear to bend. I liked his abrupt manner and his welcoming rudeness. His sharp nose cut through problems and his sandy hair swept them aside. "If I am not mistaken—"

"You're not."

"We're looking at criminal operations colluding across the capital."

"Run from bawd houses and public houses." I tapped at the centre of his map. "With one sprawling behemoth at the centre."

He nodded. "In order to fathom that influence, we've got to dig down to the roots."

My eyes roved across the map. "Where do flowers bloom?" My finger came to rest where our collected annotations were densest, right beside old father Thames.

He nodded. "In the dirt."

# LINKS

The traces were fearfully hidden. If only I had got to Groggins first. He had been deep in this business. If only I had paid him another visit, we might have known sooner. Now it was too late. Especially for him.

I must try every avenue. I swallowed my pride and wrote again to Miss Villiers. She still worked, irregularly, at the British Museum Library, which held every book ever published. I posed her the puzzle of unravelling the meaning of M—S—L—. I did not mention the list of incriminating initials, nor the coded title on Brodie's shelf. I reminded her about my reader's pass. She preferred handling her own researches, I wanted to read Felix's second volume and judge his tales for myself.

The weather had turned. The winds that had so long hounded us changed not to the spring we craved, but to something altogether more oppressive: fog.

I hurried back to Holywell Street. I would lean on Dugdale and Hotten. Even if it upset Payne's literary friends, a little shock might draw an indiscreet admission. If they were collating Groggins' work, who was printing it? Who stood to gain?

Dugdale-Hotten was no more. Gone. Not just their shop. Half of Holywell Street had been razed. I stood gawping through the lingering fog.

An urchin asked me for money.

I took out a ha'penny and toyed with it. "Where's Dugdale and Hotten gone?"

"The dirty writer men?"

"Where did they move to?"

"Back to jail." The boy clapped his hands in glee. "Someone shopped 'em in."

The far end of Holywell Street was still standing. I stopped into an antiquarian bookseller's and asked about *The Secret Prisons of Italy*. I would track down Felix's second volume somehow.

They gave me a look as if I were ordering *The Awful Disclosures of Maria Monk*. It was marked in their catalogue as a revolutionary tome. To order such books, in the current political climate, could get you noticed. Garibaldi was about to visit; republican twitterings were afoot, and anti-monarchist parades. No, they declared, they knew of no copies available.

I thought again of Miss Villiers. Normally so punctilious, she had said nothing about my reader's pass. I dropped into the museum. The principal librarian happened to spot me. "You are of the *carabinieri*, no? I am Panizzi, Antonio Panizzi."

This took me aback, as I was not in uniform.

"I saw you, at Quarterhouse, with Sir Richard. A good

cause, the Phoenix Foundation." Without pausing for breath, he grabbed my shoulder. "I have been the victim of a theft. Not here. Privately. Two weeks ago."

"Weeks?" I restrained my irritation. Little use reporting it now, when all the evidence was gone. "What was stolen, sir?"

"This is the surprise, truly. Initially, I think nothing. I think, ah, it is the addict of the laudanum, looking for the money or jewels. No good! My treasures are literary. Now I realise certain papers were taken, papers I should lament to see fallen into the bad hands."

"Tell me, sir." I raised an eyebrow. "Are you by any chance a chess fanatic?"

He was astonished by my deduction.

I assured him, without mentioning the automaton, that I was on the thieves' trail. I would find what had happened to his papers. And it might prove significant in the upcoming hearings. "I have need, sir, of upstanding witnesses. Would you testify?"

"Parliamentary hearings?" His smile froze. "That I am an erotobibliomaniac, this is no secret. I see no shame in it. The lust in literature, it is part of the lust for the life. But to testify? No, no. Besides, Brodie was strict that I not speak of the New Turk."

"I never mentioned it."

"Boh! You deduce it, I know." He was sweating slightly. "Nobody wish to jeopardise the plans of Mr Brodie."

I asked if I might be admitted, to call up Felix's book. But our interview had gone sour, and his brow clouded.

"Ah, Felix? Ha!" His air of bonhomie gave way to a hectoring tone. "The Reading Room, it is fully occupied at the moment. The foreign scholars, you know."

I could see a few empty seats. "I am pursuing police enquiries. Miss Villiers usually finds me a spot—"

"Beh! Miss Villiers, she has trouble enough. Irregular behaving for a lady so young. Good day."

* * *

Had Dugdale and Hotten been arrested? Enquiries at the Yard next day proved this not quite true. They were taken in for questioning, and their goods seized. Hotten, released with a caution, vanished. Dugdale reacted so badly to the arrest, they had to restrain him. Declared insane, he was removed to the new lunatic prison in Berkshire.

I was not best pleased. Payne was avoiding me. What pressures were being exerted on him from above? I would need special permission to visit Dugdale. Whither their stock of dirty books had been sequestered, nobody seemed to know.

I moaned to Jeffcoat about all these hidden traces.

"If they be hiding, we must seek." His chin jutted toward me. "What's the fascination with this old musician, then?"

I told him about Felix. His elation, his dejection. His foundation, and its entanglement with Brodie. His erratic behaviour, after the party, in the hothouse, at the Opera House; about Quartern Mews, and the girl, and his panic at the window.

"He has her installed there?" His eyes lit up. "And other girls on the same street, you say?"

I nodded. "Who the girl is, I know not; but she is entangled with Felix."

"And he with Brodie." He clapped his hands. "This is it. This is our way to sniff out this blooming syndicate." So many avenues were forestalled: secrecy around the Turk, Groggins dead, his file snatched away, the Oddbodies terrified, Kate's girls evasive, and Skittles... well. It was a labyrinthine route, but Jeffcoat convinced me to follow it. How else to fathom who controls the mechanism? "We watch the house, note the comings and goings, enquire discreetly. Someone will be careless. Someone will lead us back to the centre."

As we put on our coats to go and reconnoitre this vigil,

Molly materialised out of the fog.

"I was debating." She stood, disconsolate at the doorway, dripping. "Whether I might risk presenting myself. Knowing that associates of mine are under investigation within these hallowed doors." She rubbed her nose and looked up at me distractedly. "I am a harbinger of bad tidings, I'm afraid. It's Felix."

# FELIX STRICKEN

Molly wasn't given to overstatement. Sending Jeffcoat on to Quartern Mews, we took a cab, crawling through the densest of smogs. Half an hour later, we sat at Felix's bedside in St Bartholomew's Hospital. He awoke and started speaking. His tone varied, as if he were telling us an epic of woes, but in fact, he was simply repeating phrases over and over, and seemed frustrated that we could not understand him. "Flowers. Flowers. Flowers, you see. Girl. The girl. The girl. Then the flowers."

I looked at Molly appalled.

She rose with a sigh. "I'll dig out a crocus."

Until the doctor arrived, I tried to calm him. His frustration rose and fell. It was distressing, seeing those eyes still the same, full of warmth and humanity, unable to communicate. Did he know who we were? He seemed frightened, but that was reasonable. He seemed to think I expected something of him, even looked fearful that we might hurt him.

I spoke softly, reminding him who I was, where he was, what had happened. Reassured, he grasped my hand. He indicated he needed something from the dressing table. I found his cheque book.

He made out a bill for £50 with Coutts & Co. Three times he tried to write a name. Each time, he crossed it out, painstakingly initialling each change. Frustration got the better of him. He gave me the cheque, the payee still unresolved.

Where the name should be, he had scored out "Ang", then "Evv", then "Eff". He slumped on his pillow, exhausted, and fell into a profound sleep.

I squeezed his hand, wondering if he would ever rise from that bed. Who should Molly chance upon but our old friend Dr Simpson?

He was abrupt as ever. Felix had had a stroke. "Lucky to be alive at his age. Doubtless likes a drink."

"Did something prompt the stroke?"

He was dismissive. "A hundred things might contribute. A hard life. Exertion. Sleeping tablets." Felix's inability to speak Simpson termed aphasia. "It might be permanent, it might not. Whether stimulation is positive or detrimental, medical opinion is divided: reinvigorates the animal spirits or compounds the frustration."

Simpson prescribed rest, good food in moderation and a regular pipe. I determined to fetch Felix's tobacco, sheet music, and violin from Quarterhouse, though he might play it no longer.

Molly had waited patiently. I was glad of her company, for the place left me glum. As we left, she nudged me. "Down the corridor, look. Couple of blokes, see?" Sure enough, the two men did not look like they were waiting for visitors' hour. "Waiting for a pair of dead man's shoes, I don't wonder."

I picked up Felix's things from Quarterhouse. His scout stood by, sniffling miserably. "He was in the rudest 'ealth a month back. The rudest of 'ealth."

I took the chance to nose around Felix's rooms. The scout assured me nothing had been disturbed. His possessions seemed from a different time. His music stand, his violin; the bedspread and old silk ties; gilt-framed drawings of the Italian opera houses. But one daguerreotype, by his bed, had a modern frame: a studio portrait of a young woman with a heart-shaped face, the hint of a smile on her lips, dark hair billowing against a white bonnet, and eyes that looked up impertinently, as if remembering something wicked. I knew her: it was the lady he'd escorted to Quartern Mews.

The scout coughed. "Oh, I should take him that, if I were you. Most fond of that picture, he is. First thing he looks at every morning when I wake him with his tea. Frenchy-style mind: lemon, not milk. It's his daughter, I think, or someone, at least."

Someone, at least. Perhaps I was mistaken about Felix, and the Phoenix Foundation was nothing to do with the Great Social Evil but something quite private and personal.

I slipped the picture into my bag and tipped the scout to keep him quiet. The dressing table also bore a pill dispenser, empty but for a little white dust. Foul play? Had Felix become tangled in the same threads I was trying to unravel?

The scout was surprised. "Felix warn't one for pills. Unlike most of our Quarterhouse Brothers, who chomp each quack remedy the apothecaries present 'em. Prefers his tea and his wine, Felix does. Must belong to those men who visited the other day."

On Quartern Lane, Jeffcoat had bogus roadworks set up under the auspices of telegraphical diggings. He had stationed himself in the workman's hut with a clear view of the Mews: he had already seen several ladies coming and going.

I showed him Felix's daguerreotype. We sat for a moment, both taken with the girl's expression. But we must hold off accosting her and her landlady at No. 17, we decided, lest we queer our chance. Instead, keep watch and see what visitors they received.

The Commons Select Committee would convene within the week. I vouched for Molly's urchins to keep an eye on the place. Better than demanding police officers whose discretion we might not trust. We would engage the Oddbodies as watchers, aside from Bede and the Pixie, for whom I had other plans.

* * *

I dropped in on Bertie's driver, returned from Paris, and persuaded him to come for a spin. As he drove me to visit Felix, he gave his own version of Skittles's ill-fated crossing. I brought him into the hospital, where he spotted the dark-suited men waiting in the corridor.

"That's them," he said. "Them as scared Skittles at the Channel."

I thanked him and gave him leave to go.

Felix was sleeping. I longed to ask so many things, not least of the cheque and the daguerreotype. I slipped the picture into the drawer and tipped the matron to keep a close eye on him. I was ever out of pocket those days.

On my way back, I dropped in to Coutts & Co. Bank. I mentioned Felix's ill turn and his distress about a payment to a certain party, whose name he had been unable to write.

The teller eyed me disdainfully. "Acting on his behalf, are we?"

"I'm no lawyer," I admitted, "but I am a policeman, and Felix's friend."

I was sent through to a senior partner, a rotund toad of a Scot. He might have risen to greet me if his chair was not so comfortable. "Police? How thrilling. Is Felix's money being sequestered on the grounds of incapability?" He shook silently, slapping his knee.

I frowned.

"You'll have enjoyed that *Notting Hill Mystery*? Such skullduggery." He cast his eyes over an impenetrable ledger. "No, no. Nothing beyond the regular payments to Brodie for the maintenance of the Foundation. All in hand."

I showed not a trace of surprise. "Ah, yes. Brodie."

"Well. To Brodie's newspaper group. Subsidiaries of the same. They deal with the day-to-day running of the

Foundation. Sixty beds, twenty staff, plans to expand. It's all accounted for. The payments are in hand."

"And those payments continue, with Felix ill?"

"Yes, yes. Even should he die."

I drew in my breath.

Feeling he had divulged too much, he was not willing to discuss individual payments Felix might frequently make. There was no way to know for whom the blank cheque was intended; I kept hold of it, hoping I would find the girl soon enough.

I would visit Felix as often as I could. Some days he was calm, others distressed. The matron reported that some nice gentlemen had enquired as to Felix's recovery, asking especially nicely about his speech. She never knew anyone make a recovery in that department, and told them so, which seemed to satisfy them, for they left at once.

The next time I went with Molly, he spoke with the same aphasic limitations. After his customary floral refrain, he reached for another word, again and again, slapping his knee in distress.

Molly checked we were alone. She laid on the bed a sheet she had inscribed with the alphabet.

Felix's eyes lit up. He began pointing at once, letter by letter. R—S—Q.

Molly looked at him. "Rescue."

"Rescue you, Felix?" I smiled. "Are you in danger?"

He shook his head and looked askance.

I drew out the picture from his bedside table. He had not known it was there, and his eyes went round. He took it from me reverently, clutching it to his breast with melancholy love. The haunted look returned. I drew closer.

"You want to find this lady? To rescue her? Is it to her the cheque is due?"

He nodded, then glanced around, putting his finger to his

lips. Staring about in panic, he gestured to hide the portrait.

Molly slipped it into her satchel. "Poor fellow," she murmured. "Who is she?"

I whispered. "Your daughter, is it?"

He blinked rapidly, attempting a smile, but giving way to sobbing.

The matron rushed over and told us off. "Leave him be, you awful people. Tiring out an old gent. One at a time for future visits, or you'll find you ain't welcome."

# HIDE AND SEEK

Things moved quickly behind the deepening fogs. My suspicions over Groggins and Felix grew graver. Jeffcoat and I were on the right track. Bede and the Pixie were in danger, too. And the girl, the mysterious woman Felix had been visiting. If only I could unravel it in time to sway the Select Committee.

We made enquiries up Quartern Lane: surely baker, butcher and candlestick maker knew the house and who paid their bills. Not at all; none of them served the houses at all, or had in living memory. The Master of Quarterhouse said I was welcome to ask the Brothers, but he feared none would admit they knew the street, for it was infamous locally. How to prove the connections between the courtesans, the brothels and the memoirs? How to discover who held the strings of power?

Where do flowers bloom? In the dirt.

Jeffcoat and I kept up our other duties, somehow, while I slaved over my initial deposition to the Committee. Despite Skittles's vanishment, Sabine's freedom was bought her—by a mysterious benefactor, so she said—and she became Stephanie again. She founded her longed-for establishment on the better side of Waterloo: Mrs Boulton's Café. With new pride and no powder on her cheeks, she made a handsome woman. She undertook to help me, just as Skittles had promised, *in memoriam* of our friend, in hearts, diamonds, clubs and spades. Twice weekly, I took breakfast there, weary with sleep, as Steph called in favours from far and wide. Doxies all over the capital rose from their beds to tell me their tale, in exchange for tea or white satin (that is, gin), stories less rosy than I'd heard at Kate Hamilton's, stories worse than the societies'. People like to tell the truth, just as Collins had shown me, if they trust you are listening.

More from the 9.23 Club, with Molly's lot running errands; more from the societies; and these evidences I passed gratefully on to the clerks attending the Commons Select Committee. Why should your life have worth only if you're born into money? Everyone should have their chance. Each story I heard strengthened my belief: some girls might be drawn to the life by the dream of adventure, but more were lured, tricked or forced into it. If one woman could be saved from the dustheap, it was worth the struggle.

It was on my way to Mrs Boulton's, rushing to get figures for the Enquiry next day, that the incident occurred. Seeing how shaken I was, Steph insisted on my taking whisky, despite the early hour. I told her everything.

The fog was denser than ever. Fearful of delay in securing cabs, I had commandeered one of the Yard's carriages. I was hurtling down from Quartern Lane after my stint when I became lost in the unfamiliar streets across the river. I was a good enough driver all told, but everything had changed since the Tooley Street fire: at one corner, gleaming warehouses; at the next, a rabbit warren of slums and burnt-out tenements.

The whole incident took but five minutes.

The girl appeared from nowhere. She was knocked down before I even saw her, and never a moment to slow the horses.

I stopped as soon as I could. The girl was making a low noise, pale as death. She had welts on her face, but no cuts or bruises. Her sister screamed operatically. She gave me a foul look and dragged me to her house, leaving the girl lying on the road. I broke free and lifted the poor thing to the broken doorway, where repeated banging drew out an old dragon with moon eyes, ivory-faced and scab-headed, who might be anything from aunt to great-grandmother. She took one look at me and shut the door in our faces.

The sister banged again.

The door opened but a crack. I pleaded that she must let me lay the girl down. She was breathing regularly, and seemed if anything in a daze. The dragon told me to mind my own business, or she would call a copper. She spoke as in a dream, and I smelt strange smoke on her. I pushed past, declaring that I *was* a copper. If she did not want to be charged, she had best send for a doctor. That shut her up.

Where I had expected to find a kitchen, there was a kind of office. I laid the girl on the table, on top of the accounts. Feeling their hostility, I offered money and my name. Through a hatch, I could hear clacking and whirring. I saw in the semi-dark a roomful of grey-faced seamstresses silently at work, sewing, hemming, making buttons; and on racks behind them the most wondrous dresses, beautifully arrayed. It was the strangest thing to see, such lovely clothes made in such drudgery. The scabbed old dragon chased me out. She took neither my money nor my name. Even the scowling sister refused a tip for minding the horses.

I was at Mrs Boulton's within five minutes.

Steph's face darkened as I made my confession. There were warehouses innumerable along those streets. Their behaviour was strange, she admitted, but folk who make a crooked living will have crooked ways. More than that she would not say.

# PRELIMINARY HEARING

"Sergeant Lawless," said Gladstone, opening the preliminary hearing of the Commons Select Committee as pleasantly as if it were a luncheon appointment. "Sir Richard Payne tells me your report is not ready. If your researches are incomplete, let us not waste time. Do you accept that this Commons Select Committee hand over these enquiries to the civil servants, as he suggests?"

"No, Mr Chairman, sir. On the contrary, I request a full Judicial Enquiry."

Murmurings in the gallery. Though Gladstone had persuaded an impressive selection of MPs to attend at short notice, Payne himself was chatting complacently in the corridor outside, surrounded by lesser politicians. How was he to know that I'd wound up my research (with a deal of help)?—though he could have asked. How was I to know an Enquiry was the last thing he wanted?—though I could have asked.

I breathed deep. "If my witnesses can tell that Enquiry what they have told me, we shall need your judicial experience to unravel the truth behind their tales. It may be darker than anyone has imagined. May I speak confidentially?"

Approaching the bench, I passed over my deposition to Gladstone, a document I intended as incendiary. He read my notes swiftly. He had had prior view of the statistics and other documents, but not my conclusions.

The evidence I outlined went beyond prostitution. Coercion, kidnap, blackmail and Jeffcoat's discoveries. It would not be politic, nor safe, to reveal in open court the wider implications of our researches. As the investigations advanced, we would pass on the evidence.

"I see no objection. Indeed, the sooner we begin an Enquiry, the more evidence will remain admissible." His eyes flickered around. In the gallery sat Disraeli, alongside Skittles's duke;

but a Select Committee transcends normal party politicking. He nodded. "We shall do our damnedest."

Thank goodness for Gladstone and his oratory. With eloquent restraint, he there and then persuaded the Select Committee they must instigate a Judicial Enquiry. This Enquiry would be open to MPs and public, but with an injunction against newspaper reports, in order to protect our witnesses, due to the delicate nature of the evidence, with so many conflicts of public and private interest. He went on to propose Lord Chief Justice Fairchild, President of the Queen's Bench Division, as presiding judge.


Outside, the fog was hanging in, like a headache. Reporters hung around, waiting to descend on Jeffcoat and me.

Payne plucked me by the sleeve. "What the hell are you up to?"

I swallowed. "You asked me to turn over stones."

"Stones, not boulders." He was trying to maintain a jovial tone.

"Why pose a question, if you knew the answer you required?" I shrugged. "You've mugs aplenty you can squeeze into line, sir. No lies, you said. No fudging."

He turned to Jeffcoat, his wrath harder to contain. If I was ungovernable, he thought he had him in his pocket. "Solly, what's going on?"

Jeffcoat said, reasonably enough, that we had suspicions we could not yet prove, and hoped the Committee would give us grace to pursue them. We would report to him, as soon as we knew what we had uncovered. This evasion was unfaultable, and we made our escape.

Behind us, J.W. Brodie sidled up to Payne, his ash grey hair dark beside the commissioner's white mutton chops. I looked back, surprised to see him. I'd imagined Brodie far removed from such mundanity; but our investigation had drawn him from his underground lair. While Payne blustered, smoothing his whiskers energetically, Brodie stared coolly after me. Beside Payne's bulk, he seemed small. On his shoulders, though, he balanced the weight of public opinion, tilting it back and forth at will.

Gladstone prevailed. The decision was made in minutes. He banged his gavel with a grim satisfaction. "Sergeant Lawless will deliver his evidence and witness list to the Enquiry. If the judge accepts, it may begin forthwith."

Sir Richard Payne was furious. At the worst, he had imagined an internal enquiry, with himself as chair and Mauve as pet solicitor, and it would be sewn up by lunchtime on day one. I had rumbled this plan just in time.

A word to Skittles's friends had done the trick. For Skittles had had friends on both sides of the House, of course, in upper and lower chambers, not least Mr Gladstone and her spoony-eyed duke. These two had spread word of the ill done to their darling, swaying parliamentary colleagues on both sides to sign up for this minor Committee and raise a fuss. The whole thing was cast as an homage to Skittles. Justice Fairchild accepted within the hour and tabled the Enquiry to start the following week.

Fairchild was that rare thing in Westminster, an honest soul. He had qualified up north, far from the cankered claws of the establishment—and that stroke of luck would prove momentous. Risen to prominence by his own virtues, he surrounded himself with like-minded folk. Throughout the Enquiry, the clerk and ushers impressed with their impartiality. The press, annoyed at their exclusion, raised scandals over the junior counsels; complaints were made, complaints were dismissed. I prayed that the newspapers' malign spell would be quelled. Only thus, the truth would out.

If Sir Richard had expected a murmur, I had given him a roar.

* * *

The newspapers, stung by Gladstone's slap in the face, began a campaign of cheap insinuations. From low-brow pamphlets to distinguished broadsheets, they ignited a debate. Men and men's antics. Femininity versus feminine decorum. Polite society against the Great Social Evil.

Brodie's rags never quite said the police were in cahoots with the judiciary. They never quite revealed depositions from the "closed" court. But they hinted like hell. They hinted at unsavoury collusions, questionable deals and disreputable practices, hidden from the public, filed, and whitewashed.

That was Brodie's way of punishing our misdemeanours.

I no longer cared. Sir Richard might be angry as he liked; he no longer spoke to me. If everybody tried to save their own skin, we'd get nowhere. Jeffcoat and I, we were ready to fall.

Skittles's duke stopped me that first day outside the court. He thanked me for my efforts, and he agreed to testify, which was exactly the kind of courage we needed. They might do for Groggins and lock up Dugdale, they might make Cora vanish, and silence even Felix, innocent though he was; but they couldn't keep us all quiet.

# WARNING

Fortunate that I kept irregular hours, and kept no paperwork at home. The sinister men scared the willies out of my old landlady, and broke my best china. Scared enough, I took my blanket and pillow and moved in to Scotland Yard. I had avoided this expedient lodging in my early days, preferring my own company. Now, apart from the snoring, the alarum calls and Jeffcoat's cat, I liked it well—though the roof leaked.

The sinister men tracked me down the next day in Mrs

Boulton's coffee house. They came through the fog without my spotting them; it was weeks since we'd seen the sun. I knew them from the hospital. The leader slipped into the booth opposite me.

"We have an offer to make you, Sergeant." Quite who "we" were, he did not make clear; what I was to do, or avoid doing, was never stated. But the gist was clear. My life would be carefree only if I desisted from these foolish investigations. "Give it a rest. Vanish gracefully away. Enjoy life in the countryside. Back in Scotland, why not? With a little financial salve to recompense you for your troubles."

I pushed my cup away. "Why don't you vanish up your own arse? Tell your master, whoever he may be, that if he's nothing to hide, nothing will come out." My attempt at an exit was blocked by his colleague's bulk in the doorway.

The seated man smiled tightly. "You've had your offer. Let's pray you see sense. You shouldn't like a proper warning. Like your friend Felix had."

Off they went, the threat of violence hanging in the air. When I popped into Kate Hamilton's that same evening, these same villains were at the bar. I wheeled straight around and fled. I must watch my back. Mostly, we police move around in a law-abiding reverie. It was timely for me to be reminded how most people live, not by law or morality, but at the whim of fear and brute force.

$$M—S—L—$$

Miss Villiers had at last written back, about the coded titles and about Felix's book.

*The Criminal Prisons of Italy*, volume II, was hard indeed to find, though such a success in its day; if I could attend the dreaded aunt's charitable book swap on the vernal equinox in Petersfield, Hampshire, she would strive to secure me a copy.

As for the title *M—S—L—*, she had scoured the stack in search of likely abbreviations. Her surmised solution was uncertain, but rather delicate to commit to paper. Ruth's prevarication was inconvenient. Would it connect Groggins' labours with the tome on Brodie's shelf?

I visited Molly at the Adelphi Arches, to plan her deposition for the Enquiry. I complained about Miss Villiers' contrary evasion.

"Attend her blasted book swap, then." Molly shook her head. "Promise me."

The two of them had been plotting; it was irksome that Ruth communicated more with Molly than with me. "If I can, if I can."

"Miss Bilious has her reasons, though you may be blind to them." Molly sniffed. "Tell me more of these coded titles."

I mentioned neither Groggins nor Brodie, but I wrote out the two mysterious titles: *M—S—L—* and—as best I remembered—*Eflsym*.

"You loofish ecipol yob," Molly laughed. "Ain't I taught you nothing?"

*Eflsym*. I kicked myself. Backslang. I was missing letters, but it could be backslang: *myslfe*, likely *My S__ Lfe*. At Molly's insistence, I wrote then and there, asking Ruth to look up *My Something Life* in the museum stack. Did such a volume exist?

She replied by return post, rather sportively, how pleased she was that I'd worked out so much. She had already worked out so much. The volume *My Secret Life* was not listed in the catalogue—but I was not the first to request it. She could explain no further on paper but gladly in person.

Was I in for a roasting? If Ruth had tracked down a copy of the tales that tickled Groggins, she would look at my nose for seeking such filth. The darker truth behind it all, of course, she could not know.

I had better go to her blasted aunt's blasted book swap.

# FURTIVE PLEASURES

When they found Cora, Darlington was distraught. It was the last straw for him, seeing her dragged out of the river, belly swollen, that matchless body ruined by the filthy Thames. It didn't do to think of her last moments, jumping from the parapet.

I took him straight from mortuary to pub. As we passed the Evans, where hoofers stood at the stage door smoking, he ogled every skirt. The 9.23 Club would straighten him out. Strange, that my dream of befriending Felix had proved impossible; here instead I was presenting Darlington, the debauchee. His eyes were raw with sleeplessness. Reading the memoirs had infected his brain, and he was a dreadful bore, making our eyes water recounting the denouement of *Lucretia, or The Delights of Cunnyland*.

"Does erotic reading sate a man's urges," he insisted, "or stimulate them?"

Collins couldn't resist. "Is my *Woman in White* a provocation to murder?"

"That is hardly the same," I said. "Your books are entertainments; but these tales are obsessions, for some."

"I don't doubt." Collins glanced at Darlington. "The Obscene Publications Act has only heightened the thrill. Would I wish my servants to read this salacious stuff?"

I laughed. "Or your mistress?"

Darlington coughed. My candour embarrassed him, though his reading matter didn't. "Drive me potty, these stories do. Can't sleep. Sensual visions all around me."

"Laudanum," Collins declared. "That'll do it. Good for the clap, and all."

I laughed. This was Collins's remedy for everything. Damn it, his fictional characters were all on opiates.

Collins measured out a dose, which Darlington took, with a shudder. He then handed over the whole bottle, to my discomfort. "It's above board, Lawless. Elevation, the Patent One Night Cough Syrup. Most morphinomaniacs do not break the law, only the bank. I prescribe a teaspoonful at bedtime, Darlington. Beware sullied goods. A Chinaman, Appoo, gets me mine. He beats his woman, but he's a connoisseur. Buy from any old lush, and it's curtains." He rolled his eyeballs up in their sockets.

The next day, Darlington was rejuvenated. "Grateful to you, Watchman, old man."

"I didn't give it to you," I said.

"You're the broker," he grinned. "Anyway, I slept like a baby."

The Enquiry summonses were issued. All very well for those with addresses; my more itinerant witnesses I visited in person. Molly put the first steps of our plan into motion, and we ran through her routine, for she was my second witness.

Money was tight, paying urchins for watching Quartern Mews and doxies for stories at Mrs Boulton's. I had thought Sir Richard would not approve my latest expense sheet. He did worse; he approved it, so I would keep spending, then bullied the clerks not to pay up.

Felix no longer needed constant care, but he could not return to Quarterhouse, with its corkscrew stairs and regulations. They helped arrange his transfer to the Clapham House for Incurables. Felix's cheque I made out to them, to pay for his upkeep in private rooms there.

## MISDIRECTION (ENQUIRY I)

Molly entered the courtroom at her ease. She shook hands with the usher and nodded to the gallery, as a music hall comedian might take the stage. She benefited from following a dry presentation of the figures for prostitution, gathered by myself and all my helpers. These numbers drew murmurs of surprise, and Sir Richard's wrath. Though incomplete, these already far outstripped the 1857 charts, indeed, any statistics in his time as commissioner.

Knowing that MPs and judges move in exalted circles, I had arranged for experts to speak on prostitution, exploitation and theft, for you can't beat the word from the horse's mouth. I felt a pang of regret: inviting Molly was a step too far, for all her bumptious chaunter.

As she reached the bench, a little figure with a fake beard stumbled into the courtroom. The drunken sot fell on the usher, in a move I recognised from the street. General hilarity. I hurried over, as the usher set him upright. The drunk pulled at his beard and winked at me. He sauntered across the room, pointing at a couple of gents in the gallery, who shifted uncomfortably in their seats. Bumping into Molly, he entered the witness stand and stood swaying comically, as if about to pass out.

"What have you to say for yourself?" Lord Chief Justice Fairchild only now looked up from his notes. "Lawless? Is this your expert witness?"

The drunkard tugged his beard, searching for words.

"No, sir." I sprang forward. "I'll remove the offending personage."

Strangely cooperative as I dragged him out, the drunk uttered not a sound. Out in the corridor, the beard came off, and I saw, by God, it was the Pixie. I demanded the usher's wallet, which she had lifted. She gave me to understand that she no longer had it, but I shouldn't worry. I told her I wanted a word with her; if she would pop by the Yard later, I would make it worth her while.

Molly had taken the stand. She waited ebulliently.

Justice Fairchild smiled kindly. "Have you nothing to say, young lady?"

"Plenty." She scratched her nose. "But I think it best not speak till spoken to."

"A wise policy. You are our expert on misdirection. Is that right?"

She spread her hands. "Exemplar is what I offered. If you wanted a diddling expert, you should've called Noddle McDevitt or Jezzer the Stick. But an exemplar, My Lord, I can present."

Fairchild wrinkled his nose, amused. "Go ahead, young lady."

"All done, My Lord." She frowned. "That's the point."

"I'm afraid I haven't followed you."

"I should bleeding hope not, or I'd be a poor sell. I'll take you through, straightways first, then back through the chicanery."

Molly shuffled a deck of cards with the dexterity born of wasted youth. The front row of politicians picked cards from her splayed deck. She bade them follow her every move. One muttered about normal procedure; Molly gibed that he'd never fathom underworld tricks if she proceeded normally.

A joke, a jape, a lary look, and Molly transformed the court into Wilton's Music Hall when the ships are in. Cards were extracted from earlobes, from the clerk's inkwell, and from the junior counsel's wig.

With a finishing fanfare, Molly flourished five cards before us. "Gentlemen, are these, or are these not, your cards?"

The judge looked crestfallen. "Oh. Afraid not, old bean."

The others made similar apologies. With each admission, Molly deflated further.

There was a silence. I felt more shamed for Molly and her failure than for wasting the Enquiry's time. Yet I recognised something theatrical about her sobs.

"Unless of course…" She raised an accusing finger. "Unless you thieving theologists have filched 'em. What's that poking out your poche, good sir?" The finger of doom fell on junior counsel. He was so taken in by her theatrics that he did a proper double take. He took the card from his top pocket with astonishment, muttering. "But, gentlemen." He leapt, quite improperly, to his feet, crying, "Gentlemen, this is my card!"

The MPs in the gallery, to general hilarity, all discovered their cards secreted about their persons. Except for Justice Fairchild himself, who look bamboozled and a little left out. "And my card, young lady?"

She eyed him, amused. "Yours, Lord Chief Justice, is in the hands of justice."

It took the judge a few moments to notice the statue above his head, a statue representing Justice herself. Her blindfold looked painfully tight, her sword blunt but heavy, and upon her scales of justice—rested his card.

After Molly's hand had been nearly shaken off by the gallery bigwigs, the judge recovered his decorum. "Which of us spotted where the trick took place?"

"Come on, gents." Molly giggled. "I told you fair and square."

The judge turned to her. "Hold on. You said at the start it was already done."

"*Exactement*, my friend. I was shaking your hands, remember, when the drunkard distracted you, allowing me to plant cards in your pockets."

"And my card, on the scales of Justice?"

"Your one," she admitted, "I had to stow in advance of proceedings."

The judge simply could not believe it. "You are telling us that the card had sat evident before us all the time, unnoticed?"

"Why would you spot it?" Molly laughed. "The mind will contrive to ignore anything, however incongruous, unless notice is drawn to it."

The judge smiled. "Misdirection."

Moll grinned. "Sir, you have garnered my exemplary meaning."

"But how this works in the perpetration of larger crimes—"

"That you must fathom for yourselves." She stepped down,

with a nudge to the usher. "Lend us a shilling, will you?"

The man looked troubled, feeling for his wallet.

She tutted. "Is our gent in argent, or a gent of three inns? That is, in debt, in danger, in poverty. Has that naughty judge filched your pennies?"

Judge Fairchild, staggered, drew the usher's wallet from his pocket.

"Misdirection, My Lord." Molly received the spontaneous cheers with aplomb. As the applause abated, she tapped her temple. "We think we know what we seen, us as sit in judgement, well-heeled and dressed in finery, all aggrieved by the little man's crimes. But you beaks in your lambskin gowns may tell whatever tale you wish, and the Fleet Street penny-a-liners worse still, while their hands are rooting around in pockets where they've no right to root. What a lot of crimes may be blamed on the wrong parties, My Lord, whilst our attentions is misdirected, by those we trust, quite the wrong way."

## THE ALCHEMICAL SAVANT

After Molly's triumph, I hurried along to the Oddbody Confab. I found Bede alone, distraught, fumbling to chalk words upon their wall. The Pixie had vanished. He feared she had run into trouble with their employers.

I felt for the wee fellow, I really did. "Who have you told of her vanishment?"

He had told everyone, as I hoped. The poor fellow had dragged himself down to the Asylum for Deaf and Dumb Females and the Royal Association in Aid of the Deaf and Dumb. No word anywhere. "I even been to the newspapers. Begged 'em to put in a Missing Persons notice, as the editors know her, you see, and people do so love to read of a helpless mute in trouble."

The plan Molly and I had cooked up involved certain gambits; played rightly, we might convert a humble pawn into a queen.

"You have done well, young man. You could not have done better. But, Bede, you two were not straight with me." I put my hand on his poor sloped shoulder. We both knew that he and the Pixie had committed the automaton thefts. "You did it for money, I understand."

"And chess," he protested. "I do enjoy a game at chess."

"Versus drunken MPs and aristocrats? Too easy."

A smile broke through his misery. "You gave me a good tussle."

"Twenty-eight moves?" I barked, which brought him to tears again. "Please God, I hope to keep you safe from danger. Have you sent word to your masters, as you promised me, that you can do such jobs no longer?"

His eyes grew round. "Problem is, our man is killed and dead. We've left a note for them, saying we are otherwise employed."

I took pity on him. No matter if he had collected blackmail material. I must share my darker fears. His puppet shows with the Pixie were artful, but she took part in another type of show, after-hours. That night at Quarterhouse was mild enough: I imagined some private displays would have less artistic integrity. As people knew her deaf and dumb, what secrets she might know.

"Dumb. Not deaf."

"She can't talk, can she?"

"Talk, no, but—Is that what people think?"

Bede explained: Pixie could communicate perfectly well. Indeed, she understood and remembered far more than you or me. Not only could she tell Bede everything in sign language, she was perfectly able to write it down, if evidence was needed.

"But too young to give evidence in court."

"She's nineteen, only short as glass of gin." His smile froze, as he remembered she was missing. "Is she all right, d'you think?"

"Come with me. Do as I ask. It's for your own safety."

A few stray Oddbodies helped me carry their Punch and Judy stall and affix it atop the Yard carriage. Bede himself I brought up to the driving seat.

"You, Bede," I announced in plain hearing, "are moving in to Scotland Yard."

We drove ostentatiously along the backstreets, where Bede was known. They catcalled as we passed: "Under arrest, Captain Cripple? What you been up to?"

Bede flushed at the attention, but his fear was evident, which was how I wanted it. I dragged him, quaking, into the Yard. Without further delay, I shoved him into the cell—where he found the Pixie awaiting him. Such a happy reunion. For they were more than friends.

I had taken the liberty of removing the Pixie from harm's way, because I felt sure she was in danger. Once the Turk's demonstrations were done, they were both expendable, but I could not understand her answers—until now. With Bede interpreting her language of signs, the Pixie told us all she could. All about the shows she had taken part in, and other activities forced upon her. She wept a little.

Bede reported her words at times falteringly, at times with anger. She was happy to confess her sins. If the court would hear her, she would testify.

I took full notes and left the statement for her to read over and sign.

My suspicions were right, only the truth was worse. Thinking that mute meant dumb too, many men had been careless in front of the Pixie: careless with their identities, careless with actions, infidelities, exploitations, and crimes. The peepholes, the midgets and the acrobats, these were things

I might have expected. I had never expected the other tales she told us: of the children's foundations she had grown up in, where their supposed protectors allowed them to be molested; of the gangs who had bought them from the foundations to be used and abused at will; of the depraved tastes of people who should know better; and of the black rumours whispered between the inmates of these institutions about friends who had vanished.

The night was black. I unlocked their cell and escorted them to a little-used detainment room, where I left the window ajar. I said goodnight at the Yard's front office, turning for a stroll down by the river. At my whistle, Pixie lifted Bede up to the window. Never was I so glad of the foul weather, for the soupy fog enveloped the wharves, and I whisked them both out without a single soul knowing. Into the borrowed boat, and across to Westminster Pier under cover of darkness.

Thence by cab to Clapham, where I was able to install them in the back room of Felix's apartments, leaving a tip with the matron for her discretion. They knew Felix, and he them. They would be able to keep his spirits up, chatting, and keep watch for me—with strict orders to avoid being seen by any visitors, for their own good and his.

## PHILOSOPHY OF SINNING (ENQUIRY II)

Mayhew:   That, sir, is a condensation of the philosophy of sinning.

Counsel:   The Enquiry thanks you for presenting your extensive researches. Mr Mayhew, advise us whether these night houses are private concerns or a conglomerate.

Mayhew:    Investors and speculators undoubtedly own many houses.

Counsel:    Can you say which?

Mayhew:    [*glances around the court*] Kate Hamilton's, Lizzy Davis's, Sam's, Sally's, the Carlton. And many more.

Counsel:    Do such houses promote unusual illegal activity?

Mayhew:    By unusual, you mean besides prostitution? Yes, sir.

Counsel:    Which activities?

Mayhew:    Oh, I can't say. Scandalous iniquities.

Counsel:    Come, Mr Mayhew, do not turn coy on us. What else do you accuse these houses of, and why do the police not act thereon?

Mayhew:    The police regulate the night houses' sale of illicit spirits. Nothing more. They cannot reprimand women who are there of their own free will, or claim to be. But the recent census of such women shows how little we know of what brings them to this pass.

Counsel:    Enlighten us.

Mayhew:    Many, I hope, will speak to this court for themselves. Some are swindled, some seduced, others bought like slaves. Some snatched as children, kept in poverty until old enough to be introduced into the life: desperate, malleable, biddable. For this degradation, who is responsible? Many assume the women themselves. I suggest blame upon the men who demand them. And those who profit by these transactions? Even in a society where capital is king and regulation a dirty word, would we not want assurances that these middle men do not engineer the whole thing for their own gain? At one end, encouraging, titillating, licensing unruly gents; at the other, enticing, coercing, enslaving women to satisfy.

Counsel:   That would be iniquitous, if it were true.

Mayhew:   It is true.

Counsel:   What evidence have you?

Mayhew:   If women wish to leave the life, are they free to? If they become ill or lose their lustre, what becomes of them? If they have a child, what becomes of it? A woman was found beneath Waterloo Bridge only the other day. Another "suicide".

Counsel:   You suggest she was not a suicide?

Mayhew:   Such claims I leave to the police, lest I be open to charges of slander.

Counsel:   Mr Mayhew, gentleman, scholar and esteemed journalist, do you know who owns these conglomerates of iniquity?

Mayhew:   I have signed depositions from many women.

Counsel:    Depositions—from such women? We shall need more solid evidence.

Mayhew:    Also from bullies, bawds and courtesans.

Counsel:    [*looks at the judge*] There is no reason to bar such evidence, I suppose.

Mayhew:    There is every reason to encourage it.

Counsel:    And from gentlemen, have you corroborating statements?

Mayhew:    [*looks at the gallery*] This is surely the forum for such declarations. Gentlemen may unburden themselves here, assured of anonymity. In return for candour, let no one fear society's censure. If we are to tackle these crimes, to eradicate them, it matters dearly how this case is reported, and who is thrown to the hounds of public obloquy. But such matters, My Lord, neither you nor I control.

## INDISCRETIONS (ENQUIRY III)

While we watched Quartern Mews, the hearings went on in our absence. My wider remit for witnesses appalled Sir Richard. He wanted the evidence confined to temperance campaigners, with a few streetwalkers and criminal bullies to add colour. I summoned many of Dugdale's subscribers, several from Groggins' list of initials, and one or two surprises.

Mayhew and friends: Lemon, the *Punch* editor, Trollope, Dickens, Carlyle. Darlington was meant to attend and fill me in on proceedings, but he was ill. Contradictory opinions were aired on why women did it, why men did it. Edward Lear, Holman Hunt, Rossetti. Skittles's duke. Collins failed to turn up, oblivious. Bertie's sporting friends. And names less known, bankers and civil servants, industrialists and inventors.

Some denied indiscretions, others admitted, many evaded. Rather than illuminating the oldest profession, the recurring refrain was of the press intruding: reporters poking in noses, claiming public interest, sensationalising what was private and making the common man think he has a right—a duty—to read about the sins of the flesh, sins of commerce, and things that go on behind closed doors.

I popped back in time to hear Sir Richard stand up for the press. It was their nose for scandal that kept politicians honest. With regard to prostitution, he pooh-poohed statistics, which made me laugh, considering I had broken my back to gather them for him; but, of course, I hadn't pruned the numbers quite as he wished.

Counsel asked the wider implications of my new census.

Payne declined to comment.

"Are you happy with the findings?"

"Happy? With the city still full of prostitutes? Hardly."

"So there are further investigations taking place?"

"Nothing outside the Yard's normal remit."

"Is it not true that accusations have been made against prominent figures who cannot yet be named until enquiries are taken further?"

"No." Sir Richard looked uncomfortable. Though understatement is not downright deceit, he was no card player. He struggled to conceal his ire. The atmosphere in the court was thick, as we all felt his duplicity. He gave me not a glance as he strode out.

"Who will watch the watchmen?" quoted Skittles's duke, in an aristocratic bellow.

* * *

What had I hoped for from Sir Richard?

I wanted the police to take notice of any crime reported, even if by a prostitute; that she had rights. That if she was harmed, we would investigate. That if a girl came to us, we would believe her until she was proven to be lying. That we would pursue criminal justice. That no judgement of their sins would deprive them of protection. That even the dispossessed would one day trust police impartiality. That those who exploit in this way be never excusable, however their status protects them. That things must change.

That could have been Sir Richard's legacy. If he would aspire to, he could end this culture of neglect. None of his own peccadillos need ever be mentioned.

Jeffcoat had anticipated these equivocations. He had Acton follow Sir Richard in giving evidence. Acton was coherent and his evidence troubling. He presented our statistics as a call for social change so cogently that the gallery sat up, half applauding and half scowling. Acton was used to it: anyone whom his testimony offended had already been offended by his books.

He raised queries about children born out of wedlock. These figures he had used to estimate prostitution. Now Jeffcoat had investigated the mismatch between children born and births registered by parish.

Such a strange shortfall should concern us all. Doubtless many grow up as an underclass, unrecognised by the state, without the stamp of officialdom. What of the rest? Hundreds of children, vanished from record. Where were they?

The court moved on to Dugdale's subscribers. I returned to our duties, watching and waiting. Pressures were exerted behind the scenes, and the newspaper reported this stretch of the hearings as shambolic. Reported? Direct reportage was banned, of course, but the rags discovered loopholes, evaluating the gallery's reactions, the impact on witnesses' families, popular rancour about the waste of government monies. What a load of tripe.

Dugdale remained on Her Majesty's Pleasure in Berkshire and could not testify; Hotten was gone to France.

One libertarian book lover and expert on the *Index of Prohibited Books* spoke at length of the importance of free thought.

The next day, Sir Antonio Panizzi declared that his job was to safeguard the nation's books, and the nation's morality could go hang; he'd be damned if he'd fled Habsburg Italy only to endure censorship on these shores; while he didn't admire the Dugdale-Hotten catalogue, he stood by their right to publish and to be read.

Darlington was to speak further of the trade in erotica. He had struggled with his conscience, whether to condemn its provocation or defend it as prophylactic. I told him to let the Enquiry decide.

He did not show up. The court adjourned temporarily while an urchin was sent, but they could not rouse him from his sick bed, and the day was lost. We returned to our observations at Quartern Mews.

Next would be Gabriel Mauve MP.


My ostentatious arrest of Bede to Scotland Yard did the trick. Two days later, Jeffcoat's cat Thom attacked two intruders in the night. One got away, but the other was thrown in the cells.

It turned out to be one of my sinister friends from my coffee house chat. Despite long questioning, he would admit nothing, not his reasons, nor his paymaster; he was more afraid of them than jail. He got a short sentence for breaking and entering; but he had been looking for Bede and Pixie, no doubt, and looking to shut them up.

## *THE BUGLE*, 10 MARCH 1864

This summer's International Festival of Chess, at which the American challenger Morphy was due to confront the masters of Europe, Anderssen, Steinitz and perhaps even our old champion Howard Staunton, has been postponed, provoking accusations on both sides.

To top off the disappointment, the "New Turk" is unexpectedly indisposed. The automaton chess marvel has caused widespread amazement in private exhibitions, provoking accusations of witchcraft, and was expected to challenge the chess champion. The device has been recalled to its makers for maintenance. Public performances are postponed indefinitely.

## MAUVE'S FALL

In the weeks before Mauve's fall from grace, the thorns of rumour had entangled him. Barred from reporting overtly on the Enquiry, the press unleashed a storm of scurrilous revelations, almost as if prepared in advance.

Mauve, so lauded as the cabinet's *enfant terrible*, endured a barrage of ridicule. His penchant for rhetorical declaration could no longer hide his blindness to detail. One by one, experts denounced him as a blustering, rabble-rousing fraud. His repute for cutting through swathes of fusty opposition dissolved into a fame for hot air and needless offence; his proposals were dismantled, along with the government's strategy for bridging our "two nations" to spread the glimmer of aspiration to those dwelling in the darkness of poverty.

The Mauves' parties dwindled, the glamour faded. The servants were dismissed amid black rumours. The grand house was shut down. He moved to the country, she to the sea. Infidelity was whispered abroad: first he, then she, then both. Divorce was imminent. The papers pawed over the legal bloodbath, awaiting the kill.

He was spotted in a disreputable night house. Not unusual for a gent, only unusual to see it reported. His cachet was evaporated. When good will deserts, no one shields you from rumour, that beast with a hundred eyes and a hundred ears. Did you hear what they did? Disgusting. Illegal! Aren't they ashamed? Degenerates. What will be next?

What was next would have given me pause, had the details come out before the hearing. Mauve's carriage was implicated in a traffic incident.

It was late at night, south of the river. A girl was knocked down, her legs broken. The driver didn't stop. The carriage was incontrovertibly identified as Mauve's. His driver was arrested and jailed for furious driving. He swore he knew nothing of the incident, nor the transpontine streets.

The papers hounded. Mrs Mauve confessed to her hairdresser. Pursued by reporters, she declared she had told the driver to go on; her train was so late, she exhausted, the streets dangerous. Why was a girl on the streets at that hour? The imputations were clear. The Mauves were innocent, victims of a hateful campaign.

The girl's family fought back. The mother had cholera; the girl was headed for the pump in the night. The mother was dead now, the girl unable to walk, her brothers and sisters helpless in the slums, if it weren't for the community spirit of the borough drawing together to protect the defenceless from the rich riding them down. Mrs Mauve's story was undermined: she was on no train that night. Why on earth was she in those backstreets at such an hour—or was she covering her illustrious husband's back?

The day before his testimony, Mauve was ousted from the cabinet for failure to make good on election promises.

The headlines concealed further scandal: a kept woman, impregnated and paid off, now found beneath Waterloo Bridge. One of the articles was bold enough to mention the woman's chequerboard tattoo.

Mauve had been thrown to the lions. The people bayed for circuses. The papers delivered. If the thumbs turned down in condemnation, what matter? His day had passed. Fresh blood, fresh scandal.

Mauve was a shadow of the man who had lorded it over the Phoenix Foundation party, dispensing wit and champagne at the side of his coveted wife. As he took the stand, the galleries were full. Justice Fairchild's injunction against journalists was all very well, but anyone might take notes on Mauve's revelations.

The questioning barrister stated that Mauve's personal travails were by the bye. In addressing the court's wider queries, he must be candid.

He went to pieces. He recounted at length the anecdote about meeting his wife in the *maison de tolérance*, inappropriate enough when told to me at Brodie's, but here, so ill judged, it provoked uproar.

Justice Fairchild called for silence.

The barrister underlined specific points: Mrs Mauve had been seeking satisfaction outside wedlock? And Mauve himself?

Yes, yes, Mauve conceded, but that was beside the point, which was that they rediscovered the joys of wedlock.

The barrister, with misgivings, delved further into the couple's unconventional practices. Their visits to Kate Hamilton's together. (Why, I wondered, was I shown that lurid peepshow?) Orgiastic revels chez Mauve, with choice girls from select establishments; choice boys were not mentioned, but corporal punishment was.

The barrister blinked. "You beat your wife?"

"And she me, sir. Consensually. What of it? Don't you?" Mauve grinned like a daring schoolboy, confessing all. He sang, to the crowd's mirth:

> *A whelp, a wife,*
> *A walnut tree:*
> *The more you bash,*
> *The better they be.*

The deeper he dug himself, the more he seemed a monster. None of us took thought of our own sins and how they would look if dragged into the public eye. Shame on us that this man had been in government; shame on us that we had fanned his egotism and lauded his nonsense.

Asked about Cora, Mauve became maudlin. He regretted her death. He was fond of her. He loved her, he declared suddenly. This was why his marriage had foundered, his growing obsession with her. He had been a fool. They could have had a life together, hidden from his wife, hidden from public view. He should have paid up; the seeds were planted, the beds prepared, ripe to flourish.

The barrister, troubled, asked him to expound.

Mauve glanced around the court wide-eyed, like a stag caught in the hunting fences. He burst into tears, exclaiming, "Why am I pursued so? My wastepaper stolen. My letters steamed open. Maids seduced. My wife systematically demoralised by these fiends from the daily rags—"

Justice Fairchild intervened.

Mauve recovered his decorum. The questioning moved on.

The traffic incident. After evasions and expressions of sympathy, Mauve at last confessed: he himself had been driving, but his wife persuaded him not to stop. She knew the ruse: people were always getting themselves "run down" in the hopes of a handout from the quality; he had heard of families that lived entirely by blackmail, the mortified culprits paying for "treatments" for years on end. Could one complain? Could one expose them? Not without rousing the ire of the penny pamphlets. Find that girl now, he declared, and you will see her legs are no more broken than yours or mine.

Noise from the gallery: "She'll be here." Applause. "You'll see."

Peeved at this outcry, Justice Fairchild demanded an end to Mauve's evasions. What had Mauve meant, with regard to Cora, by paying up?

Mauve's cheeks paled. He had said nothing of the kind.

The judge assured him that he had.

Mauve started telling of a gambling hell where a friend once failed to pay up.

Counsel asked him to return to the judge's question.

Mauve objected that he was bloody well addressing it.

Counsel declared equably that, if his memory was unclear, the record could be consulted. Mauve's objection overruled, the passage was duly read back to him.

Feigning confusion, he continued the story of the gambling hell. He began gesturing wildly, playing up to the crowd with the flamboyance of a music hall entertainer; except he had none of Molly's charm, overemphasising his comments and telegraphing his punch lines before the jokes were halfway done.

Justice Fairchild lost patience. It had been a long day. "Mr Mauve, kindly ponder the seriousness of leading this Enquiry astray. Come back in the morning with your notions reformed, sir. Proceedings adjourned."

Mauve had planned a party that night to celebrate his public exoneration. He cast it as another fundraiser for the Phoenix Foundation. He had even sent me a brusque demand for the guest list from the Quarterhouse do; I was so occupied, I failed to reply.

The fog was filthy that night. I was reluctant to attend. So was everyone else. Though nobody admitted going, rumours soon spread about young boys present, girls on the youthful side, brandy drunk from ice sculptures' appendages.

# LAST GOODBYE

*Must speak. Please. Usual corner, 10 tonight.*
*Find another house. Can you? Please. —A*

It was this note, waiting for me at the Yard, that made me skip Mauve's party. The timing could not be worse. But I could never refuse her summons.

Ridiculous, to be intimate and know no more than her first name. It had seemed prudent, and fascinating. To be swept up in the maelstrom of desire without regard for our station in life. She knew I was in the police. I knew she was a lady, from the countryside, who was in Society but not caring for it overmuch; whether she hid a husband back in the shires I did not ask—better remain ignorant. I had never thought of the man I cuckolded, until the moment of this message.

She never suggested my rooms, or anywhere else we might be known. She lived out of town, in Surrey or Suffolk or one of those shires that sound all the same to a Scot. We spoke little of our feelings; when one of us blew cold, the other showed their love more keenly, and the thing came right about. As the man about town, I was expected to know places; I did know bawdy houses, of course, a thousand of them, but few I would take her to.

I stopped by Kate Hamilton's. She was to speak near the end of the Enquiry, on the same day as I. "I trust you'll show your face, Kate."

"Wouldn't miss it, my lover. A chance to show off to the quality."

"A chance to defend your girls," I said, "and their rights."

"And their wrongs." She licked her lips. "I'll do my duty, Watchman. You look like you have a thirst. Girls, moisten our pet Scotsman's chaffer."

As Kate could see my disquiet, I swallowed my pride: I asked, in an undertone, for a discreet place to meet. I feared she would broadcast my request in her usual cackle; she was kind enough not to.

"Usual haunts under observation, eh?" With an appraising look, she murmured an address I knew on a street nearby. "I'll send word to prepare a room fit for a king, my lover, and his queen."

As I waited at Seven Dials, I gazed at her note as if it had fallen from the heavens. We had never needed to write to each other, not since that first note.

She kept me waiting, just a little. "I shouldn't have come," she sighed.

"I shouldn't have asked you."

"I asked you, you fool."

On the short cab ride, we fell silent. En route, I spied, within the walls of a foundation not unlike Felix's, the fallen women bent over in the yard, washing clothes.

Alexandra followed my gaze. "Tempted?"

I made a face. Though, if anyone were looking in at us, they might read a dark history into it.

Denmark Street was not the salubrious haven I had hoped for. I tapped at the door of Adelphi House, my nerves rising. The door opened discreetly; the madam gave a nod. The hall was dank. Below stairs, though, was a heavenly bedroom: fresh sheets, flowers, bonbons on the pillows.

"I surmise," Alexandra breathed, "that you know that landlady."

"Yes, but through my work, not hers."

She fell silent. Lush hair. I wanted to touch it. It was as well not to return to Titchfield Street, but I did not ask why. Perhaps we had been recognised. I did not ask. I still knew nothing about her, and she little of me.

On the wall, that same print: the striving lady, the lounging fellow, torment and exaltation. Alexandra stood beside me, eyes shining. "I saw this painting exhibited ten years ago. *The Awakening Conscience.* I thought it dreamy. Lace hearts round her petticoats, rich shawl at her hips, determination on her face, and that hair. I was young and innocent."

I gazed at her, more beautiful than any painting. "Like her?"

"Don't you see? The girl is seduced; only now she repents." She put her hand to her mouth, smiling, but tears were close behind. "We must end it."

This was not our usual routine. "You've tired of me."

"Never." She was not making the usual replies. "This must be our last goodbye."

"It always is." It was not our first attempt to end it. Not our tenth.

"All this. It doesn't become you. You—" She looked at me. Her rehearsed speech faltered.

"What's wrong? Are you ill?"

"Tired. Perhaps I've caught a chill."

She reached out; I grasped her hand. I could make no sense of it, but she was in earnest. Voices sounded from the street, boots on rain-soaked pavements. I swept the ringlet from her face, trailing my finger over her cheek, lingering over her lips. We were lost. There at the dresser, knowing it was the last time, every touch was filled with aching; through the bliss, a pain in my gut reminded me I was striving to ignore the impending gloom.

"This doesn't become you." She tried again. "You're young. You should find somebody—a wife—and grow up… grow old together. We must end it. Further, and we can only hurt each other. I… I've found something out. I can't tell you. I wouldn't have come at all," she whispered, "only—stupid excuse—I have realised something. About Felix."

I was angry with her. I should have listened; I had spent so long puzzling at Felix's story, but I had not the patience for it on such a night, after such a week.

She was eager to tell me about Felix, things she recalled from his memoir, about his family. "His heart was broken, Campbell. His wife killed and his child, his daughter, gone missing in the Italian revolutions. That scarred him, you see. Poor stoical heart. No wonder he became unbalanced. Monomaniacal."

"Alexandra—"

She wanted to explain: how she saw sense in his starting the Phoenix Foundation. "His interest in fallen women was not entirely— No, I don't mean that. Can't you see? The thing is, Felix's upbringing. His mother a courtesan; like a slave. And he saw it all. While his father—not his own father—had no time for him. Then the military orchestra—no place for a boy. And now his stroke."

I could bear her indifference no longer, talking of such things that stood so far from our entire story. Stupid excuse, indeed. I barely heeded her words.

I took her in my arms; I silenced her with a kiss and I walked out, leaving her upon that bed, beneath that print, with the bonbons untouched on the pillows.

## TRANSPONTINE DELIVERIES

The next day, a girl hobbled into the gallery on crutches. Mauve's traffic incident come to haunt him. I looked closer, but whether she was the backstreet girl who I had "run over" I could not tell. She drew back beneath the protection of her forbidding protectors, her soi-disant family.

Mauve never appeared. When they found his body, later that day, it was kept secret; but Justice Fairchild adjourned the hearing for a week. We had to use these precious days to resolve our search. We had to find them.

Time was running short. On Quartern Lane, nobody had spied the girl, neither Jeffcoat nor Molly's cohort. How could I allay Felix's anxiety? A dreadful unease haunted my nights: the tapestry of sin remained obscure, and if my testimony was to hold, I must discern the threads that bound it together.

I was for strolling into the Mews and questioning the landlady: where had the girl gone? What of Felix? What of their relations? Jeffcoat restrained me. Felix's girl had vanished and No. 17 fallen silent, but girls came and went in the adjoining houses. There was every chance they fell under the same organisation. Something must out.

We redoubled our watch. Even before the adjournment for Mauve, we decided we must watch all hours, even if it meant missing more of the questioning.

Jeffcoat appeared, triumph on his face.

Quartern Mews did receive daily deliveries after all, but everything arrived before daybreak: sumptuous flowers, sweetmeats, bread, fine wines. Jeffcoat had sent urchins to follow each of the carts on their rounds of the West End, but in the dreadful fog their little legs got them no further than the bridges, as every single cart headed south of the river. Most likely everything was delivered from one place.

Jeffcoat was itching to follow himself, but to go alone was folly. He might give the game away or be despatched into the river. It must be done aright.

I joined him at Quartern Lane long before dawn. It was Saturday, and the Enquiry would not convene. We wore workman's clothes, our carriage stationed close by.

We watched the deliveries: milk, bacon, newspapers, firewood to every house in Quartern Mews. It was not until the laundry van delivered its fresh white sheets that Jeffcoat nudged me into action. The other carts went on to do the rounds of Mayfair, Kensington and Belgravia. But this, our urchins reckoned, was the laundry cart's final stop before heading back.

We headed south of the river. It was a gloomy March morning, the freezing air making it difficult to talk. The rising fog swept the bridges bare, obscuring the tilted moon. I'd never seen London so deserted. I wished it otherwise, for I feared calamity. So many months seeking; finally, we were making sense of this dense pattern. How I longed to believe Kate and her girls came to the trade willingly and thrived in it; how easy this job would be then, and the world brighter, and London equitable and just. But the world is not equitable, and our task looked darker by the hour.

The laundry cart rattled across Southwark Bridge, and we were obliged to hang back. The lamps south of the river were so poor, we could not be sure where it turned. Jeffcoat was steering the horses between the old vinegar works and Barclay & Perkins Brewery when I spotted the cart, veering into the riverside alleys.

We turned abruptly. The place must be near, else London Bridge would have been the easier route. A square, full of wind and dust; thin trees lashed against the railings, as we stopped, listening for the cartwheels' telltale rattle. On, quietly on, past a dishevelled doorway, and quite unexpectedly I clutched at Jeffcoat's arm.

I confessed it all in a breathless whisper: how I had run down the girl, right here in this spot. He understood at once. Any poor mother would bawl if their child was run over, holler for compensation; that was the spirit of the age. Why let me go? They must have things afoot they did not wish police to know of: the two girls, the room of grey-faced seamstresses. Within these buildings lurked something ill.

Jeffcoat jumped down and ran ahead. I rounded the block circumspectly.

He intercepted me, breathless, and ushered me to a nook, behind the brewery, where we might station the carriage. "It's there. This is it. These warehouses backing onto the river."

We looked at each other in utter silence. What we had found looked like an old laundry or a forgotten clothier's. But we both sensed it: this was the loose thread we had been searching for. We must bide our time. With the Enquiry adjourned, we could be patient. Pull at the thread too soon, too sudden, and the tapestry would unravel before we discerned the pattern.

Many girls had hinted of a place, a kind of nursery where they were taken to be broken in. None could tell us where it was; none seemed to know exactly, for they were taken there drugged, in darkened carriages. A scheme so bold no one would credit it. Right here, in the heart of London, two steps from London Bridge and Borough market—could this be their academy of sin?

And Acton's figures: the unmarried mothers and childbirths registered, those discrepancies must be explained somewhere.

We must not be spotted. Jeffcoat sketched out the entrances he had spotted on his circuit of the building. I would keep first watch, while he returned to the Yard for clothes and provisions.

An hour's watch was revealing. I saw blankets and towels brought in, bedding, lamps, divans, an ottoman, and fine furnishings, pots, pans, privies, bedpans, headboards. This parade I watched with awed reverence, imagining an army of cooks, haberdashers and laundresses at work. And this turned out to be the side entrance.

We must take our time and get the whole picture. With day about to break, the streets were busier, and I feared I was conspicuous. Jeffcoat returned on foot, bringing disguises,

namely hats, capes, glasses, whiskers, fishing rods, newspapers
and toolboxes that would allow us to take up positions around
the building without obvious loitering.

Having inspected all corners of the building, Jeffcoat took to
strolling around the quayside in docker's garb. I preferred the
sausage-seller's, where I overheard local tales. Though we sent
for Darlington, he remained absent. Just as well; he might
have sold us out to the papers. We told no one else, though we
discussed which officers we could trust, whom neither bribe
nor threat would sway.

Molly's best spies stood guard for us on the bridges, a
thankless posting in those changeable morning fogs, though
the days were finally growing warmer. When we wanted a
carriage followed, Jeffcoat sent one of Molly's lot after them;
with London's pollution and traffic, a sure-footed youth can
chase down the most reckless driver.

We identified more threads than imagined:

– that various ladies came and went in costume, as if
rehearsing plays;
– that most met gentlemen at the opera and the theatre,
then returned;
– that a few were transferred to residences in Kensington
Gore and Quartern Mews;
– that a very few gentlemen visited the premises, with
briefcases and an academic gait; they spent the morning
within, and left without any voluptuous air;
– that ageing spinsters attended to household purchases;
– that these same accompanied the ladies on their
outings;
– that every few days, a number of younger girls arrived
at the place, ragged and dirty, and were never seen to
leave;

– that from one shabby doorway, on the back alley of my incident, small packages were every so often despatched, wrapped in old rags;

– that dressmakers made frequent deliveries.

I followed one as he left; his pockets full, he stopped in at The Pig and Whistle on the corner of Borough High Street.

"Oh, there are some right ones," said he, "in the new batch."

It was the easiest thing to stand at the bar and listen in.

"You want to make a selection, young Henry," said the bartender.

"I wouldn't dream of it," he replied. "Destined for greater than me."

I refrained from imprudent queries, lest I give the game away.

These comings and goings were highly regulated. Never was a door opened without lists crosschecked and names confirmed. We should not be able to stroll up and visit. There was nothing untoward about the house, not a trace of malfeasance. Nobody in the environs would comment on it; only we, knowing whither their products were destined, sniffed illegitimacy. Good Lord, even the people working there might believe it was a finishing school for ladies, or a kind of hotel.

Every couple of days, three men in dark suits paid a visit. Their timing was unpredictable, yet they were greeted with distinct servility. In the brief moments I saw them, I recognised one of the sinister heavies who had "made me an offer" to vanish away and forget these investigations.

A distressed woman arrived. Her clothes were fine but disarrayed, for she was heavily pregnant. She was received at the door after some altercation between the driver and the spinster on duty, whom she knew. Her weeping hushed, she was sent inside, with a harsh word to the driver. An hour later, a muffled cry. The mother left not long after, evidently delivered of her child.

A second unexpected call was paid by a more impressive chaise. This driver was altogether more welcomed. After a short visit, the spinster herself came out, with a bundle of swaddling, to accompany the driver. Jeffcoat was particularly impressed with Molly's boy for following the carriage all the way to a Wapping orphanage, known for a quick trade in unwanted infants.

This inspired us to ask him to track those other packages from the shabby back door. These went in a cart up to Ice Wharf, and a house on the Caledonian Road, beside the Regent's Canal.

How to see inside without being discovered? We could not stop by, could not break in. A feigned inspection could end the game in stalemate. Sir Richard would not condone force. I began to feel the whole neighbourhood was in the pay of the place to keep silent.

I took Molly along to Mrs Boulton's, as storms brooded upriver. How wonderfully changed Steph was, quite liberated from her former trade; surely she might confirm my suspicions.

"There are things you cannot ask me about." She knew the place; she had been there, I could feel it. She gave us tea and went about her work with downcast eyes, steadfastly refusing to say more.

"All right, I must find out myself, and I will." I was frustrated. "There is this establishment. I don't expect you to say more. Only help me think: how can I learn for myself what goes on there? Give me some sign, damn you."

A rumble of thunder near at hand. The wind gusted down the chimney, and the ashes were scattered from the grate. Mrs Boulton, smiling, swept them deliberately into the pan, without a word.

Molly looked at me with a grin.

# INTO THE DARK

"Tuppenny ha'penny per chimney," said Molly, one hand belligerently on her hip, the other brandishing the broom. "Extra for disposal of ashes."

The dried old spinster stood at the door, arms folded. Behind her, a plaque inscribed: BLUMENGARTEN SCHOOL FOR LADIES. She eyed me warily, as if I were an idiot boy to be working up chimneys at my age.

Molly patted my back. "Don't go maligning my boy. May as he be silent, and may as he be dumb, but he's a top hand at slanting up a flue. Little ones is banned, mind. You'd have the law down on you if I brung one in, don't you know? My boy here'll buff it if he has to. There's many a littler one got stuck up a chimney, smothered for want of air and the fright. Many a one of 'em as lost their lives that way, but not he."

They admitted us just as the rain set in. I was astonished they let us in at all. But every house stands always in need of a sweeping; sweeps come and go, as good as invisible, and nobody pays them a thought.

Our story, that we were sent as proxy for their customary sweeps, they took on trust. Thus we got to view every room in the place, unattended, unrestricted. Fortuitous timing: during the fogs, all the fires had been lit; now with this freshening rain, everyone longed to throw open the windows and sweep away the long winter.

I fretted, if we were caught, what would become of us. There must be guard dogs to protect these tender saplings from harm.

Molly set my mind at ease. There could be no bulldogs, no protection ring. That would give the game away. Misdirection, remember? How swiftly a bawd house reverts to propriety, to the astonishment of intemperate young men. We had seen no sign of solicitation this side of the river; unlikely we should see anything within that was actually illegal.

"Settle your nerves, Watchman," said Molly. "A touch of play-acting is surely within even your capacities."

With my face blacked and an hour's coaching in assemblage of brushes, Molly and I got to work. I was covered in filth, forbidden to speak, and more than once thought I was jammed in a flue. But Molly was equal to it, chatting to whomsoever she could, giving me plenty of time to stick my nose in every corner, excusing my improprietous stares on the grounds of my imbecility.

Opulence. All around we saw luxury: velvet curtains; tables set with silver hardly used, like the set of a play; dining rooms, parlours and, at the heart of the warehouse, a great ballroom.

Voices recited behind a door. Molly knocked. The stern ma'am shooed us to the fireplace in the corner. She returned to exemplifying phrases to a roomful of guttersnipes from every corner of the kingdom, who squeezed their inflexible tonsils around her genteel vowels.

We walked through sewing class and singing lesson, table manners and quadrilles. Girls of all types and every shape, slouched and slovenly to elegant and elevated, gradated class by class. Some timid, others brimming with effrontery; some pert and artful, others cowering and sly.

I gazed at the coarse novices and the flowerlike sirens; even Molly stopped to watch the crème de la crème enter the ballroom, heads elegantly poised. Long eyelashes hinted at demure flirtation and suggestive submission. This was a studied poise I had seen somewhere before: Felix's lady, as she walked up Quartern Mews.

A school for courtesans, in the French style, or like the geishas. Rumours of such an academy of strumpetry had been aired before at the Yard. Skittles and Steph had hinted more; and every so often, a fallen woman let slip mention of her days at this nursery, brought south of the river for ruination, then trained into the life.

The nursery was not quite unguarded. A pair of complacent bullies squabbled over dice in the hallway. They must be on call for the whole establishment, but the place ran so much like clockwork, they were never needed. We were lucky. When the sinister trio turned up, it was the bullies' negligence that saved us.

As we trooped through from the teaching area to the sleeping quarters, the men were waiting for us in their dark suits. It was the inspection, and the men in suits carried it out with sinister pleasure. My heart raced. Though caked in coal dust, I was convinced I might be recognised. I remembered their threat of a "proper warning", like my friend Felix; and look how they had left him.

The bullies' dice-playing irked them, thank God, and while they were told off, we scurried off to the dormitories.

To one side bunkhouses, to the other sumptuous bedrooms.

At one door, we heard noises. Bedroom lessons?

A maid spotted us just in time. "I wouldn't go sweeping in there." A smile cracked her dry features. "Sweeping of their own going on."

Molly was so droll and full of stories, she could get anyone to talk. How did she do it? In the next room, a maid was making the bed: plumped pillows, hospital corners, perfectly effected. Molly stood behind her, making flirtatious comments, while pointing me to my work, as if I was her drudge. Salutary to be ordered around: I had a taste of what it was like for our constables at the Yard. I swallowed my anger, for it was an unparalleled disguise, and regretted my daily arrogances.

This maid liked the place well enough, though she envied her betters.

A second was unhappy with her lot. "We are all prisoners," she whispered, "and the pretty ones worse off than me."

We returned to the dining hall in time for their high tea.

What a palaver, like a banquet in the Great Hall of King's College. Row upon row of women, ladies, girls, served by menials in hessian gowns, primly feasting on a meal that would have been extravagant at the Grosvenor Hotel.

From the flue, I heard only patches of the ceremony, prizes doled out and punishments; but Molly took in every detail.

One menial was promoted to servant-orderly, one servant to lady aspirant, entitling her to fine clothes and elocution. One lady aspirant, her training complete, was to be delivered to her guardian on the morrow.

"To be his dead wife," whispered the maid stood beside us.

"How does that work, then?" Molly asked her, bright as brass.

"Wife died; he wishes she hadn't," the girl answered unabashed. "He buys a new one."

Molly nodded. "A pretty service."

We were hushed into silence by the other maids.

Next came a certain Florence, returned in shame. She was beaten on the soles of her feet, to make an example of her failure. Trying vainly to smile, she accepted her sentence, consigned to menial duties. Finally, an elfin girl, not even accorded the dignity of a name, was to be taken off to Lansdowne Gardens.

"Extracurriculars," whispered the naughty girl. "With the dustman."

"Need I remind you," said the spinster, brow black as the clouds outside, "that we allow no solicitation, not here, not nearby, not until you are far across the river? This shall be punctiliously obeyed, or punished."

I expected the anonymous miscreant would be struck or shamed. But this banishment was shame enough. Nobody so much as looked at her as she walked out of the room and into the hands of Brodie's men.

One final fireplace remained. Secluded behind classrooms

and dormitories, one final exquisite apartment, the four-poster bed pristine and sumptuous, where I could not help imagining girls being delivered, pale and torpid, as if to be sacrificed to a monstrous mythic deity.

O Flowers of Sin, I little thought to find you here, in the dingy backstreets of the Borough, in a rain-soaked warehouse behind the grimy wharves. Just another investment, prolific and luxuriant, but an investment nonetheless. The nursery where seeds of beauty are sown and shoots nurtured, then their blossoms plucked and delivered across the city, lighting up the night-time city with vivacity and colour.

Brushes packed and minds awhirl, we made our way back to the door. The sooner I could tell Jeffcoat, the sooner we could unravel the threads and trace them back to the spindle.

"Slow enough, aren't you?" The spinster had a disdainful manner, but impeccable vowels. "Aren't you to do next door, then? Don't touch, filthy fingers."

Molly slapped my hand away from the door handle. "Where's that, then?"

"Didn't they tell you? Ooh, they can keep a secret, those ones." The spinster pointed slyly down the street. "Shimmy up them irons on the corner, if you like."

We peered out into the deluge. The antique stairwell looked as if it might rust away any second; at the thought of the precipitous rooftops, my breath ran short.

"In this weather?" Molly shook her head. "Enough of your larks, Mrs Snooks. We'll take the low road, thank you very much."

It is hard to write of what we saw next door. The spinster led us through a tunnel and two locked doors. It did not take long to clean the flues; there were only two fireplaces in this whole draughty dungeon.

First, the room of seamstresses I had glimpsed all those weeks ago. Beside it, a great kitchen of cooks dully chopping firewood for the ovens and vegetables for the pot. The laundry, industrious and perfumed. Next, a workshop. Some women bent over intricate jewellery. Some filling bottles, mixing perfumes and tinctures by the dim light; others copying letters.

Next, hoary draggletails repaired furnishings, boxes and lamps. They were not locked in, but I knew them to be slaves, the cast-offs of the flash life, devoid of hope, devoid of light. If they were able to speak, they did not dare; it had been beaten out of them. There were seats by the doors, where perhaps bullies once sat to cajole and threaten, but the bullies were long forgotten, the workforce trained into acquiescence.

No comfy bedrooms, like the main house; here, damp mattresses were rolled against the walls, piled into closets and storerooms, where stained blankets hinted of diseases that had run their full course on that threadbare matting.

Some women were of foreign extraction: Negresses and gypsies, Hindus and Arabs. Others were so plain or so bent with toil, I could see why they had been expelled from the palace next door.

Molly and I completed our work in silence. We passed back through the seamstresses and rang at the bell, as we had been shown, to ask for payment. At the hatch of the front office the ivory-faced dragon appeared, her eyes round as the moon. I shrank back, lest she recognise me. There was no sign of the girl I had run over, nor her scowling sister; perhaps they had been promoted to the main house, or run over in earnest, or sold.

The old dragon was so elevated on laudanum—the only way to survive that deathly place—she was more likely to think I was the Queen of Sheba. Molly nudged me into the office, delaying her with chatter, as she counted out our money, befuddled.

On the table lay a book of accounts. Even in my panic, I recognised the system at once, from the intricate ledger at the Phoenix Foundation. Each line of dense laborious writing bore a date, woman's name (or two names), an address, two sums in pounds, shillings and pence, and finally a man's name. Some entries were asterisked, some were scratched out. It took moments to flick back through the months. There I found it, at the year's end, just a few weeks after the Foundation party at Quarterhouse:

30 December '63
£5 & £5     Eveline/Angelina
                5 Mill Lane, Wildernsea, N. Yorks.
£1,000      Felix Sonnabend

## RIVER OF MUTE CRIMES

It was nearing the end of our days of grace. In a few days, I must deliver my statement to the Enquiry. I hoped we could explain these discoveries; I hoped that our testimony, with Kate Hamilton's and the rest, would point an incontrovertible finger. I had discovered the secret I had so long guessed at. Now Jeffcoat sniffed a conclusion to his researches.

Molly's boy led him to the house on Caledonian Road where he had seen the packages from the shabby back door of the warehouse deposited. Jeffcoat spent the day in whiskers and oilskins, fishing from the steps, keeping one eye on the house and one on the road. He stared into the canal, reflecting on our discoveries, as the rain churned up the filthy water.

Sure enough, come evening, the cart drove up again. Our old spinster Mrs Snooks dragged the packages into the house. The donkey watched reproachfully from the cart. Soon after dark, she emerged empty-handed. The tenant stepped out on his back porch, which overhung the towpath. The moon was low; the drizzle drummed on the waters.

Jeffcoat had stowed away his rod around dark, wrapping himself under the steps in the gloom, like a vagrant.

The man, thinking nobody was around, brought out the first package. He tested its weight in his arms, and hefted it into the canal. It bobbed for a moment, then sank from view. He stood, smoking a pipe.

Jeffcoat could do nothing without being seen. He was intrigued. But to enter those waters was a recipe for death.

Why bring a package so far to throw it away? A hidden exchange, too risky to keep at the warehouse? An illicit side deal, concealed from Brodie's men: liquor, jewels or spices? Payne was away, but the Yard's diver drank nearby. A grizzled old navvy, who used to dive for the navy, he was always trawling the Serpentine, the Hampstead Ponds, and the Thames; it was he who had dragged Cora from the waters beneath Waterloo Bridge. We found him in the King's Street Tavern and promised him drink if he'd come in the morning.

We rose early that morning; the fewer who spied such work, the better. I stood guard on the towpath, Jeffcoat by the house, for the tenant would bolt if he suspected their cache discovered. The diver lowered himself into the water on the far side of the bridge.

The March mizzle concealed us. Every hue of light passed over me as I waited by the dark waters, one moment black as night, then like a bonfire, until the haggard daylight struggled through. With the lamps flickering against this mournful sky, it seemed a landscape from a nightmare.

My thoughts were sunken with the diver. I would have been in terror beneath those waters. Guilt stabbed at me: of what I had seen in the warehouse; of the accusations I would make in court; hoping I was more honest than those I condemned; wondering if I truly was.

The diver surfaced with a muffled cry. He hefted a bundle out by my feet, and pulled off his helmet. He gazed at me, eyes hooded. He must go down again, for there were two dozen more bundles the same, some fresh as this, some rotted by the years.

I nodded, uncomprehending. As he dived again, I undid the old rags and unravelled the bundle at my feet. I cried out, forgetting the man we must arrest. My heart thumped in my chest, and I heard a rushing: not traffic, not the wind, just every sound amplified clear in my head. I gazed into the mists wreathing the Caledonian Road as it struck northward; I longed to follow it, all the way, home to the haven of my childhood, where such things never happened.

Jeffcoat came to find out why I had called out. I looked up at him. He saw what lay at my feet.

# WILDERNSEA

The rain thrummed on the vaulted roof of King's Cross. The express awaited, snorting and puffing, a great iron horse—the same that had delivered me to London five years ago. I would take the train north, not knowing what I sought. I must pursue the one thread joining Felix and the Flowers of Sin, leaving Jeffcoat to map out the finishing end.

I bypassed the tranquillity of first and second class, and threw myself into the menagerie of third: dubious dandies, with cravat pins and greased hair; military penitents with muskets that scared ragged old women; a Scotch corporal pretending to read *Powder and Piety*, but inside the dust jacket *Maria Monk*; and all of us northward bound at a penny a mile.

Mrs Agnes McGarrigan was not surprised to receive a visitor, though the telegram I had sent arrived half an hour after I did. A simple soul, she did not leave the range during my visit. I asked to speak with her daughter.

Her face grew troubled. "Which?"

I smiled. "Are there so many?"

"Ten." Her eyelids fluttered. "Or thereabouts."

Angelina evoked no response; Eveline elicited a twitch of recognition, then denial. "You had better speak to Susan, my eldest," she said.

She gave me tea and bread spread thick with butter, speaking all the while of her family. Her husband was a good man, a failed farmer, who ran a ragged school in Whitby. Their numerous daughters worked about the house and the village, and there were sons too, but they were lazy. I could gather no more.

I saw around the room scanty evidence of endeavour: a basket, a cushion unstuffed, a napkin of embroidered tulle. I was thinking to depart, disappointed, when a buxom lass breezed in, soaking wet.

She deposited milk, onions and my telegram upon the table and stared brazenly. "Who do you think you are, then?"

Her mother reprimanded her, timidly. "Susan."

"I'm looking for someone," I explained. "Your sister, perhaps."

Susan's tongue flickered along her lip. "Which?"

"Eveline?"

Her scowl vanished. She shot a glance at her mother, then tugged me through to the saddle room, where she sat me on a rude bench. "Is it Effie, then?" She leaned conspiratorially close, with unexpected bonhomie. "Bin expecting next instalment. I heard as they'd changed her name, though."

"Angelina." I blinked. "That would be Angelina."

"Bloody southerners. Eh? Eh!" She hooted with laughter and stirred up the fire. "Still, done you proud, I'll wager, en't she?"

I took out my wallet and set it on the bench. "Susan, if I may call you that, what payment you are expecting, I don't know. Let us say, there has been a change within the organisation. I will pay you something, if you confirm a few details for me."

Her grumpy expression returned. She plumped down on a joint stool and began removing her sodden garments, hanging them up one by one, until she was in a blouse and bloomers. She then lambasted me with an outburst of profanity that would have shocked the navvies down Gray's Inn Road.

I interrupted. I explained that I was a policeman. That shut her up. "I hope to safeguard your sister's well-being. But I'll need help."

"What's happed her, then? It en't our fault. It's them blimmin'—" She caught herself. Blinking away her suspicions, she glanced at the wallet. The coins clinked, and out came the story. It was a catalogue of woes, but Susan told it as if it were bearable, even amusing, and I pitied her.

They lived on Wildernsea's smallest farm and least fruitful. Their mother was a cook, their father absent most of the year, and as to why he spent so much time in Whitby, her story was less academic and more amorous. For his children, he cared nothing.

Wildernsea was long troubled; nobody talked of it, but girls had always gone missing. Of course, that's what every girl wanted: to leave. Men would pass through, paying for their board on the way to Whitby; her mother never minded.

As the sisters reached womanhood, the men paid them more attention than their mother. She, Susan, busied herself with the farm; but Sookie was a beauty and Sarah a tease. One of those who passed through returned from Whitby with a contract, signed by her father, declaring that Sookie was to go into service in London. She would be paid and fed. What's more, she would join a household influential in the nation's affairs. He brought her a bonnet and fine boots, and off she went, proud as Punch.

As the daughters disappeared, how could they not rejoice? Their father was pleased with them. He brought presents at harvest. He told them what joy they brought him, needing no dowry.

"How much did Effie bring you?"

"I wouldn't like to say." She couldn't resist: playing coy was not her suit, nor swindling. "But five guineas would make it a round twenty."

I laughed and took out my wallet. "This man. Describe him."

"Grey hair. Talked peculiar." She shrugged. "Rich."

I thanked Susan for her tale, gave her a pound and said I must leave.

She scowled. "You've missed the branch line service. Sunday, in't it? No express until tomorrow." She said they would make me comfortable. I gave in.

Her mother called us to the dinner table. Besides her, and Susan, aged twenty or so, there were four little girls, and Shirley, twelve, a pretty wee thing with dark eyes and heart-shaped face, who gave me her most winsome smile.

"You need only ring, sir. Remember. Whatever you should want." Shirley's smile seemed familiar. "You need only ring."

I took dinner alone in my room and retired early.

Did I imagine the scrabbling on my door in the night? It was a struggle to sleep. The long waves rolled in on the shore and into my dreams.

I rose before dawn and left, my cape useless against the disconsolate northern rain. Dozing fitfully on the train, I understood why little Shirley's smile was familiar: she was the image of her sister, Effie, the girl in Felix's daguerreotype.

Third class was mercifully quiet. I sat thinking of Felix. Wondering about what Alexandra had told me. The family he had lost. It all wove together in my imagination. No wonder his broken mind was so filled with self-reproach. Had he paid over such a fortune? A thousand pounds, filched, most like, from his Phoenix Foundation; I thought of the cheques I had dropped into Coutts & Co. Had that thousand paid for this Effie, though her family received but ten? What had she to do with these losses of his? Even if I found this mysterious Eveline, this homely Effie, this ineffable Angelina, there were a thousand girls in the same trouble who were never rescued, never remembered.

I tumbled gratefully into sleep. I dreamed of the Wildernsea house, threatened by the rising of the sea. From the boisterous waves, gathered to crush it, a mermaid's starry face emerged, with the Pixie's features. The spume of sea bubbles danced around her. Mighty as a titan, she uprooted the house and pulled it out into the waves. Her troublesome sisters danced out onto the roof, which turned into the monotonous rocks, and called passing sailors to their doom. Each arm in arm with a gentleman, the sisters lined up in silk gowns, each the same smile, dragging us all ever further from that northern shore, the coast vanishing behind us.

I did not arise from this distracted slumber until the guard woke me at King's Cross. At last I reached the Yard, damp, and dumb with exhaustion. I looked about, fearful to go forward. I had hoped, by understanding Eveline's story, I might understand them all. I must try Quartern Mews one last time. First I would check up on Felix. Then we must swoop upon the Flowers of Sin.

# PART V
## FINAL FLOURISH
### MID MARCH 1864

The devil jerks us back, tweaking our strings.
Repugnant objects hold us in their spell;
Each day we take a step closer to hell,
Without disgust, across the shades that stink.

Charles Baudelaire, *Les Fleurs du Mal* Traffic in
Foreign Women

One of the most disgraceful, horrible and revolting
practices carried on by Europeans is the importation of
girls into England from foreign countries to swell the
ranks of prostitution.

Henry Mayhew,
*London Labour and the London Poor*

## COMPLAINTS TO *THE TIMES* RE: GENTLEMEN'S ATTENTIONS

Recently moved to London, I allowed my daughter to go shopping with a female relative. In Oxford Street, a blackguard kept walking behind and had the audacity to make observations, until the ladies took shelter in a stationer's shop. What an outrage that innocent girls cannot walk unaccompanied without being bothered by the stares and comments of scoundrels masquerading as gentlemen.

"A Northern father"

I have often walked alone in the city and never received any incivility. Perhaps provincial girls invite attention by their hats, dress and demeanour. If they adopted more modest dress and behaviour, they might escape the idlers' attentions.

"Urban lady"

Walking between my pupils' residences, I am so often bothered by middle-aged and older men that I endeavour only to go before 10.30am, which I recommend as free from unwanted harassments.

"M, a teacher and female"

The ladies in my aforementioned letter were dressed in mourning, in sympathy with our bereft Queen; and what is decency worth if a girl's country upbringing is to be blamed for an idler's advances?

"A Northern father"

There is no city in the world safer than London, with its police and attentive shopkeepers, for unaccompanied women. Every father is certain his own daughters are perfectly demure. That Blanche ever looked kindly at a strange chap who was struck with her appearance, he cannot believe; still less that Isobel showed more than her neat ankle, on purpose, to a young officer as she crossed the street. It never occurs to the father that these kiss-me-quick bonnets, loud stockings, capers, crinolines and ringlets straying over the shoulder say, "Follow me, lads." Many harmless adventures occur to such dear girls during their walks, of which they say nothing when they return home; but Blanche and Isobel are not displeased to be noticed.

"Common Sense"

Ladies, the remedy lies in your hands. Dress dowdy. Put on poke bonnets, stinted skirts and dreary grey underclothes. Saunter ye not overmuch nor look about too boldly, and ye shall be safe from my amorous glance.

"Beau"

## MAUVE FOUND

I was returning from the north when the scandal about Mauve broke. It was revealed that they had found him immolated in his bed, as if Dugdale-Hotten had illustrated a scene from *The Decline and Fall of the Roman Empire*. The week of adjournment was barely enough to let the furore die down. The newspapers enjoyed a gold rush as they pussyfooted around the portrayal, never quite describing what everyone soon knew: how he was found, *sans culottes*, handcuffed against that fold-down bed in his secret cabinet, eyes bulging out of his head, satin kimono round his neck and Seville orange in his mouth.

In death, they defamed him. I recalled what everyone seemed to forget, that he was toast of the town but six months ago, and Brodie's bosom chum. Molly's point entirely: make enough fuss of others' crimes, and nobody notices your own.

How Mauve became the villain of our times, I never understood. We all reviled him. Papers reviled him. People reviled him. Politicians spat bile upon him. How on earth was he allowed to get away with it so long? Alas, he should have been exposed quicker, had the newspapers' acumen not been blunted by the *Bugle* scandal. Oh, let them quiz servants, seduce maids, decode blotting paper, if they save us from such monsters.

The police were full of bluster, their theories void of sense. They were perhaps colluding, perhaps orchestrating this devilry. If only we'd trusted our newsmen. It was their job to scrutinise. If Brodie's fingers hadn't been rapped, he would have exposed the fiend.

Everyone forgot the days when Mauve was the toast of the town. All changed now. As each new scandal came out—prostitution, coercion, trafficking, slavery—the public imagination laid them all at Mauve's door (whereupon others, as guilty, sighed with relief). Gabriel Mauve was lucky to have died before we lynched him.

## ONE GOLDEN AFTERNOON

Arriving at The Clapham Hospital for Incurables, I found Felix asleep and alone. I called out for Bede and the Pixie. Nothing.

I sat down, fretting for the Oddbodies' safety. They leapt out, laughing, from the Punch and Judy stall; hard to credit, but the contraption served them as bunk bed.

"We weren't certain it was you, old man," Bede said. "By the way, our friend is learning to talk again."

When Felix woke, sitting upright in a panic, he stared at me in anxiety. Then the ward mistress knocked with elevenses, and he swooned with terror. We convinced him at last that he was safe. Pixie settled him and poured the tea. The warmth flooded back to his face.

"I cannot say exactly what I mean." Felix's voice was unchanged in timbre. It still wrapped you in its warmth, but the gorgeous rhythm was disrupted. "Time," he intoned, grasping my hand; his pulse beat defiantly. "Past, present, and—and—the other one."

"Felix, I have only a little time." I had to plan with Jeffcoat our tactics for the evening, but I longed to get some answers out of poor Felix first. "But if the bad men come, the frightening men, you must pretend you cannot speak."

Felix nodded.

I sighed. "Bede, do you think he follows me?"

"Hard to tell, old man. We're teaching him a bit of signing, to augment his vocabulary."

"Brodie's men?" Felix broke in.

I stared. "That's right, Felix. They mustn't know."

He tapped the side of his nose. "Shan't let on."

I couldn't help but feel joyful to see his complicitous smile. I had brought writing materials. I needed Felix to write his testimony—though I feared it might be a testament—to unearth the roots of his woes. Bede shook his head, but promised to try and extract said testimony, and the Pixie would scribe it, just as I had taken down hers at the Yard beforetimes.

"Times. Oh, yes," Felix nodded. "That's right. Time and—

the other one. Lucky, you see. Still here. Otherwise—dead."
He smiled a guileless smile of pleasure at finding himself here
with us, still touching and hearing and feeling.

I squeezed his hand. "You poor fellow."

"Oh, no, no, no, no. My own—the blame—my own." He
tapped his chest. The cup of tea Pixie delivered to his bedside
unlocked a moment of lucidity. "Isn't she d-d-d-darling? Talent.
Misfortune. Won't stay, you? *Die Childer haven promisso*—play
Punch for me—dramaticals." His concentration gave out.

Pixie and Bede grinned at each other and wriggled into
the Punch and Judy. They re-enacted for us their *Orpheus and
Eurydice* tragedy. These brief hours, spent with those three
kind-hearted fools, were the most golden afternoon I spent
in all my years in London. Felix kept nudging me at the good
bits. "Or-pheu-uuus," called Eurydice, as she vanished. "With
all thy faults I love thee still, Orphe—!" By the curtain call,
they had me cackling with laughter.

Felix's tears were streaming down his grey old cheeks. "I
don't suppose… By Jove." He clutched his tea, gone cold, and
gestured at our little stars. The Pixie leapt out, before I had
finished clapping, to settle him back on his pillows, drying his
eyes with her raggedy sleeves. "There, see!"

He looked at her, and I wondered: he thinks she might be
his daughter, this poor mute girl, so bright, so trammelled,
condemned since childhood to theft and depravity in order to
survive. Perhaps every ragamuffin girl he ever meets he thinks
might be his daughter. I leaned closer. "What is it, Felix? Tell
me what it is."

"I suppose you…" He shook his head. "Not finded? Her?"

"Oh. The girl, Effie?—I mean, Angelina?"

He became still, his attention rapt.

"I haven't found her yet. I shall search more. Can you tell
me where?"

His eyes darted about.

Pixie made signs, repeating my question.

He understood. "Sorry. No designs. Blood—dance—at her touch. Blest. So… she suffer, yes! But I—" His brows knitted. "So joy—of time past."

"What is he speaking of?" I asked. "His daughter?" Or was he speaking of the Flowers of Sin?

The Pixie gestured.

Felix essayed a reply but could not get it out.

"Time past, time present." Bede grinned. "He's altogether spoony over 'em."

I laughed a soundless laugh.

"Pain," said Felix, "pain I am. Cannot you relieve me, good apothecary? All I ask, that she be alive. I want. I wish. I not go on." His body shuddered, his eyes squeezed shut; he clenched his fists, as if to tear back the veil of the past. The tears streamed from him. Poor broken man. How I had admired him, wanted to help him, wanted to be like him; and here he was brought so low.

I slipped the daguerreotype from the drawer and studied the girl's face. Yes, she had the features of Wildernsea. How much did Felix know of the Flowers of Sin? Did he know where I would find his missing Angelina?

Bede shuffled up beside me, patting Felix's hand until the convulsions fell quiet and he slept again. "You know, perhaps we shall change our repertoire."


# FADE, FLOWERS, FADE


Across the river, cats were prowling along the old factory walls. The moon peered through tatterdemalion clouds. On the line overhead, a train echoed by, spicing the scents of spring with its smoky trail.

A hundred bullseye lanterns were converging on a Southwark backstreet. A coded knock at the door, copied from long observations. A girl opened up, her shock illuminated in the lamp light. No need for force. At the back door, a sharpened steel axe chopped at the stout lock.

That night, we closed down the Flowers.

John Crow, commissioner of Southwark division, raised a militia to bolster his constables, all sworn to secrecy. Jeffcoat and I stood by; our Yard colleagues assisted them into the vans. The bullies made a run for it; they were tumbled and disarmed. The spinsters in charge protested: it was a ladies' finishing school. So haughtily did they declaim their innocence, pointing and stamping and huffing and puffing, that they would have overwhelmed the poor constables with their sheer respectability—if we had not been immoveable. We knew the truth, and we had only a few days to provide evidence of their crimes and collusion.

What of the women? What of the slaves? Though victims, they could not simply be released—where would they go? Were they in danger? We had no idea how pervasive the whole organisation was. The girls were split up and taken in for questioning, to give them a scare, but also a meal and a bed. Those who protested were offered clemency in return for giving evidence; we gave orders to treat the meek more kindly. After that, they were offered places by various foundations; a higher number than usual were returned to their families, and more went into service.

The enslaved workers we continued to house in their dungeons, lest they be terrified. We sent doctors, food, drink, fresh bedding; Payne agreed to foot the bill, knowing I was about to give evidence at the Enquiry. They were poorly nourished, and stupefied. The opium fiends had to be jailed in John Crow's crammed cells while they kicked up a stink. Two died there in Southwark Jail; but most emerged from their nightmare and returned to the world of the free.

I had not foreseen the basement room. We had not viewed

it while sweeping the chimneys because it had no fireplace. There we found seven infants laid on a dilapidated divan bed. Their bottles by their sides, they were emaciated and dirty and neglected. These children were taken to Lambeth Workhouse; four survived.

These considerable efforts we orchestrated with the help of Acton, Molly's lot and Dickens's crowd from Urania Cottage. It was a messy business, but the Yard's coffers were not troubled, and Sir Richard could have no complaint.

We struck at each limb simultaneously. I found a trusty lawyer to consult. Just a few witnesses would sew up the tapestry of sin. Nothing tenuous would do; they must be so compelling that the Enquiry would be adjourned after their testimony and legal proceedings begun.

Steph was too afraid, and perhaps rightly. It would cost them nothing to kill her, she said, whether she testified or they suspected she'd informed on them.

Jeffcoat and I would testify, but we could not be viewed as impartial.

How many city gents knew of the Flowers of Sin? How many used their services? What price indiscretion? Of course, you might use their services without an inkling of what lay beneath, and protest yourself innocent. I had the feeling our raid would not find its way into the press on the morrow; I had a feeling a few seats would be vacated at the Enquiry during the next day's proceedings. Finally I could see the threads spinning out from the automaton: thefts, perversions, and erotica; blackmail, prostitution, enslavement. The spinster delivering her bundles of sin. The man smoking his pipe by the canal. The scabbed old dragon, face smoothed by hypocrisy: drug-addled, opium-ridden, did she not know what she was at—the accountancy of evil? At the strike of her pen, another wasted away. Mothers, shamed, abandoned their little ones, clinging to the solace that they might have a better life. What became of their children, none of them guessed, some sold on to new lives, others—but of that I have said enough.

Somewhere behind all this lurked a shadowy figure, behind these damnable go-betweens doing his filthy work at such a remove, a tapestry of nods and suggestions, protection and besmirched souls.

I vowed to call him to account. I needed Kate to come out for us, to put him on the spot. I needed to prove the link between Groggins' work and Brodie's bookcase, between Bede's thieving and Dugdale-Hotten's chapbooks. The Pixie's evidence might be admitted, the lawyer reckoned, and Felix's testimony, if coherent, after a doctor's evaluation. One more, just one more; I must pull out of the woodwork someone who would swing everything.

Early next day I knocked politely at No. 17 Quartern Mews. The servant allowed me to interview her most genteelly. She spoke with fondness of her lady, Angelina. She spoke of Felix's kindnesses, which meant his politeness as much as the tips.

What did she know about the transactions that led to their relationship? She denied everything. "No, that is not right," she said, flabbergasted. "Why, Angelina is an heiress from abroad. Mr Felix was her relation, calling upon her out of courtesy and familial fondness."

She was astonished to hear of his stroke, for he had seemed in the most robust health. Angelina, now that I mentioned it, had started behaving oddly a time ago. She looked tired. Harboured secrets. But such is the difference in cultures. A continental flower cannot be expected to behave as demurely as would an English rose.

Where had she gone?

"Heaven knows, sir. Gallivanting. Consorting."

How old? She could give me only a notion, for the girl looked twenty or more with her toilet complete, but to see her wrapped up in her shift at bedtime, with hot chocolate and warming pan, she might be sixteen, or younger still. She was a grateful soul. If they filled her with conceit, could you blame her? Such attention she drew from the gentry, men and boys. Oh, she was a winning girl, and no doubt of it.

Where was she now?

"Well, that's asking. Off she waltzed. That's the way of it."

Who paid them?

"Why, some agency or other, but we're closing up the Mews now. You've only caught us by the skin of your teeth. You'd have to ask at Coutts. Someone along the row might know, but prying don't go down well."

Who made the arrangements for the gentlemen?

This she truly didn't understand. "Arrangements? Why, you have a funny notion of the world, and no mistake."

## EQUIVOCATION

Still it rained.

Brodie was there at the courtroom, sat at the back. His presence seemed to say: "Looky here, Mr Scotland. I have the judiciary in my pocket. I have your boss, I have your parliament. If you persist, do you think you will ever work here again?"

I could not care about such things. I would testify in the afternoon, and Jeffcoat before me, with Kate and Darlington in between.

We had tried all our cards. There was no point dragging in Quartern concierges, Clink Street madams, the poor slaves, the drug-addled accountant, not even the Pixie. Not even Brodie. Not until the finger of blame was authoritatively pointed.

As I settled in for the morning session, I found myself thinking about Mauve's peculiar death; and I began to wonder where on earth Jimmy Darlington had got to.

# JEFFCOAT'S DENUNCIATION (ENQUIRY IV)

Counsel:    Sergeant Jeffcoat, will you explain your deputation?

Jeffcoat:   [*hesitates*] Concerning coercion, or the further matters for which we are still gathering evidence?

Counsel:    The former.

Jeffcoat:   That girls in poor houses, and in gangs, are persuaded or forced into the life has already been attested. I assert that girls are also imported into London from provincial towns and foreign countries in order to swell the ranks of prostitution.

Counsel:    Do you not intervene on their behalf?

Jeffcoat:   We might wish to, sir, but the laws respecting brothels are so peculiar that we can rarely extricate these unfortunates from their dire position.

Counsel:    Surely *habeas corpus* protects them.

Jeffcoat:   Only, sir, if we can prove they are held against their will. But they are scared and so zealously watched that attempts to liberate them prove futile.

Counsel:    Where are these women taken from?

Jeffcoat:   Principally the north of England. One also finds Belgians, Irish, Spanish, Italian, Armenian. I know one Tahitian, sir, black-skinned and not a word of English. Even if she wanted to be liberated, what is she useful for? Except— [*noise in the court*]

Justice:    Order.

Counsel:    How are these women enticed?

Jeffcoat:   Cajolery, sir. Promises. Lures. Threats to family. Social pressures—

Counsel:    Pressures?

Jeffcoat:   Say you are a girl, with beauty but no other assets. You step out with one boy, innocently enough. He insists that you step out with his friend, teasing, and threatening to defame your reputation. Only this friend proves more insistent. I need not spell it out. Ruined, you cannot return home. You are entered on the life already. What can you do but accept the generous offer to join their nursery?

Counsel:    This nursery. What happens when they arrive?

Jeffcoat:   They are scrubbed, shorn, given a new name. Following an initiation night, with an inspection by the... an inspection and trial run, let us say, they receive training in the arts of the night and, if biddable, the refinements of a lady.

Counsel:    Then they are sent out to work?

Jeffcoat:   It depends, sir, on their accomplishments. The unlucky are cast out to fend for themselves. Most take up residence in houses of ill fame, whose keepers derive profits from their labours. They sign an initial document—our Exhibit A, sir—which they in their ignorance imagine to be binding. They are in the hands of their keepers. But there is a loftier tier beyond this. A bespoke service, whereby the finest, most accomplished of the women are auctioned off—for extraordinary prices.

Counsel:   Prices justified by what?

Jeffcoat:   They make your dreams come true. [*scurrilous buzz in the galleries*]

Counsel:   Your dreams? I see. [*makes a note*] Does this traffic run in both directions?

Jeffcoat:   Englishwomen are ever tricked and decoyed to Ostend, Bologna, and Le Havre. Their *maisons de joie* never have enough to satisfy their patrons; they derive obscene emoluments from the prostitution of English girls. [*hubbub*]

Counsel:   Sergeant Jeffcoat, these are serious claims.

Jeffcoat:   I do not make them lightly, sir.

Counsel:   Have you documentary evidence?

Jeffcoat:   Much, sir, and it should be brought to the public eye. Women might henceforth come to police, trusting their protection, if only they may tell their tale and be believed. At the moment, they expect blame. They are told they have got what they deserve.

Counsel:   Give an example, Sergeant. Evidence.

[*Jeffcoat tells of Miss Reade, an Englishwoman returned recovered from practical slavery. Attending an interview for service, she was promised recompense for working in Dieppe. He expatiates on the horrors the girl underwent. With difficulty conquered. Submitted to her fate: Frenchmen pay well for the privilege of ruining Englishwomen. By chance, an Englishman frequented the house. He smuggled her to the consulate and thence to Britain. Her written deposition is presented.*]

Jeffcoat:    She is too frightened to testify, sir.

Counsel:    Frightened?

Jeffcoat:    We can barely conceive, sir, the hold their... employers have over them.

Counsel:    But I thought this woman has been rescued from her fate?

Jeffcoat:    Not exactly, sir. Now returned, without other support, Miss Reade has done what she never did before, and had recourse to prostitution. [*consternation in court*]

## THIS DELICATE MONSTER (ENQUIRY V)

"Miss Hamilton." A thrill ran through the gallery, as the new barrister narrowed his eyes. The Enquiry was not a court case, as such, but its procedures often resembled a prosecution; Fairchild selected his barristers carefully, specialists in various fields, to get the most out of each witness. This fellow seemed familiar to me. What kind of a match would he make for this monstrous wonder of the underworld? "Miss Hamilton, you run an establishment dedicated—how shall we put it delicately?—to the pleasure of gentlemen."

"Nuffink delicate about it, My Lord. Nor can I guarantee the pleasure's all on the side of the gentleman."

Titters around the room. Kate Hamilton, I thought, you're going to eat this poor devil alive. They had decorously installed her during an adjournment, a capacious armchair replacing the stand. Her bulk dominated the courtroom, strangely out of place away from the pink divan at London's pulsing centre. In the depths of my weary bones, I was rooting for her. Tell the truth, Kate, the whole truth and—

"Can you describe your business?"

"I'm something like a confessor, My Lord, or an alienist doctor. Don't get me wrong, I've no ideas above my station. I only mean it ain't right to divulge what goes on within the walls of my establishment." Her eyebrows flickered. "Any more than I'd reveal the names of clients and patrons."

"The court may require those details later, should they become relevant."

Kate leaned forward, like the gathering of a storm. "Oh, may we, Jocelyn? I mean, begging your pardon, sir, certainly."

The young barrister's lips continued to form words soundlessly. He shuffled his papers. A murmur sprang up. Of course. Now I recognised him: I hadn't known the intemperate fool in his wig, with trousers, and without his horsehair plume.

"Order," called Lord Chief Justice Fairchild.

"No need to jump the gun." Our learned friend recovered himself. "Names need only be revealed if relevant—"

"A lot of names, and I can name 'em. Here and now, if you ask me, I can. Drag 'em out of me, you'll have to, as I've ever assured my clients of the strictest confidentiality." She looked him in the eye. "But, as Mr Mauve has told us—rather, the late Mr Mauve—this is a brave new world. Messrs Acton and Mayhew have spoke of cleansing ourselves of the Great Social

Evil. And I'm sure you yourself, sir, have oft looked upon me and my like with, shall I say, disdain. Disgust. It ain't the moral judgement I feel the harshest, for we're all sinners, ain't we?" She came to an abrupt stop and appealed to the gallery. "Ain't we sinners, every last one of us?"

The tittering fell away as she gazed steadily round the audience, transfixing each in turn, like the finest tragedian. She looked at Acton and Mayhew; at the barrister, and Sir Richard; and at me; but toward J.W. Brodie she did not look. My heart juddered, as if something was caught in my throat. Come on, Kate, I whispered, don't let me down.

"Let him who is free from sin cast the first stone." She breathed in. "Sorry, My Lord, gabbling on like an old fishbag. What's the question?"

The barrister continued, but the fight had gone out of him. His voice was hollow. Kate described her night house, how many girls employed, how many patrons per week, how much liquor sold, how often divans recovered. Her establishment sounded cleaner than the Queen's dining table. Undesirable crumbs were brushed under the legal carpet: where the girls came from, how brought to the life, how long under her protection and what happened after their flash days were done—none of this was discussed. Gorged with useless detail, the gallery sat stupefied, still sated on the threat of scandal.

At last, Kate sat back on her throne, lips pursed in a lascivious smile. The bile rose in my gorge. It was too late. She knew it, I knew it, and Brodie, I could plainly see, was delighted.

Justice Fairchild adjourned for lunch. Amid the tittle-tattle, Brodie, unnoticed, touched his cap toward Kate, wrinkling his eyes with gratitude. She flushed, feinting at a curtsey, before she was lifted down the aisle, rather akin to the launch of the *Great Eastern*.

# FULL OF BLASPHEMIES

The court dispersed in a frenzy. Kate's chicanery left me heartsick. I had wanted to believe her place was a republic of free women, choosing the life they preferred, under Kate's benevolent gaze. I had wanted to believe it from the first time Darlington brought me there. It was easier to believe than the truth.

As they dragged her past, Kate Hamilton, that teasing, prodigious madam the likes of whom you would encounter nowhere else, I found myself muttering, "You think you're the great protectress. Standing up for your sex, against men who abuse their beauty."

Kate heard. She turned. She laughed in my face. "I don't give a sausage for you and your beautiful girls, Watchman." What a fool I was: I'd thought her a lighthouse in the seas of immorality; but she was a monster drawing all to shipwreck. She flashed me a look of triumph. "I may not be the looker I once was, but I'm the one as takes 'em, and shapes 'em. Men would use 'em or abuse 'em anywise. I'm just running a business."

"They have you." I had never expected her destructive glee. Those lost overboard, wrecked and drowned, they meant nothing to her: girls kidnapped, impregnated, despatched to the madhouse, or the Thames. "You're not your own woman. You're bought and sold. You're nothing."

"And you, Watchman, my lover, with your pompous airs, strutting round as if you own the place. You don't own nothing." She fixed me with a look, then waved her bearers onward, calling out to shame me, "Like a monk, are you? Refusing my girls! Pah. He's just like the next man, only he wouldn't know an honest desire when it smacks him in the unmentionables."

# SHAME, REMORSE (ENQUIRY VI)

As I stood to testify, exhaustion assailed me. Kate had demoralised the Enquiry: she gave them to understand not just that her establishment was nobly patronised and above board, but that the whole case against prostitution was wildly overstated, in her humble (informed) opinion. I thought she would speak eloquently on women's behalf; but she never promised that. I cursed my own deluded hopes.

As in a dream, I took the oath, fighting off the shivering fits. My mind felt sluggish; my words stumbled. So much I must make public, so much to denounce.

I'd had a dream in the night, after closing the Flowers of Sin, a dream so fearful that I awoke in the wee small hours, heart pounding. The gulls were crying at the window—what business had they here? I could not sleep. I lay, rehearsing over and over what I planned to say in court, if the questioning would allow.

The barrister indicated that I should look around the court before I answered. Little confidence I had in him, the same intemperate young man who had detained me the night Groggins met his end. Kate had got under his collar; now he was getting at me. I would not be swayed. I breathed deep, trying to steady my heart, as the courtroom's marble paving slabs shifted in my vision: black squares and white squares, a chequerboard pattern.

My dream returned to me with fearful clarity.

In my dream, I stood in this very dock. It was part of the chess automaton, larger than life and extending right across the room. The Turk studied my face. He moved his pawn to commence the Evans Gambit.

I studied his face in return: I would not be swayed. If I could only fathom those impassive features, I would triumph. Yet my pieces stayed pinned in their home rank. My pawns shifted, but slowly, shunting up the board to immolate themselves against the Turk's marauding bullies. I had to shove them across the irregular slabs to meet their obliteration, heads dashed against castle walls, rookeries and bishops' palaces. As the board transmogrified, I saw the Turk smile—a smile I recognised— and I couldn't resist walking to him across the board.

The board had become Trafalgar Square; the bishops and rooks were domes and spires all along. I hastened to wriggle away down Holywell Street, to a most urgent appointment on Titchfield Street—with her. The sewerlike passage quivered, the ground swelling...

Damn and blast. I was at Kate Hamilton's, quite the wrong place. Her entranceway plunged into a canyon; behind me, two hills rose up. I lost my footing. As I slipped down the passage, the mossy grove burst into colour with flowers. Cries resounded around me, like birds, like children. I fled.

I was aching to return to the room of love, where Alexandra awaited me. The ground was scattered with leaves and dried petals, inscribed with Groggins' florid lettering, black on black. My limbs were sluggish, as I ran on the shifting ground. The fog enveloped me, the cries behind more terrifying than the dangers ahead. A wretched wind sprang up. I dragged the door open and found to my delight that beautiful bed, sheets, pillows, bonbons, but lying in it, the wrong person: a girl, half recognised, lying still, eyes open, awaiting me—or lying ruined—or was she dead?

Before I knew it, my chance was gone. I barely knew what happened.

The lawyer began by quoting complaints against me, from Mauve and Dugdale and others. He dropped hints about a traffic incident; he mentioned a quarrel in a night house in Denmark Street. I could not gainsay these conjectures, which painted a dire picture of my competence, though they seemed beside the point.

I asked to deliver my evidence, my arguments so

painstakingly collated and rehearsed. Around the court, all eyes were upon me.

The lawyer's questions allowed me to state only bare statistics. Night houses, prostitutes; compared to the previous census, he pointed out, the figures far worse. He looked round the court, and shook his head at me. "You must be disappointed with your efforts, Sergeant?"

"No, no. You misconstrue my task," I stammered.

"Did Sir Richard Payne not commission you to—?"

"That is not the point." I tried to go further, to touch on the business behind the figures. Manipulations. Contracts. Coercion.

"Please," he smiled. "No need to explain the Great Social Evil to the court."

I countered that there was need. We had made discoveries darker than the court imagined. Through my feverish haze, I tried to tell more of the Southwark academy. Jeffcoat had given the facts, but I wanted to convey the plight of the women subdued there. I tried to speak of the damned Regent's Canal, but my voice failed me.

He deflected my challenge, as if batting away a gadfly. It was an expert smothering, as deft and deadly as any murder. First he swamped my half-hearted testimony, bamboozling us with meaningless facts. Then he swayed the gallery's attentions from my discoveries by uprooting my private life.

Lord Chief Justice Fairchild eyed me warily. "I must allow, with some reluctance, that Counsel mention allegations against Sergeant Lawless's conduct."

The self-satisfied lawyer laid out a catalogue of my misconduct. Mauve's theft I had failed to solve; and now he was dead. Groggins, who died so soon after I pestered him, sneaking in uninvited. Where was my witness, Felix? Struck down. And my colleague Darlington, for whom I had procured dubious remedies? Where was he?

"I further put it to you," the barrister began with apparent relish, "that you were often seen in an establishment in Leicester Square with one of these women, when you were not, in fact, on duty."

That would be Cora. Nothing untoward, but I could not deny it.

"I put it to you that, as a regular customer at Kate Hamilton's bordello, you were accustomed to accepting favours. Drinks. Rooms."

"I played chess with Cora. One of the girls. Women, rather," I spluttered. "No favours."

"Never?"

"They offered me whisky."

"Which you drank?"

"No." I shrugged. "Not usually."

"On duty?"

"The line between duty and not duty... It's an awkward distinction, in our work." This was not the moment to defend my methods. "But no other favours, as you put it."

"Rooms?"

"No."

"Never?"

My mouth sagged open. I could make no reply.

"There are allegations, My Lord, regarding Sergeant Lawless's relations with women. We prefer not to tarnish the other parties. Only, if I may show Your Honour these daguerreotypes. This image. Yes, My Lord. And worse—these."

Easy to shame me publicly. I stood awestruck. Nothing could have thrown me more than revealing my love for Alexandra. Threatening to ruin her. She had ended it, our imprudent indulgence; but too late. I had erred, I suppose, but that should not stop the court from hearing me.

"Whatever my folly, why should my testimony be rendered stingless?" I struggled to muster my reason. "Which of us is pure? None of you. We all—"

The judge called me to order, troubled. My deposition was concluded.

I stumbled from the court. I barely knew what I had said. Little of purpose. I had ranted, wasting our months of work, undermining our case. The damnable lawyer: Brodie's spies had told him everything. I was not even sure which crimes were imputed to me and which only in my imagination.

Jeffcoat laid his hand on my shoulder. "They've found Jimmy Darlington."

# FURTHER INTO HELL

I should have gone to see Darlington. You work and work, never imagining that one day your friend is there, and the next he will be gone.

He had been dead for days before they found him. The coroner recorded a surfeit of opiates.

They had to hold the funeral at once, the body was that degraded. Beforehand, Jeffcoat and I visited Darlington's quarters. I had never been before. What a small, tidy life he had. I expected papers everywhere, encrusted with baked potato and coffee stains, dirty books left open. Nothing. Tidy notes on life in the police, scribbled in a workaday journal; perhaps he hoped to be discovered, just like Sergeant McLevy in Edinburgh, and published to critical renown. I offered them to Hotten, but he found the prose style too sensational.

After the funeral, the 9.23 Club agreed: he was the kind of man who wouldn't be told. Collins was strict about dosage; Darlington must have doubled it. Some people are natural addicts: bibliomania, morphinomania, erotomania. You cannot save a maniac. We should have looked after him. He was weak, it's true, and gave in to many temptations; but we are all weak at times.

# WOEFUL FATES

The bodies from the canal were buried the same day in one large grave in the police cemetery at Manor Park. Simpson would not even put a number on them, the remains the diver had found in those tattered bags of bones. The doctor was reluctant to spend his valuable time without assurances; he had been duped before. Before? Why, yes. Mass graves were dug up all the time. The Artillery Ground, the Foundling Hospital, the Strand Union Workhouse: these diggings turfed up so many burial grounds, he was sick of old bones. Why, a doctor he knew in Blackheath—

I reminded him that these bodies had not been buried in the first place.

He would give cause of death for the first five. If there were a prosecution, it would be a collective one; each post-mortem required a report; the Yard would hesitate to pay his total fee per cadaver, and he was in no mood to quibble.

He thumbed through the swaddling garments. Ages: from two months to three years. Two were suffocated, he told me blankly; one starved; one had its head stove in. The last was uncertain: the fractures of the ribcage suggested violence but might be rickets, often fatal to infants.

We spoke no further of it.

The man who cast the bundles was arrested, undemonstratively. On the Caledonian Road, one can do nothing without an audience, but we gave out that a neighbour had reported a nuisance; we gave no reason to think it part of a wider investigation.

The atmosphere within the Yard was subdued. Jeffcoat and I spoke in hushed tones. We could let nobody know that we were on to the warehouse nursery: the Flowers of Sin, as Groggins' card styled it. Not yet. A few officers came to us, pledging loyalty. Others treated us like lepers. What made these colleagues treat us circumspectly was not clear, but the poison was deep-rooted. I came back to our lodgings in the Yard to find the boys taunting Jeffcoat's cat.

One blockhead grabbed it by the tail. "I told you. Not enough room to swing a cat in here." Having cracked it about the head till it stopped mewling, he threw it out the window and into the river. I am ashamed to admit that I watched it drown.

Jeffcoat was devastated to find Thom vanished. I persuaded him to move back to my old rooms, where together we should be safe from threats. I never told him the truth about poor Thom.

# ASHES

It was my darkest hour. Jeffcoat and I kept a late vigil. Dawn glimmered golden red over the rooftops. I was at my wits' end. Of my humiliation in court we said little. What was there to say? It was over.

Jeffcoat took it on himself to haul me into action. "It's not the end. Not yet." He'd appealed for a fresh barrister, beyond Brodie's manipulations; we had one last trick up our sleeve. "New lawyer, new witness. Just so little may tip the balance."

We had set up our final gambit, and we were ready to sacrifice all our pieces. To fight those with friends in high places, sometimes one needs friends in even higher places. Who? Who is left on the side of right?

I regretted promising Miss Villiers I would attend her blasted charitable book swap. Molly had strong-armed me; I could not think why.

When we heard about Darlington, Justice Fairchild had

called an adjournment. I had a day's reprieve to straighten out loose ends. Jeffcoat packed me off for the early train to Crowthorne. I hadn't slept. He reminded me to get Felix's book: I still hoped Felix could testify decisively. I walked through the rain, addled with the shame of the courtroom. The *ad hominem* attack to bury my evidence. They wouldn't need to shut me up, as they had done for Mauve and Groggins.

The clean bricks of the new Broadmoor Criminal Lunatic Asylum promised a different type of reform. I asked to see Dugdale, author and engraver. I was brought through endless bright corridors, ashamed of my muddy boots. Dugdale had been dropped right in it, after all his work on the secret manuscript and its subscription list. He just might risk testifying against them.

I saw Dugdale—but he did not see me. The electrical charge run through his temples that morning had been at a new, experimental level. It could be a month before he spoke in full sentences.


The branch line stations were a biblical lamentation: Ash, Ash Vale, Wanborough, Godalming, Havant. I slept right through Petersfield and woke at the end of the line. I walked blindly on to Portsmouth Harbour, where I stood on the pier like an inarticulate slave.

Boys were frolicking in the mudflats, as the quality hurried through the drizzle to the Isle of Wight ferry. A girl flipped a farthing into the mud below. The boy turned a somersault for her; he came up like a painted minstrel, the coin gleaming between his teeth. The girl gave a shy wave, while her father bought the tickets. How many obstacles love will overleap.

A boatload of women was ferried ashore from the hulking destroyer at anchor in the harbour: black-haired, dark-skinned, dishevelled and excitable. What they had to do with the British Navy I could not imagine.

"Why, sir," said the station guard, with a wink. "Officers' wives, them."

"Officers' wives?" I winked in return. "Any bargains?"

"Not here, sir. Nobody does business here. There's Spice Island if you wants a passing taste. For purchasing, you wants to go up the hill, to the new forts." He pointed and winked again. The chalky hilltop was pocked with half-built battlements. Palmerston's follies: I'd read of them in the papers, bankrupting the nation against phantom enemies. "Tell 'em you'd like to buy a piglet. That's it. A nice little piglet."

I gave the man a shilling. I was always out of pocket.

## MEMOIRS AND MEMORIES

It had done me the power of good to smell the sea. I did not have time now to go up the hill; I'd return later, in search of the piglets.

I arrived in Petersfield ashen, with the rain finally easing. I walked to the book swap, in a private garden filled with flowers, where Miss Villiers received me with such warmth, I nearly burst into tears. She looked lithe in an elegant aquamarine dress, nothing like her dowdy library outfits. How had I spent so long without seeing her? Molly was clever to engineer this, knowing I missed Ruth's bright company. Ruth saw I was in no state to be presented to shire society. She took pity and hid me away.

"Still, I must introduce you to the dreaded aunt." She took the liberty of straightening my hair and adjusting my lapels; it was such a heedless intimacy, I couldn't help but smile. She frowned. "What?"

"Must I meet the aunt? I was hoping to drown my sorrows." I told of my courtroom disgrace. I wanted to tell her of the canal, and the end of my inappropriate relationship, but I dared not. "What about these books you've investigated for me?"

Ruth stood conspiratorially close, and spent a stolen half hour neglecting her charitable duties.

Around the same time as my first letter, a couple of gents had enquired laughingly if she had Walter's *My Secret Life* on her shelves. "They kept asking, 'Does it pique your interest, Miss?' in a roguish sort of a way."

She consulted the catalogue. Nothing. She consulted her superior, Panizzi.

The Italian's brow darkened. "Licentious pranks," he blasted, his accent sharper when he was angry. He blamed her for encouraging them, though the gents were already vanished. The next thing, Ruth was reprimanded and her contract under question.

"Your job? I'm mortified."

"He's a rotten prig." She waved a hand. "I'm better off out of it."

It took discreet enquiries to discover that she had chanced upon a Masonic secret. Following recent donations to the Library, a battle was raging. Some said every book should be catalogued and available; others insisted certain tomes be removed to a special chamber.

Her eyes sparkling, she whispered, "Erotic books."

When Panizzi examined the catalogue of priapic exhibits from the Museum of Naples, he was decided. A cupboard amid the stacks acquired a lock. Thus began the Museum's famed Secret Cabinet. Already it was growing. Only trusted collectors were given access, upon enquiring in the right way, from the right librarian. And there was a rumour of a vast bequest to come.

Brodie's bookshelves. I knew it.

Ruth nudged me. "An eye-opening collection, this gents' flower garden."

I spluttered. "You've seen it?"

"I had a peek. Freethinking women must broaden their minds."

"Freethinking." I nodded.

Her eyes flashed. She would refuse, on principle, to be shocked by licentious material, though the degenerate scenes Darlington had shown me would puzzle her. If Ruth liked nothing more than a mystery, nothing irked her more than being excluded. "Panizzi means to dismiss me. The old goat. Not that I would allege he prefers young males. To employ young males, I mean, of course. Wait, now." Ruth peered from the camellias and called out, "Aunt Lexie, here we are. I must introduce you."

The dreaded aunt, about whom I had heard little all these years, looked over at us.

My mouth ran dry.

"Why, you must be the famous Sergeant Lawless," she said, as if we had never met, "of whom my darling Ruth tells me such stories."

I looked at her.

Ruth looked petulant. "I can't see how you didn't meet at Felix's party."

"Didn't we?" The aunt blinked her lovely eyes. She tucked a ringlet nervously beneath her hat, not to say seductively. "I don't recall."

"No, no. I should remember," I said warmly. "A pleasure to meet you." I cast a glance at Ruth. "But can this really be your maiden aunt, Lexie? You have sold her short in your descriptions."

Ruth snorted at this outright flirtation. "Because I am jealous of her beauty."

"If you'll excuse me, Lexie," I said carelessly, "or do I too call you Aunt Lexie? I must look at these fearful books. I'm after one in particular, about Italian prisons." I walked rudely away.

Ruth apologised on my behalf. "That's Scotsmen for you. Excuse me, Lexie. I spy a vicar gasping for roulade."

I leaned in the recess of the garden wall, my mind awhirl. I wanted something from her, some kind of recognition, or forgiveness. She hovered alongside me, picking at books on the trestle tables. The rain started up in earnest, spattering the awnings, and the crowds scurried for shelter. Satisfied we were hidden by the camellias, she inserted her finger through the buttonhole of my lapel, drew me to her, pushed me away, drew me to her, pushed me away. I gazed into her tear-shaped eyes with their hint of long sorrows.

She smiled.

I revelled in that smile. But I promised myself I wouldn't describe her. I said I wouldn't, and I have.

She breathed in the fresh spring air. "And Felix's daughter? Have you found her?" Seeing I had understood so little at our final meeting, she began telling me the history again: that Felix's interest in fallen women was due to his daughter, lost in the wars, then apparently found. The girl at the opera must be—

I interrupted. "When did you find out that I knew Ruth?"

She bit her lip. "I knew. From the start, I knew. I just couldn't resist." She smiled. "Wicked, wasn't it?"

We both burst out laughing. I laughed to think how I had resisted offers of Kate's girls, Skittles's charms and sirens all over London, but succumbed to her.

Ruth appeared, a book in her hand, and Alexandra walked away, without a word or a backward glance. I saw the similarity between them: the delicious knowingness in the eyes, neither sad nor ironical, but irresistible. There was no doubt they were aunt and niece.

Ruth frowned. "What was that you were talking of?"

"Oh, have you Felix's book for me?"

"You seem rather intimate with the aunt." She feigned unconcern.

"No, no." I found the inscription:

*Ruth, my darling niece,*
*To a life of rapture.*
*Love, Aunt Lexie.*

This second volume of Felix's memoirs I would devour on the train back to town. I shook my head, and looked up. "But the dreaded aunt has some good ideas."

Ruth eyed me warily, shoulders tensed to rebuff a joke. "Such as?"

I looked into her emerald eyes and breathed in. "That I should ask you to step out with me."

## WHO IS THE STRONGER?

"You were disappointed with our friend, Kitty Hamilton," said Brodie. "Right, Mr Scotland?" His accents still surprised me, the American vowels peppered through it like the grey in his hair and moustaches. We were back in his Secret Cabinet, where it all began, back in November. "Women, huh? Cleopatras, Catherines and Virgin Queens. When they're not battling and murdering, they're scheming how to sate those constant impulsive desires. Petticoat government, huh? We men would lie in the sunshine and eat lotuses, if our wives would let us. The stronger sex? The noisier. They want freedom of opinion, occupation? Let 'em. Let 'em be lawyers, prime ministers, editors, anything they like; but let 'em be goddamned quiet— if they can."

"Mr Brodie." I must unfold my final gambit. The first time I was here, I accepted his hospitality; I laughed along, I got drunk, I welcomed his open invitation. Now I felt sullied, but I kept up my smile, for now. "Mr Brodie, I know everything."

He blessed me with that rare smile of his. "No chess this time, I'm afraid. Can't get the staff. Will I suffice as entertainment?" He opened the drinks cabinet. "You want to threaten me with revelations? Oh, I'm scared. The touch of death you have. Mauve. The Irishman. Your sergeant friend. And darling Skittles. You, with your assignations, are gonna threaten me:

your questionable women, high and low; improper entry into premises; and such a furious driver."

"Oh, can't we speak plainly? I know everything that's going on. I'm not white as snow, I admit. What sins will you admit to?"

"We all like to feel a little besmirched." He brandished the decanter, grinning. "Have you a lawyer prepared to pursue these poetic convictions of yours?"

A lawyer he couldn't touch? Yes, by God, we had found one. I gave no answer.

"No? Then, frankly, Sergeant, go hang yourself." Brodie took an unholy age measuring out my whisky. "How much have you lived? I mean really lived. I'll wager that my hour is more than your month. What the hell? I realised early in life, I have a need. I felt it so strong, I was sure all men must feel something of the same. Am I not right, Mr Scotland?"

I took the glass of peaty brown liquor.

"The Apostle Paul's advice: 'Let your weakness be your strength.' His weakness was so great, he was forced to rely on God. I, too, have such a proclivity. Don't you?"

"If you mean to want women at my beck and call, no."

"Women, girls, boys. No?" He eyed me strangely. "Well, I thought that if all men desire it so, even more than they want drink and games and gossip, then, on top of newspapers, racehorses and public houses, I better invest in bordellos. People are profligate; if someone's going to profit, might as well be me. I made my fortune. Five times over, I made it. As the Lord says, I hid not my worth. To him who has will be given, and he will have abundance. I invested; I got back tenfold. And if I ever thought about sin, I told myself: see how the Lord blesses my enterprises; I cannot be sinful, or he'd punish me. The Lord sees all, and forgives all, and blesses all. Why be the moral fool, when I can be lord of all I survey? If not me, it'd be someone else running these affiliations. I tell you, a smaller-minded man could be pretty cruel."

"You don't think your organisations are cruel?"

"They could be one hell of a lot crueller."

"Taking children from mothers—"

"Buying. What else have they to sell? And why not? Reward for their sufferings. Do you blame them? How caring your own mother must have been. I congratulate you. Mine was not."

I sighed. "If you wish to play silly buggers, I have known about the thefts from the start. It took me a while to see what you stood to gain. Power over the powerful. Money from the moneyed. Felix, for example. Not just access to his charity: access to the women, access to their children."

"Are you finished with your high horse?" Plucking a volume off the bookcase, Brodie thumbed through it. "These stubborn sins of ours. Such slack repentance! Promising, always promising. Then straight back on the path of filth. Ha! Forgive my extemporary version, Sergeant. You must know your Baudelaire. *Les Fleurs du Mal.* Spouts a heap of hogwash about our sins. But the circles of the Parisian underworld, those he imbues with spiritual grace." In that small room, his gaze was fixed far off, like a beast patiently awaiting its prey. "You got to admit, there's nobility in these syphilitic veterans of Venus."

"Mayhew's women speak with more poetry than any West End playwright."

"You got it. A perverse dignity: the prostitute's trivial life acquires tragical grandeur in its fatality. The tinge of transgressive melancholy." He sniffed at his drink. "Our puritan lands consider organised vice insolent and shaming. Where is the Japanese geisha? The Parisian cocotte, that pinnacle of pleasure and imitation?" He threw back his whisky with evident pleasure. "As long as prostitution is a fecund evil, it will flourish in the dirt."

"Were you aiming to make it respectable?"

"Let's just say I liberated myself from my native Puritanism."

"Now you're liberating London."

"Look, some women are too amorous; but it's frigidity that more often ruins our lives. Wouldn't you say, Sergeant?"

"That's hardly your papers' tune. Nor does it license propositioning."

"Flirting is to marriage what free trade is to commerce. Test a woman, and you judge what sort of wife she'd be. If you conceive a passion for each other, you should be entitled to indulge it, morally. Surely you're not so old-fashioned as to disagree with that."

I managed a smile, gritting my teeth. It was hard to speak civilly with a man who in my mind was the architect of evil, careless of crimes, manipulations, and ruined lives. Everything grist to the mill of commerce: decency, privacy, life itself. I must keep in mind what I hoped to achieve. "And Felix's girl. You persuaded her family to sell her for ten pounds."

"Ten? Never so much." He laughed. "Don't take much persuading, I tell you, those northerners. What's the problem? The girl learnt a trade. She made something of her life."

"Did she? Where is she now?"

"Ain't my business, Mr Scotland. Ask your friend Felix."

I stared. "Felix will not speak again."

"No? A shame. An eloquent soul. That's the struggle for life, ain't it? The strong survive, the species develops." He poured himself another whisky; mine I soaked into my handkerchief, the trick inspired by Cora; best he think I was matching his drams. "I only give people what they want. He and his girl both."

"But you tell people what they want, in the headlines, daily."

"No, no. My influence ain't so strong. I listen to what they want, and I amplify it." He took a file from the shelf and stroked the leather cover. "Say, ain't it strange how we ban love, yet endorse murder and mutilation? Actors and novelists may give people whatever they want; courtesans not so."

What exactly did Brodie mean by his proclivity? "You mean prostitution?"

"Oh, Mr Scotland." He rolled his eyes. "So small-minded."

"What happened to Gabriel Mauve?"

"You set the plough a-rolling, you mow down flowers."

"Did he get what he wanted?"

"In spades. Mauve was a fool. He took chances; he lost out."

"Lost out?" I was not alone in suspecting Mauve's suicide was assisted. Easily orchestrated: slow asphyxiation in the midst of erotic games.

Brodie, flicking through the file, gave no answer.

"And Groggins?"

"Who, the Irish gabbler? A big mouth he had. I was wrong to choose him for such a delicate task." He tapped at the file. "Though he had talent. The twisted verbiage he churned out, it got me right here—"

"And the girl?"

"Felix's girl? You care about her?" He looked at me squarely, resting his chin in his hand. "What did you think you could do, boy? Expose me? Had your chance."

"True." I cast my eyes downward. I had suffered public humiliation; he believed I'd given up, and that was all the better. "I thought you'd be big enough to admit your crimes."

"Ha!" He looked at me. "You ain't free from sin yourself."

"Not like that. Nothing like the things you're involved in."

"Oh, that was love, was it? Extramarital, though. Not typically Presbyterian."

I sighed. "Haven't you dragged me through the mud enough?"

"I could have gone much farther." He pointed at me, as an Englishman never would point. "I still could. If you're determined to expose my services, and the good folk who enjoy my services, go ahead. I can provide you with photographic images we showed the judge, if you like. You may find the pictures distasteful."

These threats, these games—I was tiring of it all. "And Felix. What of him?"

"You go close to the fire, you get burned." He set the file down carefully beside me and sat back in his armchair. "You want to style me as some black-hearted mogul, tossing people into the ditch in pursuit of profit. It won't hold. It's a caricature." He took a cigar, bit the end off and lit it calmly. "Newspapers ain't just for profits. They're a public service. I won't pretend sales don't matter; a business has to pay. But I could aim much lower. Look at the *Illustrated Police News*, with its cat headlines. Always damned cats: cats suffocated, cats crowned, cats beheaded. When did cats become so entertaining? It's a parade of freaks, I grant you. But I take my duty to inform the public seriously. The readership has doubled during my tenure. I backed the Chartist riots in '48. I'll back the new reforms when they come."

"Don't pretend you're for reform."

"Of course I am. Enfranchised people are inquisitive people. They read papers, they get angry. Good for society, good for me."

"That doesn't follow. You hint that Mauve died in a bizarre sexual game, and your sales quadruple."

"Don't they have the right to know? The misery most men endure, ashamed of their natural urges, and their wives still more ashamed of theirs." He tapped the file. "This stuff keeps men out of trouble, just like prostitution safeguards marriages."

"Do you believe that?" The temptation to indulge these romantic versions of commercial sexuality was strong, but it couldn't stem the cruelties. I shook my head. "And the casualties?"

Brodie shrugged. "Not my fault."

"Nor blackmail. Trafficking. Baby farming." The Enquiry had not linked any of these crimes to him, not yet. I wanted him to admit it all. That was why I had come. It was a long shot, but I had thrown everything into the pot; if I lost now, I was beyond caring. "Not your fault."

He sat wide-eyed for a moment. He was actually shocked that I knew—and that shock meant I was right.

"Your web of tainted trades," I said, "you can never free yourself from. Even if you're never brought to justice, you know your heart is black. I know. And the whole of Scotland Yard knows."

Brodie tilted his head, considering me, as if making a decision. He sprang, with a spry energy, over to his cabinet of curiosities, opening it with an ornate key, as if from a fairytale. "You done your job, Mr Scotland. You ain't no big shot at courtroom bluff. But as a policeman, you done what Sir Richard asked, the cowardly bigot, and goddamn if you ain't done what he ought to have asked. You plough where you never sowed. I admire that." The cabinet was locked again; he had extracted three stones he had shown me all those months ago: pieces of the Colosseum. He tossed them up and down. "What you're saying about Scotland Yard, though, is horse manure. And those same horses are gonna trample you down."

"Threaten me all you like, Brodie. Power has to obey universal laws. I hoped to expose you in court as a charlatan, a kidnapper, a seducer." As his gaze burned into me, I brought the last drop of whisky to my lips, but did not drink it. There was a smell hidden in the peat, nutmeg or almond. "And—"

"And what?" he mocked. "You failed, if you recall."

"And the rest you know." I counted off on my fingers. "Murderer of innocents. Erotomaniac. Pederast, with a liking for—but you know your own mind. Can you be sure the rest will not come out tomorrow? Don't you wish to leave town tonight and flee the shame?"

"The Socratic option? Run before they bring the hemlock?" He snorted. What a man, comparing himself to Socrates, though the pederasty doubtless rang a bell. "I have no shame to flee from." He began juggling the rocks; Molly would have been proud. "Your testimony is done. It's my turn in court tomorrow. You can't make no reply. You can't say nothing—if you're dead."

I sat bolt upright. My heart juddered. What mischief was at play? I stared about: the door was bolted tight. If he meant me harm, he must do it himself. Did he mean to fell me with a rock between the eyes? That's David's trick, not Goliath's. I looked around, wild-eyed, as he kept on juggling. "Killing me won't help you. Everything I've said is written and witnessed, with proofs, at Scotland Yard."

Those crafty eyes. "Sure it is."

"To be opened in case of my death or disappearance. Certified copies in the possession of a lawyer, which even you cannot get at." I was afraid; I was sweating and short of breath. But I was right. If he thought me worth killing, I could still ruin his reputation; I might even send him to jail.

"Feel all right?" He put down the confounded rocks, unconcerned. His eyes twitched toward my glass, his mouth twisting into a smile. "Another Scotch, Mr Scotland?"

Strange smell of the whisky. Poison. He was waiting for me to fall; and then what? Let us find out. I stepped towards him, looking about theatrically. "The Scotch?" Raising my hand to my throat, I staggered, overdoing it a bit. "Foul play."

He jerked away, as if I would fall at his feet. "What a shame, Sergeant. If these depositions of yours are so powerful, and so safely stowed, I may yet have to retreat." He sighed. "You cast aspersions on my colleagues. Disrupt my businesses. The inconvenience alone would be worth killing you. I have enjoyed dominating London. If I must go, I'll go. New York's an improving sort of a place, and they read newspapers."

"Don't you think the scandal shall follow you? I shall make sure of it..." I trailed off, clutching at my heart.

"You, Sergeant, shall do nothing more. A few convulsions, perhaps. Your heart will stop. Your body will be disposed of by men who owe me so much, they would think nothing of assassinating the Queen of England."

I tumbled at his feet and convulsed, as he had described, before falling still.

Brodie walked right around me, breathing calmly, like he was studying a meteorite fallen to earth. He rifled through my pockets, as if by habit; it made me think of his father arriving in New York without a penny. He poured himself another drink.

I hadn't noticed, until now, the ticking of a clock in the cabinet: an old Bohemian mantel clock, by the sound of it.

"Ah, Sergeant. It never ceases to amaze me how you little men overestimate your value. It's almost disappointing. Nobody will notice you're gone. No eulogy. Your story will be forgotten: another cop, snuffed out by some whore's bully."

How and when I would be disposed of, he took no thought for. A matter for the servants, no doubt; this was a man who never needed to clear up his own mess; and he wanted me to feel sorry for him about his beastly mother?

He prodded me with his expensive shoe. "Have you even anyone who loves you? Who will miss you?" He sniggered. Brodie was still talking to me; even having killed a man, he felt the need to belittle me. Yet he feared me; he feared what I could reveal; he feared me enough to kill me. "Oh, the ageing dowager, of course. But she broke that off, right?"

This was too much. I charged at him, roaring. His eyes nearly popped out of his head as I rose from the dead, lifted him by the lapels of his jacket, and shoved him into the glass cabinet.

The fear in his eyes fed my fury. I finally knew this odious beast was as human as I am, no better, no grander, and he feared for his life, just as I had. I crashed him up through the panels, as easily as if he were a child. The lead flashing warped, the glass cascading upon him in a sparkling waterfall.

He batted it away, ducking into my assault. I grasped his greying hair, and twisted it, pressing his face to the wall.

"How is it I am to die?" I leaned close, enraged, so the breath of my anger would sting his eyes. "Vomit bile? Is that it? Spasms? My goodness, what a shame if these spasms cause me to drag a shard of glass across that tender neck of yours. If the poison somehow entered your blood. Involuntary, mind. I'd be as innocent of killing as you are. It's always been done by others on my behalf." I took out my handkerchief and held it near his face. "I've half a mind to make you drink my whisky." As I thrust it over his mouth and nose, he threw up his arms in panic at the cyanide smell, snorting and coughing. How his terror delighted me.

I would not kill him. I grabbed his head in both hands, jerking it backwards. More glass. Cuts on his face. My hands bleeding. He punched me. I was too close for him to get a good swing; in my fury, I barely felt the blow. Drinking in his fear, I threw him to the floor. He cowered away. How petrified he was at seeing me rise from the dead. All thanks to the nights I'd spent pouring away drams at Kate Hamilton's in the hope of defeating Cora at chess.

I reached into the broken cabinet and took the mediaeval scimitar. It was bright and polished.

"Do you mean to kill me, Scotland?"

I brandished the scimitar in warning. Brodie panted for mercy. How I longed to finish him off. He had ruined, rutted and killed with impunity. He had done it for years. And he had meant to dispose of me, without a thought. But there was no escape from his own black soul. These stains would never wash off. If he did flee, tail between his legs, his power was broken. If he did not, we would have him. He could not corrupt the whole world. "To ruin your name will hurt you more."

"You don't want to bring those charges against me."

"Oh, no? I have proof to link you to them all. All your

despicable trades." The Phoenix Foundation, Quartern Mews, the Flowers of Sin, and hundreds more. I was sure, almost sure, we could prove it, if they came forward to testify.

"No, no. I don't think you'll want to bring those charges against me." He pulled himself upright. He rocked back and forth, head in his hands. "Not when you see what I have in that book."

The black volume he had laid on the table was embossed *Efil Terces Ym* on the spine. On the title page, *M—S—L—*, then the same chapter headings Groggins had stashed as insurance policy. But here, beside the chapters, were not initials, but names. Names I knew. Names every Briton would know. Names I cannot write, even here. Beside, in different colours, were named the women: some courtesans, to be sure, but also madams and ladies, abbesses and actresses, countesses and dames. I flicked through the pages. The subchapter titles already made me blush:

*A frisky governess—Male & female aromas—Seeing & feeling— My prepuce, & another's—An aunt exposes herself—A tumescent bath—Forcing my cousin—Bilked by a whore—A fat-rumped Devonian—Erotic madness—Torn again—Remorse—*

This was Groggins' manuscript for the printer, which Dugdale-Hotten so longed to publish: *My Secret Life*. It was not, as presented, the autobiography of a single soul, but an anthology. Erotic recollections of a host of London gents: autonomous depositions, whether stolen or offered, reports of courtesans collated by Groggins, the whole scheduled to be printed by Dugdale-Hotten for their avid subscription list.

This subsidiary venture was to be the Flowers of Sin's eternal bloom. Brodie had enabled the capital's rakes' wildest adventures, and Groggins was capitalising on them through this lavish *magnum opus*. And Brodie kept his master copy book, with its key to this kingdom of filth.

Brodie himself sat quiet now, eyes closed in defeat. I replaced the scimitar in the cabinet and took up the file. Chapter 1 told of first viewing ladies abed, written by an earl. Chapter 2 mingled bedtime amusements with spying on an aunt's bath, by a public school headmaster. Chapter 3 began with nursery frolics (minor royalty), musings on armpits (a famous novelist) and a servant's thighs (a judge)…

On, and on. Precocious youth, through depraved manhood, into lascivious old age. All was arranged to create the story of the most voracious rakehell of our time: the pseudonymous "Walter". What a curious mix of the erotic and the everyday.

> My hand roved about her bum, belly and notch. I asked her to undress. Desire increasing by the feel of her thighs made me inquisitive.

Bawdy, strange, tawdry, familiar. Never have I read such obsessive reflections. I thought of Brodie's defence of pornography. Why should writing of it be so wrong? Why should doing it?

> Grace was always frigging herself, and after she had seen Bob frig himself, she got spoony on him. Very soon Bob spent his seed up Grace's receptacle, instead of on the floor.

Was this the story of London's gentlemen? Brodie's audacious insurance. True enough, this black book carried ammunition enough for society's destruction.

> "Let me feel it," said I. "My—God—no," said she, astonished. "You may come home with me, if you'll be quick."

How many London gents were implicated? Those who wrote their own confessions, and those whose transgressions were recounted to Groggins by the well-trained women, his Flowers of Sin. Easier to count the innocents.

"No use burning it," Brodie whispered. "I have a copy."

My anger was extinguished. He picked himself up. "And Felix? Is this how you imposed yourself on him?"

"Felix asked me to help with the Foundation."

"So you stole his money?"

"On the contrary, Scotland. He pays me."

"A good man signed his charity across to you, and you turned it to dirt."

"Good man, bad man." Brodie shook his head. "Meaningless. People ain't good and evil. Deeds, maybe."

He was wrong, he must be. I wanted to demonise him, just as his papers and his brothels dehumanised people, exalted them, destroyed them.

Brodie sat down opposite me. "Felix was lost. I offered him something beautiful. He grasped it with both hands. I gave him the first taste of happiness he'd had in fifteen years." He picked up my Scotch glass and puzzled at it. He poured the dregs on to the floor. "Your obsession with Felix is amusing. Just one of hundreds of men living out fantasies because they can afford it. Society is riddled with it." He pointed at the black file. "To make all this public—I mean, with the key to its authors—would cause an unparalleled shake. You are no fool. We both have our insurance policies." He rubbed his nose, doubtful of getting his way for once. His eyes flashed to the scimitar, and I tensed; but it was too late for violence now. "If you and I fought to the death, we'd leave a thousand reputations tattered beside our corpses. What say you we walk away?" He had seen the fury in my eyes, but he did not know the hatred he had aroused in my heart. "Face the facts, Scotland. You can't prove a thing, can you?"

"Curses upon you. You may sleep, but you have forfeited your dreams. And if you should dream, let those dreams be cursed until the last day of your life. May no doctor heal you, no priest confess you, no family mourn you, no gravedigger bury you, the devil take you. If you have deserved one thing, it is the pain of the mothers whose babies are bags of bones in the Regent's Canal. Your papers cast their judgements, but you, you shall be judged the lowest of all creatures."

How I longed to say this to him. But I must keep my secret, just a little longer, and of my curses I said nothing. I slumped back in the chair. Yes, now we could prove he was the force behind the mechanism: prostitution, pregnancies, baby farming, trafficking, enslaving, buying, selling, blackmail and fraud. I was sure of it.

Out loud, I agreed. "All right. The Flowers of Sin will never be brought to book. Let them slip away into London's dark past."

"Something will come in their place, no doubt." He chuckled. "Would you still advise me to flee? I can see you're sore, Scotland. Better climb down from your high horse. Think of your own peccadillos."

"She doesn't care about being exposed." I thought of Alexandra and her modern ways. But I would care; Ruth would care.

"And the girls?" Still manipulating.

"Girls?"

"One at the Foundation party. You recall. You were rather intimate. I'm just saying, Lawless, reveal my misdemeanours, and you'll be leaving London too." He peered to see if he had scored a hit. "And if you make revelations about so many powerful people, why, you will never be forgiven."

My testimony might have been stingless, but there was no turning back. It was out of my hands.

"You admitted you used Kate's night house, Scotland."

"That's not what I said—"

"Nobody batted an eyelid. Policeman's benefits. Drinks here, bribes there, a fumble in the dark. I know all about your integrity." Brodie jabbed his finger at me. "Then there's the girl you killed. None of them know about that."

"I didn't kill anyone."

He smirked, convinced he had found his mark. "The girl you ran over."

"She didn't die."

"You can't be sure."

"She's one of the girls we've rescued from your nursery. One of the hundreds kidnapped, or seduced, or whatever you want to call it, into your academy."

"Hey, I give 'em an education, don't I? What's so wrong with that?"

"To hang around street corners. Until she is old enough— no doubt soon—to be trained in your erotic cohorts."

"Hold on. A rustic slut, who can't write and barely speaks English? I bring her to the Big Smoke, clothe her, teach her to speak nice, make her a lady, so she can be loved by the finest gents—"

"Loved? That's a good word for it."

"Scoff all you like. A kept lady in Kensington or Mayfair is superior to any wife in terms of dignity and income. She has finery, she has jewellery, a box at the opera. She has society's respect. When the relationship ends, they go their ways, she to her next lover, he to his or, woe betide, to a wife. It's the wives who are the slaves, not my girls. Wives have no freedom: pure and self-denying forever, with a husband's chafing their only assurance, and finally his disgust. I give people what they want. What greater love can a man have than the love that he has lost? This is my venture. To give it back to him."

This was his boast of the Flowers of Sin and its ministry. "You delude people."

"I offer hope."

"For the rich. For the poor, enslavement."

"They get what they want, too: gossip, gambling, drink, sex. You puritans want everyone to live drab and equal. Why? Why not let 'em dream?" He went to the cabinet, brushing away glass and straightening his collection. "We all harbour dreams that cannot come true. Love denied, love forbidden, love lost. Things we want more than anything, more than riches and empire, I provide. I have no regrets."

I sat in silence, contemplating his crazed vocation. No regrets? Not of that beautiful, pristine bedroom to which virginal youths were delivered as if to the Minotaur; nor of the dungeon in Southwark. Did he travel the country seeking them out? Did he drop by schools and farmsteads, hospitals and poorhouses, plucking them out with a pat on the head? It struck me that we would find a branch establishment, near the Flowers, for boys. What unmentionable things had he done, right here in this secret chamber?

Brodie closed the broken cabinet, as best he could, with a fastidious delicacy. Our struggle was done. "What should we do? Arrest you for your traffic incident? Manslaughter?"

"She didn't die."

"I can produce twenty witnesses who say she did."

"She is alive and working, and I know where, because we rescued her. Or do you have a death certificate?"

He was pleased I was putting up a fight. "The girl at the party you can't deny."

"Ridiculous. Nothing happened. Nobody would believe you."

"Stories of men who should know better misbehaving with girls. People might believe it. Especially with this." He drew a picture from the shelf. "What a story it will make: the copper that's fighting depravity, caught with his pants down, seducing a little 'un." He passed me the daguerreotype.

The Quarterhouse party. It is the morning; the snow lies

thinly on the ground. A group stands at the embers, by an iron bench. None of the typical strangled smiles: these survivors are lost in gay abandon, some heads blurred with movement, gazes challenging the photographer. There we all are: Brodie, Payne, Mauve and his wife—or another's wife—even Felix, intertwined with tumblers and dancing girls. The cartwheel girl was curled up on my lap as if she were my lover. It looked every inch like I was implicated with her. "She was one of yours," I gasped. That was why there was no one watching her, no parent, nobody. Already in training, at that age.

"If you like her," Brodie nodded. "I can get her for you."

"For a fee."

"You're poorer than our normal clientele, it's true." Still shuffling the damned cards. "Throw in a mention of your lady friend and the girl you ran over, holy moly, would that make a sensational article."

He could threaten me all he liked. It was his turn to be scared. Tomorrow would close those newspapers. I hoped it would send him to jail. "And Felix's girl. Where is she?"

"Ask Felix."

"Felix can't speak," I repeated (a lie, but a canny one).

"Of course. I forgot." It was his doing, or his men's; his careless reply betrayed it.

I narrowed my eyes. "And her: what have you done with her?"

"Nothing to do with me. Felix's responsibility. Ask him. Except you can't."

I said nothing. I still hoped to surprise the Enquiry with the testimonies of Felix and the Pixie. But there was another who would do better. I must call for extra protection at court. It could be a matter of life and death. Once this one testimony was delivered safe into the public domain—one incontrovertible witness to open the gates of truth—there would be no reason to hurt her except revenge. Brodie was capable of vengeance, no doubt of it, but to pick on one beloved of princes, dukes and cabinet ministers would be foolish, even for him. Sometimes, sometimes the law works to protect those who are brave enough to stand up against power and oppression. No doubt Brodie was a foe to be feared. But he was not the only one with friends in high places.

## TRIUMPH (ENQUIRY VII)

Browbeaten, sleepless, I made terms with Brodie. Under this armistice, I was to accompany him to the Enquiry; there I would suggest to Justice Fairchild that the whole affair should be sewn up and packed away.

Rain, rain, rain, and every corner of the city ready to burst into life. These mad March downpours washed away the last of winter. I hadn't seen it until now. You can stare at the bare grassy earth and think it dead, but once you notice a movement—an ant, a worm, a blade of grass—your eye adjusts, and you see that the whole mossy bank is crawling with life. Hyde Park had been desolate for months. Now the ecstatic daffodils gave evidence how wildly the roots had flourished all winter. Above the budding trees of the Serpentine, a skein of geese glided in a V formation off to foreign skies. How I longed to go with them. Instead, I sat by this monster without complaint, him thinking I accepted his vices and endorsed them—as if they were laughable eccentricities shared between friends.

I should have been dead tired, but I had never felt so alive. The horror ran in my veins, but I would not show it. Every sinew was electric. I must travel with him; I must make certain he was there.

The rains doubled and redoubled.

Just before my long night at Brodie's, having devoured

Felix's memoir on the train up from the book swap, I had stopped at Mrs Boulton's café. The storm was looming over Waterloo, rattling at the windows.

Steph was more at ease as a manageress than she ever had been as a whore. Acton was right after all: some women just passed through prostitution, like a stop on the underground, to reach their destination more swiftly. "I'm lucky," she said, "that I have prosperous friends. Without them to pay those first bills… Well, I'll attend your trial after all. I've an old friend to return to town. She'll be here in the morning."

Brodie and I were late. He was surprised to find the gallery full, for he thought my humiliation had ended the thing for good. I was not.

In the morning, before the sensation, the societies and foundations made their reports; Brodie slept right through, though these statistics were anything but soporific. I'd studied the information: some girls are lazy, some love clothes, others drink, or pleasure; but most are ruined against their will, curtailing pregnancies or giving their children away; seduced, ruined, abandoned. Would many women choose this life?

It was this attestation, from the Society for the Rescue of Young Women and Children, that made the gallery gasp:

The age at which they fall into evil exceeds credibility. This year, of 472 fallen, sixty-two were under thirteen. This society rescues them by hundreds—3,940 destitutes in eleven years—and begs help from the public. Nearly half were placed in domestic service, 664 returned to friends, 41 emigrated, 541 otherwise assisted, leaving 224 in the homes and 679 unsatisfactory.

Still worse was a parliamentary return on bastardy cases. Over fifteen years:

157,485 summonses.

124,218 fathers came for hearing.

107,776 maintenance orders were made.

15,981 summonses dismissed.

Thus, 1,141 children annually thrown on wretched mothers, an approximate idea of the illegitimate infant population, and especially the temptation to infanticide.

In the five years to 1860, there were 1,130 inquisitions on bodies of children under two years of age, murdered.

Brodie still had men watching the entrance, even now. They were powerless to prevent the royal carriage driving through to the inner door. Prince Bertie got out first, then her special duke.

Then she herself.

An anonymous figure descended, in red-heeled boots and velvet suit with crimson lining and gold lace. She swept into the gallery just as Brodie was being sworn in. It would have been hard to knock her off. He glanced up, discomfited to see a damask rose beneath the fashionable Parisian hat. Still, he suspected nothing.

Whatever questions the barrister cast at him, and recast, Brodie had no knowledge of. Foundation monies used to buy children. Accounts returned through his news companies. Girls enslaved in a Southwark warehouse. Lives bought. Lives sold. Cruelty to children. Infanticide.

"No, sir." He was most sincere. "I have no knowledge of any of that."

If it was put to him that he orchestrated the apparatus, distancing himself from the responsibility through a network of dissimulation, what would he say?

He remained implacable. "To such fantasies, I cannot reply."

"And if I tell you there is proof?"

"Put it to me. You cannot, nor can the police."

"Maybe not," Skittles called from the gallery, "but I can, Walter dearest, and I shall."

Skittles was not dead. Far from it. Back from France at the eleventh hour, under Bertie's protection, to expose Brodie's pantomime.

Our charade at the channel had worked a treat. Brodie's men pursued her, as hoped. Bertie's driver showed a flair for improvisation, wailing in sorrow as her straw hat drifted toward Calais. In the mist, Skittles simply walked on board, even as the driver was reporting her drowned.

With Brodie's men shaken off, they proceeded calmly to Paris where she cut her hair and reinvented herself. Bertie secured her introductions to the finest salons, the top rank of cocottes, even the bally French Emperor. L'Anonyme had a ball, consorting with opera singers and acrobats, and drinking champagne right through the winter.

Now she was back.

Skittles had contracts, affidavits, dates, times and signatures appended. Disregarding court procedure, she named Brodie at once and went on to detail every aspect of his empire. Her revenge on her enslavers was exacted with the calm self-confidence inculcated in her at the nursery, while the legal i's were dotted and t's crossed by the one lawyer in London Brodie could not scare, Skittles's own spoony duke. Skittles proved it all.

She still never paid back that sovereign.

# PART VI
## LOST AND FOUND

### MARCH 25 1864, AND BEYOND

O ends of autumn, winters, mud-steeped springs,
Sleep-inducing seasons.

Charles Baudelaire, *Les Fleurs du Mal*

# HOW TO ACQUIRE A "FLASH MOTT"

1. Leave the old woman at home.
2. Go out on the lash. Choose your nightspot by the weight of your wallet. Slim pouches should keep to Southwark, or Pimlico, Wilton's Hall, etc.; in the West End, The Holborn, The Argyll, Kate Hamilton's; but the top class of lady is to be found in the Royal Opera dress circle.
3. Catch the lady's eye. (For "lady", supply whatsoever class you desire.)
4. Purchase beverage (based on the weight of your etc.).
5. Mention the amateur theatricals you are presently mounting.
6. Should she raise an eyebrow, pounce.
7. Negotiate a rate.
8. Secure accommodation (based on your etc.).
9. Visit monthly, weekly, daily or hourly, dependent upon appetite and aptitude.
10. Enjoy her charms, overlook her failings. Money cannot purchase perfection.
11. Refrain from offering marriage, parental viewings or—God forbid—cohabitation.
12. When you tire of her (or she of you), proclaim your amateur theatrical run over; clinch the separation with a

dividend: two months' pay-off, by current fashion.
13.  Repeat from (3).

> "Flash Bash Rodney", *Darkest London in the Sixties,*
> *or The Fast Gent's Guide to Shady Recesses*

## SHAME ENOUGH

Out it all poured. With the cork unstopped, the poison flowed out, down to the very dregs. Everything except for the ritual of breaking in the arrivals fresh in from abroad, from the shires and from the foundations; that was hard to prove. Most of the Flowers of Sin were so drugged, they recalled nothing of the gruntings and shuntings of their first night.

The unidentified remains found in the basements of one foundation were never called to account. Brodie claimed he had never been there; a daguerreotype proved that he had, but the court could not admit that. The managers were implicated by their negligence in permitting acts of inhumanity.

The women still believed they had signed their lives away.

Justice Fairchild concurred with Skittles's duke that one cannot enslave oneself, however fanciful the contract one has signed. Individual "owners" might challenge his judgement, if they chose to, but their claims imply immorality.

Skittles produced her own contract. Her duke gave evidence on how the bargain was arrived at and monies paid. She spoke of how they took away the child she had, soon after she arrived in London, promising him a better life. She also identified the woman I'd seen that first night near Quarterhouse, Palmerston's friend, as one of Brodie's particular favourites; it was also established that she had visited Brodie the night before we found her, Felix and I, dead in the gutter.

Two of Skittles's contemporaries from Kensington Gore, also known as Albertopolis, exposed the darker practices of high-class courtesanship. Steph's friends spoke, in Cora's memory, of the destitution with which they were threatened each day.

Two Haymarket streetwalkers, ejected from the Flowers, told how they had to make a pound an hour from as many encounters, being kept ragged, hungry and nearly naked to prevent them escaping. Diseased girls and damaged girls were shipped off to tame foundations, of which there were dozens. Any who threatened revelation were easily silenced, for who, in an asylum for fallen women, would credit such outlandish accusations?

Starched spinsters bemoaned their place in the chain of power, lamenting that they had never understood what cruelties carried on beneath their well-meaning noses. The scab-headed moon-eyed accountant was unfit to be presented in court. In exchange for a plea of criminally insane, she peaceably explained her diabolical ledgers. A system of ticks, crosses and asterisks told which children were kept, which sold, and which died—though whether of natural causes was never clear.

Stephanie at last told her story: how her child was taken, with the promise of him a better life; but she knew he was sickly. We painstakingly deciphered the ledger, and found her boy had died.

One bully made so bold as to defend his honour. "A girl who has done it before has no right to refuse it. If stopping out late, in such clothes, with perfume, they are asking for it. It ain't rape, My Lord, if it's between friends. If my girls accused me, that's the ultimate whoring, for public attention. Besides, in my opinion, many girls need a good raping every so often."

Jeffcoat brought seamstresses from Southwark and cooks who blinked like moles in the daylight. They fought to stammer out hasty accounts, in which they were always at fault: indebted, they said, not enslaved. A boatload of foreign women was rescued from Portsmouth Harbour. They told in breathless accents how they were lured with tales of smuggling and benefactors.

Victims brave enough to come forward were full of praise for the police. The newspapers saw it differently. Still today, more and more cases have been brought revealing how Brodie cultivated friends in high places, manipulated the police and used his celebrated status to safeguard these operations. That doesn't excuse us; on the contrary. But it was part of his style to control in this way, right down to the street gang who scared away prying eyes, patrolling the neighbouring streets, in return for four copies weekly of the *Ha'penny Gazette*.

At the last, I should have been called to the stand again. It was declared improper that the barrister who bamboozled me should have been allowed to quiz me, having previously lodged a complaint against me. Even if I had been there, I had little to add to this mountain of evidence. Before making his recommendations to parliament in the strongest terms, Fairchild took the chance to thank me, Jeffcoat, and Molly and her lot, for our pains.


We cannot prevent every seduction, every misfortune, but we could start by fighting against trafficking and forgiving the ruinated. How to fight a culture of coercion and enslavement. How to safeguard women. How to teach a better way of life than flaunting their bodies. How to save unwanted babes. Are these questions of educating, or punishing, or wealth, or love? These puzzles, I cannot solve.

Pontificating about these horrors became *de rigueur*. Society ladies would bring up Mauve's name, then trail off halfway through a sentence; for nothing polite could be said about him.

Men would go further, growing bold over whisky in the drawing room. "The surprising thing is not that it happens. Wherever there are weaker and stronger, it will keep

happening. The surprise is that it doesn't happen more." A pat
on the back to the man so boldly pontificating. Indignation not
only sells newspapers but salves our irredeemable consciences.

What I do know is that to leave all in the hands of earnest
benefactors is to licence caprice. Until it is the right of all to be
protected by society, equally and fiercely, then the abject day I
spent on the Caledonian Road will be repeated, not just in our
nightmares but as commonplace, horrors we speak of only in
order to distance ourselves from them, never conceiving that
we share in the blame.

The great irony of the Enquiry was the consequent demand
for Dugdale-Hotten's books. We drew attention to the erotic
genre. *Maria Monk* outsold *Lady Audley*, and when *Rosa Fielding*
came out, Dickens was green with jealousy.

*My Secret Life* was never published, not openly, but
everyone knew it existed. I got hold of Groggins' manuscript,
but somehow it was circulated. Was Brodie's the only other
copy? How else did so many clandestine editions appear? The
demand to know the dark secrets of the mysterious "Walter"
would keep it in print forever. Those in the know loved to
speculate who had done what with whom—despite nobody's
ever having read the interminable epic, which made Wisden
Cricketers' Almanack seem a vague and slapdash romp. All
those famous witnesses with their prettified perversions, we
all knew they could have told more; now anyone could seek
out their chapter from the bookstalls under Waterloo Bridge.
Ah, London. People think it austere, but it is filthier than
Naples, the capital of European filth.

The sub-chapter titles are enough to make the faint-hearted
blanch:

*Foul-tongued & hot-arsed—Sodomites & catamites—On the
qualities of different cunts—Lolotte's gamahuche—Reflexions*

*on the change in my erotic tastes—French, fat, red-haired &*
*thirty-five—A sphincter dilated—Lingual delicacies—Kid*
*gloves & cold cream—Dildo buggery.*

Sometimes of a Sunday, I pour a glass of gin, to mortify
my taste for malts, and take to my armchair. I extract the
manuscript from the dusty top shelf, and peruse it, with
Groggins' key alongside, revealing who wrote what.

I am on her, up her, a slight sob as my prick goes up
with the thrust of a giant, and we are spending in each
other's embraces, mouth to mouth, belly to belly, prick
to cunt, ballocks to bum-cheeks. All is oblivium and
elysium. There is no uncunting; but with rigid prick still
up to its roots, on again we go fucking in earnest.

At the end of Groggins' chapter list was a coded note, which
I transcribed for Miss Villiers (not wanting to be indelicate) and
she decoded. That is how we found the envelope deposited
with Coutts: the full manuscript, stashed by Groggins just
before they got to him. Brodie got the redraft, edited for the
printers; but perhaps such a work takes more than one draft,
to harmonise the style of the narrators, and that is how the
clandestine publishers got hold of it.

H*l*n pronounced mine to be a most wonderful
amatory career, when she had read the manuscript,
or I had read it her whilst in bed and she laid quietly
feeling my prick. Sometimes she'd read and I listen,
kissing and smelling her lovely alabaster breasts,
feeling her cunt, till the spirit moved us both to
incorporate our bodies.

I turn the pages with strange fascination, as phrases leap

out. I cannot bring myself to read more than a few lines at a time. On some pages I recognise Mauve's holograph and wash my hands afterward.

> The grip and tenacity of her Paphian temple seemed wonderful—what muscular force, what a nutcracker! But that indeed I knew, for her cunt was perfect in every way, a pudenda of all the virtues, powers, and beauties for fucking—a supreme pleasure-giver.

Groggins' endnotes (unpublished) confirmed that he transcribed stories from gentlemen and from the Flowers of Sin themselves, and that he was paid by Brodie. Everyone was writing erotic memoirs, but it's clear that Groggins fancied himself the Baudelaire of Leicester Square.

> Is it any surprise that revered pillars of the community have fallen to buying and selling girls and boys at will? It is the culture of the day. We all read of abasement and abominations. If the next man is tailing madly and devil take the consequence, why shouldn't I?

It's not in my nature to be disgusted at what another man calls natural. I can see how poor Darlington's head overflowed with it. I find myself hoping much of it is fiction. Such strange fictions, though: some arousing, some disgusting, some illegal, but so many details, menial and touching.

> She lifted up her clothes freely, and I saw her cunt. It was surrounded with fine, chestnut-brown, soft, thick hair. How is it that at a glance all this was seen and remembered ever since? Strange that a mere gap close to an arsehole should have such power. I held a candle between her thighs. "Hold your quim open—do—do."

If truth, it tells things a man should never admit to his dearest friend, let alone on paper.

Following Fairchild's recommendations, prosecutions were later brought, not against politicians or financiers, but only actors and singers of harum-scarum popular songs. What opprobrium heaped upon these caricatures. The cases were dismissed, of course, playing out like popular melodramas. What a fuss the papers made. The doting audience rallied round the accused, vilifying the prosecutors as the cases unravelled in shambolic confusion. "If they are guiltless, let us ruin no more lives." It was almost as if innocents were unjustly persecuted in order to make the public lose its appetite for justice, so that the real perpetrators might go unpursued.

At first, nobody spoke of anything but these cases. Then the months passed and we scrubbed our hands of dirty thoughts, as these unthinkable crimes were overshadowed by the usual nonsense: Garibaldi's tour, the Sheffield Flood, the District Line, *Mazeppa* nude at Astley's Theatre, and Müller damnably hanged.

Some say we should be ashamed of our society, where the poor are forgotten, women ruined, the streets unsafe. But ignorance is a great tonic. Read but a page of yesteryear's newspaper, and you learn that each scandal today, each shooting and beheading, is twice outdone by those of the past. You can delude yourself through life, regurgitating stale aphorisms from a lost era, or else wake up and accept this is the only time you can live in; you may as well channel your vitriol into making it endurable.

Sir Richard retired and, within a couple of years, died.

Panizzi retired and died.

Palmerston died in office, clearing the way for Gladstone and Disraeli's ding-dong duelling.

Dugdale was moved to the Clerkenwell House of Correction,

where, deprived of books, pen and paper he died. Though his death was ruled "from natural causes" the jury recommended that books of "high intellectual character" should be made available to prisoners.

I would not suggest they were knocked off, but all were tainted by scandal.

Hotten lived longer. His publishing venture ultimately became Chatto & Windus, which has fared tolerably well.

Felix's Phoenix Foundation was investigated and the board sacked; it was renamed the Foundation for Fallen Flowers.

Quarterhouse flourished, providing refuge for thirty or so Brothers amid the sins of the city, though the Glasshouse fell into disrepair and was dismantled.

Those who helped me were tarred with accusations. Gladstone endured malicious talk about fallen women up to his death. The Prince of Wales was dragged through the courts. I was viewed with suspicion until the day I left the Yard.

Kate Hamilton was condemned and sent to Millbank Penitentiary. Her bulk could not save her from the Tench prisoners' vengeance.

Skittles, at least, went on to a glorious career.

And Brodie?

Brodie made to leave as Skittles commenced her testimony. He found his way from the gallery blocked. It would have made a scene to fight his way out. At the end, he came quietly. His papers fell quiet. His competitors had a field day. The punishments proposed ranged from capital punishment to mediaeval torture. Of course, with threats made and palms greased, Brodie found himself transferred to Southampton Prison. Thence to the docks by night, and the ocean liner to New York, first class.

I fumed about it. His gift to the British Museum clinched it; what is justice, after all, beside a first edition *Don Quixote*?

It seemed just that he lost so much, though, despatched to

the Americas. In New York, he was hounded from town, his reputation destroyed in articles by Dickens and Collins. Half his papers closed, half were sold. I believe he ended up on the West Coast or Mexico, where his proclivities (the weakness he spoke of) were more tolerated.

Yes, Brodie was despatched. And his sins with him? I never knew. I would love to believe that such a tangle of sin could never again be spun. But I know human nature.

I didn't see the triumph in court played out to the finish. Molly tugged me by the sleeve mid-morning.

"Felix is talking. Telling 'em everything. He's desperate we find the girl, old cove." She wiped her nose. "And I may've found her."

# MEAN TEARS

By the time we rescued Eveline, it was too late. Foolish overstatement. It was already too late when Felix had his stroke; even when I first laid eyes on her at the opera. Caught, then ruined, now doomed.

Molly worked it out from our visit as sweeps. The counterpart of the courtesans conveyed to Quartern Lane was the doxy despatched to Lansdowne Gardens.

As we arrived in the syphilitic back alleys of Stockwell, the weather was changing at last. A whiskery Irishman hitched up his trousers with twine, looking at the clearing skies. "Same time next week, darlin'?"

"She won't make it to next week, you devil." The old bawd yawned. Three pups yapped at her heels; she kicked them back. "Nor'll you, if you catch what she has."

"Ah, well, Queenie. Beggars can't be, et cetera."

Lansdowne Gardens looked respectable enough. But within

lay a decaying morass of humanity: laudanum fiends, poxed doxies, squeezed into interstices.

If the Flowers of Sin were the gleaming frontage, No. 9 Lansdowne Gardens was the dirty rear, where cast-offs were left to rot. The opposite of the refuge Felix had founded, this was a compost heap of misery.

Eveline was laid spread-eagle on a tawdry bedspread, festooned in taffeta, as if she were part of this drear garret's furnishings. Her dress was torn. She tugged at her décolletage, perspiration dripping down her collarbone. Her body seemed drawn with effort; yet her face—that face—shone with the radiance of an angel fallen from grace, descending toward her last end.

"Just in time." Molly sighed. "I hope."

"What the devil's wrong with her?" I said roughly. It was indecent, as if some monster had tossed her there, weary of her attentions. The bed was barely made up.

The old bawd bustled in, buzzing like a fly. "I'm sure I don't know, sir."

I snorted. "Someone had better."

"They're brung 'ere from scrapes of every sort. Beatings. Disease. It's habitual, sir."

"How did she come to be here?"

"I'd say she'd have been on the street, sir. But I've not seen her before. Working up the West End, she said. Many do. Whatever the nuns say, it's reasonable a young girl should want the gay life and make the most of her glorious youth. Better than hiding such a face in rags—"

There was a noise on the street below. I glared at the old bawd. "Go on."

"Can't I speak for myself?" The girl turned on the meagre pillow. "Just this final once, mayn't I?"

I looked to Molly astonished. I had seen this phantom just

twice and never heard her speak. Those poor, gravelly tones took me aback.

"She's all burned up." Molly tugged my arm. "Get that window, will you?"

I drew back the pitiful curtain. Damp mushroomed across the ceiling, creeping in from the roof. The vapours in the room were enough to give you tuberculosis in five minutes. I forced the skylight open. The rain was done. The aroma of onions cut through the air, and distant piano music, as a shaft of sunlight pierced the clouds.

Molly liberated the girl from her crinolines. Her pupils were small as she flinched in confusion. She quivered, clinging to her underskirts. She raised her heart-shaped face to me, pale with exhaustion. I had despaired of getting anything from her but recovered my determination. Those eyes I had seen in Felix's daguerreotype, and in her Wildernsea sisters. There was even something about her gestures and expressions that I recognised.

"We've come to hear your story," I said, "if you can be so bold as to tell."

"Must you harass her?" Molly chided. "We've come to help you."

"Oh, but there is a hurry," Eveline said.

Five minutes later, she was ready to tell us her tale, propped up on plumped pillows and fortified by tea, with lemon.

"The Frenchy way, if you wouldn't mind."

She was recovering her colour, but oh, she was frail. Molly brushed her hair from her forehead, settling the sheets, and performing countless ministrations that neither I nor the dunce of a bawd had the wit to think of. Thank God Molly was there: I was beyond exhaustion and felt a poor witness to eternity.

Noises on the stair, and Simpson blundered in. I had sent word to the college hospital with little hope, for he had refused to treat the Flowers from Southwark. I viewed the doctor's arrival with astonishment and dismay. I longed to hear Eveline's story, for we did not yet know if Skittles's gambit would play out.

Brusquely, Simpson examined her pupils. He put his stethoscope to her chest. I found myself fascinated by the pearly lustre of her skin, her raven hair tangled with sweat. There was something about her, something light and magical, an ineffable welcome.

Simpson tossed down his instruments. He pulled me from the bedside and spoke, white-faced, in urgent appeal, a tone unusual to this most arrogant of men. "Let us pray, Lawless, that you may ask your confounded questions. First leave me to examine this poor wretch and treat her."

He kept Molly to assist him. I passed a wretched quarter hour with the harridan of a landlady. "A cup of scandalmonger?" she offered, and made me the filthiest cup of tea I have ever imbibed, speaking all the while of her gentleman callers. The moment I asked of Eveline, she shut up like a Whitstable oyster.

Simpson pushed the door open and collapsed against the wall, holding back tears. I had never seen him care one iota for any creature, living or dead. It made me fear for her. She would tell him nothing, fearful of recriminations; but she was badly bruised and had bled considerably—"Externally and internally," he said. "You mustn't tire her."

I went back in and sat by her. Simpson loomed up, preparing the injection.

"I was a good girl," she said, "a milliner's step-daughter, you know."

As Simpson held up the syringe against the skylight, Molly stood up, knocking it from his hand. The bottle tumbled to the floor. It did not shatter, but the sedative poured out on the floorboards.

Simpson cursed. "Damnable girl. That's the last of my

opiates. You shall have to run along to the chemist's for me."

Molly ducked his hand. "Run along yourself, you cracked old crocus."

"Simpson." Eveline hushed him with a contemptuous glance, like a lady long used to ordering professionals around. Her dark eyes unnerved him. "Get out, you dirty sawbones. You are no longer welcome. I have something to tell Molly here."

Simpson huffed and puffed and stormed out. He would return within the half hour.

"My name is Angelina. An orphan with neither parents nor siblings. Childhood a mystery. Born in Italy. Uncle used me reasonably. Taught me to mend clothes. Transported from Naples to the London docks—"

I nudged Molly, appalled. This was not the Effie I had heard of in Wildernsea, and her native freedom in speaking was quashed in the retelling.

"You doxy fishbag," Molly said kindly. "Cheese your tosh and flam. You're well trained, you are, but save that bosh for the bigwigs. We know about the Flowers, see, and we know about Brodie, so you've to have no fear that you're welching. We want the truth of your flash life, and your vocation, and most of all the truth about Felix."

Eveline blinked, shyly, but the light danced in her eyes. She reached for Molly's coat sleeve, nodding. "Thank you, Molly. Some tales, if not told, fold in on themselves and disappear. I'm not just any girl. A ruined girl is like every other ruined girl, unless she tell her tale aright."

It was true: I had heard so many tales of ruination that I was inured to the tellers' tears. They were numbers on a census, headlines in the *Illustrated Police News*, or stories in Mayhew's reports, stories that might end in resurrection but more likely in abandoned love. This poor soul deserved a better redemption.

Angelina was haughty as you like to Simpson; but to Molly, in those last hours on earth, Effie confessed her tale, trusting entirely to this smudge-nosed ginger-mopped tyke.

She told her tale, and I wrote it all down: of gentlemen who stopped to see her mother or her sisters. She told of leaving the north. Uncertainty arriving in London. The training. Her weakness for the elocution teacher, who taught other things, too: practical biology, he called it.

Then, oh, the glorious time before her fall. She might have gone back to her parents, to shame and good works; more like, she would have been shut in a home for fallen women, with no hope for larks. It was bad enough being poor, but she feared losing her larksomeness more than her health.

She spoke of Felix, and I wrote that down too: how he showered gifts upon her, time and attention. He loved her. He was the first ever to love her. Now she was ill and feared she would never see him again. This was the terrible part. That this beautiful girl should not have been loved. Not just beautiful; irrepressible and unvanquished by hardship and injustice. She should have been loved by princes; she was sold into slavery.

I prayed that she would survive to know better. I thought of the woman I saw that first night walking with Felix, fallen dead in the gutter. Another of Brodie's Flowers of Sin, tossed in the compost, with a story that would never be told.

I gazed down at Eveline. As I lowered my head, I seemed to rise into the sky and look down into all the apartments; and in each another Effie told her final narrative; higher still, peeking under the Stockwell slums and Waterloo whorehouses. So many untold testaments to a city of sins uncounted, unaccountable.

Who can say that Felix's love for Effie, even if deluded, was not real? Her bubbling, intemperate voice, telling this implausible tale: this was the sound of no mythical lyre, but of life itself.

At the end she murmured, pale as death, "Take me to see him."

## VOWS OF FAITH

Simpson returned in a fluster. Saying nothing of his telling-off, he took the girl's pulse and insisted she could not be moved.

I insisted she would be. We could not leave her. I would take her to the Clapham Hospital and—though I did not say it—to Felix. Simpson might give her something to ease the pain, no more.

Shuddering, she reached out for my hand. She held my shirt cuff, rubbing it between her fingers for comfort. I recalled the girl at the party, in Brodie's photograph, pinching a fold of my trousers, transporting me back to my childhood.

Eveline was not that naive girl, turning cartwheels, unaware of herself and the ill-meaning gents ogling her. But, dear God, Eveline was not so much older. This elegant flower had been just such a girl a year or two before, transformed from child to adult not by stays and petticoats and make-up, but by the arts of the Flowers of Sin. Brodie had seen she would soon be a woman: men would stumble over one another to declare their love for her. In that time, she had grown fulsome and lustrous—an irresistible beauty who brought Felix such love, who brought Felix so low—only for that lustre to fade.

I saw now what I had recognised in her gestures: Skittles's grace. Schooled in the same nursery, with the same cultured laugh, half covering the mouth, Eveline was a life-size study for Anonyma, the most famed courtesan in London.

Why she was dying I never understood. The violence done her so carelessly in those weeks at Lansdowne Gardens was enough; on top of that was a wasting disease that set her coughing. Whatever Felix had done to her, we would never know; but I knew that Brodie's jackals had dropped her here, where they knew she could be silenced, and anything she did say would be ignored or ridiculed. We shall never know.

As she slipped into opium dreams, she repeated her wish to see Felix. To my surprise, Simpson yielded. In the cab, he wept. I thought I had seen everything, but this man weeping I had never thought to see. For Groggins he had shown no emotion, nor even the bones dredged from the canal. Now, over this lost girl, he was broken.

In a funk, he admitted he'd treated Eveline before. First, with the Flowers, where he conducted medical checks; then in Quartern Mews, laid low by Felix's passions. I have no doubt that he genuinely felt for her, but he was also ashamed at having forsworn his Hippocratic Oath. He had seen the punishments she endured; he had not stirred to save her; now she could not be saved. But he was told not to interfere, and threatened that his personal affairs would be revealed to the police. Besides, what was she anyway but a whore—even if a winning one?

There it was: this venerable medic, our mortician for murder cases, and all the while, he was one of Brodie's underlings. What sins had he helped to hide? I could sense the shame he had suffered, enduring blackmail to value silence over his medical duties, this man without scruples. He deserved to suffer.

Spring had arrived overnight, packing the winter back to its mothballs and mildew. The day was warm. Families were picnicking on Clapham Common. As we sped past, six girls were singing in a ring beneath the blossom of a cherry tree.

> *Sparrow, come, the first spring morning.*
> *Will you take my garland?*
> *Sparrow, come, your girl is calling.*
> *Will you take my ring?*

The daffodils reared rampant, the narcissi close behind. All over the city tonight, flesh would be on view again, like these garish blooms, as women threw off their inhibitions along with their winter coats.

The Clapham Hospital for Incurables was in mayhem. I had not foreseen reprisals from Brodie's men, that they could move so fast. Our closure of the Flowers of Sin sparked it, I suppose. Somebody had welched. That morning, before Skittles testified, Brodie's jackals could not have imagined that within a few hours, he would be jailed and his empire fallen.

As we hurtled into the courtyard, people huddled around a pile of blankets. I saw Bede's withered hands rubbing the silken hair of that august head. I ran to him, fearing we were too late. We could not piece together what had happened from the conflicting reports. Felix did not fall from the window: he would not have lived.

We lifted him gingerly back to his room, while Molly carried Eveline.

Bede sat in the corridor, quivering. Smoke billowed out under the door of Felix's room. When I reached out to him, Bede flinched away.

"Bede, where's the Pixie? Bede?"

His eyes darted around wildly. He scrabbled at the door, then fainted. I had to pull Bede away and barge the door down. The flue was on fire. But why a fire? This was the first warm day of the year.

By the time we found the Pixie, it was too late. Despite my precautions, Brodie had got to them. How she suffered with the flames and the smoke, we shall never know. She could not scream for help. I sat on the floor with my head in my hands, as the orderlies took her little body away.

The birds were singing in the courtyard.

# IN DEATH AS IN LIFE

We laid Eveline and Felix side by side on the bed. I stood gazing at them: the old man with his lustrous silver hair disarrayed, the young woman with the irresistible heart-shaped face, both of them ruined by this dreadful sink of a city. Effie's story was magical and strange, a tale of deception, and yet, in the end, I wondered which of them was the less deceived.

Simpson tended them intently. A ladybird fluttered above the bedposts.

Felix's breath was short, but he took her hand. Effie seemed at peace, her smile beatific, but she was never conscious again. Her tale was told. Now I should never hear Felix's. I fell to my knees by the bed.

Molly settled Bede on a blanket by the window. He was shuddering with fear and cold, trying to talk. Molly told him to shut his trap and breathe. Now at last, he was coming back to his senses.

Still shivering, he tried to sit up. "Where's the Pixie, then?"

Molly looked to me. We turned away, unable to reply.

"She must have got away, then," said Bede, eyes wide with hope. "I told her to run. She's a fast little slip of a thing when she wants. Where's the violin case?"

"Bede, settle down." Straining to steady my voice, I rose from the bedside and brought him the case.

"Lovely." He heaved a sigh of relief. "Felix has been in cracking form. Oh, his logicality is all sewed back to a totality. Pixie has him learning her sign language. Didn't he pick it up easy! Musician, ain't he?"

With Felix on his way to complete recovery, Bede and Pixie between them had been piecing together what Felix wanted to say.

"You got his testimony?" I meant to sound sceptical; I sounded impatient.

"Oh, we've notated his whole bleedin' memoir for you, Watchman."

I attempted a joke, my voice choked. "More in Groggins' style?"

"No, no. No erotic memoir, this."

"And where is said memoir?"

He blinked brightly. "That violin case: there's a false back panel."

I opened it. The violin had not even a scratch. The inside panel, though, was ripped out. There was nothing there.

"See?" he said. "There's your manuscript."

Not till then did I realise how thorough Brodie's men had been. Someone had threatened to unravel the yarn that led to the monster; if it was Felix and the Pixie, they must be silenced. Not content with doing for Felix, they had burnt his story and snuffed out the poor soul who wrote it down. Lost, all lost. I took the violin and held up the empty case. "Oh, Bede."

"Where is it?" Bede looked puzzled. "Felix himself had writ a bit about his old life, then he added the extra bits, which the Pixie wrote down. I do like a love story."

The fire was still smouldering. I knelt at the grate with an involuntary shudder as the last flames shot up the flue. Sure enough, a remnant of foolscap glowed in the embers. I pulled at the edges and drew out a scrap, written in the Pixie's hand:

I must mention two stretches of particular turmoil.

They had burnt it all, all but these cinders. The few words that remained I could imagine in Felix's clipped accent, more English than the English. The outer envelope had not taken. On it I read the legend, in Felix's flowing holograph: *Memoirs of Music and Rapture*. Inside, nothing. All Bede's efforts, and the Pixie's final labours, these idiots had destroyed.

Simpson sat back heavily by the bedside; there was no more he could do.

I stumbled to Bede and clasped his poor, withered shoulders. Molly laid one hand on Bede's forehead, the other upon my shoulder. Together, we gazed over at Felix and Effie, laid side by side like a mediaeval knight and his lady, staring up into eternity, with nothing remaining of their outrageous lives except this moment and the memory of love.

Bede shrugged. "No matter," he said. The poor boy was beyond fear. He turned his bright eyes upon me, eyes that had seen too much for any young man. "I can remember it mostly."

"Like our chess game?"

"That's not fair, Watchman. When it's important, I remember it."

"Go ahead," I stammered. Could he possibly mean it?

He told me sternly to sit myself down with a pencil, and he would recite. "I won't just do the gist. You'd rather every word, wouldn't you? I'll start with his bit he'd writ beforehand, then what we wormed out of him fresh."

"Don't tell me you have it by heart?"

"I used to think everyone remembered like that. It was the Pixie told me I was odd." Bede said he could remember an epic poem, when he paid attention. "Mr Groggins had me listen to the odd confessional session, so as I could fill in blanks in his shorthand. I should prefer if you'd write this down, though, as you know I'm unable."

I shook my head in wonder and stroked the hair from his face. "You wee genius."

"Lucky, ain't it?" He smiled. "I just seem to remember these things."

# PART VII
## ON A BED SO WILD

### EFFIE, 1848–1864

Causes to account for lax morality of female operatives:

1. Low wages inadequate to sustenance.
2. Natural levity and the example around them.
3. Love of dress and display, coupled with the desire for a sweetheart.
4. Sedentary employment, and want of proper exercise.
5. Low and cheap literature of an immoral tendency.
6. Absence of parental care and the inculcation of proper precepts. In short, bad bringing up.

Henry Mayhew, *London Labour and the London Poor*

# A POOR LIFETIME (EVELINE'S CONFESSIONS)

I was the twelfth, and named Effie, or mayhap the fourteenth; depends which of my sisters you believe or how many that died do you count. My mother was sick of childbearing and my father sick of children, so as there wasn't much care taken of the little ones, except by the others. And if chores were undone, or food scarce, which it often was, the little ones got it bad. My first memory is cowering under the stair, in terror, not that Father would beat me, but that Susan would beat my brother, William, for passing me buttered bread under the table, like a dog.

The smallest did the housework, my mother being exhausted of life. The elder ones went out to work at the farms where Father did odd jobs. Though what the girls did, I could never get out of them. Cooking or cleaning or making beds, I imagined, for I learned these as soon as I could walk; but Sookie hinted at other things young women might work at. I was fascinated for her to tell me. Every time she came home, I would harangue her to tell us how she had earned those gleaming pennies off the squire, until she got the habit of slapping me, and I desisted.

Not to say my upbringing was harsh; more that it was careless. Father had work; Mother was ill and oft abed. So we had to care for each other, looking out for ways to survive. Once Sookie had been noticed down the Coach House, she started bringing home gifts and luxuries: dried fruit, cocoa and, once, a book. We became known. A different sort of gentlemen took to visiting. Sookie upped and vanished. Then Sarah. Wouldn't be so strange, except that they were never, ever spoken of. Not until a big man came, from down south, with news of the girls and how they were thriving. You may imagine, the whole family was up to high doh about his dropping in, except for Father, who knew nothing about it, or cared nothing, perhaps.

There was a gent, so we were told, coming to view us. My mother kept to her room. My father was at work; he was always at work these times. As Susan was presenting, I was to bring in the tea.

Straightaway, the grand London fellow caught my eye. He was a Mr Broody, or Moody, or perhaps Bridie; I was never sure. Anywise, he took a fancy to me. His coat was different to any I'd ever seen—not the fur or the material; I know now it was the cut of it, modern and tailored.

Of course, it was me he bought. I didn't know at the time I'd been bought; only now I look back at it and remember Susan squirrelling the money away, and my mother, agreeing I must go, full of shame.

The others were dismissed, grumbling. I had to stand there in my milkmaid's pinny and pirouette for him while Susan answered his questions. Could I read? Write? Sew? Cook? All tolerably, but I was quick to learn, if he should like to return in a sixmonth. He said he would return on the morrow, with a bag of gold.

That night, I endured such a scrubbing as I never had before. All was hushed tones, and instructing me in flirtation, so as to raise the price. Father couldn't be told what was to become of me, because he was right upset whenever Susan sold one of us. How could I have told? I hadn't the faintest. He couldn't stop her doing it, you see, because he didn't send enough to feed us, so Susan would lambast him for his weakness and dole him out a few pennies, keeping the lion's share for us and herself.

Next day, sure as eggs is eggs, the man came again, on his return from Whitby. Susan asked should he like to be alone with me.

He laughed. To test the goods? No, thank you very much. I would be kept fresh for others' eyes—and hands. Effie, he said, and my name sounded exotic in his accent. That'll have to change; what do you make of Eveline?

I liked it tolerably enough.

Henceforth, you are Eveline—at least, until we find you a station in life. Can you learn? Can you make believe? Can you please?

I can, sir, I replied. I was always eager to please; it was the way to avoid a beating in my family.

And so I flew the nest.

It seemed to me a tremendous lark. Third-class compartment with his valet, while our Mr Broody travelled in first. I knew not where I was going. The city, with its vast, unwieldy fogs. Every inch of the way, my head filling with excitement and conceit, for which I'm justly punished now. I would learn, I would read and write and draw; I would acquire the accomplishments of a lady. I was pretty, after all, everyone said, and I had been chosen above my sisters for—I knew not what.

So much did they teach us. If you think I speak strange now, you should've heard me back then, when I were a child and spake pure Yorkshire, and should have been laughed straight back up Ermine Street. Now I've got my education, learnt off old Grogbags, of how the quality speak and how I ought to speak; but I am ever so tired of it. And this story I'm telling, I wouldn't have had words to tell then, so that I am grateful for all they gave me. I'm a Frankenstein's monster, my voice created by studying from books and listening in doorways. Yes, this is a voice quite changed from the one you would have heard then.

I never think of my family now. I suppose as Susan did something with the money. And Father will have missed me, if nobody else.

## A DEMON NATION (EVELINE'S CONFESSIONS)

I was took past all the sights of London in his very own carriage—I heard the valet tutting—Euston Arch, British Museum, filthy Thames as has took girls less wickeder than I. I was all a-flutter. Then I was deposited all alone I'm sure I don't know where. The nursery, the girls called it: nursery because you were grown into flowers there. No, sir, Flowers as with a capital F, if you're taking dictation. The Flowers of Sin. Don't you know about it? I suppose you don't, for it was a secret sworn and guarded as well as any in London.

When I arrived, a starchy matron bustled me inside, looked at me askance, told me to sign something, or put my mark on it at least, and take off my clothes.

Don't be prim, little miss, she said. You'll have clothes enough if you behave.

I thought it a lark. How do I know it was Mr Broody that night? I didn't. But later we'd spy on him, in the evenings, coming by when there was a new girl.

Protecting his investment, said my friend Helen. Proper businessman. A poor country girl like me couldn't fathom what business there was in a house full of tender lasses, or rather of foul-mouthed wenches being reformed into the elegant young women as made it worth their efforts.

That first night was the only night we slept alone before

joining the dormitory. Helen said they slipped something in our tea, before the gentleman came to view us. After the matron took our clothes off, he would come when we were sleeping—and maybe there was something in that nightcap the night I arrived.

View us? Dirty Gertie laughed. Is that what you call it? It was ever impossible to have a private chat among the Flowers.

Don't be potty-mouthed, said Helen. This one is innocent as a daisy.

I am not. And to try and impress them, I told them Sookie's adventure in the upstairs room at the Coach House on the road to Whitby, but something in how I told it made them laugh, I suppose because I yet knew nothing of the ways of love.

I did my service. I saw that some vanished quick and some stayed forever; some got regular beatings, and some were never noticed. Looks is a lot, but they aren't everything. More is to be smart and biddable. Show you can learn. So I am biddable. I am invisible. That way, I avoid the worst. Some are ruined quick and tossed away. You see them going downhill, and there's nothing can save them once the rot sets in. And there they go, Lansdowne Gardening.

Thus we blossomed. The Flowers of Sin. How far from the drudgery of my childhood.

I knew they would pick me out. Sure enough, as soon as they came to choose the next bunch, I was promoted from the seedlings into training for the Flowers. Which is an honour, being as how the Flowers service the finest gents in the country: poets and admirals and politicians. So we are trained up, nicer than ladies, finer than princesses: etiquette and elocution, dancing, singing, writing, French, German and a smattering of Aye-tie. I took a liking for the fiddle and learned gypsy waltzes.

They brought former pupils to give talks—a discourse, they called it—to inspire and improve us. My heroine was Miss

Skittles, who didn't take no tripe. How to Keep Your Man and Enjoy Doing It, was her topic. She could marry any day she liked. She enjoyed the respect of all society, with the freedoms of the gay life.

I wanted to be like her. I wanted to be her. If they demanded what she would not give, she didn't give it, and—this is the best of it—they wanted her all the more for it. All those lessons in etiquette, the tutoring from Groggins and schooling of my lips, tongue and teeth, not to mention organs unmentionable, but this, this was the best lesson I ever learnt. Men want us, and if we too readily give what they desire, they won't want us long, but if we tarry and dally, and dither and delay, they will want us forever. Heavens, they will marry us.

Now and again, a girl was thrown out. Gertie hadn't come up to scratch in her pronunciation. Her table manners were uncouth, and her toilet manners; then she was dallying in a side street talking of our training, secrets we know must never be whispered. She was sent to Lansdowne Gardens and never seen again.

Helen said that Gertie died on the street within a few weeks.

I see now what an investment it was. They had people sewing for us, cooking, teaching us to walk, to talk, to please a man, no less. Our Mr Broody was a wily one. To find a real lady and make her whore for you is a tricky game, but to raise up twenty guttersnipes and make them seem like ladies is safe—a charitable action—and altogether cheaper.

Seek them far off, beyond the rule of law, in backwaters such as Poland and Portsmouth, Yorkshire and Ypres. Life is cheap in the provinces. Pick up a bargain with a bit of potential, toss her to the trainers (kept discreet through threats), and within a year—six months, if she's quick—you have a debutante, a society wife or—in my case—a long-lost daughter.

Have you rumbled the plot? Fulfilling impossible desires is a lucrative business. A confession here, a jotted note, a peccadillo admitted. Collecting such secrets was Broody's vocation and Groggins' joy.

## WASH AWAY OUR STAINS (EVELINE'S CONFESSIONS)

I was to go to the opera. I was told where to promenade. I must be poised and beautiful. If it came off, everything would change.

Sure enough, I caught Felix's eye. No one told me what to do, or who to look for; but I knew my business. I shan't forget the astonishment in his eyes when he spotted me. Then I was gone, on the arm of a young swell. Ooh, I had studied all about it, learnt which operas to compliment and which to deride, but nothing prepared me for the glamour of the West End.

We had him. My training redoubled.

I was to style myself a Milanese lady exile. We knew only so much of her. The girl went missing in 1849, at the age of three, in some revolution or other. She would be seventeen, nearly eighteen now.

I was younger, but tall and slender. She was fair, but my dark curls would have to serve, for the Flowers distrust dyed hair. I do not like my bulging moon face, but others find it pretty enough, and that should do. Dark eyes, big nose, near enough. For the birthmark, a burn from a hot coal, soothed with calamine lotion.

Italian was her language; she'll have heard German, too. I know only English, and even that dubious with my brogue. Where I hail from in the moors, all is utterance; words are abbreviated and lengthened at will. There is no theatre or poetry or music, beyond the banshee wails at the Coach House on the northern turnpike, where Mr Broody first spotted Sookie.

I learned some lingua franca to serve for Aye-tie, a few words of German thieves' cant, and a smattering of Frenchy argot. Too little, too late. Talking posh would serve, which I didn't mind, as it makes me feel like quality, the same as the silk drawers they gave me.

My training as a Milanese lady was done, my fiddle-playing to be kept a secret for the moment. They had us nicely prepared. They taught that if we were overwhelmed by our lovers and by London, that's as it should be. We Flowers had more right to decent treatment than any whore, than any wife. Oh, we were privileged. Groggins taught us to be mercurial, and capricious came easy to me. I was imaginary, you see, come back from the past. Back, even, from the dead.

Dear Felix. Thought he'd seen a ghost. After that first tantalising view, they fed him a line about me: that I recalled nothing of my early life, I was an orphan learning a trade, found in a milliner's shop. To make sure, he would have to pick me out in Cremorne Gardens, on the promenade.

I held my breath as I walked past. I'd been told to say nothing, but I couldn't help practising in my head. How do you do, sir? Why, how do you do? My petticoats were comfortable, but it was always the silk underneath that gave me shivers.

The other girls smirked, said I was too young, too gauche, apart from Helen, who loved me. She told me I would succeed; she told me other things too, about my body, and how he would want me, and she showed me, and read me stories about men and women that she kept in the drawer of her dresser, which were adventures she'd had with her gentlemen and persuaded them to write down, and a few she'd told to Groggins, shameless of the secrets. Telling it back made it worth all the more, she said, because then the gents would enjoy us over and over again. Years from now, they would still remember our youthful skin, when they were old and couldn't get it up any more, and we were dead and gone. Perhaps I would be luckier. I was to be given to one man who would love me and keep me all to himself, whereas Helen was shared far and wide among her gents and their friends.

Felix picked me out at once, to my everlasting delight. We'd framed it just right. He was transfigured. He believed. It was ridiculous and should have been shaming. But I didn't mind that. I would play my role and bask in his attentions. How he loved me. Filled me up from my boots to my bodice to my bows. One day, he would see through me, I knew it. Northern Effie was bugger all like his darkling Angelina, and someone must surely tell him so. I think his friends did, early in the madness; but he cut them off and withdrew into the solitude of our indulgences.

How he loved me. Such merriment. Oh, to be someone else, anyone other than useless Effie McGarrigan, with her countless siblings and barren upbringing. To be someone. I liked being high class, I'll admit, but most of all, I liked being loved. Have you ever been adored? I loved being adored. He wanted ever so much to look after me, I felt guilty, almost.

He kept me hid at first, as they'd instructed, fearing to be found out, fearing to transgress their rules. As the months passed and his amazement gave way, he shared with me his pleasures in life. We feigned I was a long-lost niece for a while. He forbade me to dress too fine and hated my make-up; he'd hide me on his arm and sneak me up to his box after the shows started. I didn't care. It was a luxurious life, and I revelled in it.

At last, he began to whisper the story of my return from the dead, even—alas—to whisper the name of the Flowers of Sin. He thought to do them the honour of thanking them; for in returning me to him, they had returned him to life. But they brook no indiscretion. He received a visit from Mr Broody's jackals, who can be heavy-handed, as you know.

If I say that Felix was gentler than I had imagined, will you take my meaning? I had been warned that, sold off and signed away, I should no more expect the Flowers' protection. We must negotiate our own rules.

If I say Felix was less thrilling than I had imagined—how unkind of me—you will think me shallow. I am ungrateful, I'm sure. Life with him was not as I had imagined, for the Flowers trained us in the arts of love. I could never get used to it, however he loved me.

If I say he was strange, poor man, well, such strange things had befallen him. I made him tell me, over and over, so I would know the story better than he. I was a good student that way. Yet I tired of the deception, or perhaps, if I am honest, simply of him. I had everything; I risked everything.

I wanted to niggle him. That, I suppose, is what good daughters do. He always insisted I go out without make-up and finery, and if I had learnt one thing from the Flowers, it was that a woman must use all her weapons, and invisibly. As our story went, I'd survived this long with no father to chide me, so I snuck a little rouge in my bag and applied lipstick in the dark of the theatre. Though I was his darling long-lost daughter whom he would forgive anything, I found the one thing he could not forgive: infidelity.

How I had feared at the first to be found out. Now the role required me to play up. If he forbade me to go out and make friends, that was fatherly. Any daughter worth her salt would disobey such dictatorship. He began to look at me more closely. His wonderment turned to criticism.

Let me say nothing of the opera, the young gent in the box, and Felix's raging outburst which disturbed *La traviata*. I had never seen his eyes so dark. He wasn't to blame. Dear Felix. The fault was mine. We were taught this in the Flowers. It was always our fault, and I must improve.

When he came back, after our estrangement, he was bristling. He apologised, but the way he looked at me—I could see—he knew. Maybe he had known all along. He's an artist, a visionary dreamer, but he isn't a fool. The truth he'd denied, in his anger, became obvious.

You know his public persona. Everyone thinks him such an angel, and he is; but he is good after long struggles. He has endured things you can't imagine.

I used the only defences I had. Our time was almost done. He was disabused of that fanciful mystery: my reappearance. If I wished to keep him, I must resort to more feminine wiles, lessons learnt with the Flowers.

In France, poets revere the prosperous courtesan. In Turkey, harem ladies have respect and power. Japanese geishas are admired for knowledge of music and refinement in the arts of love-making. The purchase price does not include the right to make love; to earn this is out of reach except for the most expert lovers.

This is how I envisaged Miss Skittles. Now I fancied myself her equal.

I saw in his eyes something I had not seen before. I realised he was still a man, with a bellyful of life. He'd been badly used as a boy, in the army; and then there was what the soldiers did to his wife. Now he would use me badly.

I feared I would be cast from his heart, and cast from the Flowers. He was beside himself. He took me home and punished me. He grabbed me, as he had never done before, and threw me to the ground: I was no daughter of his. I had no choice; I used the only defences I knew. If I could no longer hold him by being his daughter, then it was time to be his wife.

After the seduction, he was like a little boy. Delighted. Disgusted. He must have known I was no maid. The Flowers of Sin were trained in that, too; Mr Broody's vision, to rival Paris bawd houses, where no wickedness is too much, everything is indulged and gratified to the point of perfection. I was out of practice, after my months of celibacy. But it did not take long to recall the art of so-far-and-no-further.

He fell to me. Once he knew himself to be consigned to hell, he behaved like the devil, and we enjoyed rapture undreamt of. He clung to my bosom, wept tears of lust and shame when he went too far, and stormed off in disgust—but I knew he would return. No one can abandon the pleasures we shared.

The final end came quickly. The opera box: *déshabillée* again. I knew he was spying. I did it to rile. He no longer believed my protestations. He marched me home, a strange light in his eyes. I saw what nobody else sees in him: that all his art and refinement and kindness was held in place by the merest threads, taut and ready to snap after years of pain. This charitable hero, money all spent, with his silky hair and endearing old jacket.

Give in to it, I told him, for we'll soon be dust, all of us. When I finally persuaded him to give in to lust, he was a beast, worse than I foresaw, because he knew what he was doing. Oh, yes. Felix struggled to be good. He used me as badly as he had been used. He had me as a girl and as a boy, if you'll pardon my saying. Artful make-up I needed, and I was so sore I couldn't sit down. Sodom and Gomorrah, and every heresy in the good book. This was how Broody sold us: we would admire our gents, love them, refuse them nothing, not even if they used us as the filthiest whore or a sailor boy.

His lusts redoubled. What did I care? I was dead to normal love. With each abuse, he loved me more, and where's the harm in that? I was my own enslaver, and he my salvation. I harboured the hope he'd marry me, or somebody should, one day. Laugh all you want. Many Flowers have managed it. Too late for me now.

When he left me for dead one day, they called the doctor, I suppose. I don't recall. I didn't feel anything. The landlady gave me dirty looks. But I recovered. Only, when he didn't return, I became afraid. The money stopped. I was flung out. I couldn't sell my wares on that patch. I was bruised, and the local girls beat me.

When I knocked at Quarterhouse to enquire of my beloved, I was told Felix was in the hospital, all but dead. I went to go and visit him, but I collapsed, I'd had so little to eat, and never got there. I woke up here, a Lansdowne Gardener, God forbid; and old Queenie, she isn't so kind, blaming her troubles on us.

It's fast I've been brought low, and nobody's fault but my own. I don't feel it too deep. I'm used to it. I did once, especially when I heard my brother William had died. My sister Sookie, who I never cared for, visited Quartern Mews to tell me, and beg money off me. I did cry, but why? I get enough gin and victuals; the gin's my preference. I won't live long. I don't have regrets. I feel less than some do, perhaps.

If you have any regard for me, give Felix my fond wishes, now that I'm dying or dead. Tell him I bless him despite it all. If you think I'm still playing my role, oh, think what you will. I've had it hard enough. I have had a harder life than you can know, until my months with Felix. He was my one place of peace.

# PART VIII
## TO PUT OUR GRIEFS TO SLEEP

### FELIX SONNABEND, 1801—1864

For hearts to which the frost is so long tethered,
Nothing more sweet for hearts of deathly grace,
O sombre seasons, queens of our weather,
Than your pale shadows' immutable face,
—Except, on moonless eves, we two, just we,
On a bed so wild to put our grief to sleep.

Charles Baudelaire, *Les Fleurs du Mal*

## MUSIC AND RAPTURE
## (FELIX'S TESTAMENT, RECOUNTED BY BEDE)

I was born in Vienna in 1801. My mother moved in society circles. I never knew who was my father, but many men attended her and paid court to her. I believed myself an Austrian, though I often heard men admire my mother's Hungarian cheekbones.

She being busy with her work, I was brought up by Nanny, whom I loved. Mother was beautiful, but Nanny was warm and wifely, though she had no children, and I sometimes wonder if she loved me too much.

When I showed an aptitude for violin at a tender age, I was wrenched away from Nanny and sent to the conservatory school. The day I had to leave her, I threw a sort of a fit, banging my fists upon the ground and gnashing my teeth; I remember, my mother thought I was wilful, ruining my best clothes to shame her. The passion that overwhelmed me then I do not understand. Only I remember that the thought of a day without Nanny seemed an everlasting winter, and even though I returned to her every afternoon, it was never the same as those first paradisiacal years. When, later, I realised it was the violin that had taken me from her, I felt it as a pain, like pinpricks in my heart, for I loved her dearly.

I made progress at the conservatory. In the vibration of the strings I rediscovered the first magic of my life: in the half notes and breves, dominant sevenths and flat fourths. This made school tolerable. Though I was not sociable, I got on with my fellows. I was astonished, thinking them my equals, to be singled out at the age of twelve to go on to the Musikschule, that became the Konservatorium.

My mother strutted with pride into the principal's offices. I was pleased to have pleased her. She now started to pay me more attention, even attending some concerts, often with the same man, whom she introduced as my uncle, whereupon teachers and friends would catch each other's eyes significantly.

Of course, the greater world changed utterly in those first years of my life, but I remember nothing of Napoleon's arrival or departures. I first learned about the army when a general spoke of the fine Austrian music our troops needed to inspire them. He brought the conductor of the military orchestra, who listened to our *St Matthew Passion*. He invited me to join the military band, at the age of thirteen.

The principal was sorry to lose such a talent as mine, but the chance to contribute to Boney's downfall was too glorious to miss, and I should not regret it. That is how I came to entertain the troops on the way to Waterloo.

I found myself in the clutches of that savage beast, the conductor, who thought his military status gave him complete power, as if we were a tribe of marauding apes. I became the butt of jokes about soft skin and dimples, along with more ribald comments. The shared accommodation where we young musicians were bundled alongside the veterans gave me some protection. But the conductor had his own tent and liked to summon me, as he put it, to play him to sleep.

I will not say what happened after the serenade, except that I did not return straight to my berth; candles were extinguished, my cries were dampened with a resin wrapped in cloth while he did what he pleased. Sometimes, the conductor, shamed by his actions, would throw me in the cart with the instruments to be pulled by the horses. That is what I was to him, I suppose: another instrument that sounded sweetly enough to soothe his blackguard heart.

Of life after the wars, in Habsburg society, from Vienna to Verona, and finally Milan, I will say nothing, for the history books shall record those shining eras—for even Garibaldi's nationalist tomfoolery will not eclipse that glittering era. I prospered. I played in the best orchestras, the finest operas and ballets, in such concert halls and amphitheatres as you cannot dream of. I was feted as a musician, and feted in society as a bohemian. Finally—though I had never thought of marriage, still less of love—I fell for a wonderful Italian lass.

We were quickly blessed with a daughter, and I thought that the sun could never shine more brightly than upon me and my happy clan. I was at the height of my powers, leader of the finest orchestra in Milan, when the storm clouds gathered.

There had been political agitations before. The year 1848 was different. Italian patriots managed to throw the mighty Habsburgs out of the city. As a mixed couple, we were anxious, but the Italians treated us well enough. Musicians are loved and considered honorary rebels.

When the Austrians returned, they showed no mercy. Buildings were razed, families executed. At one baker's house, when his bread was not ready for the troops, they murdered his wife and put his daughter into the oven. In this climate, I began to fear. I knew people on both sides, but my associations with artistic Italians weighed against me. Early one morning, we were packing our bags for the safety of our countryside. Then came the dreadful knock.

My wife pleaded with me not to open the door. She was distraught. They would kill us, she said; and perhaps her family were with the rebel brotherhoods, Young Italy or the Carbonari. I never knew about that.

I opened the door and was manhandled into chains. My wife threw herself at them, wailing and weeping about our little child. She beat the commander's chest with her hands. They ran her through. At that moment, all my love for my wife exploded in my heart.

I heard myself telling them, in a voice void of music, that our daughter was upstairs. Would they give her to the neighbour? Their hands stained with blood, they fetched her down. A soldier carried my little Angelina down the road, and that was the last I saw of her. Where she was taken, nobody could say. Later, I made every enquiry possible. So many were killed and lost, nobody knew what became of these wretches. Some survived, some died, some were exiled.

In the square fortress of Mantua, I lay four days without eating or drinking. Such a fury arose within me that I was ready to cut the throat of every soldier I saw. In my delirium, I found a kind of perspicuity. I must be stronger. Their brute strength, so ill-directed, had destroyed my world. If I wished to fight such evil, it was fruitless to kill one or two; I must tell the world.

Accordingly, I ate, I drank. I slept, I planned. I sawed through the bars at night, knotted the sheets and made my escape. Then the serendipitous fisherman—but all that you may read in my book.

I was lucky. Even after my escape, my story could have stayed untold. But I had friends. Italy had friends, and eloquent ones. Ruskin, Carlyle, Tennyson, Swinburne. Music is like that: it leaps boundaries. When I reached London and began, fearfully, to tell my tale, the disbelief subsided. Public opinion was swayed. When the Italians rose to take their nation, none applauded more than the British.

I settled quickly; I was invited to join a prestigious orchestra, the London Exiles. My enquiries of Angelina got nowhere.

Friends showed me London's darker side. In those months of grief, I gave vent to the darker passions. Sometimes I barely knew myself. Careless of my life, I volunteered for the musical corps entertaining the Crimean troops. A rash fit of fervour. Of my accident I cannot speak. Whoever was at fault—whether the Austrians stooped so low in revenge for my revelations—it sounded the knell for my career as a violinist.

On my way home, still hobbling, I chanced to pass through Milan. My enquiries were fruitless. Every child I saw, I thought it was my Angelina. I dreamt she had found a better life, but I knew she was more likely dead or sold. My friends sent me away. It would never be safe for me there. Italian bigwigs never vanish, they transform themselves like chameleons to the political colour required of them.

In London, I could no longer support the life I had been living. The Quarterhouse Brotherhood welcomed me among their faded luminaries. I put my woes behind me, thinking to live out this shadow life without pain.

At least, I thought I had put my woes behind me. The Brotherhood are wont to discuss weighty topics at dinner. I learned more of the Great Social Evil. Fellow Brothers speak of it as a fact of life. Men naturally desire women. Men being powerful and women being poor, commercial transactions are inevitable, for the benefit of both. This, I do not doubt, is sometimes the case. But often, that wretch collapsed in an inglenook, why, she might be as pure as your daughter—or mine—wronged by life and with no recourse but to sell herself.

This injustice struck me so hard that I was persuaded out of my torpor. Last autumn, I got on my high horse. My friends converted my musical reputation into charitable capital. Lo, the Phoenix Foundation for the Fallen. Nobody need know, but it was a way for me to commemorate my lost daughter.

Walter Brodie was one of those who offered his support. A

man of strange insight, he accosted me in the quadrangle, that night of the Quarterhouse party, with the oddest of questions.

"Tell me, Felix, who are you trying to save?" he said in that Atlantic twang of his. "Did you ever look for that daughter of yours?"

It is a peculiar thing to report, when you are bereaved, that people avoid speaking of that loss. When the pain subsides, which you thought would last forever, you do not have to strive to keep from weeping, because nobody ever mentions it.

When Brodie asked me, I said nothing. I supposed he had read my book or had his people read it—for I am convinced the man has no interest in words or politics or the ideas his papers espouse.

I felt unmanned. I could not speak.

Brodie was kind. "I'm sorry, my friend," he said, though we were by no means friends. His understanding moved me. It unseated my judgement. I was too ready to believe the hope he held out. Impossible hope. "I know people who find missing persons. Let's say they find what has happened to missing persons. But, often, they find the persons. Come and see me."

Later that evening, the little mute played her fiddle. I was overcome, remembering the little fiddle I had bought for Angelina. She threw a tantrum on her third birthday because her fingers were small. All these details I recall: her fingers, so tiny, so perfect, when she was born, on the feast of St Sebastian; her little elbow, her shoulder, her toes.

The next day, I went to see him. Brodie told me about the Flowers, a detective concern he acquired from that fellow Pinkerton. Their rate of detection was remarkable. The police were useless, claiming that missing persons may have gone voluntarily.

I objected that his sleuths could not know Milan and the world beyond. Who could say where my little angel had been taken?

He laughed. "Perhaps. Do you know how many Italian

children were shipped into London in the 1850s? Enough that they made a law against it. How old would she be now? Seventeen? Children from Naples are sold around the world. But they especially come to London. They work as dockers, sweeps, printers' runners, clowns, beggars and..." He did not spell out all the possibilities. "Shall I send a man?"

The temptation was too great. Yet I had no money. My savings were gone on my hospital treatments. I had only my meagre pension. I told Brodie as much. For a friend, he insisted, initial enquiries came free. If it went further, we'd discuss it then.

I was dazzled, ashamed, confused. Could my little angel be found? I was ashamed I had not sought her longer. I feared discovering her dead.

Brodie's man came to me, an expansive Irish poet. He drew me on Angelina's looks and personality. He told tales of the Italian quarter, the bordellos and workshops. I told him all: her eyes, her hair, her nose, the birthmark. He annotated it all, as if he were trying to recreate a submerged civilisation. He told me to wait.

I waited.

I could do nothing useful for weeks. I fretted, I worried. Sergeant Lawless saw me at the theatre. What a state. He must have wondered what had become of the refined old chap he had previously met.

I received frequent reports at first: of their enquiries abroad, the trafficking route, Naples, the East End, Little Italy, children sold, children apprenticed, and worse. The whole thing became clandestine after the scandal in '58, which stopped the trail dead. But I should not give up. Here in London, lines of enquiry often took time to bear fruit.

A known trafficker, in Millbank Penitentiary, was discovered to be running his agency from within those bleak walls. With persuasion, he could be prevailed upon to have a long memory of past transactions.

Daily we expected news, so Groggins told me. He checked with me again her birthday, her love of singing, her sullen moods, her quickness to laughter. Fool that I was, I told him every detail, never considering how little a young child in 1849 would be like a young lady in 1863, in a different country, with a different name.

Daily, Groggins came to me and reported that enquiries, though hopeful, had yet to prove fruitful. December was torture.

At last, torn between hope and despair, I intruded upon Brodie's calm office. I demanded what I should expect from the garrulous Irishman. Why torment an old man unless to annihilate my heart and my savings? For I had insisted on paying their fee, and there were tips enough.

Brodie took me seriously. He removed Groggins and installed another man on the case, a model of discretion, whom I would never meet. I should not expect results on the instant. Instead, I should return to my daily round of visits and concerts and the club and the opera. He by no means encouraged me to be hopeful, but he promised news within a six-month—and he would take no more payment from the Phoenix Foundation until we had that final news, one way or the other.

This impressed me and allayed my terror. It was a tremendous pressure, keeping my excitement from my fellows for so long, for the Brothers are a close-knit group, and we notice each other's excitations and improprieties.

This is a story I have never told. I am old. Forgive me if I repeat myself. It is the most extraordinary thing, but when I lost my family, I had no time to mourn. I was quickly snatched into dulling solitude. Incarceration pierces the soul. Only those capable of suppressing their feelings survive, as I learnt at a tender age. I prevailed. I grew strong in my desire for survival—and requital. I never suffered the true pain.

In December, so many years after the despair and deprivation, I was granted hope. And it lacerated. I longed to speak to friends of my lost daughter, but I could not.

For years, I have woken at four in the morning, my heart beating, fear and longing slapping me in the face. I am afraid to tell what has woken me all these years. She stands by the fireside, diaphanous, unattainable. Is it a dream? I care not if it is. I am overtaken by a joy I cannot describe in my waking hours.

Dr Simpson talked of insomnia. Neurasthenic anxiety. He prescribed pills to soothe the blood. And then I saw her.

A ghost of the past. At the opera. I knew it was she. I had seen her in my dreams, I knew her for sure. I seemed to move but could not move. I seemed to speak and could not speak. I stood dumbly and watched her walk away, but my heart was singing.

I roared around the town. I hid away and wept. Imagine how that feels after so many years. But the fury of my suffering abated, and in its place came hope. I gave in. I believed the unbelievable. And I have suffered the consequences.

Two days later, I waited in a gazebo in Cremorne Gardens, respectable enough of an afternoon, as you know. It was one of those clear winter days, free of the sleet, and the scent of lavender filled the air. Brodie had arranged everything. I thought I might explode with waiting. At last, Groggins arrived to prepare me. I could barely comprehend: they had told her that I was a relative, from her distant family; that I would ask questions; that I might help her in life. She knew nothing of her past, but she knew she was not from London.

Sure enough, an ugly chaperone drew near at four o'clock in funereal black. On her arm, a delicate butterfly, in chenille and lace.

My Angelina.

In the light of day, I knew her for sure. I leapt up; I had to restrain myself from sweeping her into my arms. Groggins and the chaperone sat decorously apart, and we talked.

The sound of her voice thrilled me, that dusky timbre resonating through elegant cheekbones. I had not heard that voice for fifteen years, and my heart leapt into my mouth; it was her mother's voice, reborn. I stayed calm as we chatted, but inside, my thoughts danced a polka of joy. She was delightful, after an initial reticence. Free and natural, she spoke of opera and theatre, and her musical hopes, while I nodded like a nincompoop, sure that she took me for some old fool.

Finally, as if her nerves had become frayed, she mentioned a book of old Italian songs she had seen in a Charing Cross bookshop. I said I should like to buy it for her, if she would allow. When was her birthday?

A shadow obscured her brow, and she exclaimed, "Sir, I think you know that I am an orphan and know little of my earliest life; but, I'm told, my birthday is nigh; it is three weeks hence, on the feast of St Sebastian."

"Then, my child, my sweet and lovely child, I remember dearly the day of your birth." I grasped her hand, careless of propriety. "For I am your father."

When it proved true, and the unhoped-for became real, I hardly dare to believe it.

On our second meeting, as I bought her tea and scones under the eye of the chaperone, I tentatively asked her what life had dealt her. She began stumblingly to disclose the deprivations she had endured. I began to see her in these terrible places: the mouseholes of Naples, where life is so cheap they do not bury their own; the dockyards of London; the slave ship; and the milliner's whence I had rescued her. She spoke of her sisters, their carelessness of her, and her mother's—not real sisters and mother, of course, but the thieves' republic who adopted her. My heart ached.

She said, over and over, how she was not worthy of the kindnesses I bestowed on her, of the luxuries I lavished. Mere tea and scones.

I wanted to scoop her up in my arms and fly her high over the streets of this wild, welcoming city to deliver her safe to her home. I wanted to light her way in the darkness so she need not fear, to light a thousand candles in her bedchamber that she might see at last her own beauty in the glass.

It was too great a gift from a God I had long cursed. A Christmas wonder. A miracle. I nodded to the chaperone. I signed, I promised, I paid.

A week later, after the wonder and disbelief, she was installed in apartments off Quartern Lane. Her people were paid off. She had an income, a servant and modest garments to shield her from any who had a claim upon her. From the demure hat to her well-hidden ankles, Brodie's Flowers arranged all.

Brodie himself urged continued discretion. I should not initially be seen with her, not more than was necessary. We cooked up the story that she was a long-lost niece, reunited through European family. I paid Brodie's lot a bonus; or rather, they took it from the fund; and that, I understood, concluded their involvement.

I was walking on air. At night, I had to calm my beating heart, knowing that she slept just five hundred yards away. In the morning, I took coffee with the Brothers, but refused my bacon and eggs; in twenty minutes, I would be knocking on her door with pastries, perfume or whatever gift my fond old heart had settled on.

I learned of her early life, the little she could recall.

A kindly old Judaeo-Italian, now deceased, kept a house near the river for Neapolitan orphans. He had favoured her, a Milanese girl with musical inclinations, and schooled her tolerably, but refused to teach her Italian, calling it a barbarous tongue, insisting on English. When she was twelve, he died. She subsisted on her wits and the kindness of charitable societies, who finally placed her as a milliner's apprentice. She hoped that she might one day enter society and marry, though that seemed a distant dream.

I enjoined her to sing for me. Her voice was vigorous, but untrained. I asked if she would learn violin. This gave her pause. I thought it was sullenness, but it was the very way children behave with their parents. They do not like to be tutored in something they will always be worse at, to be forever corrected. Believe me, I know how belittling it is to have a famous teacher.

Nonetheless, I contrived to leave an old fiddle with her servant. One day, I arrived to hear a lively air played in rustic fashion. I burst into the drawing room and saw to my amazement that my Angelina could play in the gypsy style. Her posture and hands were barbaric, but to hear those angelic hands strike out a tune so irrepressible made my heart sing. Truly, though her tender years had been lost and lowly, she was my own daughter.

On the surface, calm. Within, a tempest of emotion. My life was filled with fresh joys from morn until night. Soon enough, fresh troubles. The best melodies hide discord deep within their harmonies.

I lived to all appearances the same life as before, only instead of going out with my fellows, I was bold to step out with her. Her: my Angelina, and such I called her; she called herself Eveline, as the old Neapolitan Jew had named her when he bought her. We kept to places where we were not like to encounter any who knew us: Hampstead Heath, Burton's Colosseum, the Park Square Diorama. These were far from her stomping ground by the river and little frequented by my friends.

Finally, the itch took me to see a new production of Gluck's *Orfeo* at the Opera House. She begged me to take her for her birthday. What a joy to me that was, to be sat there with my daughter—my daughter! How my old heart swelled, as the years of tribulation fell away, and I watched my darling Angelina delight in the foolish comings and goings onstage. At the intervals, I was taken aback how many raffish young gents passed close to us, some pleasant enough, but some with ribald jibes aimed at her beauty, or suggesting our relations improper. Angelina did not react appropriately, which irked me; this was the first time I found myself telling her off. To be familiar did not become a lady. She ought to restrain her gaze and her pert replies.

Angelina was instructed, by Brodie's lot, not to venture too freely from home. A single lady in London may nowadays walk unaccompanied, it is true, as far as the Post Office, or to purchase a crumpet, or even to church. Any further, for one so young, and she seems not quite a lady. Besides, I had a hovering fear—without delving deeply into her past—that there might be someone who had a hold over her or wished her ill. I repeated Brodie's injunction. I tipped her servant to remind her of her duty as a young lady and to inform me of her movements.

Her housemaid informed me, in hushed tones, that when I was not expected, Angelina was in the habit of wandering whole afternoons abroad. Blow me if Angelina didn't sack the woman on the spot. I bribed the next with more circumspection. This is when I learnt the watchful spying that is the mark of fatherhood, especially of a lass. In today's thought-tormented age, when girls vanish and societies are dedicated to their ruination, fathers will fret. I, though old, was no different. I had missed so much of her upbringing, I was determined to make amends. Those first days were sweet, a rediscovery of Eden: the perfume of my wife's hair, the memory of her soft cheek. What was to come was a bitter hell. I had dealt with the devil; now I should pay for it.

Angelina begged me to take a box at the Opera House. I am a tired old man. I can only stomach the theatre twice or thrice a fortnight. She longed to go every night. I gave in. I was still in the way of spoiling her.

But something in her manner made me suspicious. After a few days, I turned up at the Opera House without warning. Rather than go to our box, I took a seat nearby. Cloak and daggers, indeed. She sat alone, rapt with the drama. It was as if, after long deprivation, she could not get enough of that other world, the world of glimmering hopes and wild passions, a world we may but glimpse beyond the pillars for a careless hour of which—if we are lucky—this world is but a pale reflection. As I was about to leave, sure enough, a young bounder appeared in the back of her box, our box. She greeted him decorously enough, then the two of them repaired to the back room. I stormed up, hot-headed, demanding admittance from the theatre manager.

"The locks are worked from within, sir. On this is the popularity of the Opera House founded."

I fumed. I felt the tantrum well within me, but I waited, without knocking, without pounding the door down, until the very end. Whereupon, decorously enough, Angelina and the young cad emerged. She laughed to see me and introduced me to her friend, Angelo, whom she knew through her millinery work. He seemed to hold her in esteem, without the predatory looks I had grown accustomed to seeing from younger men. He suggested we go to the Holborn. My rage abated. They gave me to understand that Angelo was of another persuasion and no threat to Angelina's honour.

The next week, I came again unannounced. The story was less sweet. I cannot say what I saw her doing, for my eyes were full of rage. It was the bloody Irishman, Groggins. He had the decency to be discomfited. He had used to give her lessons, she said. She owed him thanks, and so should I, if I was at all grateful that she was alive. Again to the bloody Holborn. But this Groggins was decidedly not of the other persuasion. He insisted upon flirtation, touching her elbow, right there, in front of her old father. The impudence of the modern generation.

So I learnt the pains of fatherhood. I am afraid I behaved badly that night. Angelina did not upbraid me there but suffered me to walk her home after we had despatched the frisky Dubliner.

The next day, she would not receive me. I laughed in the face of her new housekeeper and strode past her, as well as I can stride.

She launched into such a stream of invective as I have never heard: how I held her back, I tied her down; I dressed her like a princess, I treated her as a slave; so much fun she used to have before she met me; and she preferred being poor, when you could cadge off the world, rather than being one of the quality, when everyone looked to cadge off you. Besides, what was the point of being a society lady but to bag a man? Which made you as bad as the Haymarket whores, only for a steeper fee.

"Chuck me out of the coop, if you want. Call me ungrateful, but I can't live how we're living. All your wittering about the past. Wars on the continent. A girl today can't be expected to care about all that, can she?"

"Angelina, my love, my life—"

"I am no daughter of yours." She slammed the door in my face.

I returned to the Brothers in disarray. We were estranged.

The days passed. The feast of St Valentine came and went, and I did not see her.

I had learned something. That my aching desire to be a

father, to be a good father, had prejudiced my sympathy with her. Perhaps she was flirtatious, perhaps she was uncouth. But what torments she had undergone. A tiny child ripped from her loved ones; a youth brought up in vilest squalor by an exploiting old Semite—lucky he died before she was of the age he could sell her or charge for her or otherwise use her.

I went to her to make amends. She was not there. This was the end of February, and Lawless saw me on her balcony in a panic.

Groggins came to see me. He was in a state. He reminded me of my vow to the Flowers. I must not divulge any word about finding her. I sent him away with a blessing. Whatever his misdemeanours, I had found new peace.

I went to abase myself before her.

She received me warmly, more like a tolerated old uncle than a beloved father. I apologised if I had upset her, and her friend, but I was a foolish antediluvian zealot. I had spent so long without her that it hurt like the devil to see her drift away, this time into adulthood.

She was changed. More grown up, more familiar than before, she spread her hands. "Don't brood so, you daft ha'porth. We both know it, plain as day."

I did not comprehend her fully.

She said it clearer, bold as brass. "I'm not your daughter. I never was." She explained it all: the Flowers of Sin, where girls are taken into service, trained in all the arts of a lady, all the arts, on the French model; and for each of Groggins' classes in elocution and comportment, they underwent training twice as rigorous in satisfying gents' more unacceptable demands.

The sweat went cold on my neck. My hand trembled. My tongue lay dormant in my mouth.

She described, in too much detail, what she had been taught. With those desires awoken, what a disappointment it was to be saddled with a stiff old lizard like me. Not only did I talk so endlessly, and insist on our convoluted pretence, but I refused to lay a hand on her, so that she was driven mad with pent-up desires. Could she be blamed if she invited the odd gent of her former acquaintance up to our private box to make her feel loved?

I sat without hearing, without seeing. "What have you done with Angelina?" I hissed. I do not remember hitting her. I recall her impudent gaze as I hit her a second time. "You are not my daughter."

More, she seemed to say. That is what I deserve. That is how you long to treat me. "I could see it in your kindly old eyes," she said, "that somewhere inside was a devilish old goat chomping to get out and punish me, as I deserve."

Blind fury took me. The rapture turned black. I avenged myself on her for the thousand sins that life has done me. Her insults stirred me so, and her impudent gaze, those impish eyes, the heart-shaped face framed by such perfect ringlets of hair. There she lay, crumpled on the floor against the divan in such a wanton pose. My fury redoubled and turned into something carnal and loathsome.

Once we had rearranged her dress, I called the maid. She decided the doctor must be summoned. He treated her bruises and said she must stay in for a week, wear high scarves and broad hats, and say she had fallen. Simpson spoke cantankerously, frowning at what I had done. "And you, sir, will do well to becalm yourself, or you will have a fit."

"For God's sake, have pity, doctor," I protested. "I was told this was my daughter. I believed it until today."

"You need say no more, sir. I have seen much darker stories. All I would say is this: if this is not your daughter, it is hardly the fault of the Flowers. I would remind you that you signed the contract and pay the bills, otherwise I should not be so precipitously summoned. Secondly, I remind you not to break your promise. To criticise the Flowers is reckless." He let his warning hang in the air. "Tell the same to your daughter, or whatever you choose to call her now."

I stumbled back to Quarterhouse, but could not endure the society of my fellows. On I went to the river. Oh, the futility of man's wishes. I had wanted an impossible thing. I had been deceived; I had let myself be deceived. I should have known that things were not right; her accents were not as they should be; so many other hints. But I longed to believe. If I spoke to Brodie, he would laugh at my naivety; of course, the deception was plain. Nobody could have believed it, to find a girl lost fifteen years ago, halfway across the world, in another age.

That should have been the end of it. I resolved to pay her off, give her notice and her maid, and be quit of the diabolical affair. I had ruined her; I must toss her aside. Such was my disgust at my own depravity. I was ashamed, too; I had squandered the Foundation's funds on my fruitless indulgences. I had wilfully been taken for a fool. I had believed her my daughter. Then, despite her so young, I had done unmentionable things…

She received me, dressed in softest silks. Her drawing room was draped in the purples and lavender of a Turkish harem. Candles, fruit bowls, silvery apples and golden pomegranates. I fell again.

When it was done, and the beauty and wonder all faded, I was disgusted. She bade me punish her for this seduction, and I did. So we went on, day after day, yielding to each other. I was revolted, to find such angers within me. And she, she received my tantrums with love. It stoked her passion.

She showed herself expert in the ways of love. Self-denial thrown to the winds, she abased herself in the most unladylike ways; thrilling, erotic ways. We explored pleasures ever more wayward, beyond the pleasures I had known before, beyond my marriage, beyond the depravity of my London debauches, and, at the last, beyond the degradations I suffered at the hands of the filthy army conductor. Beyond any woman, she knew how to please. I enjoyed her and punished her for that enjoyment. She revelled in the abasement. I had finally learned the rapture offered by the Flowers: not the angelic love I sought but a fervid venality that torched my soul. Yet still I loved her.

One day, I truly hurt her. I told the servant to call Simpson. I left in a panic, like a thief. I meant to return the next day. I could not return. I ordered more of Simpson's pills and doubled my dosage.

The parliamentary Enquiry was soon to begin. I sent word to Lawless that I should like to make a deposition. I thought to expose the sordid deception. I do not know what I intended to disclose. But I must unburden myself. Yes, I must reveal to the Enquiry what I knew. I could not avenge all the lost girls, but I could at least confess how I had wasted the Foundation's funds on private purposes, ill purposes; and I could publicly repent. I must be punished, however it ruin my good name. If you are reading this, Lawless, the matter is resolved or I dead in its cause.

I have no regrets. The passion in these last months, the hope and the wickedness, was worth it. I once believed it was our duty to seek rapture. Epicureanism is not about drink and merriment. Pleasures of the flesh may spark rapture. But the touch of that ineffable magic, the wonder of love, this is the majesty that, to know for a moment, justifies a lifetime of seeking.

Lawless did not come. I fell into restless slumbers.

I awoke to find Brodie's jackals at the door. The knock was brutish. They had intercepted my message. They did not need to berate me. I took Simpson's pills to calm my nerves, and a dram of gin to wash them down. I suffered the stroke straight after, I suppose.

Hours passed before they found me. I was lucky that they did. I often dined with Angelina, but my neighbouring Brother was in all afternoon and knew that I had neither gone out nor taken dinner. In the silence of this solitude, I lived a thousand ages of remorse. I relived every moment of my time with her, the splendour of finding her, the despair of her rejection.

I lost the power of speech. I am recovering my thoughts. These brilliant cripples are digging from the corners of my mind the phrases I devised in that long solitude, never knowing if I would be able to share them. I know the men will come to make certain of my silence. I have begged Bede and his little friend to secrete these texts in my violin case, where the jackals will not seek, and flee. I fear the recriminations Brodie's men may exact on them.

If I must die—and I must soon—let me declare this: I loved, I lost. I never thought I could love again, but I did. I did, with a wild rapture unthought of in common hours. I am a man thought admirable, when I know none more debauched.

I will ever reserve in my memory a cherished palace for you to dwell. I wish I could believe that I shall walk with you in the hereafter. Oh, how I long for the possibility of meeting you again. How did I stay sanguine through all those years? The truth is, I did not. I despaired of life and thought often of ending it. Now I resume my discourse with death.

I shall not look upon the sun again. I am a man divided. The world esteems the gentle artistic half; blessed few have suffered the beast behind this carapace. She, who filled me with such joy, unearthed the childish lustful furious vengeful raging ugly monster that is in me, that is me; she faced it gladly, and still she seemed to love me.

I must leave you now. Useless to prolong this damnation, and the time awfully fails me. I hope that Lawless, that any readers of these poor pages, may try to understand, through their disgust. Unless you are one of the dead people, I think you will understand me. I think you may forgive me. We are predators hurled through this world by forces we cannot fathom. We are all romancers and fools.

And, oh my heart, Angelina, my sweet, sweet Angelina, I hope you may live—

A knock.

Little ones, hide. Hide yourselves, please. And hide these tender pages.

Knock, knock, knock.

Bring her back with your knocking. If only I could. Hide now. Soon, love, we shall come to that finishing end—

(*Here Felix's Testament ends.*)

# DRAMATIS PERSONAE

**SERGEANT CAMPBELL LAWLESS**, also known as Watchman
**FELIX SONNABEND**, musician
**MOLLY**, leader of street urchins
**BEDE & THE PIXIE**, the Oddbody Theatricals
**SIR RICHARD PAYNE**, commissioner of Scotland Yard
**SERGEANT SOLOMON JEFFCOAT**
**BERTIE**, Prince of Wales, son of Queen Victoria, and his wife
**PRINCESS ALIX**
**GABRIEL MAUVE MP & MRS MAUVE**
**J.W. BRODIE**, newspaper magnate
**ALEXANDRA**
**MISS RUTH VILLIERS**, librarian
**SERGEANT JIMMY DARLINGTON**
**KATE HAMILTON** (also called Kitty), bawd house madam
**CORA**, prostitute
**SABINE**, otherwise Mrs Stephanie Boulton, prostitute
**WILKIE COLLINS**, novelist
**HENRY MAYHEW**, social commentator
**CHARLES DICKENS**, novelist
**SKITTLES**, or Anonyma, or Catherine Walters, courtesan
**WILLIAM DUGDALE & JOHN CAMDEN HOTTEN**, erotic booksellers
**SHERIDAN GROGGINS**, elocutionist

**Dr William Acton**, social commentator
**Sir Antonio Panizzi**, librarian
**Lord Chief Justice Fairchild**, judge
**William Gladstone,** MP and Chancellor of the Exchequer
**Dr Malachi Simpson**
**The McGarrigan family:** Agnes, Susan et al.
**Eveline**

In addition, manifold unnamed servants, glaziers, doxies, dollymops, fourpennies, zuches, bobtails, jawbreakers, lushy betts, cast-iron polls, dirty salls, dancing sues, pineapple jacks, fancy men, bullies, followers, bawds, procuresses, pimps, panders, children, socialites, lords, dukes, parliamentarians and intemperate young men.

# AUTHOR'S NOTE

The characters and situations in this novel are the fabrication of the author, apart from the ones that clearly aren't. Skittles, Collins, Mayhew, Payne (actually Sir Richard Mayne) and Kate Hamilton are real, Mauve and Brodie palpably not.

Many of the women's tales are adapted from Henry Mayhew's interviews with the London poor, as is Bede's story (see "The Crippled Nutmeg Grater Seller"). The figures of the Society for the Rescue of Young Women and Children are genuine (*The Times*, 23 December 1864); Jeffcoat's evidence is adapted from Mayhew.

Knowing that readers of *Lawless and the Devil of Euston Square* enjoyed distinguishing the historical from the fabricated, I give more hints at *william-sutton.co.uk*.

I have stolen most from *The Strange Case of Dr Jekyll and Mr Hyde* by Robert Louis Stevenson, Henry Mayhew's *London Labour and the London Poor* and Baudelaire's *Les Fleurs du Mal*.

*My Secret Life* by "Walter" was published, in the end; its author remains a mystery, though *The Oxford Dictionary of Biography* has suggestions. I have misconstrued its origins for my own purposes, but the quotations are genuine, if abridged. It remains an extraordinary document, shocking and tawdry by turns, guaranteed to embarrass anyone reading it over your shoulder on the train.

Brodie's novella in a yellow jacket is *Phoebe Kissagen*. The volumes in the Flower Garden Catalogue, Ancient & Modern, are all genuine, except for *Mutton Walk Cyprians*, as was the British Museum Library's Secret Cabinet. See *Private Case— Public Scandal: Secrets of the British Museum Revealed*, Peter Fryer.

Further significant sources: *Dictionary of Modern Slang, Cant, and Vulgar Words*, John Camden Hotten. Peter Quennell's introduction to *London's Underworld* (selections from Mayhew). *A Dictionary of Victorian London*, Lee Jackson (see also his legendary website victorianlondon.org). Jonathon Green's Timelines of Slang website. *The Victorian City*, Judith Flanders. *The Austrian Dungeons in Italy*, Felice Orsini. *'Orrible Murder, Selections from The Illustrated Police News*, Leonard de Vries. *London: the Wicked City*, Fergus Linnane. *Poor Things*, Alasdair Gray. *The Less Deceived*, Philip Larkin.

# ACKNOWLEDGMENTS

Thanks to Caroline, Phil Patterson, Miranda Jewess, Emlyn Rees, Bryon Quertermous, John Sutton, Doris and Nina, Mum and Dad, Chris and David, Rebecca my map guru (rebeccawilliamsart.com), Andy and Carolyn, Jamie, Lucy, Alfie and Megan, Sally, Romily and Dexter, Lucy Holmes, Jamie and Ben, Siân and Jeremy, Vikki Cookson, Mirko Sekulic, John Lloyd, John Waltho, Sarah Salway, SJ Butler, Jason Bermingham, Charlie Loxton, Tim and Sonya, Katherine May, Greg Klerkx and Samantha Holdsworth of the ReAuthoring Project @NimbleFishArts, Andrew Powney, Roy Leighton, Jennifer McCoy, Chris Myles Kennedy, Tara and Martin Knight @southseacoffee, Dom Kippin, Tessa Ditner, Jo West, Diana Bretherick, Matt Wingett, Zella Compton, Tom Harris, Christine Lawrence, Charlotte Comley, Fark and Lilou @TheTeaTray in the Sky, Portsmouth Writers' Hub, New Writing South, Seán Moore, Pedro Monteiro, @AuthorsCC, Alwyn James, Dallas Campbell and George Cochrane.

# ABOUT THE AUTHOR

William Sutton comes from Dunblane, Scotland. He has appeared at CrimeFest, the Edinburgh International Book Festival, High Down Prison and CSI Portsmouth. He compères *Day of the Dead* in Portsmouth's Square Tower, dismaying audiences with his ukulele nonsense. He writes for magazines across Europe on language, travel and futurology. He has had articles published in *The Times* and plays produced for radio and theatre. He teaches classics. He plays in chansonnier Philip Jeays' band. He played cricket for Brazil, and now plays with The Authors Cricket Club.

*william-sutton.co.uk | twitter.com/WilliamGeorgeQ*
*facebook.com/WilliamGeorgeQ | pinterest.com/wgq42*
*soundcloud.com/william-george-sutton*

# LAWLESS
# AND THE DEVIL OF EUSTON SQUARE

## WILLIAM SUTTON

It is 1859, and novice detective Campbell Lawless has just arrived in London. He is summoned to the scene of a deadly act of sabotage at Euston Station by the illustrious Inspector Wardle. Wardle believes that the man found dead amidst his handiwork is the culprit, but Lawless is not so sure. So begins his hunt for elusive revolutionary Berwick Skelton. Aided by a gang of street urchins and a vivacious librarian, Lawless must capture his underworld nemesis before Skelton unleashes his final vengeance…

"Highly original and engaging"
*Scotland on Sunday*

"Fine, extravagant and thoroughly enjoyable"
*The Scotsman*

"First-rate victorian crime fiction"
*The Herald*

TITANBOOKS.COM